AN
ALEX
SIGHT
THRILLER

KILL
SIGHT
BOOK ONE

GEOFFREY SAIGN

BOOKS BY GEOFFREY SAIGN

Jack Steel Thrillers

Steel Trust

Steel Force

Steel Assassin

Steel Justice

Alex Sight Thrillers

Kill Sight

Magical Beasts

Guardian: The Choice

Guardian: The Quest

Guardian: The Sacrifice

Guardian: The Stand

Nonfiction

Smile More Stress Less:
A Playful Guide to End Anxiety, Be Calm,
& Achieve Happiness with Awareness

Green Essentials: What You Need to
Know About the Environment

African Cats

Great Apes

Interior design by Lazar Kackarovski

Printed in the United States of America
ISBN: 979-8-611368-41-1

For Kathy...

"We do not inherit the Earth from our ancestors, we borrow it from our children."

~ Wendell Berry ~
(1934-   )

CHAPTER 1

THE LATE MAY SOUTHERN California sun was a raging fireball in the clear sky, sending sweat running in rivulets beneath Odysseus' black Lycra suit. The other three men also wore black hoods that covered their faces; goggles covered their eyes. They observed Odysseus carefully.

Odysseus checked his watch. Noon. He took a deep breath, the image of Kristen tightening his jaw.

Reaching up, his fingers and toes found the small indentations and outcroppings he had already spotted. Years of climbing gave him strength to move fast. He quickly inched his head above the ten-foot stone wall.

His heart pounded. Laughter and a splash came from the distant pool. The guard was approaching from the far left on the grounds, walking along the inside of the wall. The guard's suit jacket was open, his holstered gun visible.

Lowering himself back down, hanging with one hand with his toes dug in, Odysseus pulled the silenced Glock from his waist pouch. After counting to ten, he silently swung himself atop the wall, and waited until the guard walked by just below him.

Jumping down from the wall, Odysseus' knees bent when his feet hit the plush grass. Straightening, he jammed his gun barrel against the whirling guard's neck and held a finger over his lips.

The guard's eyes widened and he nodded slightly.

Odysseus pulled off the guard's ear piece and throat mike and tossed them to the side. Then he whispered, "If you want to live, on the ground, on your stomach."

The guard paled and complied.

Odysseus put a knee on the guard's back and said softly into his neck radio, "Go."

Rubber-coated grappling hooks made soft sounds as they sailed lightly over the top of the wall and snugged into the stone. In seconds the others joined him. Six-foot-four, Menelaus' rounded shoulders and square back bulged beneath his Lycra. Patroclus, five-eight, had a thick torso, and Achilles stood six feet, his lean frame approximating Odysseus' height and size.

From his backpack Achilles pulled a Glock. Patroclus already held a Heckler & Koch MP5 submachine gun. Menelaus dug out a syringe and injected its contents into the guard's arm, and then armed himself with a Desert Eagle. All the weapons had silencers.

The guard went limp. Achilles zip-tied his wrists and ankles, and then gagged him.

Odysseus led them across the tennis court single file in a crouched run to the six-foot-high patio wall. Built out of designer cored brick, it separated the court from the pool area.

Odysseus looked through the brick, past the pool, at the glass doors at the back of the house. He prayed there would be no surprises. Waiting until the girl was swimming away from them, her head down in the water, he strode around the north side of the patio wall, his gun level. Patroclus followed him.

Achilles and Menelaus rounded the south end of the wall and headed for the house doors, running undetected behind Wheeler and his wife.

Wheeler was in his bathing suit, lounging on a chair and listening to his iPod, while watching his daughter swim. His plump body revealed his easy lifestyle. Sunbathing in a chair next to him, Wheeler's trim wife wore a yellow bikini. Her eyes were closed and she looked asleep.

Odysseus' lips pursed. The good times were over for Wheeler. It took Wheeler five seconds to notice them. By then Odysseus was in front of him.

"What the..." Wheeler sat up, looking at each of them. His face quickly turned several shades of darkening red, before turning pale. Sweat beaded his forehead. He didn't reach for the cell phone on the table by his drink, but he did pull out his earbuds and tap his wife's arm. She woke up and sat rigidly, her eyes wide.

Standing in shallow water, Wheeler's teenage daughter had stopped swimming. Her face blanched as she crossed her arms across her chest.

A twinge of pity struck Odysseus. The girl reminded him of Kristen. Innocent.

Muffled shots of the MP5 came from the house. Achilles and Menelaus. Odysseus listened, relieved when the gunfire stopped. Menelaus' whispered voice came through his ear piece; "House secure."

Odysseus glared at the two terrified people in front of him. "Mr. And Mrs. Wheeler, you're going to reap what you sow."

CHAPTER 2

A LEX SIGHT FELT DEATH hanging in the air—like a fading memory. He wanted to ignore it but couldn't. Pausing in the living room, he stared out at the patio, swallowing over what was coming.

Persian rugs, expensive wall art, and pottery on pedestals betrayed Wheeler's wealthy lifestyle. None of it meant anything to them now. He wondered what they thought it had done for their lives.

Taking the last few steps to the patio doorway, he stopped when his senses exploded with sensual details. Like the million bursts of sunlight dancing off the surface of the swimming pool in the backyard, and the hundreds of fiery points the late-morning sun created on his arms and face. Even the holstered Smith & Wesson M&P Shield 9mm in the inner waistband of his jeans felt extra hard against his skin, as did the ankle sheath holding his OTF Microtech double-edged blade. The notes of a nearby singing warbler seemed acutely crisp and sharp.

Walking through the open glass doors, he noted a large blood-red numeral 5 spray-painted on the patio. *They were making a game of it.* His arms stiffened over the chalk outlines of the victims beside the pool.

He walked to the left.

FBI Deputy Director Joseph Foley was sitting with a woman at a small white table with an enormous purple umbrella shading it.

Three glasses of pink liquid were on the table, coffee and a manila folder in front of Foley.

Alex reached the shade of the umbrella and stopped, staring at Foley.

Foley took off his sunglasses. Smudges beneath his eyes indicated a lack of sleep, but his six-three, solid frame seemed alert. Dressed in a dark blue suit and tie, his graying hair swept back above commanding eyes and a jutting jaw.

Alex hadn't seen Foley for nearly a year. Wrinkles lined the corners of the man's eyes and mouth, betraying his forty-eight years and lack of sleep. Alex wondered if at thirty-eight he appeared older too, and if his lined forehead gave away his own weariness.

Foley extended a hand. "Good to see you, Alex."

Not wanting contact, he kept his hands to himself and nodded.

Retracting his hand, Foley's eyes narrowed. "Alex Sight, I'd like you to meet Special Agent Megan Detalio. She's an information analyst. One of the best."

In her mid-thirties, she wore an expensive blue suit and white blouse. An olive complexion added to her striking, unconventional appearance. A mix of Caucasian and maybe Pacific Islander, long, dark curly hair framed her soft-featured face. Alex found her attractive, but what held his attention were her dark eyes. Smoldering emotion.

Something threatening surged at him from her, details that he couldn't quite grasp. It felt oddly out of place with the calm woman who sat in front of him. Try as he might, it was an elusive thing, evaporating before he understood it.

"I'm pleased to meet you." Her voice was slightly husky, her tone genuine and easy to read. She stood, five inches under his six-foot height, and extended a hand.

Ignoring her, Alex turned back to Foley. He was aware of the woman frowning. "Get on with it."

Foley cleared his throat. "Megan, could you please wait inside the house?"

"Of course." She looked annoyed, grabbed her sunglasses from the table, and left.

As she walked away, Alex noted that her athletic frame made a distinct V to her waist. Loose fitting slacks tightened around her ankles, above low-heeled shoes. She moved like an athlete, with good balance and a smooth stride.

Alex skewered Foley with his gaze. "The case. Show me."

Foley put on his sunglasses. Rising fluidly, he strode around the pool, taking several mints from a small tin. He didn't offer Alex any.

Foley gestured at the stone wall surrounding the estate. "The killers came over yesterday at noon. Maybe from Avenida Primavera. They knew the layout..."

As Foley talked, Alex's eyes were drawn to the wall, and settled on one round, coarse stone. *Anger*. It leapt at him, clamping on his throat like a vise. He grasped at the word, trying to hang onto it. The emotion changed subtly, expanded, and he felt the rage as it swept into his chest like a hot brand. *Revenge*. That emotion slowly withered away as he listened to the deputy director.

Foley handed over a sheet of paper. "Here's the statement this Threshold terrorist group put on the Internet. A blogger informed us last night of the possibility of foul play with the Wheelers. I happened to be in Los Angeles. Thanks for taking a late flight."

Alex glanced over the words, looking for anything that might trigger a reaction. Some phrases he absorbed, while others slid out of his perception like water through open fingers. *Denton and Patty Wheeler...selling toxic agricultural chemicals...toxic deaths and sickness... victims avenged...no compromise until guilty... brought to justice.*

Nothing jumped out at him so he handed it back to Foley. They strode back to the table.

Foley continued talking. "The killers left footprints made by climbing shoes and wore black Lycra with hoods and red-tinted goggles. Wheeler's teenage daughter said they talked to each other using Greek names from the Trojan War. Menelaus, Patroclus, Achilles, and Odysseus. She had a course in Greek history so the names resonated.

"She said Achilles dragged one of the dead dogs into the pool, but Odysseus stopped him from throwing the second one in. Achilles made some sarcastic remark. Then Odysseus gave the sentencing speech, accusing the Wheelers of poisoning the planet. They sedated and removed the daughter so she didn't have to watch her parents die. One guard and the maid were tranquilized too."

Foley grimaced as he sat down again. "So we have one slightly compassionate killer and at least one psycho who enjoys it. And they don't like each other. The daughter described Odysseus and Achilles as slender and tall, Menelaus big and strong, Patroclus short and stocky."

Sitting at the table, Alex closed his eyes, not focusing on anything, letting his gift have its way with him. He heard Foley's words in snatches and listened for something beyond them.

"Two guards killed...Heckler & Koch MP5 machine gun... Glock..."

Billings. The word hung in his consciousness and had deep anguish attached to it. Before he could explore it further, black and white images filled his mind, surrounded by darkness— *bullets spraying everywhere, men and women toppling over, shouts...*

Desperately he grasped at the vision, trying to return to it, wanting more of the small taste he had.

However his senses abruptly closed down, shrinking back to the mundane as he dropped out of his state. He made a feeble effort to cling to the fading imagery, but it dissipated like rising smoke.

Dismayed, he opened his eyes. Joseph Foley sat in front of him, seeming a bit more solid and perturbed than he had been aware of earlier. Waves of heat rose from the surrounding patio stones.

The atrocity he had witnessed, a small-scale massacre, curled his hands on the arms of the chair. He always witnessed death or its possibility in his imagery, but never of this magnitude. And never precisely where it would occur. Not knowing the details always left him feeling anxious. The word *Billings* wasn't attached to the site of the massacre, but made him curious.

Relaxing his shoulders, he sagged into his chair, his throat parched. Sweat ran beneath his casual short-sleeved pullover and his tennis shoes suffocated his feet. Lifting the glass of lemonade in front of him, he drained half of it, and then looked at the lawn. "I bet that takes a lot of water in a heat wave like this."

"I know you like print for your skill set." Taking a pencil from his shirt pocket, Foley rested its eraser against the manila folder on the table. "Threshold named several hundred company executives and owners that they're holding personally responsible for national and international environmental crimes. Climate change, toxic chemicals killing people and wildlife, GMO pesticides and herbicides, and plastic pollution. They also faxed details of Wheeler's company operations to the press. Obviously to sway public opinion. We've had quite a few panicked calls from the named CEOs."

"Why did Wheeler have armed guards?"

Foley shrugged. "He was a billionaire living in Del Mar with the Pacific Ocean for a backyard view. I guess he thought it came with the territory."

"Cause of death?"

Foley grimaced. "Respiratory failure. The Wheelers were forced to swallow a cup of glyphosate and clothianidin. Glyphosate is a common herbicide used worldwide, clothianidin is a neonicotinoid pesticide. Both are used on genetically engineered crops. The terrorists blame clothianidin and glyphosate for killing pollinators and insect populations worldwide. Glyphosate is linked to cancer."

"Wheeler's company manufactured them?" asked Alex.

"Yes. In Asia." Foley lifted a few fingers. "Glyphosate is available at lawn and garden stores. Roundup, a common brand from Monsanto, relies on glyphosate. Farmers also use it and clothianidin. We'll talk to Wheeler employees, see if anyone stands out."

"They went to some effort to spare the guard, maid, and daughter." Alex didn't ask how the daughter was doing. She would have to live with this hell for the rest of her life.

Foley's eyebrows arched. "Some twisted idea of killing only those they claim are guilty. The two guards who resisted and the dogs were expendable. They tasered the live-in maid, then sedated her. The sedative used on her, the guard, and the daughter was a mix of ketamine and xylazine. Both are used illegally for recreation, and used as sedatives by veterinarians, among others. Someone had to know what they were doing to mix the two."

"A veterinarian." Intuitively that fit for him.

"Or someone who works with big animals." Foley tapped his pencil's eraser once against the folder. "We pulled together a list of large animal vets in California and neighboring states that use xylazine, alphabetical by states and last names. We'll interview many of them in the coming days."

"How about an environmental extremist file?"

"We're working on it." Foley pushed the folder across the table. "There's also a dossier on Wheeler's company. Phone calls for the last year, acquaintances, friends, and business contacts. We've already moved on a lot of it, but it seems Wheeler was a random target. He just happened to be in the wrong business. In the folder there's a Bureau credit card, FBI photo ID, and the number to my office manager in Washington. She'll be able to locate me immediately."

Alex opened the folder and quickly scanned the list of company executives and owners, letting his eyes wander down pages. Nothing. He moved through the Wheeler company information just as fast. Lastly he scanned the veterinarians listed by state, pausing on California. *San Diego.* It felt intuitive too, and obvious. He stared at the names listed beneath it. *Dr. Frank Crary* stood out, but no images came.

He looked up at Foley. "I want to see phone records on veterinarians around San Diego, especially Dr. Frank Crary."

Foley raised an eyebrow. "Good. We'll get warrants."

Alex sat back. "Why kill Wheeler's wife?"

"She ran the business with him so they considered her equally responsible." Leaning on the table, hands clasped, Foley's steady voice matched the firmness of his expression. "Megan Detalio is your partner."

Alex clenched his jaw. He should have guessed. He recalled sensing something threatening about her. The idea of a partner brought a sour taste to his mouth and memories of Jenny flooded him. Recovering, he tried to sound nonchalant. "What's her history?"

"Phenomenal information analyst. Out of the San Diego office. She volunteered and convinced me of her assets."

Alex kept his voice calm. "Great. Tell her to review the information you have. I'll call her daily to see what she's put together."

"She'll be with you in the field. It's nonnegotiable."

Alex sensed Foley wouldn't budge, so he said, "Look for a motive of revenge."

Foley frowned. "Don't you think that's obvious?"

He shook his head. "A personal motive. Beyond the environmental concerns, and not necessarily directed at Wheeler. Has Billings, Montana, come up in your investigation?"

"Why?" asked Foley.

"Keep it in mind." Alex paused. "I saw a massacre, but it wasn't there. They're connected somehow though."

"A massacre?" Foley pursed his lips.

Alex turned in the direction of heavy footsteps.

A burly, nearly bald man approached them from the house. A tan suit stretched over his wide shoulders and thick arms. He held an unlit wooden pipe. The man stopped at their table, chewing gum and squinting against the sun.

Alex looked at Foley expectantly.

"Alex, this is Bill Gallagher. He directs the FBI's counterterrorism division and will be your contact if I'm busy or detained elsewhere."

Noting the man's surly frown, Alex stuck out his hand. "Nice to meet you."

Gallagher grunted and took his hand in a quick shake. "Likewise."

"I wanted Gallagher to meet you in person." Foley fidgeted in his chair. "You need to work together as the case develops."

"I look forward to it." Alex didn't see any friendliness in the man's eyes. "I'm sure we'll be a great help to each other."

"It should prove interesting." Gallagher nodded, wheeled, and walked back into the house with heavy steps.

Alex shook his head. "Did his dog just die?"

"It seems to be contagious, doesn't it?"

Alex waved a hand. "Sorry. Earlier...that wasn't personal. Hand contact would have interfered with my ability to focus—"

"Don't worry about it." Foley straightened. "Gallagher's the best intelligence analyst we have. He doesn't appreciate bringing in an outsider. You can understand that, can't you?"

"Of course. No one likes to have a partner forced on them."

"Alex, I brought you in because of your ability to deliver fast results." Foley tapped his pencil's eraser rhythmically against the table. "But I want everyone on this case communicating with each other. Understood?"

Foley's words carried a bite and it annoyed him. "Perfectly."

"You need to toe the line too, Alex. Nothing except standard procedure unless you check with me first."

"Fine." He had to work to not react, reminding himself that Foley, besides having a need to spell everything out, always had to tap his stupid pencil like a drumbeat everyone was supposed to march to. Not much had changed in the last year.

Foley leaned back. "I want immediate updates on anything important, and I'll contact you if anything significant develops from our other efforts."

Alex picked up the folder as he rose. He waved at the painted numeral five on the patio. "It's a countdown. The next murder will be tonight and will have a four, the next murders three, two, one."

"You're certain of this?" Foley gaped at him. "Then what?"

Alex grimaced. "Maybe they disappear or go out in a big battle."

Foley rose stiffly. "And you're sure the next one is tonight?"

"I'm guessing after sunset. They did this first one in daylight, but now they'll need to be more careful." He eyed Foley. "A lot of people are going to die before this is over, Joseph."

Foley's eyes widened. "Is that written in stone?"

"I'd bet on it." He strode past the pool, his own words filling him with revulsion. Drained, he needed rest. And his thoughts churned over Megan Detalio.

Walking through the cooler house, he noticed Gallagher talking to several agents. The man avoided his eyes as he went by. Alex wondered how Foley expected him to have good communication with someone who didn't even want him on the case.

Worse than that, the images he had experienced reverberated deep inside. He abruptly realized that he didn't want to do this kind of work anymore. For the first time ever, he wanted off a case. Wanted to walk out of this mansion and forget about it. His curse was that it was too late for that. His conscience wouldn't let him.

CHAPTER 3

*J*ENNY YELLED FOR HIS *help from the room, her voice frantic. He ran up the wooden stairs of the old house, knowing he wouldn't be in time, gripping the handrail with one hand, his gun in the other. There were too many steps and he was too far from the room...*

Alex woke up, the nightmare fading but leaving him edgy. He leaned back in his seat. Soft music played—Pink singing *Just Give Me a Reason*. Sitting stiffly, Megan was driving his rental Corolla, sleek black sunglasses hiding her eyes. She had taken off her suit jacket, which lay on the back seat next to her laptop. She turned down the music on her iPod.

After telling her what he had sensed at the Wheeler estate, he had crashed. Bringing his seat vertical, he glimpsed the Pacific Ocean through the trees out his open car window. That surprised him. His sunglasses gave the water a greenish tint. A red-tailed hawk circled in the sky.

The AC was off and hot air roasted his skin. His watch read eleven a.m. The promise of another murder tonight sent his thoughts racing. He had to work to calm himself.

His eyes widened as a black and white CHP Charger pulled up alongside them in the opposing traffic lane, lights flashing. No siren.

Megan slowed down and moved their car over to the right side of the lane, biting her lip. The shoulder on their side of the road was nonexistent, with trees and shrubs growing right up to the edge of the pavement.

"What happened?" he asked.

Not answering, Megan stared at the police car keeping pace alongside them as she braked to a stop. The police car stopped beside them, the passenger window open, two male officers in front.

The passenger police officer, wearing sunglasses and tight-lipped, flashed a palm down at Megan. His sun visor was against the window and hid part of his face.

While Megan searched for her driver's license in her small purse, for one instant the driver of the police car leaned forward and scowled.

Alex wondered what Megan had done to make the officer angry—his expression didn't fit a speeding ticket. Maybe the guy was having a bad day.

The CHP quickly accelerated and disappeared around the next bend.

Megan took a deep breath and sagged into her seat. "I was going a little fast. They probably ran the plates and found your name on the rental agreement. And I'm not you."

He glanced at her. "They must have another call. Lucky you."

"No kidding." She tossed her purse into the backseat.

"Where are we?" he asked.

Turning off the music, she pulled back into the lane and continued driving. "Torrey Pines Park Road. The county highway had road construction. We'll pick it up halfway through."

He clutched the armrest as she took the next corner. Twisted pine and chaparral covered the dry countryside. Dust filled the air. He could taste it. Just west of their lane, the rugged landscape dropped three hundred feet. In his side mirror he watched a Subaru Outback with tinted glass roar up fast behind them.

The speed limit was thirty, but Megan pushed the sedan to thirty-five to accommodate the following car. Double solid yellow lines prohibited passing on the winding road and there wasn't a shoulder she could use to let the car pass.

The Subaru hugged their bumper for a few moments, and then dropped back twenty feet.

Alex glanced at Megan, surprised she was speeding again after just being stopped. "Thanks for driving. I needed a rest. Want a break?"

"I'm good." Wind played with strands of her hair while she fingered a silver dolphin at the end of a thin necklace.

He wiped sweat off his brow. "Can we turn on the AC? We're in the middle of a heat wave."

"Sure." She powered up the windows and turned it on.

He opened the glove compartment, which was half-filled with mini dark chocolate bars. "Want one?" She shook her head, and he unwrapped one and started eating.

"I like milk chocolate." She smiled. "One of my few vices."

He winked at her. "Better than drugs and alcohol."

"It goes to my butt."

"Yikes."

Alex's phone played the U.S. Army's *Call to the Post* bugle riff that began every horse race. Taking it out of his pocket, he answered it. A *WhatsApp* call. A man with red curly hair, thick eyebrows, ruddy cheeks, and a reddish beard appeared on the screen.

Alex smiled. "Hey, Harry. What are the names?"

Harry had a deep Irish accent, and Alex murmured the names after him, "Passion, Best Yield, Down Under, Snowball, Spring Step, Constant Effort..." He paused, his forehead wrinkling as he closed his eyes. "Ten on Passion to win, Harry." Two to one odds.

"Don't worry, lad," said Harry. "We'll do her."

"Thanks, Harry." As he put his phone away the Subaru closed on their bumper again and honked. "Impatient," he muttered.

Megan accelerated to forty. "Seems like a lot of effort to bet ten dollars." She brushed strands of her long hair off her cheek and gave him a quizzical look.

He felt an unexpected tug on his emotions. He hadn't had a relationship for three years. Since Jenny. Even so, his reaction bothered him. "Ten thousand." He immediately regretted telling her that.

She gaped. "I never liked gambling. I hope you're not playing with your pension. Do you gamble on everything?"

He smiled. "Just horse racing. There's always one running. Harry does the work for me."

She studied him for a moment. "What you detected at the Wheeler's today, well, are you always right?"

Looking out his window, his mouth was suddenly as dry as the parched air. He grabbed his water bottle from the floor and took a sip.

"Most of the time?" she prodded.

"Yeah, too often."

She glanced in the rearview mirror. "How long have you been able to do it?"

He looked out the window. "I have a vivid memory of an old person dying in my neighborhood when I was ten years old."

"Wow. Must have been a rough childhood." She sounded empathetic.

"Highs and lows, like most." Finished with the chocolate, he tossed the wrapper into the glove compartment and settled back. He remembered the guilt he felt when he was young, having visions of people dying, and then witnessing their actual deaths. Sometimes running to a house to see if he was right—hoping he wasn't. In his teens he tried to prevent the deaths from coming true, but he had always failed.

"That would have been a nightmare for anyone that age," she added.

"Understatement." He wondered how much Foley had shared about him. Megan was an analyst so she might have investigated him. That idea made him uncomfortable.

The Subaru dropped back fifty feet, but immediately raced up to their bumper again.

Alex pushed his feet into the floorboard. Maybe it was a stupid teenager playing around—or on drugs. "How long have you worked for the FBI?"

"A few years as an analyst," she said.

"Any field experience?" He eyed the sideview mirror.

"Not with the FBI." She glanced into her rearview mirror. "I can take care of myself."

Surprised, he turned to her. "What did you do before the FBI?"

"Not now, all right?" Her voice had an edge.

"What's the big deal?" His throat filled with words he wanted to spit at Foley for forcing her on him. "I like to know who I'm working with."

"Megan Detalio," she said stiffly.

"Great."

She glanced at him, her voice changing gears from irritated to curious. "How do you do it? You know, get your information."

"A crystal ball."

She frowned. "Is it only related to cases? What you're focused on?"

"Gambling's intuitive. The other stuff is triggered by my emotions or what's left over at a crime scene. I don't have any control over it." He swallowed. "Once I'm focused on a case everything is related to it. I usually see people die or who are going to die, but never the exact kill site."

"That frustrates you."

"Of course." The Subaru honked again and he looked into his side mirror. "Someone's in a hurry."

"So are we," she quipped.

He pursed his lips. Stubborn too. Damn Foley.

Her voice softened. "I'm glad you care enough to get involved. You could have remained retired on disability."

"You investigated me." It pushed his irritation further.

She glanced at him. "It's called Google. You came up fast through the ranks and earned a rep as a detective who always solved his cases. You retired from the force after you were wounded and only work freelance now. The last case you solved for the FBI on missing women in Seattle is well-known, as are your psychic abilities."

"Are they?"

She added, "This case will be explosive for the nation. Threshold is murderous, but getting attention for legitimate concerns."

His eyebrows arched. "Sympathizing with murderers?"

"No, but Wheeler wasn't much better. The chemicals he made are carcinogens for humans and killing our pollinators. Many countries and U.S. cities have banned glyphosate. I wouldn't eat GMOs."

The Subaru finally dropped back a reasonable distance and remained there.

Alex didn't know who he was more annoyed with, Megan or the Subaru driver. He choked back a comment about her driving. "You're an environmentalist."

"Activist all through college. The USDA, EPA, FDA, Congress, and the presidency are in the pockets of corporations so people feel they have no representation. We're back to the rich and elite running everything. That's what started the American Revolution, and that's why GMO test plots have been burned. It was only a matter of time before something worse like Threshold evolved."

She gazed at him. "I suppose you're a conservative?"

"I eat organic, worry about climate change and endangered species, and gave twenty grand to Greenpeace last year."

She began to say something, but clamped her lips shut and braked before a turn. "When are we going to Montana? And why bother with San Diego?"

"San Diego felt intuitive."

She waved a hand. "You had a clairvoyant hit on Billings. How does intuition trump that?"

Not used to being grilled, he had to admit the question was insightful. "Billings wasn't attached to the kill site. The goal is to stop the next murder tonight, and it won't be at Billings. Maybe Threshold is based in San Diego. If Wheeler was a random target, as Foley thinks, it makes sense the killers would use a convenient location like Del Mar. People know their own backyard best. I also want to meet Dr. Frank Crary in person to see if I get any further insights."

"I like that logic." She looked at him, her voice eager. "Are we going to Dr. Crary now? Foley showed me the veterinarian list and I memorized their addresses and phone numbers, along with California street maps."

"Really?" Alex stared at her. Foley hadn't exaggerated her abilities. "Foley is obtaining warrants for phone records. Let's see if Crary has any connection to Billings before we approach him."

"Sounds good."

He glanced again at the sideview mirror. The Subaru was closing in again and pulled up within a few feet from them. His stomach tightened as the car crept closer in the mirror. "Geez."

"Idiot." Megan glanced at the rearview mirror.

The car smacked their bumper with a crunch, jerking Alex against his seat belt. "Damn."

Megan scowled and eased off the accelerator. "Great. Just what we need."

The Outback pulled into the opposing traffic lane as if to pass them.

Alex wanted to snap at Megan for not letting the car go by earlier, but instead said, "Probably underage kids drinking. Get the license plate if they don't stop."

A road sign showed a hairpin curve up ahead. Megan braked and drove their car partly onto the narrow shoulder.

The Subaru was taking a huge risk if it was going to pass them now. Alex turned to glare at the driver, and saw something protruding from the car's open passenger window.

"Get down!" He gasped and spun around, hunching low in his seat.

Already ducking, Megan punched the gas pedal.

A blast struck the rear passenger window, scattering glass shards throughout the interior. A burst of warm air swept through the car.

Taking off his seatbelt, Alex drew his 9mm. A hill loomed up in the windshield and he shouted, lifting his free arm in front of his face.

Megan looked over the dash and twisted the steering wheel. The tires bit into dirt, jerking the sedan left.

Turning around, Alex looked between the seats. A man in the front passenger seat of the Subaru wore a nylon stocking over his head and gripped a shotgun. The Outback accelerated into the opposing traffic lane.

"He's coming again!" snapped Alex.

Megan jerked the sedan left and cut off the Subaru. She powered down her window.

Half on his knees, Alex fired three shots, shattering their car's rear window. The reports rang in his ears and bullet holes appeared in the front windshield of the Subaru. The Subaru veered back into the right lane.

Megan swung the sedan sharply right to keep the swerving wagon behind them. Alex slid sideways. Megan drew a SIG Sauer P320 and set it on her lap. She swung the car left again to block the Subaru.

They entered the hairpin curve in the wrong lane, the Subaru following.

Alex scanned ahead as the Toyota's tires screamed around the corner. "Hey!" he yelled.

An oncoming red minivan sounded its horn—the woman driver gaped at them.

Megan wrenched the sedan right. Wheels squealed on pavement. Alex slid against her shoulder, jamming her against the door. The minivan clipped their back fender, jolting their car a few feet sideways.

"Get off me!" yelled Megan.

Their Toyota veered across the road with Alex's weight still trapping Megan. The Subaru veered out of the way of the van, which ran off the road and crashed into a tree.

Turning, Alex shouted as pine trees loomed over them. Gripping the wheel, he wrenched the sedan left. The turn slid him against the passenger door and he swore. Tilting sharply, the Corolla fishtailed briefly before Megan steadied it.

Alex glanced back. The Subaru had lost ground to avoid the minivan.

When they rounded the curve, relief swept him. Fifty yards ahead of them, the CHP Charger was parked in a tourist lookout on the right shoulder.

CHAPTER 4

MEGAN SLAMMED ON THE brakes and spun the steering wheel. The tires screeched and their sedan did a one-eighty in the road and jolted to a stop. The engine died.

Alex gaped. The Outback was approaching them head-on.

Megan stuck her arm out the window and squeezed off three shots.

"Get down!" shouted Alex.

Megan leaned sideways. Alex threw himself over her as a hard jolt pushed their car toward the east side of the road amid crunching metal. Air bags exploded, pushing them against the front seat.

An engine whined.

Alex peered over the dash. The Subaru was racing backward, its engine hood crumpled like a camel's hump. Three bullet holes marred its windshield. The car made a reverse turn in the middle of the road, and then sped around the hairpin curve, quickly out of sight.

Alex sat up. The front end of their car was pushed in on the passenger side and their car rested at an angle in the road.

Partially rising, Megan peered over the dashboard out their windshield.

Wiping a forearm across his forehead, Alex said, "California drivers."

"Get out of the car with your hands on your head!"

One of the CHP officers stood in the turn-off twenty feet from them, a Smith & Wesson M&P pistol held stiffly in his extended hands. Dressed in a khaki shirt and pants, the trooper wore a wide-brimmed tan hat. A radio hung over his shoulder. The driving officer stood behind his open car door, his left hand already on his radio as he talked into it.

Alex was irritated at the officer holding a gun on them. But the patrolmen had seen Megan shooting at a car. Maybe they assumed it was road rage. He hoped the officers were calling to intercept the other car.

He slid his gun back into the holster beneath his shirt. Taking a deep breath, he opened his door and stepped onto the road, holding his badge above the hood. Dust and the scent of steaming blacktop hit his nostrils. Sweat coated his skin.

"FBI," he said to the officer. "We need you to get on the radio and set roadblocks at the..." He looked in at Megan. "Do you know where?"

She spoke softly. "South end of Torrey Pines, and both directions on the 5 and Ted Williams Freeway out to ten miles. Better do Camino Del Mar ten miles north of the park too."

Alex repeated the information to the officer.

The officer didn't lower his gun, and instead lifted his chin at Megan. "I want to see her badge too." His voice was hard.

Megan cracked her door, still hunched over in the seat.

Alex glanced in at her. She was moving slow, appearing a little dazed. Softly, he said, "Holster your gun, Megan."

Straightening, he shuffled to the rear of the car. The trooper in the road eyed him closely, but had his M&P trained on Megan's door. Megan sat motionless, her door still only cracked opened. Alex stopped near the trunk, wondering why she wasn't getting out. Maybe she was hurt.

The officer in the road swung his gun from Megan to him.

Alex frowned. "Hey, are you deaf? We're FBI." He spotted the SIG Sauer in Megan's hands behind the door as she stared at the trooper.

At the same moment, the standing officer swung his gun back to Megan, his face hardening. "Show your badge and hands."

Alex blurted, "It's all right, officer. I'm a special investigator on assignment with—"

An explosion cut him off.

The trooper crumpled, red darkening the belly of his brown shirt, his arms dropping as he stumbled back.

Alex gaped, lowering his badge. He swung to Megan; she lay on her back on the front seat, arms extended, her gun aimed at her window.

"Get down, Alex!" she yelled.

The officer standing behind the open CHP car door held a MP7 silenced submachine gun. The nonstandard weapon sent adrenaline into Alex's chest.

Megan shot three times at the officer, who ducked down while firing the MP7 at them through his open window.

Alex crouched behind the rear tire as bullets ripped dull pops along the car's frame. Twisting to sit behind the tire, he drew his gun and pushed his back against the hubcap, keeping his head down. His shoulders and arms were rigid and he jammed his shoes into the tar. Bullets punched through the rear car door near him and bit the road past the trunk.

Megan belly crawled out of the front passenger door down to the asphalt, and then scrambled behind the front passenger tire.

Alex rose slightly and risked a look over the trunk.

The wounded trooper was falling into the back seat of the police car. The other officer rose and sprayed them again with the MP7.

Alex ducked as bullets ripped into the sedan in dull thuds. When the shooting stopped, he glanced at Megan. She was still crouched behind the front passenger tire.

Tires spewed gravel.

Alex glanced over the trunk, and then scrambled around the car to the driver's side to get a better line of sight on the fleeing patrol car. He stood and fired three shots; Megan didn't fire. After the cruiser disappeared around the corner, his shoulders slumped, the sudden quiet at odds with his emotions.

He leaned against the car, his left knee aching. His shirt was drenched and his stomach heaved. "Megan?"

No response.

"Megan!" He quickly limped back around the trunk.

She stood up near the front end, her face ashen, her gun holstered. Blood dripped from her left hand, staining the cuff of her white blouse.

Walking along the car in a rush, he stopped in front of her. "You're shot?"

"Just grazed my forearm." Using her right hand, she took off her sunglasses and ran her gaze over him. "Are you all right?"

Relief swept his limbs and he exhaled. "I'll make it to dinner. Sit down, keep the arm elevated. I'll call it in."

Dialing 911 on his cell, he gave a quick report while retrieving a clean T-shirt from his suitcase in the trunk. He strode back to Megan.

She sat sideways on the front car seat, her feet on the pavement. The sleeve of her blouse was mostly red.

Pulling out his OTF knife, he cut her sleeve to make it easier to pull back. She had a thin, jagged scrape along the forearm. He folded the tee into a rectangle and gently laid it against her wound. "Put pressure on it."

As she placed her palm against it, her eyes searched his, the emotion in them reaching him. "Thank you, Alex."

He stared down at her. "How did you know the cops were fake?"

The corners of her mouth turned down. "I caught a glimpse of the MP7 that the officer was hiding in his right hand. When he lifted it, I fired."

"I should have seen that." She was sharp and it impressed him. Or was he getting sloppy?

Sirens blared in the distance.

He thought about Threshold. "It's a big risk for the terrorists to attack us. But if not them, then who?"

Her face darkened and she didn't answer.

The set-up had been so elaborate that it felt bigger than a personal vendetta. Also why not just shoot them earlier instead of playing bumper cars? None of it seemed logical. And when he ran through his past, he came up empty for suspects. "Do you have anyone in your past that would try something like this?"

"I ran through possibilities," she said. "Nothing fits. You?"

"Nothing that makes sense."

She looked up at him. "I saw you limping."

"Left knee acts up sometimes. An old wound." One of the bullets he had taken from Jenny's killer.

He gestured to her. "Thanks."

"For what?"

He shrugged. "Saving my life."

She reddened with an awkward glance that didn't quite meet his. "You're welcome, Alex." Her voice lowered. "I've never shot anyone before."

"You had no choice." He wondered again what she had done before. Maybe she had never been in the field. Still, she had handled herself well.

In a moment her intense eyes probed his.

"What?" he asked.

"I guess this means I now have field experience."

CHAPTER 5

ALEX'S CELL PHONE RANG. He answered it. The harsh voice on the other end was monotone, but the punctuated words had a gleeful quality.

"Psychy, got a message for you."

Alex became still. "I'm listening."

"Road kill can't run." The man chuckled. "Remember that, if you can."

"Can you speak English? Or find a translator? Maybe get your GED."

A short laugh, and then, "Lovely sense of humor. Lovely. Sure, for you, Psychy, here's some English. Get off the Threshold case or you're dead. You and that hot island piece."

The phone went dead in his hands. Alex looked at it in surprise. A cold sensation settled into his stomach. Why would Threshold give a threat after they had already attacked them? Just a reminder? And how did they know he was on the case? Also his cell number was unpublished and unlisted. The first thing that came to him was that there was a leak at the FBI. That unsettled him, but he couldn't think of an alternative that fit.

He watched Megan walk down the block across the street and disappear into a boutique. An EMT had cleaned and bandaged her arm. Police had questioned them, and then driven them into the FBI field office in San Diego. They did a short interview with an agent at the station before securing a pool car and driving into the city.

Deputy Director Foley hadn't returned his call yet.

Megan hadn't said a word during the drive. Alex didn't blame her. His stomach had been washboard tight all the way in, but now he was just angry. Attacking them only made sense if Threshold already felt threatened by them—or him. Maybe his past successes made them nervous. He had a host of questions but no answers.

He sat in their car parked a block away from some clothing boutiques on University Avenue. They were making a quick stop for Megan to buy a new blouse. She lived thirty minutes away, which they both agreed was too much driving time, hence the ten-minute shopping trip.

Dr. Crary's big animal vet clinic was only a mile away and Alex was impatient to meet the veterinarian. They were still waiting for the veterinarian's phone records before they interviewed him.

He picked up the apple that he had bought and finished it off, its juice tart on his tongue.

His thoughts turned to his last partner, Jenny. She had died while they were on a stakeout of a serial killer. Those memories still assaulted him too often. After going freelance he had decided to never work with a partner again. It allowed him to handle the few cases he took without the added stress of worrying about someone else.

His cell played the *Call to the Post* bugle riff. Deputy Director Foley. Alex explained the threatening call.

Foley said, "I'm having Leon Mason from our San Diego office back you up. He'll introduce himself this afternoon."

An instant objection was on Alex's tongue, but he bit it off. "The more the merrier."

"I don't have much for you," said Foley. "Four hooded men carjacked the patrol car. The officer was tied up, but unharmed. Maybe the four men were Threshold. There doesn't seem to be any other possibility. The Subaru Outback and police cruiser were abandoned. No prints. The woman in the van that hit you and crashed is okay. Anything new on your end?"

Alex didn't like the lack of leads. "Another possibility is an FBI leak."

Foley sounded doubtful. "Is that something you're certain of?"

"No. Just logic working here."

Foley didn't reply for a few moments. "Let me talk to Gallagher about that."

"What did you say Megan used to do?" Alex tried to sound nonchalant.

"Why?" asked Foley.

"I'm looking at all possibilities for who would have a reason to attack us."

Foley's voice was level. "Like I said, I can vouch for her. Whatever else she chooses to share with you is up to her. Don't press her." He hung up.

Annoyed, Alex put the phone away. Megan's refusal to tell him about her past reminded him of his older brother, Jack. When their father had died from a heart attack, Jack had walled himself off from any sharing and trust. Defied anyone to enter into his mind and rebelled against any authority that tried to make him do anything.

Their mother had been unable to control Jack, and he had died of a drug overdose at the age of sixteen. Alex remembered the funeral. Only twelve years old, he had cried, feeling helpless and already knowing he wanted to be a police officer. Back then he believed law officers could prevent bad things from happening.

He spotted Megan exiting the boutique. She wore a new white blouse. He was impressed. A speed shopper. He was about to start the car when she walked farther down the street, away from him, looking into another window. Needing to stretch his legs, he got out and walked along the sidewalk on the opposite side of the street. Megan had a store bag in hand and she was talking on her phone. In a minute she continued down the sidewalk.

Alex noted that a short, bald man in his forties had also stopped fifty feet behind her, and continued when Megan did. He wore jeans, white tennis shoes, and a flowered Hawaiian-style shirt. A folded newspaper was wedged beneath his arm. The man stopped in front of another woman's boutique. Maybe shopping for a woman in his life. Maybe not.

Alex crossed the street and walked down the busy sidewalk, keeping the short man in sight. Megan entered another store. The bald man went up to the door, answered his phone, and then gave a quick glance back at Alex. Quickly putting his phone away, the bald man hustled away down the sidewalk.

Alex decided the man had been alerted. That indicated a second man somewhere. As he quickened his pace, he glanced at cars on both sides of the street, and behind him, but didn't pick anyone out that was obvious. At the end of the block the bald man looked once more in his direction, before rounding the corner out of sight. Alex ran to the corner, weaving through the crowd. At the corner he looked down the street.

Pedestrian traffic filled the block, but he didn't see the bald man. Walking down the street, he looked across the road and ahead. The man had to have gone into one of the stores or restaurants. There were two bars across the street, and a larger tavern on his side.

The tavern grabbed his attention. Walking inside, he took off his sunglasses and hung them from his pullover. He scanned the full counter and table chairs as he walked through the bar. No sign of the bald man.

At the back of the room a short hallway led to the restroom. It was bigger than he expected; three stalls, four urinals, and five sinks. Maybe they had bigger evening crowds. Polished tile glinted under bright fluorescent lights. The pungent odor of chlorine filled the air.

Two men stood at the sinks, one at a urinal. Alex walked toward the stalls. The first was cracked a few inches. Cautiously he nudged it open. Empty. The second stall hung ajar a few inches. He bent over to look beneath the door. White tennis shoes. He gripped his gun hilt and gently pushed open the door.

A teenager with glasses sat on the toilet, staring up at him.

Mouthing, *Sorry*, Alex hurriedly shut the door.

The last stall door was also ajar. When he bent over, no shoes were visible. He pushed the door. It jerked back hard. Something blurred at him. Twisting his head to the side, he partially avoided the foot aimed at his jaw. He was barely aware of the bald man standing on the toilet seat.

Staggering back from the blow, he gasped as the small of his back rammed into the sink counter. He tasted blood. Off balance, it took an act of will to remain upright.

The bald man jumped off the toilet, and aimed another straight kick at Alex's stomach. Alex twisted sideways, grabbed the man's leg, and charged, pushing him back against the stall frame. He threw a quick punch at his attacker's face.

Taking the blow on the chin silently, the bald man swung at Alex. Alex released the man's leg and blocked the punch.

The three men ran out of the restroom, but the teenager remained in his stall.

Lowering his head, the bald man butted Alex in the chest. Falling backward, Alex landed heavily on the tile floor, grappling with the man's shoulders. His sunglasses slid across the floor.

The bald man punched Alex in the ribs. Grunting, Alex pushed the man off, facing him sideways. He kicked the man in the stomach. Taking the blow, the bald man groaned and rolled away.

Alex drew his gun, but the agile man had already scrambled to his feet and bolted from the room.

Alex rose and hurried out. Quickly retracing his steps through the tavern, his gun against his thigh, he reached the sidewalk in seconds. The bald man was nowhere in sight. He put his gun away. The sun was in his eyes. He decided to retrieve his sunglasses and went back inside.

In the restroom the teenager was staring in the mirror, trying on his shades. The boy saw him and backed up against the wall.

Alex pulled his badge. "You're safe, I'm with the FBI. But I'm going to need those glasses."

The boy timidly handed them over.

Alex put them on and forced a smile. "Now you have a good story to tell someone."

Limping slightly, his smile disappeared as he headed back to the car, a dull throb in his jaw and a sharp ache in his side. He hoped he didn't have a cracked rib. He also hoped the bald man was feeling some pain. After the exertion, the heat felt oppressive.

Megan was waiting for him, standing by the front bumper, her forehead lined. She eyed him closely, her voice going lower, revealing empathy. "What happened, Alex?"

"A short bald guy was following you. I chased him. We played footsie."

He took the driver's seat and she got in. Sitting back, he said, "The bald guy didn't try to kill me. Never pulled a knife or gun. And he had a chance to." It didn't fit, especially after the earlier attempt on their lives and the phone call. None of it fit any kind of pattern.

"Too many witnesses?" she asked.

He shrugged. "Maybe. But it doesn't track the fake cop attack. And I don't think Threshold would hold back."

"You're not afraid, are you?" She said it as a statement of fact.

He looked at her, unable to tell her what he did fear. "Tell me one thing. Why did you ask Foley to be on this case?"

She shrugged. "Same reason as you. I want to make a difference. I might agree with Threshold's environmental views, but not murder. I want to take them down as fast as possible."

He nodded slowly. "Fair enough."

"Between the two of us, we can do it, Alex."

He liked her confidence. "Foley called. He has no leads for us. The police car was stolen." He swallowed. "Some guy connected to Threshold called me and warned us off the case. If we don't walk away, he threatened to kill us."

"That's odd." Her expression didn't show any fear. Just anger. That made him feel better.

"There's more." There was no way for this to sound anything but psychotic. "The caller said, 'Road kill can't run.'" Megan pursed her lips, and he asked, "Any ideas?"

Her eyes searched his. "Threshold has a lot of resources."

She opened her laptop. "Foley called me while I was in the store. I can access Dr. Crary's phone records."

He leaned back, the sun on his face feeling pleasant. "I'll drive there while you look at them."

"Wait a minute." She punched keys.

He glanced at her, noting the sunlight on her hair as she scanned data on her screen.

In a minute she looked at him. "Done."

He raised his eyebrows. "Dr. Crary's phone records first."

She eyed him. "I was able to check out all the vets in San Diego. I'd like to run some patterns by you."

"That fast?" He was impressed again with her skills.

She continued. "Some of the vets had consistent calls with private individuals around the country, excluding family, institutions, hospitals, clinics, or other veterinarians. Two of the vets with those phone patterns live in northern California. Three are closer. There's a Dr. Tor up the coast, who's made calls to Mr. Sull in Georgia, Mr. Willern in Miami, and Mr. Vadnas in Nevada. "

He massaged his knee. "Recently?"

"In the last two months."

None of those names or states resonated with him. "Who else?"

"Dr. Peterson. He made recent calls to Mr. Jansen in Maine, Mr. Shou in Philly, and Ms. Waters in Mississippi."

"Keep going. And give me two aspirin. In the glove compartment."

She found the aspirin and handed him two pills and his water bottle. "Dr. Frank Crary made personal calls to Dr. Seth Joulie in Rochester, Minnesota, and to U.S. Senator Brett Dillon in Montana."

Alex looked at her sharply. "What city in Montana?"

"Billings."

He frowned. "You knew we were looking at Dr. Crary and Billings. Why the game?"

She closed the laptop. "I wanted to see if the other names or connections might trigger something in you. We have no idea how many people are involved with Threshold, but we already know they have a lot of resources behind them."

He shrugged. "Okay. Not a bad idea."

"I'm good at what I do, Alex."

He couldn't disagree. "A-plus. You earned extra credit."

She tilted her head, a glint of humor in her eyes. "What does that get me?"

He gave a brief smile, wondering if she was flirting with him. "I'll think about it. Can you direct me to Crary's office now?"

"I called Dr. Crary's office while I was shopping and pretended to be a client. He took his fishing boat out two days ago for a week of vacation and told his staff he wouldn't answer phone calls."

"Interesting." He eyed her. "Is withholding going to be a pattern with us?"

It was her turn to smile. "I hope not. I was going to tell you sooner but a bald guy got in the way."

His gaze stalled on the smooth skin of her neck. "If Crary's involved, maybe he wants to be unavailable for questioning."

"I made another call while shopping. Senator Dillon is at his ranch for the week." Her eyebrows arched. "Now do we go to Billings?"

"Now we go to Billings."

CHAPTER 6

THROUGH HIS GLASS OFFICE door, Deputy Director Foley glimpsed Gallagher approaching from the far end of the hallway. The man's heavy footsteps preceded him. He tapped the pencil in his hand against the desk, bare except for his laptop, black ceramic coffee cup, and phone. His lips pursed. This wouldn't be pleasant, but it was necessary.

He and Gallagher had flown up separately from San Diego to Los Angeles and they hadn't had a chance to talk about the attack on Alex and Megan. The brazenness of the attack unsettled Foley, bringing a host of questions to mind. Thus he had decided to stay in California a little longer before returning to D.C.

Swiveling his chair to his computer, he cut the volume of George Strait's *Amarillo By Morning* in half. Slowly he rotated his chair in a complete three-sixty to take in the large framed wall photographs of himself. Climbing the Alps of Austria, snorkeling a reef off a small island in Fiji, hang-gliding off the dormant volcano of Mauna Kea in Hawaii, and bungee jumping off a bridge in California. Memories that exhilarated him, from a younger age when he had taken more risks. Those memories excited him almost as much as his current position in the Bureau.

He stopped his chair and faced the door again. Lifting his mug, he took a quick sip of cold coffee, then took out his mint tin and popped one in his mouth.

Gallagher burst into the office and slumped into the chair in front of the desk. He wore the same rumpled tan suit he had worn for over a week and he carried the same unlit pipe.

Foley found it all a distraction.

"Don't you ever get sick of that crap?" Gallagher nodded at the computer.

Foley's brow furrowed. "What's wrong with it?"

"Can you turn it down?

"I already did." Turning, Foley adjusted the volume to a whisper. He cleared his throat and rested his forearms on his desk. "What's your take on the attack on Alex and Megan?"

Gallagher pursed his lips. "Someone worked pretty hard to set it up."

"Even if the Wheeler estate was under surveillance by Threshold, they didn't have enough time to set up that attack." Foley tented his hands. "Alex and Megan also had a phone call from someone who threatened their lives if they don't get off the case."

Gallagher's expression didn't waver. "Do you really think Alex Sight has a psychic gift that the terrorists are afraid of?"

Foley didn't want to have this discussion. Gallagher thought Sight was just lucky with detective work and didn't buy the psychic stuff. "Alex has solved cases quickly that others couldn't."

Gallagher grunted. "So have good analysts."

Wanting to change the subject, Foley said, "Do you think someone in this department funneled information to the terrorists?"

"No way." Gallagher shook his head and his eyes narrowed. "I'll have people check for surveillance on the Wheeler estate and I'll give it some thought myself." He pulled two sticks of gum from his pocket and peeled off the wrappers. Shoving the gum in his mouth, he casually dropped the wrappers on Foley's desk. "It's interesting the carjacked police officer wasn't attacked or injured in any way."

Meeting Gallagher's gaze, Foley tapped the pencil against his desk. "Maybe Threshold doesn't have a beef with law enforcement." Gallagher's cheeks looked even more puffed with the gum, like a big hamster. "I want Alex and Megan updated with information as soon we obtain it." He steeled his jaw. "Is that understood?"

"That'll be tough to do with the way they move around." Gallagher chewed noisily.

Foley frowned. "Funnel everything through me. I'll be in touch with them daily so I can keep them abreast of everything."

Gallagher nodded. "I'll do my best, but delays are part of life around here and—"

"Bill." Foley wondered why Gallagher could never just take an order and follow it. He found it intolerable.

Gallagher swallowed his words and his face darkened.

Tapping the pencil slowly three times against the desktop, Foley felt a surge of adrenaline rush into his upper body. "I'm in charge, Bill, and I won't accept any delay of information to me. Understood? Or do I need to write it out for you?"

Gallagher grunted. "Anything else?"

"No."

Gallagher rose to go.

"Bill."

"What?" Gallagher turned with a tilted frown.

"Please take your wrappers."

"You're worse than my wife." Gallagher gave a hard smile and swiped them off the desk.

Foley leaned back as the burly man left. If Gallagher didn't have such a good reputation, he would have transferred him long ago. Foley wanted him on this case so for now it was to his advantage to put up with the man's crudeness. It had been a year since he had been appointed to the FBI deputy director position and maybe Gallagher was a sore loser.

He didn't understand how a man who never missed a single detail in his work was such a slob. It also made him wonder what kind of woman would put up with Gallagher. More plausible, perhaps Gallagher's ten-year marriage had fallen apart. A bad marriage could make your life miserable. Foley had already gone through a divorce. Never again. And never again to marriage either. Affairs made more sense. Then he could maintain control.

He wondered how Alex and Megan were getting along. Alex Sight was strange—Foley didn't know how to relate to someone who was psychic. It wasn't that he didn't believe in it, but it made him wary about what Alex could pick up about himself. Megan Detalio had her own oddities. He shook his head. Including Gallagher, all three had excellent track records and he wanted this case solved ASAP—it would look good to the director.

He slowly tapped the desk with his pencil, realizing the Threshold case already felt out of control. Like a runaway roller-coaster he didn't know how to stop.

CHAPTER 7

G ALLAGHER WANTED TO YELL at someone as he stomped away from Foley's office. The problem was he had never found the right dirt on Foley.

When the national director had appointed Foley to the deputy director position, Gallagher had worked hard to find something sleazy on the man. He thought he had succeeded after discovering Foley had been a hell-raising demonstrator in college. But his efforts had backfired. Foley's previous environmental activism had matched the mood of the country.

His research, which he had leaked to the press, just made Foley more appealing to the director.

Even more annoying, Foley tapped his stupid pencil in nearly every conversation. People in the Bureau had learned to pay attention to Foley's pencil. Otherwise they didn't stay around long.

But that was personal. The real stink of it was that Gallagher had slaved thirty years in field operations and as an intelligence analyst, finally ending up in counterterrorism. He had busted his butt and succeeded on some pretty big cases. It still hadn't been enough to beat a freak of nature like Foley. Foley had managed to float to the top with several advanced degrees and fewer years of experience under his belt. Some days it made Gallagher want to scream.

And Foley had brought about changes that weakened the Bureau. He had ordered some of their files on activists, including environmentalists, discontinued, shifting the focus solely to terrorist organizations like ISIS and splinter groups. Foley viewed files on legitimate demonstrators as harassment, whereas Gallagher embraced it as survival.

Demonstrators were potential terrorists, and Bureau files on environmental activists weren't up to date. He would have to find out what they did have. The important thing was that they wouldn't be current, and who knew how many bodies Threshold might stack up while they scrambled to get them up to date.

He hoped to find answers in the analyst center. Just entering the room took some of the weight off his heavy footfalls. At his request Juanita had arrived from D.C. an hour ago. The top analyst in his department, she was one of the few people who never tried to ingratiate herself with Foley. Gallagher appreciated that fact as much as her abilities.

The room had dozens of computers, numerous phones, faxes, copiers, scanners, and other electronic paraphernalia Gallagher barely noticed. He found Juanita sitting at a computer in a cubicle, her gaze locked on the screen. Other analysts were working with databases on different computers.

Juanita appeared younger than her twenty-five years. Long brown hair framed her small brown eyes and face. Slacks and a blue blazer over a white blouse covered her five-eight, trim body. Her only unattractive quality was that she always appeared sleepy. When he had first met her, Gallagher thought she used drugs. The reality was she had unlimited energy—maybe due to her minimal emotional responses.

He didn't care how she appeared. What mattered was she always found answers. All he had to do was provide the right questions. He stomped up to her side and asked, "Anything interesting in tracking xylazine customers?"

She didn't answer and instead saved what was on the screen—a database Gallagher didn't recognize—and punched some commands. On the computer flashed a list of companies and big animal vets. She hit a print button and a nearby laser printer spit out the file.

Gallagher ignored it. "I want to be updated on how many distributors, customers, and vets have been questioned. Inform me when their backgrounds have been run. List any that had shipments stolen or lost.

"I want to hear anything concerning Wheeler customer-reported thefts of glyphosate." He wished she would at least turn her head and meet his eyes so he knew she was listening to him. Even though she never missed or forgot any of his requests, it annoyed him.

"When you complete the list of environmental extremists, get a case history of all of them, current addresses and phone numbers. Check their alibis for the day Wheeler was killed. Take a look at the GMO Right to Know state groups that want GMO labeling and ask if they had anyone proposing violence.

"Make sure we contact Earth First! and any small radical environmental groups to see if they have any past employees or members who were dropped due to violent talk or actions. Ask if anyone will set up contact with Earth Liberation Front, to see if they have any members who would be part of something like this."

"Do you think they'll talk to us?" she asked.

He grimaced. "We have to try. ELF might support arson and sabotage, but they don't support murder and won't want to be associated with Threshold's methods. Also ask environmental magazines—online and print—for any letters they've received supporting violence. Contact the companies on Threshold's target list. Find out if they've received any aggressive letters or calls in the last year.

"Determine if Wheeler's company had any disgruntled employees that had an environmental bent, or any who were fired for opposition to company policy regarding pesticide use and sales. Cover all van and car rental agencies within a hundred miles of the Wheeler estate, and see if anyone remembers four men renting one. Ask the airlines to look for groups of four too." He thought about what else would be useful. "Any ideas?"

"Nothing else comes to mind." Her voice had a slight accent and sounded as if she tried to save energy even with spoken words.

He paused. "Get it all to me ASAP." The last sentence was unnecessary. Juanita always got everything to him ASAP. All he could figure was that her demeanor always inspired him to say those four letters.

Juanita turned to him. "Deputy Director Foley said he wanted the list of environmental extremists sent to him."

Gallagher froze. "Foley called you?"

Juanita nodded.

Jerk. "When the report's finished, bring it to me. I'll make sure he gets it."

Juanita gave a slight smile and Gallagher walked away. Foley was in his head again and it made him stomp even louder.

CHAPTER 8

"HOW MUCH LONGER?" ALEX drummed the arm of his chair with his fingertips. "We've already waited two hours."

"They're not sure," said Megan. Slumping in the seat across from him, dark circles underlined her eyes. Her hair lay on her shoulders in wild curls.

Alex found her beautiful even when she looked tired. He checked his watch; three p.m. The Salt Lake City concourse was filled with people waiting for flights.

Agent Leon Mason sat in a chair fifty feet away reading a magazine. The ebony man looked like a football linebacker. In his late twenties, he had short hair and wore a black cotton pullover and slacks. He had met them at the San Diego field office. After quick introductions they took separate cars to the airport.

Leon tailed them to watch for anyone who might do the same. The earnest man appeared good at what he did. After what had already happened, Alex had no complaints.

A cramp slowly developed in his left calf, which begged to be stretched. They had taken a flight to Salt Lake City, but their flight to Billings was delayed. Aside from being tired, his whole body felt agitated, as if he was wired with caffeine jitters. "Why didn't they inform us before we left San Diego?"

Megan's eyebrows arched. "Apparently the storm outside of Billings came up fast with little warning."

Getting a hotel room and possibly missing their flight held no appeal, but neither did a long night in the airport. He pursed his lips over the idea of Threshold preparing for their next murders, while he and Megan sat in an airport.

He didn't feel he was wrong about the terrorists' countdown or that they would kill again tonight. His conclusion of a nighttime attack was supported by the fact that nothing had been reported anywhere in the country thus far. Of course it was possible the bodies hadn't been found yet.

Megan leaned over to pick up a teddy bear that a noisy two-year-old had tossed on the floor. Handing it back to the parents with a tired smile, she spoke to them in a language he didn't recognize. Maybe Portuguese. Smiling, she settled back in her chair.

Alex eyed her. "How many languages do you speak?"

She stretched her arms up with a yawn. "Fifteen."

"Fifteen? I have enough issues with English."

She shrugged. "I grew up speaking English, French, Italian, and Fijian at home."

"Where's your family?" he asked.

"Parents and grandparents are in Colorado. My sister is in Boston, studying to be a doctor. I miss all of them. We're close. You?" She rested her elbow on the arm of her chair, her chin in her palm as she gazed at him.

"Minnesota's home base. Mom lives in St. Paul. Dad died when I was young. My grandparents died before I was born."

"Brothers or sisters?" Her voice sounded subdued.

He wasn't sure he wanted to talk about it, but he said, "My older brother OD'd at the age of sixteen." Emotion crept into his voice. "Drug rehabs are a favorite charity of mine."

"I'm sorry, Alex."

"Yeah, me too."

Her face darkened. "I lost a brother in Afghanistan." She lifted her head, her voice softer. "I was a teenager and it still hurts."

He noted the effort it cost her to say that. "I'm sorry."

She looked away. "I try not to think about it."

"Yeah, I can relate."

"I'm going to get some rest." She closed her eyes.

Never able to sleep in a chair, he didn't try. He surveyed the huddles of people, while his thoughts wandered to Threshold. Often terrorists continued their actions until they were killed. A suicide run ending in a big splash of violence. But Threshold felt different.

He nudged Megan's leg with his shoe. "Hey."

She stirred, her eyelids barely opening.

He leaned closer. "The murders will get Threshold massive media attention, but what good is that if it's short-lived and ends when they're caught?"

"Extremists usually think publicity is worth it," she murmured.

"But these people are smart. Very organized with lots of support, and aware of how to maximize news from the media. Everything's been well orchestrated, possibly for quite some time." He waited for her response.

She yawned. "So?"

He tapped the arm of his chair. "So what happens if they get all this exposure?"

She sat up and blinked. "Maybe they're trying to bring attention to an upcoming event."

"Such as?" He liked that idea.

She dug out her laptop. "We could look at the next U.N. meeting, ecological symposiums, environmental conferences, or upcoming congressional decisions."

"Get Gallagher to help track it down."

She paused. "Every event in the next month?"

"I don't think they plan to stay active that long. I'm guessing that they're aiming at something happening in the next week. Then they might go underground and hide until the next opportunity."

"Sounds good, Alex." She began punching keys.

"I'm going to stretch my legs." The only reply he got was a grunt. He rose and walked away.

Groups of people stood scattered throughout the terminal and many people slept in chairs, waiting for flight plans to clear. Leon's eyes flicked at Alex as he walked by, but the man's solid face didn't move a fraction.

Alex had a slight headache due to lack of sleep. A few aspirin hadn't helped. Frustration added to the pressure inside his skull. The image he had at the Wheeler estate of figures toppling under a barrage of bullets haunted him.

He walked into a restroom and checked his jaw in the mirror. Scraped, it had a bluish-gray spot shadowing it. There was no way to hide the bruise. Next he lifted up his shirt and carefully explored his ribs. They felt all right, but the bruise along his side would soon complement his face. The bullet indentation on his torso was a grim reminder of three years past. Scowling, he left.

He spotted vending machines farther along the concourse and had just enough change for oatmeal cookies. Breakfast had been his last full meal. Pocketing the cookies, he walked on.

Something caught his attention to the left. Stopping, he turned and looked up. A flight schedule monitor was mounted on a wall. A small group of people stared up at it.

Feeling an urge to get closer, he shouldered his way between a large woman and an even bigger man. Both gave him annoyed frowns and comments, which he ignored. Oblivious to everyone around him, he scanned the list of destinations on the monitor. Austin, Dallas, Las Vegas, Los Angeles, Mexico City... His eyes continued running down the list, then darted to the top again, stopping on Austin. The departure time was nine p.m. and the flight was on time.

His body turned rigid as his gaze repeatedly read across *Austin 9:00PM, Austin 9:00PM, Austin...*an image superimposed itself over the monitor...*the shadowy form of a truck, woods, and four darkened specters running over grass...*He closed his eyes, trying to focus...*a large house loomed in front of him, a door flung open, a pale face, hands raised in alarm...*The image faded, replaced by a silent word; *shadow*. He wavered there, waiting for more, but there was only darkness.

When he opened his eyes, the monitor showed in large letters *Austin 1:00AM,* making him blink. Abruptly the monitor showed *Austin 9:00PM* again. His body settled like a stone weight into his shoes.

Waiting to see if anything else would appear, he noticed people staring at him as his senses slowly dissolved to the world of the mundane. As usual, the Austin imagery hadn't given him the exact location. That knotted his stomach. He looked up at the monitor and verified again; Austin, nine p.m. Hours before they could fly out of here to Austin. "Hell," he murmured.

Energy drained from his limbs. His shoulders sagged and his mouth felt chalky. He needed chocolate. Then he needed to call Foley. He had no idea how long he had stood there. People standing nearby were still staring at him so he shuffled a few steps away. Slowly he allowed his tired gaze to wander around the terminal. Leon and Megan were visible a hundred feet from him.

His eyes paused on a knot of people not far from Leon, some sitting, some standing. A tall, large woman sat next to a small man wearing a baseball cap.

The woman got up to go to a restroom, moving with a dignified gait. She wore a brightly flowered dress and wide-brimmed felt hat. The man remained in his seat.

Alex walked closer, his gaze glued to the side of the man's face. He stopped as the man nonchalantly turned his way. All doubt vanished. It was the bald man he had fought in San Diego.

The bald man didn't reveal the slightest flicker of acknowledgement. With a trench coat draped over one arm, the man stood and walked down the concourse in the direction of Leon and Megan.

Walking faster, Alex's lips pursed as he gazed ahead. Megan was on her phone. She would never see the man coming.

The bald man walked past Leon, picking up his pace.

Alex moved faster. He tried to catch Leon's attention, but the young man was staring in another direction. Megan didn't see the bald man either, so he yelled, "Megan!"

She twisted in her seat as the bald man approached her. Pausing, the man gazed back at Alex, and then turned and walked briskly away.

Megan and Leon rose from their chairs as Alex ran past them. He had to weave around individuals and small clumps of people. He lost sight of the bald man and was forced to pause at every departure gate he passed to scan the crowd. Nothing. Too many places to hide. He saw Leon working the other side of the concourse.

Hurrying through the crowd as fast as he could, he reached the end of the concourse and looked left, down another concourse. Vanished.

Leon hustled up alongside him, and Alex said, "You look left, I'll take right."

Together they ran down the concourse. At the end they still hadn't spotted the bald man.

"Let's call it." Alex walked back down the concourse, Leon beside him.

"I'm sorry I didn't notice him sooner." Leon looked genuinely upset. But he wasn't sweating or breathing hard.

"No worries." Alex studied him. "You played football?"

"College. I thought about going pro." Leon shrugged. "I decided fighting crime was a better use of my talents."

"Yeah, who needs all those cheerleaders harassing you and all that money."

Leon smiled. "Money and fame are overrated."

"I'm glad you're on our side."

Megan was waiting for them and looked at Alex expectantly. He shrugged. He didn't have anything to say. Too many unknowns about the bald man left him silent.

***

Later Alex said, "The bald man's starting to get on my nerves."

Megan sat beside him, her brow furrowed. "Why would someone keep following us?"

"See what we're up to. Show us that the phone threat is real. Try to kill us again. Take your pick." He glanced at her.

"What's the plan?" Her voice was matter-of-fact.

Leaning back in his chair, he took another bite of dark chocolate. "Get to Austin and try to find them."

"How likely is that?"

"I don't know." That part knotted his stomach.

"Would it help to call ahead?" she asked.

"I can't give them enough information to act on." Foley had called and said they couldn't get a jet to them any sooner than the nine p.m. Austin flight so they were stuck waiting.

Megan pulled back her hair. "Have you had visions like this before?"

"Yeah, a few." He stopped tapping his fingers and took a deep breath.

Her eyebrows raised. "It gives us a shot, so what's the problem?"

He turned away, weary. "Some things are harder to let go."

"Such as?"

It took him a few moments to speak. "A year and a half ago I hunted a computer pedophile. He was good at kidnapping ten to twelve-year-old boys, abusing them, and then killing them." He swallowed. "I found him one hour after he had killed his last victim. I'll never forget the faces of the boy's parents."

"At least it was his last victim," she said softly.

"Yeah."

"But you feel responsible." Her tone betrayed empathy.

"It's always there now if I'm on a case." Her eyes met his, and he added, "Knowing every minute counts, and that it's up to me to get it right."

Jenny's words floated back to him: *But what if you didn't see the whole picture?* When Megan continued to stare at him, he leaned back, uncomfortable. "Married? Kids?" She didn't wear a ring.

She shrugged. "I don't want to have kids. My boyfriend wants to get married."

"Do you?" He wondered what that would be like, to be married. He also found it silly that he was disappointed she had a boyfriend. *Get real, you've just met her,* he told himself.

Her eyes returned to his. "Maybe. I sometimes wonder about reaching fifty and still being single."

He wondered about that for himself at times. "What does the boyfriend do?"

"He's a doctor in L.A. Sometimes it's hard to connect due to our jobs. I was talking to him when the bald guy ran by. What about you?"

"No doctors or kids. Single." Hearing his own words gave him an empty feeling.

She regarded him for a few moments, and then settled into her chair. "I'm going to get some sleep."

Studying her face, he realized he had been without the simple comfort of touch for too long. Trying to save a never-ending stream of victims had consumed everything else that might have been in his life over the last two years of freelance work. Lonely sometimes, he also wasn't sure if it was the fact of being alone or his grief over Jenny that still defined his emotions.

Maybe after this case he would take a break. Meet some people. Take some chances. He checked the time. Hours before more bodies piled up.

CHAPTER 9

ODYSSEUS LOOKED AT HIS watch. Eleven-fifteen p.m. Overcast with no moon. Dark like oil. Perfect.

The warm air was thick with humidity. He pulled a piece of strawberry chewing gum from a pocket and offered a piece to Patroclus, who shook his head.

The coarse rumble of a diesel engine drew his attention to the twelve-foot-tall mesh fence fifty yards from the side street where their empty cargo van was parked. He peered across the wide truck entrance in front of the gate. The darkness forced him to concentrate.

Headlights from the truck pierced the night as the gate swung open mechanically. Odysseus took a deep breath as the Isuzu diesel truck rolled through. The semi moved steadily through the gateway and onto the street.

Patroclus started their van and slowly drove out of the side street, following the diesel. Menelaus and Achilles were in another van behind them.

The truck turned right onto a freeway frontage road.

Immediately Patroclus floored the gas pedal, swerving around the same corner, then passing the semi in the oncoming traffic lane. Menelaus' van trailed the truck. Reaching into the nylon bag at his feet, Odysseus withdrew an MP5.

Once past the truck, Patroclus pulled in front of it and slowed considerably, forcing the truck driver to slow too. Odysseus waited until they were in darkness, midway between two of the bright streetlights evenly spaced along the frontage road. "Now," he whispered.

Patroclus braked hard to stop the van, then shut off the engine and turned on the hazard lights.

With a squeal of rubber, the truck drew up close to their rear bumper, its horn blaring.

Odysseus couldn't see the other van. The diesel blocked it. The truck driver confirmed he was boxed in when he blew his horn several times. After receiving no response, the driver climbed down from his cab.

Odysseus said into his neck radio, "Get ready." In the side mirror he spotted Achilles running along the passenger side of the truck.

Odysseus touched Patroclus' shoulder and handed him the MP5. Taking it, Patroclus swiveled out of the driver's seat and climbed into the back of the van. Odysseus slid over to the driver's seat and looked into the sideview mirror.

The truck driver had his shoulders hunched and his fists bunched. When he walked past the rear bumper of their van, Odysseus said, "Now."

Patroclus slid the van's side door open.

Odysseus saw the truck driver's face register surprise. The MP5 in Patroclus' hands would convince the trucker to cooperate. When the truck driver climbed into the van, his weight rocked the vehicle slightly.

Odysseus turned, watching Patroclus club the man with the rifle butt. The truck driver grunted and collapsed.

Achilles' voice came over Odysseus' radio. "Truck secured."

Odysseus released the tension in his chest.

Patroclus remained with the trucker. Menelaus would drive the other van, while Achilles drove the semi.

Starting the lead van, Odysseus drove on. The truck and second van followed.

They were soon on the freeway, but instead of driving south, as the semi driver had originally intended, Odysseus headed north, toward Austin. He set the cruise control and sat back, his shoulders bunched.

CHAPTER 10

THEY TOUCHED DOWN AT Austin-Bergstrom International Airport a little before midnight. During the flight Alex feasted on cookies and chocolate, and then napped restlessly for a half-hour. He was too wired to do anything else but stay awake during the remainder of the flight.

Megan was able to grab a few hours of sleep. He nudged her shoulder when they landed.

A wave of heat blasted them as they exited the terminal. A film of sweat covered Alex's face.

Four Bureau cars waited for them, three filled with field agents wearing dark shirts, Kevlar vests, and slacks.

The special agent in charge, a stocky mustached forty-year-old, quickly introduced himself. He had a narrow, alert face. "Pleasure to meet you, Mr. Sight, Ms. Detalio. I'm Jake Pridlow, out of the Houston office. I've heard a lot about you."

Alex grabbed Pridlow's extended hand. "Call me Alex."

"Megan." She shook his hand next.

Pridlow nodded. "Deputy Director Foley says we're all yours. Leon will drive your car. I'll ride with you. The others will follow and communicate by radio. We've brought vests and extra firepower for the three of you."

They threw their luggage into the trunk of the sedan and put on the vests. Alex sat in front with Leon, Megan in back with Pridlow. Leon drove them out of the airport.

Rolling down the window, Alex inhaled the stale air rising off the pavement as the empty expressway flashed by. Turning around, he watched Pridlow shove a loaded magazine into a MP5A3 submachine gun. He found it ironic that the FBI used the same basic weapon as the terrorists. "Foley said you know Austin like your own mother."

"Were those Foley's words?" Pridlow asked with mock indignation.

Alex couldn't smile. "Foley used *backyard*, but I like my cliché better."

Pridlow nodded. "Actually I do know this city better than my mother. And it doesn't tell me what to do either. What are we looking for?"

Alex thought on it. "A neighborhood with woods, big lots. Large houses set far back from the street.

Pridlow arched an eyebrow. "Old or new homes?"

Alex shook his head slightly. "Maybe an older design, but I'm not certain."

"Anything else?"

"No," Alex answered dully.

Pridlow lowered his voice. "There are a few areas that fit your description. Trouble is, we'll never be able to check all of them."

"Let's go west for now," said Alex.

Pridlow nodded. "You're sure?"

"Yes." Alex caught Megan watching him.

"All right," said Pridlow. "Leon, stay on this road until you see East Ben White Boulevard."

"You got it." The big man hunched his large frame over the wheel.

Alex checked his watch. Twelve-thirty p.m. "Let's forget about the speed limit."

"Right." Leon accelerated.

Closing his eyes, Alex tried to recapture details from the imagery at the airport. "Does the word *shadow* mean anything to you?"

Pridlow didn't hesitate. "Shadow Glen Golf Course, thirty minutes northeast. It's wooded around there. Some houses might fit."

Alex looked at him uncertainly. "I don't know."

"Shadow, shadow...does it have to be an exact match?" Pridlow extended the MP5A3 between the front seats.

"Why?" Alex took the gun, his palms sweaty.

"There's an older wooded development similar to the one you mentioned, southwest of Austin, called Shady Hollow." Pridlow sat back and handed a weapon and magazine to Megan.

"Shady Hollow," murmured Alex. "It feels better. Let's try it."

Megan loaded the magazine into the weapon. "How long will it take to get there?"

"Ten to fifteen minutes." Pridlow looked out his window. "If we're lucky."

"And then we have to find the house in the dark," muttered Alex.

Pridlow loaded his own gun. "Don't worry, if they're there, we'll make the event."

Pridlow's confidence didn't match what Alex felt.

"What about backup?" asked Megan.

"They've been alerted. As soon as we're sure where they are, we'll throw a net so tight around the area a fly couldn't escape." Pridlow tapped Alex's shoulder. "Should we hedge our bets, send some units northeast to Shadow Glen?"

Alex grimaced. "Do it."

Pridlow made the call on his cell phone, and then gave Leon directions.

Glancing back, Alex saw Megan inspecting her weapon. He slid the gun between his legs and gripped the armrest as Leon swerved onto the interstate. Pressure welled up inside his chest. It was twelve-forty.

At twelve-fifty-one they reached the neighborhood. Pridlow instructed the other cars to peel off and run a search pattern.

They slowly cruised along each block, windows down, looking for anything out of place. The darkness made the task difficult. Alex gripped his knees. When they entered the eighth block of their hunt on Shady Valley Drive, he worried they should have gone north. He rolled down his window, letting in the hot air.

They rounded a corner onto the second leg of Shady Valley Drive, which ran east-west. A stand of forest covered the next lot on their side of the road. Alex's gaze raced along the street and soft noises pricked his awareness.

"Slow down," he whispered. "Turn off your lights."

Leon killed the lights, easing them to a crawl, slowly rolling the car into the deeper shadows of the overhanging trees of the wooded lot. As they nosed forward, the lot beyond the trees became visible.

"Stop," whispered Alex. "Wait here."

Opening his door quietly, he jogged ahead several dozen steps to the edge of the wooded lot. The pavement still radiated heat. A great horned owl hooted from the nearby trees.

Even with the humidity of the night, Alex's mouth turned dry when he saw two vans backed far up the driveway on the next lot. They were parked alongside a semitruck that had been backed up even closer to the house.

He took a few more steps. Behind the truck, dark figures stood next to barrels in the center of the driveway. An urge to charge up the sloped yard made him waver. He could take out one or two of them before they even knew he was there. It looked like they hadn't been into the house yet. Conflicted, he didn't move, gripping the MP5 tightly.

His legs jittery, he backed up. Returning to the car, he ducked his head in his window and whispered, "We'll go through the wooded lot to the back of the house. You bring your men up from the street, Jake. We'll have them in a crossfire."

Pridlow was already talking quietly on his radio. Leon cracked his door quietly.

Megan grasped her automatic and exited the car on the driver's side.

Pridlow swore as he got out, his voice soft. "Someone called in as myself, said everything was taking place in a suburb north of here. The whole Austin police force and other FBI units rushed north. There's no one here to immediately cordon off the area." He got into the driver's seat of their car.

Alex swallowed. Without waiting he jogged back to the adjoining lot, then sprinted up the lawn along the tree line. Megan and Leon followed. He was aware of Pridlow backing up on the street to rendezvous with the other agents.

The night was silent except for their footsteps on the dried grass, the sounds like alarms in Alex's ears. His hands felt clammy on the automatic, his shoulders tight. He thought about what he had seen—the figures and barrels—and guessed what they were planning.

At the back of the lot he plunged left into the woods, picking his way between the darker shapes of trees. Their branches and leaves formed a thin canopy that blotted out much of the clouded sky. Only their footsteps and chirping crickets broke the night's quiet.

Alex hoped they were far enough away so their approach would be muffled, or at worst taken for a dog in the brush. Every piece of vegetation rubbing against his jeans, and every footfall the three of them made that snapped a twig or crushed a leaf, startled his senses and tensed him further.

They worked their way to the backyard. Glad to be on short grass again, Alex quickly led the others along the fringe of the woods and then down the gently sloped lawn to the back of the two-story house. Its pale siding appeared ghostly in the dark.

Pausing at the rear corner of the house, Alex hurried along the narrow strip of grass along the side of the house. The wooded lot was a few yards away.

Halfway to the front corner, Alex could see the street fifty yards distant at the bottom of the sloped front lawn. The center of the yard was still hidden from view, but he heard soft voices ahead. He listened for any other telltale warnings.

Engines roared from cars converging in the street below. Edging around the corner, Alex spotted four dark shapes beside two barrels on the driveway behind the semi. Someone lay on the ground sobbing.

Alex yelled, "FBI!"

The figures near the barrels crouched.

Not wanting to risk hitting whoever was on the ground, Alex fired a short burst of automatic fire above their heads.

Return fire from the terrorists ripped into the corner of the house. Jumping back beside Megan and Leon, Alex heard automatic gunfire erupt from the street. Pridlow and his agents.

Alex glanced around the corner again. The figures had fled the barrels. Engines started—the vans alongside the truck. A crouched figure near one of the vans executed an arm motion toward him.

Alex shouted, "Grenade!" Megan and Leon followed his lead as he threw himself to the ground. He scrambled a few yards back from the corner on his belly and covered his ears as a deafening explosion sent a shower of dirt and debris over his prostrate body.

Ears ringing, Alex rose and darted back to the corner of the house. Machine gun bursts came from the road. The terrorist vans raced down the grass lawn at an angle, away from the FBI sedans but firing machine guns at Pridlow's agents to keep them pinned down.

Running, keeping low, Alex ran toward the barrels, past a prone woman who was zip-tied and gagged. He didn't pause as he sprinted along the side of the semi, keeping the truck between himself and the vans. Megan ran beside him; Leon sprinted along the other side of the semi.

Alex knelt near the front bumper of the truck, sighting on the terrorists' vans. But he paused as yells erupted in the street near the FBI sedans.

An unmarked police car with a single flashing bar on its roof was parked behind the Bureau cars. Bursts of automatic gunfire came from two figures standing beside it. Chills swept down

Alex's back. The gunfire was directed at the Bureau agents. Alex couldn't fire without risking hitting agents.

There was a short exchange of staccato bursts between everyone in the street. FBI agents fell. The street firefight lit up the darkness in bright spurts of explosive light. Sickened by the sight, Alex aimed at the terrorist's vans and sprayed them. Megan knelt and fired beside him; Leon shot from the other side of the semi.

The vans had stopped in the street at a sharp angle fifty yards beyond the FBI cars. Using the vehicles for cover, the terrorists sent automatic fire down the street.

Alex flattened himself on the grass as bursts of machine gun fire arced across the lawn at them, punching the front end of the semi. Lying on the grass, he continued to spray the vans. In seconds the terrorists retreated back into the vehicles and raced off into the night.

Scrambling to his feet with Megan, Alex ran the remaining yards to the street, staring after the fleeing terrorists.

He turned his attention to the FBI agents. A few injured agents sat on the grass against cars. Others were helping the wounded. Several glanced at him as he strode past them.

The sight in the street made his stomach sink.

Eight men and women lay motionless in the road. Six lay along the line of parked FBI cars. Two bodies were beside the police cruiser—the men who had fired on the FBI agents. Bullet holes traced lines in the car frames, the patterns interrupted in places where they had struck flesh instead of metal. All the cars had their tires shot out.

The massacre fit Alex's vision from the Wheeler estate, but it hadn't helped stop any of it. Numb, he regretted not rushing the terrorists earlier when he had the chance. Jenny's image returned, her words drifting back to him again; *But what if you didn't see the whole picture?* Feeling inadequate, he wondered if he would forever see too little too late.

He walked through the strewn bodies, searching until he found Jake Pridlow. Quickly kneeling, he checked for a pulse. Not finding one, he slowly stood, watching Megan kneel to check the pulse of another downed FBI agent. She looked up at him, her lips pursed, and shook her head.

Remembering the woman, Alex jogged back up the grass, past the semi to the barrels. Leon had his cell phone to his ear as he knelt and held the woman—she cried softly against his shoulder.

A sweet gasoline-like scent from the barrels permeated the air, forcing Alex to cover his mouth. One of the barrels had a naked foot partially visible above the surface of the liquid it held. Alex backed away, swearing.

Megan hurried past him toward the house.

Leon's face was taut as he finished his call. In a subdued tone he said, "Mrs. Palmer said the terrorists killed the driver of the semi and her husband—they put them in the barrels with her watching. She said the semi is part of their company." He stared in bewilderment at the street. "God in heaven, what are we dealing with?"

"Murderers." Alex left Leon with the woman and limped up to the house, his knee throbbing.

He paused to look at the blood-red numeral four painted on the large front window of the house. There was a clean-cut hole in the decorative glass of the front door. Bright lights drew him inside into the living room.

Megan sat on a sofa between two young, wide-eyed children in pajamas. A boy and a girl, both maybe six years old. Megan had her arms wrapped around them, her face drawn.

The numb expressions of the Palmer children would haunt Alex. He didn't want to see their reactions when they learned their father was dead. Nor think about how that would affect the rest of their lives.

Megan looked at him. Her eyes betrayed that she now understood why everything weighed so heavy on him. Why a few minutes less meant so much. And why he couldn't help but always feel responsible for that lost time.

CHAPTER 11

MAX FOLDED THE SIX-INCH-SQUARE piece of paper as fast as possible on the meal tray. His brow furrowed and his lips pursed.

His morning check-in call verified that Threshold didn't like him very much. It was obvious even over the phone, but they needed him. When it came right down to it, you didn't have to believe in their righteous cause to pull a trigger. He appreciated that, and so did they.

What annoyed him was that they wanted his services, but believed they were above what he did. As if murder and mayhem could be ordered but kept off the conscience of the customer. No matter. A paycheck was the leveler that brought them all to the same table.

His father had impressed that on him. Just using his cell phone, his father had run a string of expensive call girls. When Max was sixteen, his father had shown him photos of some of the men who paid for the girls' services. Men of power. Men of the judiciary. Men of money. Everyone operated on base impulses, especially for survival.

Max saw the survival side first at age eighteen. His father had taken him along to pay a visit to someone who had hurt one of the call girls. He had allowed Max to use a hammer on the man's legs, and Max had gotten carried away, taking things farther than warranted. That day he found out his talent lay in hurting and killing. His father had hit him for killing a customer, but later said to him, *You've found your gift, son. Now control it and excel at it.*

"Would you like something to drink?"

He gazed up at the stewardess. She was in her twenties, well-built, and stirred him almost as much as his reveries about the coming game. Lifting his hand, he gave her the white crane.

"Origami," she said, smiling. "It's beautiful. You've made my day."

"Lovely." He smiled. "Lovely."

Watching her walk away, he admired her legs. He didn't have time to socialize after they landed or he would have made an attempt to engage her more.

He rubbed his hands together. The coming evening was going to be lovely too. There were many ways he could accomplish his objective, but he preferred closeup. There was nothing quite like seeing someone's face for the last few moments of their life.

CHAPTER 12

GALLAGHER WANTED ONE LEAD, anything to break the case open, to have something to pursue.

He sat on a stool at Juanita's computer station, opening a turkey sandwich wrapped in plastic wrap. Juanita punched numbers and letters as if he wasn't there. Every now and then a call or fax came in, or she made a call or sent a fax. Her orderly professionalism never ceased to impress him. She was as efficient as the computers she punched all day.

The analyst center in the J. Edgar Hoover Building in Washington, D.C. was three times the size of the one in Los Angeles and contained more of everything. Computers lined the walls, and more faxes, phones, and analysts filled the cubicles in the room. It was also noisier, with more people on the phones and more faxes coming in.

Juanita stopped to eat some chips out of a bag and sip a soda.

Gallagher didn't think he had ever seen her eat a regular meal. "I hope you eat good food at home. I'd hate to lose you to something stupid like diabetes or cancer."

The corners of her mouth barely turned upward, her voice lethargic. "Nothing yet. Wheeler's company received no threats, but they fired one senior chemist who disagreed with their approach. He wanted them to focus on safer chemicals. He has a solid alibi. None of their customers reported any break-ins or thefts."

The fax machine printed a transmission.

Juanita continued. "Palmer's plant made formaldehyde, chlorinated solvents, BPA, and benzene. The drums he and the truck driver drowned in had benzene. The truck driver was making a delivery and appears to have just been in the wrong place. No ties to anything useful."

"What did Threshold say?"

She softly rattled off, "Threshold's press release said they killed Palmer to bring attention to industrial toxic chemicals and plastic production, all of which kill people and are killing the oceans. They favor zero toxics and an end to all single use plastics. Palmer employees are being questioned. Nothing significant from the Palmer estate or from vehicle rentals in California and Austin. Phone history audits of airline passengers and rental customers are negative."

Gallagher swallowed his food, glancing at the plastic wrap in his hands. "See if any names on the flights into Billings are duplicated with the Austin or California car rental lists. I also want to cross-reference car or van rental names used in the last days in California with names on flights to Austin in the last week, and with passenger names on outbound flights from Austin today or tomorrow.

"For any matches, do background checks, and if warranted, look at alibis. Run the same complete investigation on the Palmer company as you did with Wheeler's. And tell me when the Palmer house has been processed and the neighbor interviews are finished."

Juanita barely dipped her chin in acknowledgement.

Gallagher ground his fists into his thighs. In the course of two days Threshold had left one child an orphan and three with a lifetime of sick memories. More, the terrorists had massacred agents, many of whom had families. He had two children. The thought of what it would be like for them if he and his wife were murdered made him clench his fists even tighter.

That same sense of protection had pulled him into the FBI. He had picked it up from his father, who had been on the D.C. police force for forty years before he retired.

Ironically it was also his father who had given him such a bad taste for authority and orders. His father had tried to order him around nearly every day of his life up until his death, three years ago. "Anything on the two phony police officers killed at the Palmer house?"

Juanita shook her head. "No I.D.s. No prints—they were burned off their fingers. They're checking dental records, but it will take longer. Their photos were run against driving license data bases, but no leads thus far."

"How can that be?" he asked.

Juanita raised an eyebrow. "Someone deleted records?"

That worried him. "How's the progress on the environmental extremist list?"

"The environmental groups were hesitant to label any past employees or members as radicals. But we have a few names we're investigating. We're going over backgrounds, alibis, and phone records as fast as we can. We'll see if there's any correlation with the passengers on the flights or vehicle rentals we've already looked at."

Gallagher snorted. The environmental groups would be as anxious as they were to have Threshold out of the way. Threshold furthered the image of environmentalists as radical nuts. Yet the country had polarized over the issues Threshold had raised. And the current heat wave sweeping the country played in the terrorists' favor.

Still it seemed demented to him that the terrorists gained press from the environmental information they released, regardless of how accurate it was. The list of executives that Threshold considered criminals was a *Who's Who* of corporate America.

Juanita continued. "We had a call from someone in Earth First! saying a member of the Earth Liberation Front contacted him, saying none of their members were murderers. They refuse to talk to us. They don't want any of their members revealed to law enforcement."

"Idiots."

"Environmental magazines were reluctant, but they gave us a few leads," she added. "We're also searching for smaller publications, fly-by-night operations." She pulled a fax from the machine. "And we have one possible strong lead."

Gallagher's chest tightened. When Juanita said something was a strong lead, it was just that. "Let's have it."

"This fax is from the editor and owner of a small online environmental magazine that's now out of business. She sent us an article a writer did for one of their blog columns. A few years ago, the writer submitted several articles to them over a period of six months." She handed it to him.

He stared at the copy.

A TIME TO DIE

This is a time to die. Either a time for nature to die, a time for us to die, or a time for the evils of our society to die. We must choose. And we can choose only if we open our eyes, and then we will have no choice. The power must be given back to the innocent. We must strike at the corporate and political evil that is ripping our planet apart. We must fight.

The fight must be in our hearts, but it must also be in our hands and in our actions. It cannot be left to rhetoric and pen and paper, but must be carried to the streets, to their businesses and elected offices, and to their homes until they suffer enough to realize we and the planet are also suffering.

Gallagher stopped reading and looked up. "I can't believe anyone published this crap. What kind of press was it?"

"*Earth Haters News.* An environmental newsletter that fingered the worst polluters in the nation. We had them in one of our old files on environmental activists."

Gallagher grimaced. If Foley wasn't in charge those files would have been kept current. Stupid environmentalist.

Juana continued. "I talked to the editor and it was only by luck she happened to have a copy of this blog post. She used some of this guy's work mainly out of fear. He routinely contacted her with thinly veiled threats, asking if she was going to use his writing. He hinted that he knew where she lived and she was frightened. If we find him, she asked that we don't use her name. She's still scared of him."

Gallagher was intrigued. "Who is he?"

"Jerry Peiser. We're trying to track him down now. Apparently he's on the move a lot and has no friends to speak of. A loner. His family is in Louisiana. We couldn't find any phone service or numbers listed. Someone was sent to contact them in person, to see if they might know where he is. He's not on any of the usual databases and seems to have dropped out of sight."

Gallagher doubted it was coincidence. "Ask the editor to send us anything else she has from writers backing violent action. Talk to her about anyone she knows who could provide us with hangouts of these people. Clubs, bars, or other connections."

The fax machine began humming again.

Gallagher leaned forward, but he was too far away to see the print clearly. It was on the other side of Juanita and she ignored it.

She said, "We found two guys involved in the IMF-World Bank D.C. demonstrations in 2019 who were trying to get everyone interested in violent confrontations with the police. At one of the demonstrators' meetings one of them showed up drunk and went so far as to shoot a gun he had brought. No one was hurt, but the police were called. The two men took off. It may take a while to find them. This was called in by someone who said the two men were spouting a lot of extremist environmental threats."

The fax machine stopped. Juanita slowly swiveled and picked up the transmission. "Nope, not the one we want."

The fax machine began again.

"The demonstration guys don't feel right." Gallagher wiped crumbs from his lips as he finished his sandwich. "Unless they went through some pretty disciplined training."

"I agree." Juanita inched her chair around as the fax stopped. She plucked it off the machine and turned to him. "Too bad."

"Why?"

She looked up at him. "Jerry Peiser died in a car crash a year ago."

The fax machine began again.

Gallagher sighed and rose to leave. "A guy like that could have solved a lot of our problems."

Juanita pulled out the next fax, glancing at it. "You might be interested in this. You wanted to find out if Senator Dillon, Dr. Crary, and Dr. Joulie had any previous past association with each other."

His excitement rose. "And?"

She raised her eyebrows. "I think we just got another break."

"Really?" He wanted to rip the sheet from her hands as she slowly nodded her head.

"It appears they all graduated together in nineteen-eighty from Macalester College, a private liberal arts campus in St. Paul, Minnesota."

CHAPTER 13

ALEX FELT ANOTHER THREAT looming. He couldn't sense where it would come from, but it put him on edge.

Leon drove him and Megan to Houston's FBI office. They gave a report and waited for a flight. He also received a late-night call from Deputy Director Foley who sounded as weary as he felt.

Foley informed them that the Coast Guard was broadcasting an emergency message for Dr. Crary, telling the veterinarian his house had been ransacked. Though true, it was being used to draw the doctor out. The body count was forcing them to pursue any leads, no matter how slight.

Alex didn't expect anything to come of it. He doubted that Crary was on a fishing trip. The fact that the veterinarian was ignoring the emergency message seemed to make a stronger case for his involvement with Threshold. But they had no proof.

Later Gallagher faxed more files to them at the Houston office. Megan scanned them immediately. Alex could barely keep his eyes open. They all caught a few hours of uncomfortable sleep in chairs before Leon drove them to the airport.

Their late morning flight stopped in Denver for a layover. The only good thing about it was Alex had time to call Harry. Megan stared wide-eyed while he learned he had won twenty thousand on Passion. She shook her head and turned away as he placed a bet of fifteen thousand on a horse named Shadow to win at three-to-one. Even if he lost, he would still be up five thousand.

He noted Megan was texting someone. Probably her boyfriend. He didn't ask.

In the early evening they left Denver for Montana, arriving at Billings Logan International Airport two hours later. Warm air bathed them as they walked out of the terminal. Alex was surprised it was as hot in Billings as it had been in Austin. He was sick of it.

Leon shadowed them.

They had reservations for three adjacent rooms on the second floor of the Doubletree by Hilton. Foley had arranged an appointment for them the following day with Senator Dillon. Alex was impatient to talk to the senator. The mounting deaths, and the fact that each day the terrorists promised to create new victims, pushed relentlessly through his mind.

They walked to their rooms in silence, too fatigued to start a conversation. When they reached Megan's room, she unlocked her door and turned to him. She gave him a sleepy, vacant look, her hair in disarray, her dark eyes revealing sadness.

He couldn't think of anything to say to ease her pain or his own. They hadn't talked to each other about what had happened.

"You did everything possible," she said.

Her acknowledgement touched him. "We both did."

"I trust your abilities, Alex."

"You're not bad yourself." Wavering, he said, "See you in the morning."

"Goodnight, Alex."

He waited until her deadbolt clicked and then went to his own room. After swallowing two aspirin for his knee, he pulled the curtains closed. Kicking off his shoes, he sprawled on his bed, staring at the door between their rooms. Something still bothered him about her, but he couldn't fathom what it was. Maybe it was his issue.

For a moment he imagined going to her door and into her arms. That idea faded fast. He didn't even know her. And she had a boyfriend.

The images from Austin floated through him. It was a cruel joke that his gift had given him only enough information to end up little more than a spectator to murders. And they were no closer to Threshold because of it. At least they now knew that Threshold wasn't just four terrorists. The phony police officers in Austin proved they were a larger group. The question of how large haunted him.

Crumpling the pillows into his body, he curled up around them. Mercifully, sleep claimed him immediately.

The hotel phone woke him later. It rang a number of times before he managed to undo the grogginess wrapped around his mind. After putting the receiver to his lips, he mumbled, "Hello."

"Is this Terry?" asked a deep male voice.

"Wrong number."

The line went dead. Alex put the phone back in its cradle. He called the front desk and asked for a wake-up call for six a.m. His watch read ten p.m. A headache was building. Pulling off his clothes, he groaned and buried his face beneath his pillow.

He drifted into sleep, but loud sirens woke him. His head throbbed. Swearing, he threw off his covers and stumbled to the window. He tossed the curtains aside. In the street below he saw a fire truck race by, followed by several police cars. In the distance a reddish glow lit the night.

He drew the curtains, took two more aspirin with a slug of water, and went to bed. Waiting for the pills to work, he clicked on the TV. The late-night news talked about a large, five-story apartment building fire. As the story unfolded, Alex's eyes closed. Nodding off, he turned off the TV and his head dropped to his pillow.

There were several loud knocks on his door. He groaned and waited.

The knocking came again, louder and more insistent. Swinging his legs out of bed, he stared at the door. He grabbed the M&P 9mm on the nightstand. His eyes bleary, he shuffled to the side of the door and glared at the doorknob. "Who is it?"

"Leon."

Alex opened the door, letting his tired appearance speak for itself.

"Sorry." Leon didn't look the least bit tired. "I got a call from the lobby. There's an urgent message for me. I'm going to get it. Told Megan, now I've told you."

"Fine." Alex swung the door half-closed, then stopped. "Have you been in the hallway all night?"

The ebony man shrugged. "I usually don't go to bed until one or two anyway."

"Insomniac?"

Leon grinned. "Video games, late-night TV, or biorhythms. Take your pick."

"Thanks." Alex shook his head. "See you in the morning. And unless it's life or death, don't bother me again."

Leon grinned. "Gotcha. Try to get some sleep. You look ragged."

Alex stared as Leon left. He shut his door, locked it, and wearily crawled into bed.

The hotel phone rang again. Rolling over, he stared at it as if it were a viper. Stretching a hand, he picked it up and pressed it to his ear.

"Is Terry there?"

Alex beat the man to it and hung up first.

***

Max stood halfway between the third and second floor landing of the fire exit stairway. A hotel porter bounded up from the lower floors toward the second-floor landing. The gangly young man stopped when he saw Max. Dressed in the blue and white livery of the hotel, the man was perhaps twenty. His eyes widened as Max slowly walked down the stairs with a brown paper bag held in one hand, his other hand stuck inside it.

The youthfulness of the porter reminded Max of the Army. He had volunteered at a young age, thinking he would find kinship in killing. Instead they had sent him home, declaring him mentally unfit. Angry and violent, they said. It had been for the best. Killing freelance was a much better fit for him anyway.

Hotel guests weren't usually in emergency stairwells, and Max noted curiosity and suspicion on the young man's face. He stopped on the step above the porter and gave a broad smile. "Can you help me?"

It seemed to put the man at ease. "Certainly, sir."

Max frowned, looking at his paper bag. "I better set this down." He carefully placed the bag on the step he stood on, resting it on its side.

The porter craned his neck, able to glimpse the stock of the Mossberg 500 shotgun protruding from the bag.

"It's a big gun." Max stepped down to the next stair, lightly poking the porter in the stomach with one finger. "To kill someone."

The porter cringed.

That made Max feel better. It was going to be a lovely evening, he thought. He put an arm around the man's shoulders. Simply lovely.

***

Leon gave his name and showed his I.D. to the hotel clerk at the front desk. "I was told you had an urgent message for me."

"Yes, sir." The clerk retrieved an envelope from the message boxes. "A young man came in and said this was urgent and should be given to you ASAP. He didn't leave his name and left immediately."

"Well, here I am." Leon stuck out his hand.

The clerk handed over the envelope.

Opening it carefully, Leon saw a small slip of paper inside. He took it out. On it was written *Road kill can't run*. The words were so unexpected that he stared at them in silence. Alex had told him about the calls. There was something odd-looking in the envelope. He pulled it out. Some kind of folded paper.

"Origami," said the clerk.

Leon looked up sharply. "Who gave this to you?"

"Like I said, a young man."

Leon looked at the message again, feeling there was something else he should be able to see beneath the words. "Tell me again exactly what he said."

"He said, 'This is an urgent message for Leon Mason.' I asked if he wanted to wait, and he said, 'No, please have Mr. Mason come immediately for this message. Tell him it's urgent.' Then he left."

The hotel fire alarm blared.

Leon's eyes widened. He reached over the counter and grabbed the hotel phone. "What's the extension for room two-oh-seven?"

"Two-two-zero-seven." The clerk grabbed another phone.

People poured from the restaurant, bar, and elevators, all hurrying to the front doors.

Leon dialed, but the phone line was dead. "This phone's out of order." His jaw tensed as he regarded the clerk.

The clerk looked puzzled as he lowered the phone he held. "This one's not working either." He produced a cell phone and ran around the counter toward the front entrance, directing guests.

Running for the stairs, Leon dug out his cell phone. Sweat beaded his brow as the bizarre message *Road kill can't run* replayed in his mind. He dialed Alex's cell phone.

Alex answered on the first ring. Leon filled him in.

***

Alex stumbled against the wall as he pulled on his jeans and T-shirt. Grabbing another shirt, he draped it over his 9mm. Voices and hurried footfalls sounded in the hallway.

He hurried to the adjoining door to Megan's room. It swung open. Wearing a knee-length dark blue nightshirt imprinted with a gorilla, she stood with loose hair falling on half-bare shoulders. It caught him by surprise to see her in something other than a suit. He followed her right arm down to her hand, which clenched the butt of an olive-drab Glock 23. That made two guns she owned.

"Leon received a message," he said. "Road kill can't run."

Her eyes narrowed. "We can't wait here."

"Come on." He ran to her room door, noting items strewn across the floor and surfaces. Messy. He pressed flat against the wall. Silently he gripped the knob and cracked the door, glancing out.

Light smoke swirled through the hallway. It was heavier to the right. To the left, people wearing nightgowns and bathrobes were shouting and running toward the stairs.

Alex stuck his head out and peered to the right. He was startled to see an elderly man and woman walking arm in arm out of thick billowing smoke, coughing. The wife trailed her hand across the opposite wall to guide them.

The fire looked close and already out of control, but Alex didn't feel any heat. No flames. And the smoke was too white and didn't carry any scents of burned objects.

As the older couple passed by, Alex stepped into the hallway with Megan. She kept watch to the left, her gun raised in both hands, while he watched behind them. Movement in the smoke, more a shadow than anything of substance, forced him to crane his neck.

An apparition appeared, looking like a character out of a B-movie. Tall, stocky, with short brown hair, the man had small eyes and puffy cheeks, and wore a blue western suit and western boots. A handlebar moustache framed his mouth. One of his hands held a large grocery bag by the handles. The man's other hand was hidden inside the bag.

Eyeing the man, Alex gripped Megan's elbow and steered her ahead of him toward an open doorway across the hall. She looked past him and didn't object.

With a quick movement the man lifted the bag horizontal.

"Gun!" Alex shoved Megan in front of him and they leapt through the door. Two muffled blasts sounded as Alex landed hard, partly on top of Megan. She gasped. They rolled together to the side.

The gun fired again. The slug struck the floor to the side of them.

Pushing himself off Megan, Alex swiveled on his butt and kicked the door shut. Scuttling sideways, he jammed his back against the wall, his gun held vertical in both hands.

Megan crouched alongside him.

Two more shots tore through the door, scattering splinters into the room. Alex's ears rang, his hands sweaty on his weapon.

Rolling away from the wall, Megan came up in a kneeling position, swiveled, and shot six rounds through the door at an angle.

Chest heaving, Alex stood up.

Megan rose to her feet, her gun aimed at the door. Alex nodded to her, then grasped the doorknob and swung the door open. Carefully he glanced out, but the mustached man was gone. Thick smoke billowed through the hallway.

Alex looked in the other direction and his stomach heaved. The older couple lay prone on the hallway floor next to the wall by the door. Red wounds marked their backs. The shotgun lay on the floor beside them.

Sidling along the wall, Alex stepped up to the bodies. While Megan covered the other end of the hallway, he crouched and checked pulses but found nothing.

"Come on." He ran down the hallway, away from the smoke, and took the first emergency stairway down. It was clogged with people, but he shouldered his way through, holding his gun up, while repeating, "FBI, let us through!"

When he reached the lower floor, he squeezed through people in the lobby. He kept going until he stood outside. There he finally stopped to look up and down the street.

After a few moments he lowered his gun, his hand still tight on it.

Megan stood at his shoulder, her eyes hard. "He's going to come at us again."

"Next time it's his turn."

CHAPTER 14

LOUISIANA STATE SENATOR BUFORD felt great. No, better than great. High. Without using. Given he was fifty, it wasn't such a bad place to be. Missy looked up at him, her eyes full of adoration. Her blonde hair fell over her shoulders, her arm locked in his.

Buford owed his mother for his glib tongue and cheerful, beguiling smile. She had used it with his father and he had learned how effective it had been. Women never seemed to be able to resist his tongue and smile. Neither could the voters. His graying hair and tanned, pleasant face played its part. And he always dressed smart in a white sport shirt, black slacks, and expensive shoes. But he knew it was his smile and tongue which worked the magic.

He stepped out of K-Paul's Louisiana Kitchen restaurant. A little oasis of Cajun fare in the French Quarter. New Orleans' warm humid air hit him and his skin crawled with excitement. The heat did that to him.

The shrimp had been excellent. After the restaurant had closed, they had spent two hours with the chef, sharing a bottle of wine. Buford was ready for dessert.

They crossed the street, empty after midnight, and walked to his silver BMW M4 convertible. When they arrived at the driver's door, he slid his arms around Missy's tiny waist and eagerly drew her in for a quick, tight kiss.

A truck engine rumbled.

Pulling back from Missy, Buford was annoyed as a brown truck rolled toward them. The size of a UPS delivery van, the vehicle was too close. He wondered if the driver was drunk. Worried about being hit, he hustled Missy to the front of his car.

The truck lurched to a stop alongside them.

The side panel door of the truck slid open and two men in black Lycra suits with black hoods jumped to the street.

Buford gaped.

A massive man grabbed him bodily in a bear hug and threw him into the darkened truck. A taller, thinner man grabbed Missy. She cried out.

Angry words filled Buford's mouth as he hit the van floor with his shoulder. The pain made him grunt. "Damn you!" he shouted, finally finding his lungs. "You'll pay for this."

The big man who had thrown him into the truck towered over him and kicked him in the stomach.

Buford groaned and doubled over. When he could, he lifted his head. Through watery eyes he saw Missy lying beside him, her creased forehead revealing as much fear as he felt.

The truck door closed and the vehicle jerked forward. A small, dim light came on inside.

Buford looked around. The truck's interior was six feet wide, ten high, and had a twelve-foot-long bed. It was unbearably hot inside. Two coffinlike structures on stands three feet above the floor took up most of the space.

The two abductors stood silently near Buford's feet. Another man, also dressed in hooded black Lycra, came through a partition that hid the driver.

Buford's arms tensed as survival alarms went off in his head. Abruptly realizing who these men were, he knew his tongue would have to work as it never had before.

"Gentlemen," he began in earnest. "I care about the environment as much as you do. Check my record. I won compromises on the last three bills on Mississippi River sewage, industrial effluents, air emissions, and industrial toxics usage."

As he talked, one of the abductors zip-tied Missy's hands and gagged her. Tears welled up in her eyes.

The massive man zip-tied Buford's hands and he didn't resist, instead adding, "I've done more than most. Much more than my predecessor, and I've promised to do more than anyone running against me on the next ticket."

The muscled man stepped away from him.

Buford sensed a small light at the end of the tunnel, so he focused on the man who had come through the partition. "I understand we need to do more. I'm the man who can and will get it done."

"Senator Buford."

His lips clamped shut involuntarily at the sound of the cold, unforgiving anger in the voice of the man in front of him.

"You're charged with obstructing all reforms for energy efficiency and alternative energy. You seem to have made it a passion to support anything that increases climate change."

"I've done much better recently," he croaked.

"You've voted consistently for big oil drilling in Alaska and coastlines, against higher fuel standards, and for big agricultural concerns, including biotech. Often against the wishes of your voters. And long ago you fought against banning ozone depleting chemicals. You don't care if glaciers melt, seas rise, and coasts and islands are flooded, as long as you get corporate money for your reelection campaigns." The terrorist leaned closer. "So you're going to feel what it's like to have the world heat up."

The man turned to Missy, who had tears flowing down her cheeks. "You picked the wrong company to keep."

It was the first time in many years that Buford found his tongue frozen. He searched in panic for words. "Listen. Compromise is the name of the game. If I refuse to barter, nothing happens. Bills I guided through would have failed. The problem is the system, not me."

The tall man pulled Buford's hair, jerking his head off the floor as a gag was whipped around his mouth. They couldn't be serious. Not him. Not in the prime of his life. He was turned over onto his stomach and his jacket and shirt were torn off. They undid his belt and pulled off his pants too. That sent a wave of vulnerability through him and his imagination created images that he had to fight off to keep his sense of reason.

Two men lifted him. Twisting, he thrashed in their grip. He was carried a few steps and dropped onto a table on his back. Straps were yanked tight over his ankles, arms, and chest, but he managed to kick one foot free.

The tall man hit him twice in the jaw, snapping his head back. Dazed, he watched as they lowered a clear, curved lid over him, making him feel like a bug in a display case. Through the case he watched the terrorists carry Missy to the other container. They had taken off her dress. She didn't struggle.

There was a dull hum as a bright light on the inside of the lid came on, blinding him. Sweat ran over his chest.

The tall thin man tapped his fingers against the lid above Buford, and pulled up his hood just enough to reveal his smile.

Buford finally understood. A tanning booth.

Tears rolled across his cheeks as he struggled once more with his bonds. Dear, dear Missy. He couldn't see her, hear her, or comfort her.

In fifteen minutes his skin was burning, his thoughts frenzied. The truck stopped. He could hear the side door open and slide shut. He and Missy were alone.

His gag didn't prevent him from screaming.

CHAPTER 15

TENSION SEEPED FROM DEPUTY Director Foley's limbs as he sat at his desk. The Washington office did wonders for him that way. Larger than the Los Angeles office, it was wood paneled with a comfortable black leather chair. His spacious desk was again bare except for his computer, phone, and black ceramic coffee cup. The Dixie Chicks' *Not Ready to Make Nice* blared. One of his feet slowly tapped to its beat.

Surveying the room, he wasn't sure if it was the familiarity or the actual furnishings which made him feel at ease. He decided it was both. For one thing, he had more privacy in this office. The walls were solid wood, as was the door, and it was quieter. No noisy keyboards or other distractions to bother him.

More importantly, on the walls hung large photographs. A moonlit beach in Maui, a slice of the Great Barrier Reef, a mountain peak in the Cascades, and a spotted owl in a dark forest in British Columbia. He found all four beautiful. Just as with his photographs in the Los Angeles office, he had visited all four locations. Wind surfing, diving, climbing, and backpacking. Each adventure had its own level of risk and excitement, but each effort had been worth the attained goals. Goals defined all his choices and determined how much he would put on the line.

The Great Barrier Reef photo caught his attention. His gaze drifted over the brightly colored reef fish. He wondered how safe they felt when, at any moment, a bigger fish might come along and eat them. Of course, fish were too primitive to anticipate danger unless it was immediately present. Besides they had to stay exposed to obtain food. Some things couldn't be avoided.

A buzzer sounded on his phone. His office assistant's voice came over the intercom: "Mr. Gallagher is here to see you."

His shoulders hunched as he adjusted the music volume lower. He hated the fact that Gallagher always seemed to get under his skin.

Pressing the intercom button, he said, "Send him in." At least for once Gallagher was punctual. It was seven a.m., and though Gallagher was often in his office early, he wasn't known for being prompt to meetings. Foley took his pack of mints, shook three into his mouth, and leaned back.

Gallagher came through the door chewing gum, his suit disheveled. But he didn't have his empty pipe.

Foley had wondered how long the man would carry the pipe, since Gallagher had quit smoking a month ago. He waited for Gallagher to seat himself in the solitary chair in front of the desk before speaking. "You look tired, Bill."

"I am. And my patience for country music is at an all-time low."

Foley turned off the Dixie Chicks. Anything to appease the man so he didn't start an argument. Foley found his patience also worn thin. "Threshold struck again."

Gallagher's face screwed tight. "Where?"

"New Orleans. They fried Louisiana State Senator Buford in a tanning booth. A little after midnight. His girlfriend was locked up in one too, but other than being hysterical she was left unharmed. They were both found in a truck in a warehouse. No witnesses."

Gallagher gaped. "Their ingenuity is only outdone by their sadism. What did they say were Buford's crimes?"

"Supporting corporations and bills causing climate change and hindering those that would slow it down. They also left the number three painted on the truck."

"Shoving it in our faces, aren't they?" Gallagher shook his head.

Foley lifted a few fingers. "Threshold's new list of criminals includes politicians with the poorest environmental voting records, along with those like Buford who took political payoffs, i.e. campaign contributions, from what they consider to be dirty corporations. They released their list of one hundred of the worst political offenders."

"Moral hypocrites." Gallagher's eyes narrowed.

"We can count on them killing someone else tonight."

"Dependable too," scoffed Gallagher.

Foley clasped his hands on the desk. "Any patterns show up yet?"

"We haven't found any. Anything helpful in New Orleans?"

Foley shook his head. "No, but our office there will update me this morning. I'll send you anything I receive."

Gallagher grunted. "We'll look for the same patterns in New Orleans and continue to cross-check flight and vehicle rental names."

"Anything come up yet for the attack on Alex and Megan in Billings?"

Gallagher shrugged. "No."

Foley wasn't surprised. "I'm assigning a second agent to provide cover for Alex and Megan. Whatever they're doing, Threshold is spooked."

Gallagher snorted. "If someone wants to kill Alex Sight, one more agent won't help."

Foley frowned. "Are you against it?"

Gallagher flicked his hand. "It's your call. Threshold must have considerable resources to be able to send someone to Billings to murder two of our people."

"It's hard to believe. It poses a few questions."

Gallagher stared at him. "Such as?"

"I thought you might be able to help with that."

Gallagher straightened. "Sight and Detalio were identified in California and could have easily been followed to Billings. Sight caught someone following them twice already."

Foley considered that. "Has anything else turned up?"

Gallagher wagged his head. "We've had some interesting leads, but nothing solid yet. Every time we find someone who's a possibility, they're either hard to locate or dead."

"Alex and Megan will see Senator Dillon today."

Gallagher smirked and popped a bubble.

Foley ignored it. "When will you brief them on the file you have?"

"I fly out late tonight." Gallagher took out a stick of gum, unwrapped it, and dropped the wrapper on the desk. Hesitating, he glanced at Foley, and then swiped the paper off the desk and stuffed it into one of his pockets.

Foley was glad Gallagher didn't need a reminder. "Explain to me why you want to bring the file to them in person, instead of faxing or emailing it."

"I want to toss around some ideas, maybe jog something loose."

That surprised Foley, given Gallagher's disrespect of Sight. "Anything new with the research on connections between Dr. Crary, Dr. Joulie, or Senator Dillon?

"Actually something quite startling." Gallagher didn't blink.

Foley waited, annoyed over Gallagher's melodrama. "What is it?"

"Dillon, Joulie, and Crary all graduated from the same college in the same class of nineteen-eighty. Phone records show they've been talking regularly. They've known each other a long time, and they're still buddies."

Foley's eyebrows went up sharply. "When did you learn this?"

"Yesterday. Would have told you sooner, but I was busy."

Foley hid his annoyance. "We don't have anything solid against any of these men, do we?"

Gallagher hunched his shoulders, his voice even. "I thought you wanted me to work with Sight. That's why you brought him in, right? Or do you think his premonitions should be ignored?"

"Of course not." Foley knew Gallagher doubted Alex Sight's abilities and resented relying on them, so he found the question hypocritical. Yet he couldn't argue the point.

Gallagher nodded. "Well, he pointed us at Billings—and thus Senator Dillon. And Crary is a vet, Joulie a doctor—either of them could have supplied the drugs used at the Wheeler murders. It's too much of a coincidence to ignore them. We don't have anything solid right now so why not at least look at them?"

"I don't want you to make any assumptions, Bill. I want things handled carefully. No press leaks. This office will not smear anyone without solid evidence. Dr. Joulie and Senator Dillon have national reputations."

"Fine," snapped Gallagher. "Anything else?"

Foley tapped his pencil rhythmically. "I hope you won't try to interfere with Alex and Megan."

Gallagher rose and sneered. "I hardly think I'm the one who's an outsider here." He started to go but paused. "I'm a bit concerned about you though."

Foley met Gallagher's stare.

"All that cold coffee you drink. It'll do you in." Gallagher left the office, his footsteps banging heavily in the hallway.

Foley gazed at the painting of the Great Barrier Reef. Gallagher would scare some of those little fish.

CHAPTER 16

Aʟᴇx ᴀɴᴅ Megan met Billings Police Chief Bixby on the sidewalk in front of the Billings hotel. The sun beat down on their skin and they all wore sunglasses.

In his forties, tall, and with a droopy moustache, Bixby had a relaxed demeanor. "I'm going to pull my men from guard duty."

After interviewing them, Chief Bixby had volunteered to provide security at the hotel overnight.

"Any sign of the man who left the message at the hotel last night?" asked Megan.

Bixby squinted against the sunlight and shook his head. "None. He was a teenager. Doesn't match your description of the killer in the hotel. My guess is some junkie that the killer paid to deliver the note. The killer was busy. We assume he set the fire as a diversion—it's been ruled arson. The internal hotel phone line was cut too. The origami and shotgun were free of prints."

"Thanks for your help." Alex's stomach tightened. The killer could be anywhere and strike anytime. Over one night Threshold was responsible for the murder of Senator Buford, the older couple in the hotel, and the young hotel porter killed in the stairwell. It all weighed heavily on him. He was glad Threshold hadn't killed Senator Buford's girlfriend, even if it was a ploy to mute public anger.

Megan drove. Leon followed in a Ford Focus with his new partner, Peter. Foley had insisted on sending another agent. In his late twenties, Peter had short brown hair, a square jaw, broad shoulders, and a serious expression.

The U.S. Army's *Call to the Post* bugle riff sounded and Alex pulled out his phone.

Harry grinned at him from the screen. "Shadow's a winner, Alex. And so are you."

Alex calculated he was now up sixty-five thousand. "Great, Harry. Give me the names." Pausing to glance at Megan, he selected White Star, settling on seventy-five thousand at six-to-one. At worst he would be out ten thousand.

Megan glanced at him. "You don't look happy for winning forty-five thousand dollars."

"It's not about the money." He put his phone away.

"Why then?"

He gave an awkward smile. "Maybe trying to prove something to myself."

She studied him. "We all want to believe in ourselves, but you want the impossible. You want to save everyone. No one can do that."

He didn't know what to say to her. And he wished he had been more aggressive in going for the driver's door. Megan was heavy on the gas pedal again. She sped up to make it through a yellow light, which turned red as they passed through the intersection. He gripped his armrest, his feet pressed into the floorboard.

"Did you used to race?" he asked. She frowned, and he added, "You know, stock cars or the Indianapolis 500?"

"Everything's under control." She sounded annoyed.

"I want to place another bet tomorrow."

She slowed her speed. "Sorry." She glanced at him. "You have to be more direct."

Colors abruptly snapped out at him. Pedestrians were etched in cartoonish clarity and the traffic around them seemed slower, as if his eyes were scanning faster back and forth over the moving shapes. Surprised, he stared out his window until a massive tug on his senses urged him to look behind their car. "Turn around."

"Dillon's ranch is north," said Megan.

"Turn around," he insisted.

"Why? There's no reason—"

Reaching over with his left hand, he clutched the wheel and gave it a wrench to the right. The tires squealed around the corner. Several oncoming cars honked their horns as he came close to sideswiping them.

He let go of the wheel and Megan completed the maneuver, her face taut. Ignoring her, he gazed along the street. Nothing out of the ordinary struck him, but after one block he again felt the urge to move right, see right. "Turn right."

This time Megan complied. They drove another half-mile south. Megan's cell phone rang and she answered, saying, "Just follow us, Leon."

Alex's attention was pulled right a third time and he directed Megan to turn again. They drove west, past blocks of houses and a few local businesses. But his eyes raced farther down the road, as if drawn by a magnet. Hands on the dash, he craned his neck, straining against his seatbelt.

His focus shifted inward to a blurred image...*a decomposed body wrapped in rotting cloth.* The sensation of cold swept through him in a wave which made him shiver. As the image of the corpse strengthened, he tried to concentrate...*tattered shrouds, a black disfigured face,* and he smelled...

"Left!" He looked in that direction, sliding woodenly into the passenger door as the car tilted sharply.

Megan straightened the vehicle as they passed through the entrance to Mountview Cemetery.

Alex glimpsed grave markers. The stronger image of the corpse clogged his vision, while the odor of something burning filled his nostrils. The cold was bitter now. Biting his hands and feet, sweeping into his chest, and burrowing into his marrow. Dizziness gripped him as he looked along the drive.

Megan slowed the car, but he uttered, "Keep going."

"Where?"

"Go!" His eyes roamed along the graveyard road.

Megan followed the curving drive into the cemetery proper.

Alex's chest heaved and his eyes finally focused on an area off to the side of the road. "Stop!"

Megan braked hard.

The image of the corpse occupied his senses, the cold enveloping him in a cocoon of ice. He tried to open the car door but his first attempt failed. His hand felt as if it was gloved in mittens, his fingers frozen together. Trying again, his digits barely parted and he managed to grab the door handle and get out.

With clumsy, deadened stumps for legs, he walked across the sidewalk and over the grass, past tombstones. They weren't the object of his gaze or what drew him forward.

He stopped at an open burial pit. As he stared at the dark hole, the vision of the corpse intensified. The cold made him shiver, his lips trembling. The burning scent filled his mouth and nose—cloaking every square inch of his skin—choking his throat and spreading through his blood like fire until it spilled over his drowned senses like the wild gush of a waterfall. It was then that he recognized it.

He fell to his knees.

Kristen.

The name was surrounded by deep sorrow and framed by unquenchable hatred. He sought a face to attach to the name but everything evaporated, leaving him exhausted and shivering by the empty gravesite.

Megan came to his side, resting a hand on his shoulder. When he tried to rise, she helped him to his feet. Fatigued, he stumbled back to the car with her at his elbow. Peter and Leon walked toward him from the other car, but Alex raised a palm to stop them.

"Do you need anything?" Peter's voice was gentle. "Food or something to drink?"

"We'll get it," said Leon.

"I'm good, thanks." Alex avoided looking at them, but appreciated their offers.

Megan opened the passenger door and he dropped into the car.

She squatted in front of him. "Do you want to go back to the hotel?"

"No." He glanced at her. "Strawberry ice cream."

She frowned. "What?"

He swung his legs in. "Get me some strawberry ice cream. Then drive to Senator Dillon's."

She scrutinized him, then shut his door, got in, and started driving. He shut off the AC and retrieved chocolate from the glove compartment. The chocolate helped. Finished, he slid back in his seat and was asleep instantly.

***

When he woke, they were on the highway, heading north. A female vocalist sang a love song, but the volume was turned down to a whisper. The AC was on low, the interior comfortable.

Drained, he noticed a Dixie cup of ice cream in the cup holder between the seats. A wooden spoon rested atop it. He peeled back the cover and took a bite. It was half-melted. "Thanks."

She turned the music off. "What did you see?"

He swallowed. "A completely burned corpse, out of a grave. And the name Kristen."

She frowned. "Do you know what it means?"

He shook his head. "Not yet."

"Foley might have a lead on the name."

He shifted his legs. "Let's hope so."

"A corpse burned beyond recognition," she murmured. "Was it connected to Kristen?"

"Maybe." He paused. "Unsure."

"Does that particular grave matter?" she asked.

"No."

"A future victim?" She glanced at him. "A past victim?"

"I don't know." He stared at the soft lines of her face and lips.

"What?" she asked softly.

He cleared his throat. "The questions help. My previous partner used to do that."

Her brow knitted and her voice took on a personal tone. "How are you?"

"Better than that corpse." He appreciated her concern and saw the intensity in her eyes.

"One thing is for sure, Alex Sight."

"What's that?"

Her lips betrayed the hint of a smile. "When you're clairvoyant you don't have any problem being direct."

He shook his head and got out his phone to call Foley.

CHAPTER 17

A LEX FELT IMPATIENT FOR a break in the case. He hoped it would come during Senator Dillon's interview.

Dillon's ranch was near the city of Roundup, forty miles north of Billings. Megan drove them through the Bull Mountains, a low mountain range. The Rockies huddled on the western horizon. Pine trees and prairie mixed on both sides of the road as they climbed in elevation.

The air was clean, crisp, the bright spring sun making it unseasonably warm at eighty-eight degrees. The usual spring rains were absent. Thus the ground was parched, the grass brittle, and the trees limp. It made Alex thirsty just looking at it. He turned the AC higher.

Ranch Big Horn—Dillon's estate—soon appeared, abutting the lower elevations of the north side of the Bull Mountains.

In minutes they reached the open metal driveway gate.

Megan pulled through the gate, but Leon and Peter parked their car on the road shoulder.

A quarter-mile up the dirt driveway sat a large, ranch-style brick house with tinted windows and solar panels on its roof.

Alex rolled down his window and gazed over Senator Dillon's ten thousand acres. The brown landscape stretched from horizon to horizon, with scrub brush interrupting tufts of grass. Pine trees and poplars dotted the rolling and sometimes jutting hills that blended into the higher slopes of the mountain ridge. A warm breeze pushed clouds across a blue sky and further dried the topsoil. It felt like a big oven with an arid quality that seemed to suck the moisture from his lungs and nostrils.

A black-tailed jackrabbit sat up, fifty feet from the driveway but staring their way, and a golden eagle drifted high in the sky. Alex wondered if the rabbit even knew the eagle was up there.

As they approached the house, they heard gunshots.

Megan frowned.

"Relax." Alex smiled. "Target practice. We're in Montana."

Megan pulled into the empty circular drive of the senator's house. A four-car garage was attached to the south side with all the doors closed. The shots continued from behind the house.

Alex walked to the front door. Megan followed. The inner door was open but a screen door blocked their way.

"Hello, anyone home?" Shading his eyes with a palm, Alex looked inside. There was no answer, but the gunshots continued.

"They can't hear us," he said. "Come on." He pushed open the screen door and walked in.

Megan entered behind him. "I don't think this is a good idea."

"The senator is a public servant." Alex appreciated the coolness of the interior and was glad to be out of the heat. The house was spacious, with log beams running across a high ceiling and cedar and oak framing the walls. A wide, stone floor hallway led to a back door propped ajar by a wooden chair. Several other doors led off from both sides of the hallway.

"Hello!" Alex called out. "Senator?"

A dog began barking.

Alex turned to Megan. "Welcoming committee."

A massive, mangy-looking dog jumped over the chair propping open the back door and bolted through the hallway toward them. Its thick coat was a mixture of black streaked with brown, its dark eyes glinting like black pearls.

Alex waited for the dog to stop. Instead it came at him in a dead run. Unwilling to exit through the screen door—and expose his back to the dog—he lifted an arm for protection, taking a clumsy step back and smacking the back of his head into the wall.

The dog leapt.

Alex shouted.

Megan twisted, launching her palms into the side of the animal.

Yelping, the dog flew to the side where it struck the floor and rolled over, scrambling to regain its feet. Head lowered, it snarled at them but stayed put.

Lowering his arm, Alex stared at the dog, breathing hard, his hand going to his gun. He was aware of Megan at his side in some kind of martial arts stance, but he didn't take his eyes off the animal.

The back door opened wider.

Two broad-shouldered men pushed the chair out of the way and strode through the door. They wore suits and held leveled SIG Sauer M17 9mms. Alex thought they were ex-military. Short hair. Precise movements. And M17 pistols had been used by the Army.

An older man flanked them. He wore a yellow silk shirt, yellow sunglasses, black jeans, and a black felt Stetson cavalry hat. Two pearl-handled pistols were strapped to his waist in a black two-gun rig with dual holsters and bullets lining the belt.

"We're the ten o'clock appointment for Senator Dillon." Megan carefully took out her badge. "FBI agents Megan Detalio and Alex Sight."

"That's right." Alex left his gun holstered and pulled out his badge, still watching the dog.

One of the bodyguards strode up and checked their badges. "They're good, senator." He turned to them, eyes narrowing. "Next time, knock."

Senator Dillon came closer, his expression friendly. "I was expecting you."

Alex immediately recognized the man's craggy face, thin eyebrows, and strong chin and cheekbones—the senator was often on the news and Gallagher had faxed them his photo in Austin.

Alex removed his sunglasses, gesturing to the growling dog. "You could tell Rover to take a hike."

"Sorry, Senator, we should have stayed outside." Megan glanced at Alex. "My partner was impatient."

"We were having target practice." Senator Dillon nodded. "It's all right, boys. I'll be fine."

The bodyguards put their guns away and walked through the front door, their jaws set hard. One of them glared at Alex as he passed by.

The senator turned to his dog, which had its hackles up. "Shooter, go on!"

The animal immediately stopped snarling and trotted back through the hallway into an adjacent room.

Alex relaxed.

Taking off his sunglasses, Senator Dillon stepped up to them. "Shooter is part wolf and it comes out in his protectiveness. When someone enters the house, without me or any of my troops present, he's trained to attack. He was just following orders."

"Good little soldier." Alex shook the senator's hand.

"Come." Senator Dillon placed a hand lightly on Megan's shoulder. "We have tea and croissants waiting for us."

He ushered them into a large panel-lined study with deep brown colors and soft leather furniture. Shooter lay in a corner, eyeing them intently.

Senator Dillon motioned them into chairs, then unbuckled his pistols and laid them on the desk. The guns shone under the ceiling light.

Dillon patted the weapons fondly. "Colt Peacemaker forty-five six-shooters. It's a hobby of mine, collecting old guns and using them. These are replicas of the single action Colts manufactured in the 1800s. I like to think of myself as one of the fastest draws in the west. I guess I'm still a kid at heart."

A maid entered the room with a tray of croissants and tea service for three. A bottle of whiskey and three shot glasses also sat on the tray. She set the service on a small table and looked at the senator.

"Thank you, Anne," he said to her.

She nodded and left.

Senator Dillon took off his Stetson, revealing a bald pate. He sat in a chair opposite theirs and poured tea for the three of them. Picking up the bottle, he looked at them. When they shook their heads, he poured one shot, which he downed immediately. Helping himself to a croissant, he motioned them to do the same.

"Did Deputy Director Foley tell you why we wanted to speak with you?" asked Alex.

Senator Dillon wiped his mouth with a napkin. "Vaguely. He believed it might be useful for me to talk to you about the Threshold terrorists. I didn't understand why, but he said you would provide an explanation."

Staring intently at Dillon, Alex leaned forward. "You're one of Dr. Crary's closest friends?"

Dillon frowned. "You're saying Dr. Crary is involved in this case?"

"We're not certain." Megan gestured. "Threshold used the veterinary drugs ketamine and xylazine at the scene of their first murders. Dr. Crary has access to them."

Dillon waved off her words. "I'm sure thousands of vets use them. You can't possibly believe Frank Crary has anything to do with those murders."

"We have evidence, which unfortunately we're not at liberty to disclose." Alex glanced at Megan.

She frowned at him.

Alex leaned forward. "You don't think Dr. Crary would keep any secrets from you?"

Dillon hesitated. "No, I don't."

Alex nodded slowly. "We've learned Dr. Crary has a Threshold connection in Billings. Can you tell us if he has any close friends in town?"

Dillon's eyes narrowed. "None that I'm aware of."

"No one else he comes up here to see?" asked Alex.

"No." Dillon lifted a hand off the arm of the chair. "Whenever he comes, he visits me."

Alex leaned back, aware of Megan staring at him. "Really? Just you, huh?"

Dillon's face darkened. "Have you arrested Dr. Crary?"

"Dr. Crary left on his boat," said Megan. "He hasn't returned a Coast Guard emergency message which has been broadcast repeatedly over the last days."

Senator Dillon studied her. "What's the emergency?"

Alex studied the senator's features. "His house was ransacked several days ago."

Senator Dillon raised his eyebrows. "Did you find who did it?"

Megan shook her head. "It appears whoever did it was searching for something."

Dillon waved it off. "Dr. Crary's not a killer. He's just concerned about environmental issues."

"You've been a strong environmentalist for your whole career." Megan took a drink of tea.

Dillon's voice was terse. "It's easy to take a stand on the environment if you get skin cancer."

"I'm sorry," said Megan.

Senator Dillon's face softened. "No, the cancer was a small thing I had removed." Taking a deep breath, he dropped his napkin on the table. "When my wife died, I had to have something of value to hang on to, to keep my life full. Environmental issues are part of that." Pausing, his voice quieted. "But all I've found is that she was irreplaceable." He wiped a hand across his face. "All the years she's been gone and it still hurts."

"She must have been very special." Megan momentarily rested a hand on his knee.

Alex was amazed by her boldness, but her empathy seemed genuine. The senator's emotion also reminded him of the years he would never have with Jenny. He had to shove down the sadness that swept into his thoughts. "Senator, what do you think of the new list of legislators Threshold has charged as criminals?"

"They are criminals for what they've allowed to happen. But threatening them is certainly not the way I would do things. Threshold needs to be brought to justice as quickly as possible."

"If you hear from Dr. Crary, please let us know." Alex got up. "Thank you for talking to us."

"You would make a good politician." Senator Dillon looked up at him. "You say you want to shake hands, but you go for the jugular."

Dillon's maid entered. "There's a phone call for Megan Detalio."

Dillon pointed to a handheld landline phone on his desk. "A relic that I turn off when I have guests."

Megan picked up the phone, her face clouding over as she listened. She hung up and said, "Nothing important."

"Good day," said Senator Dillon.

Dillon's maid led them out of the study and to the front door.

Outside, the heat was oppressive. Hurrying to the driver's door, Alex sat behind the wheel.

Megan took the passenger side and slapped the keys into his extended palm. "You're overreacting. I hope you don't have visions while you drive."

"I can drive with my eyes closed." He followed the driveway out, leaving a trail of dust behind them.

She flipped off her shoes, crossed one of her legs beneath her, and put her bare foot on the dash. It annoyed him.

"What was the phone message?" he asked.

She grimaced. "Road kill can't run."

"Hell." He powered up the windows and put on the AC.

"How is he keeping tabs on us?" Megan put on her seatbelt.

He sped up. "It wouldn't be hard to guess where we were going. The question is how he got the senator's private phone number. It's not impossible, but..."

"An FBI traitor?" she asked.

"Or maybe Senator Dillon is involved."

"Let's run both by Foley. Gallagher has to do a security check of his staff." She paused. "You practically accused Senator Dillon of complicity with Threshold, and we don't have any proof Crary is involved. You lied to a U.S. senator."

"If I had a close friend at sea ignoring an emergency Coast Guard message, I'd be worried. Dillon didn't seem bothered by it." When they passed through the gate, Alex nodded to Leon and Peter. Peter gave him a small nod in return; Leon gave a thumbs up.

Releasing her hair clip, Megan shook her hair out and ran her hands through it. "Maybe Crary often goes fishing on his own. Dillon didn't think it was serious."

"He's an alcoholic, drinking in the morning." He glanced at her, enjoying seeing the wind play with her hair.

Megan's voice softened. "He's still mourning his wife."

"Thanks for the help with the dog. Is your arm okay?"

She shrugged. "I have a high pain tolerance."

Alex hesitated, and then said, "The dog freaked me out."

She twisted to view him. "Why?"

"When I was a kid a pit bull chased me down a sidewalk. Knocked me over and chewed my ankle. I needed stitches and was terrified of dogs for years. Now I'm just not a fan."

Megan drummed her fingers on her knee. "I was in a hurricane once in Fiji. Strong winds still make me nervous."

"Where did you learn to move like that?"

"I studied kung fu for five years." Megan looked out her window. "A friend of mine was raped in college so I was motivated. And I like the complexity of movement in kung fu."

Alex glanced at the rearview mirror. A black Mercedes aggressively passed Leon's car and slid in behind them.

Off to the far left, the black speck of a helicopter flew low over the mountaintop, on an intercept course with the road they were on.

Alex looked at Megan. "I've thought about the corpse at the cemetery."

Her brows arched. "You solved it?"

"For one thing the corpse wasn't in the ground, it was out. The victim died in a fire. That was obvious. But I saw the corpse first. That's the key."

"Why would it be out of the ground?" asked Megan.

"I'm supposed to see it above ground."

She brushed strands of hair off her forehead. "You usually exhume bodies to verify identity or to determine cause of death."

"Exactly." He looked at her. "And I already know the cause of death—fire aided by an accelerant. Most likely gasoline."

"How do we decide who to exhume?"

He had already considered that. "We ask Gallagher if he's found any likely environmental extremists who died in a fire in the last year."

Megan's forehead furrowed. "It won't be enough to get a judge's order to exhume a body."

"Maybe." Alex didn't want to share his own disappointment. He had hoped for another premonition at Dillon's. Something concrete that would put a stop to the killing.

They descended out of the hills and the road straightened, empty of traffic.

Much closer now, the helicopter still flew on an intercept course with them.

The Mercedes made a bid to pass them, speeding into the opposing traffic lane.

Alex clenched the wheel.

Glancing back at the Mercedes, Megan bit her lip. Drawing her gun, she rested it on her lap and dropped her foot from the dash. Alex pulled out his gun and held it on his thigh.

Whipping around, Alex watched the Mercedes roar up. His foot hovered over the brake pedal and the hair on the nape of his neck stood up. The oppressively loud chop of helicopter blades filled his ears.

Twisting in her seat, Megan lifted her gun with both hands, aiming at Alex's window.

Alex dropped his hand to a lower position on the steering wheel. His neck stiffened as he glanced at the Mercedes. It had tinted windows and he couldn't see the driver or passengers.

The helicopter blades drowned out everything else.

"Hell with this." Alex braked hard, the wheels protesting on the pavement.

Behind them Leon slammed on the brakes, going around their car into the opposing traffic lane to avoid a collision.

The Mercedes passed them and raced away.

The helicopter crossed the road and kept going, quickly fading in the distance.

Alex swallowed.

Megan sighed and holstered her gun. "I think I need some ice cream. Vanilla."

CHAPTER 18

MAX HIT THE MIRROR with a gloved fist, sending spider cracks shooting across it like radiating arms of a star. With red lipstick he wrote on the mirror in big letters *Road kill can't run.* How he loved those four words. Just off kilter enough to unsettle anyone, no matter how strong they were.

His vast experience in unsettling people told him that anyone's fortitude could be tumbled, given the right kind of persuasion. His father had taught him that.

After the mirror he moved to the vanity. He pulled out each drawer, leaning on them until they broke. With a rubber hammer he banged on wall and floor tiles. Tore the shower curtain. Cracked the toilet tank cover. Ripped off the toilet seat.

It wasn't difficult. He prided himself on his strength. Writing another message on the door, he fervently hoped lipstick wouldn't come off with cleanser.

The living room was even more fun. He used his knife, a six-inch switchblade, on the sofa and chairs. Down came the curtains, along with clocks, tables, and framed photos. It was a good workout and he was sweating. He was happy the furnishings were expensive. Simple in taste, but not cheap.

He worked like a whirlwind, considering his options as he moved through the house. Revenge played no little part in his efforts. Billings had been a disappointment and he wanted Detalio and Sight to pay for his wasted efforts. But no matter.

He had thought ahead, seen the course of things, and now was far enough in front of them that he had time to spare.

While smashing a picture frame beneath the heel of his boot, he searched for some small element to create the perfect unnerving effect he always strived for.

He discovered it in the kitchen.

A meow came from outside the kitchen window, which had been left open eight inches above the sill. It surprised him that people still left invitations to trouble. But when the cat arrived, such a beautiful cat, he understood why. A quick check showed the window was locked in place. It couldn't be shoved higher from outside without a break-in.

A food and water tube sat on the floor. The containers refilled automatically as they were emptied and there were several weeks of food and water available for the animal.

"Here, kitty, kitty."

The cat crouched to squeeze beneath the window, then leisurely walked onto the table, watching him intently.

"What am I thinking of, kitty?" He winked at the cat, which eyed him, and then turned to the fridge. Grabbing a carton of milk, he walked over to the table and poured it onto the wooden surface. The cat licked it up at once.

Max gently stroked the feline's back. The perfect touch. Lovely.

CHAPTER 19

ALEX'S MIND CHURNED WITH thoughts about Threshold's next victims. He sensed the same tension in Megan. Someone would die tonight and they had no leads to stop it. Hoping to hear of a breakthrough, he called Foley from the airport. Nothing had materialized.

They landed in Minneapolis in early evening. The next day they would go to Rochester, Minnesota to question Dr. Joulie.

After retrieving their luggage, Alex said wearily, "Let's go to my house for the night. I'm tired of hotels and wouldn't mind a good night's sleep." He paused. "If it's all right with you. I'd like to see how Pierre's doing anyway."

"Pierre?" Her head tilted.

He smiled. "My soulmate. My life wouldn't be the same without him."

Megan stared at him with a blank expression.

He added, "I've known Pierre fourteen years."

She frowned. "I don't have to sleep on a couch, do I?"

As they walked to the Uber pickup site, he said, "We'll manage."

"I'll cook if you're stocked."

"You just earned a bed." Leon and Peter would follow them in another Uber. After Billings, Alex didn't mind having them in his home for the night.

His house was on the frontage road of Lake of the Isles, one of the city's lakes. The driver had to go halfway around the one-way lakeshore road to reach his address.

It was a sweltering night. Yet people walked, biked, and rollerbladed along the paved paths circling the lake, seemingly without a care in the world. The beauty of the lake and the relaxed pedestrians belonged to another world, divorced from the violence Alex knew he was chasing.

The driver dropped them off under the carport of his house, a white, modern two-story with a large upper balcony and rooftop patio.

Megan eyed the house, and then him. "It must be worth two million. Did you inherit money?"

He smiled. "Gambling plus some reward money."

She shook her head. "You don't have to work for a living, do you?"

"I know, I'm crazy." Walking to the side door, Alex stopped in front of it. Across the oak door in bright red, sloppy lettering was written *Road kill can't run.*

His shoulders tensed as he set down his luggage. The door was ajar. He drew his gun.

Megan was right behind him, drawing her weapon. Leon and Peter were just exiting their Uber in his driveway, and they came up fast.

After toeing the door open, Alex stepped through the hallway into his shadowed living room. He turned on a light and his jaw tightened. Everything looked like it had been fed through a shredder.

The sofa pillows were slashed and strewn across the floor, the bookshelf toppled and splintered, and his dumbbells thrown into the TV. An easy chair showed knife gashes, a coffee table was broken in two, wall pictures lay fractured, and the balcony door curtains had been ripped off the hanging rod. On two of the walls the same message was scrawled in red lettering. The adjacent open dining area was just as tortured.

Alex assumed whoever did this was long gone, but he still kept his gun raised. With a jolt he called, "Pierre? Pierre!"

Leon had his gun up in both hands and headed upstairs with Peter.

Alex strode into each of the two lower bedrooms, one after another. Both were just as mangled. Hidden in one of the bedroom closets, the security system had been disabled. In the bathroom the same disturbing message marred the mirror and the back of the door. Swearing, he hesitated before leaving. A small origami white crane rested on the vanity.

Leaving it, he returned to the living room, walking past Megan. He followed her gaze up. Leon and Peter stood at the top of the stairway, staring down at them. They had their guns holstered.

"Looks like the upper level wasn't touched," said Leon. "We'll inspect it anyway."

"Then we'll check outside," said Peter.

"Thanks." From the dining area Alex entered the large, modern kitchen. The odors that greeted him made him gag. Refried beans, sardines, milk, ketchup, and other canned foods covered the table, floor, and walls as if a child had been finger-painting. The refrigerator, near the entryway, was open. He kicked it shut in disgust and crossed the room to the window over the kitchen table. Its pane was shattered, the frame pushed all the way up instead of the eight-inch space he had left.

"Pierre!" he called.

A meow filtered back to him, relaxing his shoulders. Megan strode in, watching.

An orange tomcat appeared on the outer window flower ledge. Arching its back, it stared at him, and then walked onto the table.

"Pierre." He gathered the cat into his arms.

"That's Pierre?" Megan rolled her eyes. "Your soul mate, huh?"

He smiled. "Yep."

Leon and Peter arrived.

"I'm glad the cat wasn't harmed," said Peter. "I hate seeing animals hurt."

"Pierre's too smart to be caught by a stranger." Alex hugged the cat.

"We better take another careful look at every room for anything out of the ordinary," said Leon. "Electronic bugs, bombs, whatever."

"Good idea," said Alex.

Megan followed Leon and Peter into the living room.

Alex took two steps, when Pierre hissed and jumped from his arms onto the kitchen table. The cat sat there, refusing to budge.

"The creep must have scared you, huh?" He stroked the cat until it purred, and then left the kitchen.

Leon and Peter had left to check out the upper bedrooms more thoroughly. Megan stood in the middle of the living room, her expression drawn.

Walking across the room, Alex kicked a broken lampshade lying on the floor, sending it flying into the wall. It fell, clattering over broken glass. "Damn them."

He waved a hand at nothing. "My cat doesn't even feel welcome in his home anymore."

"It would bother anyone, Alex."

"Yeah." He sighed and began picking things up.

They looked carefully through the lower level of the house for any signs of hidden tampering. Alex appreciated that Megan tried to straighten things as they went. He walked into the attached garage, surprised and relieved to find his black Porsche and eighteen-foot Hobie Cat untouched. The selectivity of the person responsible for the damage was beyond him.

Returning to the living room, he opened the patio doors and stepped outside to get some fresh air. Megan joined him.

Light traffic moved on the street. Tire noises slid in and out of his hearing like muffled breaths. Across the street, Lake of the Isles glistened like a black pearl in the early moonlight. The scent of lake water drifted in. A robin sang from a tree and a hot breeze ruffled his hair as he stood there, gathering himself.

Something brushed his legs. Pierre had arrived via the outside patio.

"This is nice. Lakes in the city." Megan bent over to lift up Pierre. The cat purred in appreciation. "He's friendly."

"He has his moments." Their shoulders touched and for a moment he found himself wishing they had the house alone for the night.

The wind blew Megan's dark curls around her cheeks. Her face was drawn. "This isn't just to scare us."

"I know."

She glanced at him. "Were your visions just as strong when you were a kid?"

It took a few moments for him to answer. "It was usually a ghostlike death scene involving people I knew or strangers. At first I thought I was hallucinating. Along with the emotions I sometimes picked up, I thought I was going crazy. Doctors didn't find anything wrong with me. When people died the same way I saw it happening, it freaked me out even more. After the first few deaths I thought I could save people. It didn't work. Eventually I couldn't handle the pressure and kept it mostly to myself."

"What changed?"

"After I joined the police force, I had more success using the visions. More resources and focus." He hesitated. "But I got overconfident."

"About making assumptions from what you see?"

He was surprised at her insight. "Yeah. I'm more careful now." He wanted to change the subject. "How was it being the brightest bulb in school?"

She looked at him over the cat. "My abilities made me a geek early on. I was moved up a few grades so I was always with older kids. I had difficulty relating to kids my age, and older kids didn't want to be around me. It wasn't until I graduated from college that I made some friends and felt like I fit in with people." She paused. "Did you ever marry?"

He swallowed. "I only wanted to marry once and she died."

"I'm sorry."

"You?" he asked.

"Once. I was too young. Quick divorce."

He cleared his throat. "I think about that though. Meeting someone, getting a sailboat, hanging out in the Caribbean." He scratched Pierre's neck. "Any dreams?"

"My boyfriend wants to go to Europe this summer. He likes to hike mountains."

"What do you like?" His gaze lingered on her eyes.

"I grew up around the ocean so I miss that."

He noticed her soft lips as Pierre purred in her arms.

"Tonight..." She didn't finish.

"Yeah."

Leon and Peter came out onto the balcony.

"Upper floor is clean," said Leon.

Alex turned to them. "We'll clean the kitchen."

Leon nodded. "We'll take a look outside." He and Peter left.

Alex strode across the living room. It was tidier, which gave him some comfort. He didn't want to deal with the kitchen, but he didn't want to put it off until tomorrow either.

Megan followed him, but Pierre hissed and clawed his way out of her arms. Landing on the floor, the cat ran back to the patio.

Alex stared after the feline. "He doesn't like something in the kitchen. Probably the smell." He studied Megan. "Are you all right?"

"Sure, but you'll have to replace my jacket." She pulled at a few loose threads.

"I'll place a few more substantial bets." He gave a thin smile.

Shaking her head, she walked past him.

The cupboards were empty so they wiped the walls, floor, and counter first, putting utensils in the sink and dishwasher. While they worked, Pierre entered the kitchen again from the outside window. The cat sat on the kitchen table and watched them.

"Maybe he smells the scent of whoever was here." Megan stacked dirty pots and pans near the sink.

Alex eyed the kitchen carefully. "Maybe."

Wiping her forehead with a forearm, she stood up and opened the refrigerator. "Something smells in your fridge, Alex."

"Rotten produce, since the door was left open." He began filling the sink with soapy water for the pots.

Megan gasped. She covered her mouth with her hand as she stared at the produce bin, which was pulled out.

Alex turned off the water and stepped over, frowning.

Pierre hissed and arched his back from where he stood on the table.

Alex glanced at the cat, and then checked the bin.

From beneath a clump of Romaine lettuce, two green, glazed eyes stared up at him. His head snapped back. Lifting the limp lettuce, he uncovered a brown and white cat stuffed into the bottom of the bin, its head twisted.

Megan turned and walked into the living room.

"Yours?" Leon stood next to Alex.

Alex didn't move. "Mooch. A friend of Pierre's. A stray that used to come over for handouts."

Leon shook his head. "Anyone capable of this is one sick guy."

Peter walked in, his face darkening when he saw the cat. "That's a shame."

"Yeah." Alex thought about how he was going to take the cat out, and what he was going to do with the body. "I don't think Megan will be cooking tonight."

"Pizza," said Leon.

"I'll order it." Peter got out his phone and walked out of the kitchen.

Alex stared at the dead cat. Another message from the killer. He wanted the man dead.

CHAPTER 20

DEPUTY DIRECTOR FOLEY KNEW he was taking a risk, but he wasn't going to back away from it either.

Sitting in his office chair, one of his feet slowly tapped to the beat of Shania Twain's *You're Still the One*. His thoughts drifted back to a dive he had made on the SS Yongala wreck off Townsville, Australia. Down one hundred feet. At one point the water had turned murky, suddenly filled with algae or particulate matter. Visibility had dropped to fifteen feet.

In the space of a minute a bull and tiger shark had wound their way through the dive team. The bull shark moved so fast Foley barely saw it. But the tiger swam more leisurely, eyeing each of them like lunch platters as it carefully angulated around them.

The dive master then motioned all the divers to the surface since everyone's air was close to five-hundred psi. But Foley had delayed going up a little longer. It was worth the risk.

In and out of the murkiness, banded sea snakes swam beneath him. And then the prize showed itself. A dozen twelve-foot-wide manta rays swept through the water around him, their mouths gaping as they fed in the current. Foley swam alongside them, almost touching their graceful wings with his fingertips, enraptured by their beauty.

It was the most exciting part of the dive, those seconds of risk where any threat or beauty could appear in the shadowy water surrounding the wreck.

That was how he felt now. Something dangerous or wonderful might come at him from an unseen place. His exhilaration over this unknown was matched by his curiosity over the risk that would accompany it.

His phone rang. He waited until the third ring to answer.

"The National Museum of Natural History," said a male voice. "Thirty minutes."

The line went dead.

Foley slowly tapped his pencil against his desk, got up, and left the office. The elevators carried him to parking. The air was stale. From there he found his car and drove. Rolling down the window, he stopped at the street exit. The warm evening air ruffled his hair. He put the car in park and got out to take off his suit coat, and then turned on the AC.

Instead of driving directly to the museum, he drove along Pennsylvania Avenue to see if he was followed. Satisfied, he drove to Constitution Avenue. Twice he circled the gallery, looking for anything unusual, still checking to see if anyone followed. Traffic was minimal. Only a few people ambled along the sidewalks in the dark.

Parking on Constitution Avenue, he listened to Terry Clark's *Girls Lie Too.*

On time, a limousine pulled over in front of his car. Two big men in suits exited and stood near the front doors.

Foley got out, slipped on his coat, and strode to the parked car. The pavement still radiated heat. One of the men nodded to him and opened a rear door. Foley climbed in and the guard closed the door.

The window separating the driver from the passengers was up and curtained. The car began to move. Softly lit, the interior was cool and comfortable. As he settled into the cushioned leather seat, Foley studied the man across from him.

Senator Dillon wore a western suit, boots, and a large pewter belt buckle bearing the image of a buffalo. The first thing that struck Foley was that Dillon looked older than his age. Haggard and beat down to nothing. He wondered what had happened to the senator.

He wasn't sure what he could gain from meeting Dillon, but at an intuitive level it had felt important. If it was discovered, meeting privately like this with the senator would allow Gallagher to paint him as showing favoritism to potential suspects. But he had taken precautions, and he doubted Dillon wanted Gallagher to find out either.

"Joseph Foley." Dillon extended his hand—covered with a thin leather glove.

Maintaining a serious expression, Foley grasped the senator's hand. "Good to meet you, Senator Dillon."

They shook firmly. Foley was forced to meet Dillon's eyes. He sensed this was one person he shouldn't turn away from. Retrieving his tin, he took three mints.

"I've come to ask for a favor," said Dillon.

Foley waited.

"First, is there any reason why Dr. Crary, Dr. Joulie, and I are being hounded? Do you have any concrete proof of any wrongdoing by any of us?"

Foley shook his head. "No. There's no evidence against you. I've instructed my office to be careful with their investigation."

Dillon sat back. "I hope your questioning of us stays out of the press. If there's even a hint of connection to a case like this it would tarnish our reputations. And weaken Dr. Joulie's and my own credibility and damage our work."

Foley nodded once. "As I said, at this point we don't have anything."

"But you know how it is. Once the story gets out the damage will be done. Can you keep it from the press, Joseph?"

"Yes." Uncomfortable with the senator using his first name, Foley waited. "Is that all?"

Dillon glanced out one of the darkened windows. "You've had an ambitious career."

Foley waited, unsure what the senator was implying.

"Do you remember your appointment to deputy director?" asked Dillon.

Foley hadn't thought he had any chance at the time.

Dillon continued. "You probably recall I wrote a letter of recommendation to the director for you."

Foley fidgeted. "I wrote a letter thanking you."

"What you probably don't know is that I influenced fellow members. There were enough that respected me." Dillon paused. "How do you think the director came to appoint you?"

Foley shrugged. His appointment had always been a puzzle. He hadn't had much of a reputation then, and he certainly didn't have contacts that amounted to anything. More and more interesting.

Dillon pulled a folded sheet of paper from inside his suit and handed it to him. "That's a copy, Joseph, of a letter of recommendation for your nomination to the FBI deputy director position."

Checking the date and seal, Foley concluded that the letter was genuine. He found his gaze glued to the paper as he skimmed the sentences. *Dear Director...We would appreciate it if you would consider Joseph Foley for the position of FBI deputy director...can't stress his qualifications enough...He represents our needs...*The letter continued with more superlatives, ending with the signatures of several dozen prominent senators, including Dillon's.

Foley finished the letter and looked up. "You never said anything."

"I am now."

Uncertain what this was about, Foley handed the letter back and rested his hands on his thighs. Wary, he remained calm.

Dillon pocketed the letter. "You've been observed for quite some time. I'm pleased, everyone is, with what you've done with yourself and this position."

"Who's watching me?" This time Foley couldn't keep the sharpness out of his voice. He perceived a threat he couldn't name. Who did Dillon think he was talking to?

"Names aren't important." Dillon's lips pursed. "In two years there will be another presidential election."

Foley's anger evaporated. Blood rushed to his ears and his heart beat faster.

Dillon continued. "What you probably don't know is that the vice president is considered a liability and will need to be replaced. He'll be asked to step down for health reasons."

Foley's gaze steadied on Dillon's lips and he gripped his legs.

"You would be a prime candidate, one who a lot of people would support." Dillon emphasized his next words. "If you continue to show good judgment."

Needing to ease his arched back, Foley sagged into the cushion. His mind jumped ahead two years. He had never considered such a possibility. Dreamed, yes, but never taken it seriously. Of course, he never expected to find himself in his current position either. *Vice President Foley.*

The cold voice of reason gripped him. If there was one thing he was sure of, there was always a price.

Dillon continued. "Threshold obviously represents a much larger issue than just a few terrorists, doesn't it?"

Instantly on guard, Foley said, "They're murderers."

Dillon nodded. "Of course."

Foley grew impatient. "What's the point?"

"You're following what's happening, aren't you, Joseph? I don't have to spell out everything to a smart man like you, do I? Pretty soon nature will be limited to photographs and paintings, or to places like our National Museum of Natural History. Wildlife will only be in zoos. It must strike a person like you, one who goes to these God-blessed places, as a pretty frightening scenario."

"It bothers me," he said slowly.

"You could do more, especially in a higher office. Probably my last great contribution to this struggle is to fight for legislation that will make a difference for the next generation, since my generation has trashed the planet. It's a debt, Joseph. One we must all pay."

Hiding his caution, Foley asked, "What do you want?"

Dillon leaned back. "How close are you to stopping Threshold?"

The question startled him and he answered carefully. "They're organized and we don't have the kind of leads we need right now."

Dillon looked out the window. "Some of my fellow senators are scared. They're frightened of the justice Threshold says they deserve for destroying the planet with their votes."

Foley wished Dillon would get to the point. "We're trying to keep them as safe as possible."

"Unlike my colleagues, I'm not afraid. I don't like the killing, but the publicity for the information that's being disseminated across the country by Threshold is priceless. This opportunity can't be repeated and we can't let it pass without taking advantage of it." Dillon looked at him with narrowed eyes. "No matter what happens on this case, in two years the public will forget it. Don't you think this extremist thing is almost over?"

The senator pressed an intercom button and said, "Take us back, please."

Foley couldn't believe what the senator was asking, but he wanted it spelled out. "Why did you ask to speak to me?"

Reaching into his suit coat, Dillon pulled out a white envelope and handed it to him. "It was good to see you again, Joseph. Remember, two years will pass quickly." He lifted a hand. "One more thing. This meeting never happened. I have an airtight alibi."

Foley stiffened.

"Just to be sure you understand." Dillon tipped up the armrest to his left, revealing a panel of small red lights. "This car is fitted with electronic surveillance. If you had come wired tonight, I would have known." He closed the armrest as the car came to a stop.

Foley's mouth turned sour as he wondered if their conversation had been recorded. No matter. He had been careful. With a neutral face he took Dillon's extended hand and shook it. When he got out, the limousine drove away. He hurried to his car.

Once inside he opened the envelope. In it rested a thin cigarette lighter and a small slip of paper with ten numerals scribbled on it.

He sat back, remembering the Great Barrier Reef photograph in his office, and in particular, one small fish living on the reef. That specimen represented the whole of nature. Its vulnerability, its beauty, and its fragility.

There was also a shark in the picture, at the edge of the reef, representing the unpredictable power and ferocity of nature. It seemed to him that some people were like sharks, able to control the destiny and lives of the masses. Deciding who should live or die. But most people were like the smaller fish, slaves, to some degree, to the decisions of the shark. Senator Dillon was like the shark; he wanted to choose who should be sacrificed to serve the good of the whole. The arrogant, cold-blooded bastard.

Pulling out the cigarette lighter, he lit the piece of paper and watched it burn.

CHAPTER 21

U.S. REPRESENTATIVE CAMERON LOOKED at his wife, Sheila. Her bifocals slid down her nose a little, but she didn't seem to care, so intent was her interest in the book she was reading. The luminous numbers of the clock on the bedside stand read one-thirty a.m.

"Must be a barn burner," he said softly.

"One more paragraph," she said quietly, patting his hand.

Finished, she closed the book, set it aside, and turned off the small bedlamp. She snuggled close to him and he reciprocated, stroking her back.

A small sound in the hallway outside their bedroom stopped him. Had to be Jen, their twelve-year-old daughter. Sometimes she got up late at night to hit the bathroom or the fridge.

Muffled footsteps. Their bedroom door clicked.

Cameron tried to turn around, but someone flipped him over like a pancake. A knee in the middle of his back pushed him into the mattress, muffling his exclamation. Shock engulfed his limbs.

He glimpsed Sheila tossed over by a hooded man as she yelled. The man struck her in the face and she quieted. Fear gushed into Cameron's throat, along with embarrassment and shame. Panic froze him. He told himself it was better for all of them if he was passive.

His wrists and ankles were zip-tied, his mouth gagged. In less than a minute the weight in the small of his back was lifted.

Burglars? God, please don't let them hurt Sheila. And not Jen. He listened, but he didn't hear other voices.

A rock-hard gloved hand gripped his arm and dragged him off the bed. He gasped as he struck the floor with his knees. Sheila's weight thumped off the other side of the bed.

Cameron had a dog's-eye view of the world as he was pulled across the bedroom carpet, through the darkened hallway, and down the carpeted steps to the main floor. His attacker slid him across the wood floor hallway into the living room. He was dumped in its center. No lights were on.

Sheila and Jen were dragged to either side of him, both gagged, but only their wrists were zip-tied. Sheila instantly buried her head in his shoulder. Jen curled up against his chest. Trying to be brave for his daughter, he watched the four men wearing Lycra hoods.

A scent he couldn't identify filled his nostrils, but he knew he should recognize it. His thoughts were jumpy. His senses too scattered to focus. One of the men, the apparent leader, sat in an easy chair and gestured to a short, heavyset man.

The powerfully built man stepped forward and lifted Jen like a sack of potatoes. She whimpered. Cameron followed her eyes with his gaze until she was carried out of the room.

"Representative Cameron," the leader said quietly. "We charge you with supporting the coal and oil industry, working against the Endangered Species Act, and fighting to allow industry to mine and drill for oil in pristine habitats. You've added greatly to the human legacy of ocean acidification through climate change. In appreciation for your fine work, we've brought you a gift. We hope you enjoy it."

Cameron swung his gaze to the other men. One massive, one tall. He had known immediately at some level the identity of the attackers. The idea had been too terrifying to admit it to himself.

Hopefully they wouldn't kill Jen. He tried to focus on that blessing. He didn't want to acknowledge the terrible idea now lurking at the fringes of his sanity. Sheila was beside him. To give her a sign of support, he rested his chin lightly on her shoulder.

The big man pushed their heavy oak dining table into the room. Using nylon rope, they tied him tightly to one of its legs. He couldn't move an inch.

The tall man walked by and flicked a finger against his forehead, as if swatting a fly. Cameron cringed when the muscular man approached him.

But the terrorist gripped Sheila's arms and slid her across the floor and out of the room. Cameron returned his wife's shocked gaze until she was gone. At least Jen would have her mother. Tears misted his eyes.

The leader remained sitting.

A surge of hope sparked Cameron. Maybe the man had doubts and would let him go. As if in answer to his thoughts, the man got up and walked toward the hallway leading to the kitchen.

Cameron teetered on the verge of relief. But all doubt vanished when the man lit a cigarette lighter. Bending over, the terrorist touched it to something on the floor. Cameron held his breath, finally recognizing the odor he had sensed earlier.

The gasoline-soaked paper burst into hungry flames, quickly jumping as high as three feet.

The terrorist walked deliberately around the perimeter of the room, bending over to light paper every few steps until he had made a complete circuit. Past the large oak hutch, the matching easy chairs, the tall vase in the corner, the sofa, and lastly the matching floor lamp. Without even a glance back, the man walked out of the room.

The fire joined along the perimeter into a wall of red, sending heat and smoke throughout the room, watering Cameron's eyes.

Wanting to believe it was a nightmare, all he could do was shut his eyes, hoping he would wake up with Sheila next to him, with morning sunlight streaming through the windows. He tried to focus on that image. Then he started to pray.

***

Odysseus ran back through the garage, picked up his hidden silenced MP5, and stopped.

The woman and her twelve-year-old daughter were tied to the garage door track. The mother sobbed quietly, but the girl stared at him wide-eyed. He glanced at the house, then back at the girl and woman. He drew a switchblade.

The woman gasped and cringed. The daughter leaned back but didn't take her eyes off him.

He cut the rope tying them to the track. Pulling on their arms, he dragged them to their feet and out of the garage to a small tree ten feet away, quickly retying them to it. The woman turned away from him, but the daughter looked at him defiantly.

"I'm sorry," he said to the girl. Then he ran.

Flames already flickered above the living room's bay windows. Stopping on the driveway, he grabbed the small canister sitting there. Quickly he sprayed a large red numeral two on the cement. Finished, he dropped the can and ran to the backyard, heading for the back of the house on the next street over. The lawns were spacious with nowhere to hide, but no lights advertised his presence.

The night was warm and the exertion sent sweat running down his torso. The others waited for him at the back of a large, two-story brick house.

Menelaus jerked his chin to the street. Adrenaline spiked Odysseus' chest as he peered around the corner.

A blue striped, white Collierville police car—with its flashing lights on—was parked behind one of their vans on the far side of the otherwise empty street. An officer was shining a flashlight into the van's front window. In the squad car a female officer was talking into her radio.

Odysseus signaled to the others to follow him single file. He ran for their second van parked on the near side of the street, keeping it between himself and the police officers. When he reached the vehicle, he brought his gun up, motioning to the others.

Walking around the rear of the van, he held the MP5 level in both hands waist-high. He moved directly toward the officer looking into the van's window. The officer in the car got out, drawing her gun and yelling a warning to her partner.

The policeman in front of Odysseus whirled.

Firing a very short burst from the waist, Odysseus aimed for the officer's chest, then his leg, the muffled thumping staccato loud in his anxious ears.

The officer fell to the pavement, his eyes open.

There was a simultaneous burst from another MP5, and the female officer toppled to the ground, also wounded, but not dead. Achilles ran up to the woman and hovered over her, his gun aimed at her head.

Odysseus swung his gun at Achilles. "Don't." They stared at each other, while Patroclus and Menelaus leveled their guns at Achilles from the middle of the street.

Achilles lifted his gun, stripped the radio off the officer, picked up her weapon, and got into the back seat of the police car.

Odysseus released his breath, then bent closer to the policeman's face and whispered, "We don't kill the innocent if we don't have to." After yanking the radio and gun off the officer, he ran to the police car and took the driver's seat.

Menelaus climbed into the front passenger seat, while Patroclus jumped in beside Achilles in back.

Lights came on in houses up and down the street.

Odysseus turned off the cruiser's flashers and lights, put it in reverse, and floored the accelerator. Backing around the corner, he rammed the shift into drive and raced down the street, taking the first right they came to. The tires squealed as they flew around the corner.

Menelaus turned on the AC and monitored the police radio.

The dispatcher repeated, "Officers need assist. West Bray Park Drive, Braystone Park. All units respond."

"Idiots," said Achilles.

"Be quiet and watch the streets." Odysseus shut off the radio and gunned the car along the block. He took a left at the end of it, driving west. Police and fire departments were less than a half-mile to the south and west. He wanted to avoid both by staying off major thoroughfares until they were farther away.

Needles of adrenaline raced through his chest and arms. They had succeeded, but at what cost? If the police officers had been more alert they might still be back there, involved in a shoot-out. He stopped that train of thought and shook his head. Panic wasn't justified. It wasn't the lack of vigilance by the police that had allowed their escape. It was their rigorous training, their discipline, and their planning that had protected them.

Nevertheless his stomach felt queasy. He wasn't scared of confrontation, but he didn't want to take any risks this close to their final goal. And right now there was an element of chance in their escape over which they had no control. After a mile he drove into another housing development on the north side of the street, taking a series of turns leading northwest.

After rounding one corner, he found himself nearly on top of a bicyclist. He would have missed spotting the biker if not for the reflective tape on the man's vest. Swearing, he jerked the wheel violently to the left, moving into the opposing traffic lane.

The others in the car were jolted to the left, then back to the right as Odysseus pulled the wheel sharply again to avoid hitting an oncoming car. When he straightened the vehicle, he exhaled.

"Should have run him over." Achilles gave a harsh laugh.

Odysseus glanced in his rearview mirror, clenching the steering wheel.

There was little traffic and his frenzied driving gained them distance from Cameron's house. Sirens blared. Odysseus couldn't tell if they were from the fire department or the police.

They covered a mile of quiet streets in another housing development before Odysseus began to relax. When sirens sounded closer, he turned on the car lights.

A police cruiser veered around the far corner. It was obvious from the car's flashers and siren that it was responding to the summons.

"They're tracking our car," said Patroclus. "GPS. More will be coming."

"Get ready." Odysseus powered down both driver side windows, slowing the car from fifty to ten miles an hour. Heat poured in from the street. Gripping the MP5 on his lap, he steered with his left hand.

The other police car slowed as it drew closer.

Twenty feet from the other car, Odysseus sped up alongside it and braked hard. The other car also braked so it wouldn't pass them, its driver-side window already down.

Odysseus brought his MP5 up to the window as Achilles brought up his. For one instant everything was frozen.

The two officers in the car gaped at them.

"Get out," said Odysseus.

Achilles inched up the muzzle of his gun.

The officers saw it and went for their weapons.

Odysseus squeezed the trigger.

Muffled bullets shattered the windows of the police car. It was over in seconds. The silence surrounding them was at odds with the ringing in Odysseus' ears.

Both officers in the car slowly slumped against the dash as the vehicle rolled down the street, up the curb, and into the side of a garage where it stopped with a dull crunch.

Odysseus put his MP5 on his thighs and sped off into the night, his hands sweaty on the steering wheel. Keeping to empty side streets, he drove faster.

After a half-mile a large sedan drove toward them. Turning sharply, Odysseus swerved the police car broadside in the road, forcing the sedan to stop.

They all exited, guns trained on the wide-eyed middle-aged man in the sedan. Menelaus pulled the man from the car and struck him over the head. The man crumpled, and Menelaus dragged him off the street behind some bushes on a lawn.

Patroclus drove the police cruiser to the side of the road, parked it, and killed the lights. Odysseus got into the driver's seat of the sedan, and the others joined him. He raced off.

He knew they couldn't afford any more mishaps. Each block seemed like a marathon. He counted them off. Another few miles swept by and they finally reached the highway. He took it west until they reached the interstate which circled Memphis, and took it southwest.

In a half-hour they were off the expressway, in south Memphis, cruising a darkened neighborhood of warehouses and businesses interspersed with rundown and boarded-up houses. Driving off the road into a lot, Odysseus circled up to the front of a large warehouse door.

Menelaus pressed an automatic garage door opener and the large door rolled up. Racing the sedan inside, Odysseus parked it with a jolt as the garage door closed.

They sat in silence.

Slowly Odysseus' hands fell off the steering wheel. His knuckles hurt. Patroclus and Menelaus seemed as shaken as himself and didn't move or speak.

Achilles exited first.

Getting out, Odysseus waited for Achilles to face him, and then swung on him without warning. Fists to the stomach and head.

Achilles fell to his back, gasping.

Drawing his pistol, Odysseus knelt on Achilles' chest and shoved the barrel into the side of his face mask. A hand gripped his arm. Menelaus.

Menelaus said, "We can't afford this."

Odysseus returned Achilles' glare. "He provoked those cops, made us kill them."

"What's the matter, are you soft?" Achilles asked quietly.

Odysseus put a hand around Achilles' neck and pressed the barrel between his eyes, grinding it into his mask. "What happens, you fool, when the press talks about dead cops, huh? What happens then to the public sympathy for our cause? We've already killed FBI agents, out of necessity. But we don't do it for fun. One more stupid decision and I'll kill you."

Releasing him, Odysseus stood, breathing hard, staring at Achilles until the man rose and left for his car. Odysseus lifted his gun, aiming at Achilles' back.

Patroclus shook his head.

Hesitating, Odysseus nodded, then ran with the others to the four separate cars waiting for them. Driving a two-door Hyundai Accent, Odysseus sped out after the others. The garage door closed behind him.

As he drove away, he considered following Achilles and finishing him. Only the fact that he had nowhere to safely hide the body kept him from doing it.

When the others were out of sight, he pulled off his Lycra mask and allowed his long, bleached hair to fall to his shoulders. He wiped the sweat off his face. Soon he was on the interstate. Heaving a deep breath, he turned on the AC. But he couldn't stop his shoulders from shaking.

CHAPTER 22

ALEX SWALLOWED. THEY MIGHT only have one more night to catch Threshold.

He had spent the night in restless sleep again. He couldn't remember any nightmares, but he sensed they had been there, just below the surface. A shower, a fresh black pullover, and a clean pair of jeans helped wake him up. While he listened to Gallagher, he drummed his fingers on the arm of the easy chair.

Leon and Peter were checking the garage and car again. Gallagher had asked them to remain outside.

"What you've seen on the news is about all we've got too." Gallagher sat on a torn sofa, facing Alex and Megan. Unshaven, he wore rumpled clothes and had bags under his eyes. Sweat stains were visible beneath his armpits.

He continued. "We held two things back. Representative Cameron's wife said the man in charge moved her and her daughter to safety, saving their lives. And one of the police officers said the leader stopped one of his people from finishing them off. Odysseus and Achilles."

He shrugged. "They keep trying to play the public for sympathy, yet they killed two cops and a U.S. representative. Even with one of the biggest manhunts in Tennessee's history, nothing significant has turned up. The numeral two was left painted on the driveway."

Gallagher motioned to the flash drive and folder on the coffee table between them. "That's what we have to give you. I downloaded some new files to the flash drive on the way here and haven't looked at all of it yet myself." His eyes narrowed. "Foley seems to think it's a waste of time to use his regular people these days." He cleared his throat. "We'll check the origami left here, but I doubt we'll find anything. Whoever tore your house apart didn't leave any prints anywhere."

"Did Foley tell you my theory?" Alex leaned forward.

Gallagher grunted. "Explain it again."

Alex leaned forward. "What if the terrorists have assumed new identities and killed their old ones?"

"Yes, he mentioned it." Gallagher gestured dismissively. "You want us to exhume every suspect who's died in the last five years?"

Alex ignored Gallagher's sarcasm. "Only the strongest suspects. Especially any who died in a fire and might have a personal motive."

"We need a legitimate reason to convince a judge to dig up a body or we need family consent." Gallagher paused. "I assume you found some kind of proof that prompted you to request this?"

Alex quieted his fingers on the sofa arm. "Let's call it a strong hunch."

Gallagher lifted an eyebrow. "That's not good enough."

"Shrink your list down to a few likely suspects who have died in the last year," said Megan. "Then see if you can get family consent." She wore the same suit with a white blouse and looked rested. Her feet were bare, her legs crossed yogi-style on the couch.

Alex had found her on the patio in the early morning practicing kung fu in sweats and a T-shirt. Sitting on the sofa, he had watched her for a while, enjoying it. Enjoying having a woman in his house. Her skill level looked exceptional. And he had wondered what it would feel like to wake up with someone in his life every day again.

"What do I tell the family?" Gallagher smirked. "Hey, we think your son is a member of a radical, bloodthirsty, extremist group.

We don't have any solid evidence, but would you mind if we dig up his body just in case he faked his death?"

"You figure it out." Megan gave him a cold stare.

"You figure it out, sir." Gallagher glared at her.

Megan's eyes narrowed but she said nothing.

Alex saw that Gallagher, though irritated, was at least intrigued. "My guess is you've already run into one suspect who might have died in the last year, right?"

Gallagher leaned forward. "There's one fellow by the name of Jerry Peiser. A real nutjob. He wrote some violent articles for a small radical online press. We also learned his little sister died of cancer caused by an upwind chemical plant."

Alex sat up. "How did Peiser die?"

Gallagher leaned back. "Burned in a car accident."

"What was the name of the sister?" Alex held his breath.

"Kristen."

It was Alex's turn to glare. "Didn't Foley mention the name, Kristen?"

Gallagher looked annoyed. "He did, but we have no proof for digging Peiser up."

"It's him." Alex became rigid.

Gallagher's eyes widened. "You can't be certain of that."

"The terrorist made sure Cameron's daughter was safe because she reminded him of Kristen." Alex tried to hold back his mounting frustration.

Gallagher grimaced. "His family is in rural Missouri and they don't have a phone registered to them. It'll take a few hours to get an answer. If they say no, that's the end of it. Unless you come up with some incriminating evidence and not just wild hunches."

"Do you have a photo of Peiser?" asked Megan.

Gallagher stood up. "I'll have one emailed to you. What's your next move?"

"Dr. Joulie," she said.

Gallagher strode to the door. "I'll meet you here later this afternoon." He slammed the door when he left.

Alex's phone rang. He answered it, swearing when the same monotone, gleeful voice uttered the four words that had haunted them for several days. Pocketing his cell, he saw from Megan's expression she already knew who had called. There was nothing he could say.

Impatient to get moving, he and Megan left in his Porsche for the Mayo Clinic. The world-renowned clinic was eighty miles south of Minneapolis, Minnesota. Leon and Peter followed in a Corolla. The sky was bright and sunny, and the day warmed fast like a furnace kicking in. Even so, Alex kept the top lowered on the convertible.

Megan kicked off her shoes, crossed a leg beneath her, and put her other bare foot on the dashboard. Alex thought about telling her to take it off, but instead just stared at it a few moments.

"It's clean," she said.

"Great." Her slacks slid up her lower leg a few inches, revealing a flower tattoo with a heart in the center. "Only tattoo?"

She glanced at him. "I got it in high school. But I still like it."

He did too. "I don't like needles."

"No pain, no gain." She glanced out her window.

Construction on the main freeway south had slowed traffic to a standstill so they took Highway 61, which meandered along the Mississippi River's curves. Relieved to see the blue water flowing toward the Gulf of Mexico, Alex was happy to be near something sane and calm.

Marshes bordered the river in some places and train tracks ran inland of the road. Open countryside separated the small towns they passed. The river eventually became Lake Pepin, the widest part of the Mississippi River; two miles wide and twenty-two miles long.

On the way Megan put on Annie Lennox singing *Into the West*, while she used her laptop to scan through the flash drive information that Gallagher had left them.

"Anything?" he asked at length.

"Yes." She shut off the music. "I think we've found what we were looking for."

"What?"

"There's a public Senate hearing coming up on a bill requiring mandatory prison sentences for CEOs and owners of companies who commit serious violations of national and international pollution limits. The bill is called S.229. It would extend U.S. pollution limits and environmental laws globally for companies headquartered in the U.S.

"Other restrictions include banning certain toxics and GMO herbicides, with the option of including major foreign corporations wishing to trade with the U.S. It includes four clauses for a massive ramp up of green energy, banning GMOs in the United States until long term health studies are conducted, ending throwaway plastic production, and moving to Green Chemistry."

Alex shook his head. "The business community ought to love it."

Her voice hardened. "It's about time."

He glanced over. She was scrutinizing him.

"Anything else?" he asked, caught off guard.

She kept reading, and then said, "It looks like they have very little support for the bill at present. A public hearing is in one week."

It sounded right to him. "Should be intense."

"Every environmental group in the country is lobbying for the bill." She continued to read the report. "Senator Dillon sponsored the bill and guess who's speaking at the House hearing."

"Dr. Joulie?" He glanced at her with raised eyebrows. "What's he going to say?"

She closed the laptop. "The report doesn't say."

"We'll have to ask him."

They sat quietly for a few minutes until she said, "You must feel bad about Mooch." Her eyes and voice carried empathy.

He was surprised how fast his throat choked up. Mooch was a stray, but he cared. And he knew what it really signified. "Mooch was around a lot. I kind of adopted him, though I never let him stay the night."

"I'm sorry it happened, Alex." From her purse she retrieved a pair of sunglasses with blue lenses. The color made them seem even thicker, as if she had small aquariums in front of her eyes.

Alex barely held back a smile.

"I broke my new ones." She turned away. "This old pair is all I had."

"It's a different look. I just have to get used to them on you."

"How long does it take you to get used to things, Alex Sight?" Her lips showed a hint of a smile as she stared out her window.

"Depends." He looked back at the road, wondering how sure she was of her boyfriend. More importantly, Mooch's death reminded him of Jenny. He didn't want to lose another partner.

CHAPTER 23

MAX WAS SULLEN. BECAUSE of his mood he kept the air conditioner off. After an hour on the road they were south of the city of Redwing.

Max sat in the passenger seat, annoyed with the driver he had hired for the day. Billy. A young man with straggly, greasy hair, greasy jeans to match, a dirty T-shirt, and unshaven beard. Max liked cleanliness and tidiness. Just looking at the man irritated him. Had to be a druggie. "What kind of name is Billy for an adult, anyway?"

"Why can't we turn on the AC, man, we're roasting." Billy's voice was whiny.

"Because I want to smell the river, you idiot." Max ignored Billy's glare. He knew what really burned him. On the check-in call in the morning Threshold had been terse with him, informing him that this was his last chance. If he missed again, he was off the assignment. No fee, a tarnished reputation, and no more job offers from them. Worst of all, no finality to a much-anticipated conclusion.

He consoled himself with the fact that no matter what, there would be another job soon enough. There always was. He had stretched this one out more than most. Maybe that was why he felt so attached to it and didn't want it to end.

Billy tromped on the van's accelerator and swung into the opposing traffic lane to pass. The first car was easy. Billy slid back in behind the black Porsche. As Max observed his targets through tinted glass, his mood perked up. It would be fun to see their expressions.

He had spied on them with binoculars this morning. It had been amusing to see them check the street and their cars, watching their surroundings with suspicion. He had done his job well. There was no doubt about it. They were scared.

Now that the game was almost over, he felt a surge of eagerness. The opposing traffic ceased and Billy swung out again, punching the accelerator. When they passed the Porsche, Max smiled as Alex Sight—his face taut—tried to see past their van's tinted glass.

Billy passed the black Porsche and continued to accelerate.

Max's employers had notified him that Sight was going to Rochester. He had scouted the other two freeways leading south. Both had heavy construction and delays. Thus he had hoped Sight would take the river route on Highway 61. Sight had, and Max had already assessed the road for the proper place.

He wanted a fairly sharp curve. It arrived six miles south of Redwing. A tree-covered bluff rose along the road to the right, the road curving around it. The river lay a half-mile to the east, and there were signs for Wacouta beach and Frontenac State Park, which adjoined the beach.

"Hey, could we go for a swim later?" asked Billy.

"Sure, you moron. We'll kill two people, then flee the scene of the crime to a river beach less than a few blocks away. Brilliant plan, Billy." Billy's face turned red, but Max ignored him. "As soon as we get around this bluff, pull over onto the shoulder and stop. Do you think you can manage that, Billy?"

He ignored Billy's angry gaze and climbed from his seat into the back. To the right, a canary-yellow Suzuki dirt bike was strapped to the inside wall of the van. On the carpeted floor near the bike rested a Carl Gustaf recoilless rifle with an optical sight. Next to it two antitank rounds were strapped to the floor.

Set up just in front of the rear doors was a M240B machine gun mounted on a tripod with a hundred-round ammo bandolier already attached. The rounds for the Gustaf were antitank HEAT 655—designed for use in confined spaces—but the van was too small to risk it. Max had decided on the M240B.

Lying down on the carpet, he put on ear protectors, pushed the M240B stock against his shoulder, rested his cheek against it, and stared through the telescopic sight.

"Give me a countdown, Billy. From five seconds before you stop." He had given Billy simple directions; Stop, climb into the back, and push open the rear left door.

He was anxious to see how Sight and Detalio would react to heavy fire at point blank range. He imagined, as he had repeatedly since last night, how it would look. Shocked faces. Open mouths. The high caliber rounds tearing the car to smithereens, while cars careened into the Porsche from behind. He gave a delicious sigh.

The van started to slow.

"Count me down, Billy."

"No can do."

"Billy, be professional." Once Billy opened the door, he needed one second to sight on the curve. By the time Sight saw the van a stream of bullets would be screaming into the front of his windshield.

"No way," said Billy.

A spurt of anger tightened Max's chest. He quickly set the gun stock on the carpet and pushed to his feet, ready to slap Billy on the side of his head. His anger was cut short when he looked out the front windshield. Just ahead of them, a quarter-mile-long line of stopped cars filled the road. If they attacked Sight now, they would be trapped here with no escape. He gazed disappointedly at the construction equipment and road crews, which squeezed the road to one lane.

He returned to his seat again, quickly calming. Things always worked out for the best. Adjusting his side mirror, he decided to crank up the air conditioning.

"Finally," said Billy. "AC."

He smirked. "You deserve it after all the hard work you've done, Billy."

Billy glared at him again.

Max's grin broadened when he realized he had another opportunity for one more message.

CHAPTER 24

ALEX WAS CERTAIN THAT someone in the Bureau was feeding information to Threshold. The timing of the Billings attack and his vandalized house matched their movements too closely. The idea that there might be a traitor spurred all kinds of terrible possibilities.

At Lake City they passed the marina and scores of docked sailboats. Alex stared wistfully as they drove by.

"What?" asked Megan.

"I've been looking at boats for years." He wondered what it would be like to sail to any destination with no timetable.

She looked at him quizzically. "Why don't you buy one?"

He didn't have a good answer. "Sometimes dreams pass you by."

"You have to make your dreams happen, Alex."

He glanced at her. "Have you?"

She avoided his eyes. "I'm working on it."

A little later he stopped at a gas station. Megan went for snacks.

"Get me an apple," he called to her.

Without turning she gave a thumbs-up.

He watched her walk away, wondering if she felt anything for him, and what he really felt about her. After filling the tank, he left a message with Deputy Director Foley's office assistant. Foley called back immediately.

"Anything new?" asked Foley.

"I think we need to minimize the number of people who know what we're doing."

Foley cleared his throat. "I can talk to Gallagher and make it clear that only the four of us will be aware of your plans as they develop."

Alex hesitated. "What if your communications are being tracked by someone inside?"

Foley paused. "Doubtful, but I'll have everything in our offices gone over immediately. I won't use office phones anymore."

Alex hung up. Megan joined him in the car and handed him an apple. She had a cup of chai tea and a bag of nuts for herself. The *Call to the Post* bugle riff sounded and he dug out his phone.

Harry looked somber.

"Tough luck, Alex. White Star lost." Harry's face brightened. "Surely a small setback. Want the list?"

"Yeah, why not?" He was down by ten thousand. Megan eyed him, frowning. It annoyed him. "I thought you were Ms. Positive?"

"About things we can control. Not chance events." She shrugged. "It's your money."

After choosing Blue Shoe to win, he considered the amount. Seeing Megan's lips purse, he said, "Let's do a hundred." He had ten-to-one odds.

"You're certain you want to go that high, lad?" Harry fiddled with his beard.

"I need a boost," replied Alex.

"Why not?" Harry beamed and signed off.

Megan stared at him. "You bet a hundred thousand dollars, Alex."

He put the phone away. "You think it was too low?"

Her eyebrows hunched.

He needed air. "Gotta stretch my legs."

Leaving the apple, he exited the car and took a few steps. His eyes traveled to the far end of the lot where Leon and Peter stood by their car, watching him. Heat from the parking lot radiated up in a choking haze.

His gaze wandered up to the blue sky, which instantly seemed blindingly bright. Something made him turn involuntarily. It was as if someone placed a palm against his skull and forced his head to swivel. His eyes danced over pavement, spying little pebbles and stones in its latticework, the gray, white, and black colors vivid. His gaze was pulled across the lot to the corner of the building.

Impulsively he walked past the trunk of their car, his vision sliced to a narrow margin as if he wore blinders. The vertical line of the corner of the building took all of his attention. Arms glued to his ribs and thighs, he felt squeezed from both sides. He shuffled over dry, baked asphalt. Sweat beaded his face, running over his back and arms in tiny rivulets that tickled his skin.

A butterfly fluttered by, a bright speck of yellow dancing in the air.

He was aware of a car entering the lot, heading toward him, its horn blaring. Megan called his name but he didn't turn or slow his steps.

Again Megan yelled his name. Tires screeched. Someone shouted.

Ignoring everything, Alex felt compressed over every square inch of his body—as if the world had caved in on him...*dirt fell over his forehead and legs, covering his body.*

Concentrating, he searched for something to clarify the image. Vulgar words floated to him from the driver of the car that had been forced to stop. His limbs felt wrapped like a mummy, his lips locked and nostrils pinched. He gulped air.

The corner loomed closer. He rounded it. His gaze darted to a small bulldozer fifty feet distant, its beat-up, rusted blade on the pavement...*a bright burst of fire shot upward, surrounding him. He gasped, trapped in a small enclosure, surrounded by screams and yells...*

He desperately focused on that image, even as he collapsed to his knees, then his belly. The pavement bruised his chin, hot to his cheek as he lay there, not breathing, no part of his body seeming able to respond to his commands.

Strong hands turned him over. Megan's face was blurry. His eyes filled with tears he didn't understand. His chest convulsed, shuddered to life again, and he sucked in air with heaving gulps as he stared up at her. Somewhere to the side running footsteps approached him.

"Are you all right?" Megan scanned his body.

"Help me up," he mumbled. Clumsily he gripped her arm for support.

Leon and Peter arrived and lifted him to his feet like a rag doll. Deep fatigue hit him and it was all he could do to remain upright, wavering. He wiped his eyes.

"You all right, Alex?" Leon steadied him. "What happened?"

"Do you need an ambulance?" asked Peter.

"No." He shook his head. "The heat." He didn't have to pretend fatigue. Everything was still out of focus.

"What do you want to drink?" asked Leon.

He felt faint. "Water and grapefruit juice."

"I'll get it." Peter jogged away to the gas station convenience store.

Megan hooked one arm through Alex's, and she and Leon slowly walked him back to the Porsche. Megan clasped Alex's hand, looking at him with worried eyes. Again he sensed her empathy, and something else beyond it.

Nearby a man swore loudly; the driver of the car he had walked in front of. He was glad the man's image was blurred. It made it easier to ignore him.

"You almost hit him!" Megan snapped at the man.

Leon opened the front passenger door.

It took all of Alex's focus to fall into the seat and lift his legs into the car. Leaning forward, he grabbed dark chocolate from the glove compartment. Leon shut his door, and Megan took the driver's seat.

Peter returned with bottles of juice and mineral water, shoving them through the window with a nod. "Here you go, Alex."

Alex took the bottles. "You're the best."

Peter nodded. "Anytime."

Leon patted Alex's shoulder. "You better keep your fluids up. I learned that in football double practices."

Alex glanced at them. "Thanks to both of you."

"Anything else?" Peter sounded earnest.

"We're going to the famous Mayo Clinic. If I fall apart there at least I'll be surrounded by doctors." He drank some grapefruit juice, in his side mirror watching Leon walk with Peter back to the Corolla.

Megan drove the car out. "Well?"

"I'm not completely sure." He licked his lips and allowed his head to sag against the headrest. "I was buried. And I saw a fire and an explosion." He stopped when her face paled. A sense of foreboding pulsed in his veins.

He was thankful she didn't ask more questions. "Foley will talk to Gallagher. From now on only the four of us will know where we're going and what we're planning."

"Great." Megan bit her lip as she pulled onto the highway.

He closed his eyes against the sunlight streaming in through the windshield. "Yeah, great."

CHAPTER 25

ALEX CAME OUT OF a restless sleep with Megan tapping his shoulder.

She had her laptop open and turned it toward him, showing him Dr. Joulie's driver's license photo.

"You couldn't park closer?" He looked tiredly at the coming walk. They were near Central Park, downtown Rochester, beneath an overhanging tree. The top was up on the Porsche and hot air blew through the windows.

She closed the laptop. "You need something to wake you up."

Sighing, he left the car. Megan walked beside him as they headed to the Mayo Clinic. Leon followed them at a discreet distance, and Peter remained with the cars.

Alex remembered reading somewhere that Rochester was once rated as one of the top three places to live in the U.S. A population of one-hundred-sixteen-thousand with a mix of old buildings amid some very modern ones. The traffic was light, the atmosphere of the streets relaxed. The sidewalk radiated heat into their faces.

As they walked, Alex looked up at the towering buildings housing the world-famous clinic, wondering if they also hid a terrorist. The Mayo Clinic took up about eight square blocks in an imposing array of buildings. Pedestrian subways and skyways connected all of them.

Megan gestured to it. "Fifteen million square feet with thirty-five-thousand employees serving one point three million patients yearly."

"It takes a village." He had heard Mayo was catering to wealthy Middle Eastern patients.

Megan eyed him. "Are you ready to do this?

"I'll manage."

They walked into the twenty-one-story Gonda Building. Alex thought it resembled an art museum. The ceilings were high, the waiting room furniture spotless, the curves and artwork on the walls modern. Statues, paintings, and eclectic art designs. The lobby was as large as a small airport terminal. Live piano music drifted through it. All Alex cared about was that it was cool. The inside of the building was a busy beehive compared to the streets outside.

They checked in at the front desk, located what floor Dr. Joulie worked on, and then found an elevator. It had a glass door.

The Division of Medical Oncology was on the tenth floor. They found the waiting area, which again had modern chairs, lounges, and massive windows overlooking the city. The walls were spotless. It resembled a large hotel lobby.

Several customer service workers manned the desk, servicing patients for over fifty doctors in the department.

The receptionist they approached glanced up from her computer. About fifty, with wavy brown hair and sharp eyes, she smiled at them. "May I help you?"

"Yes." Alex pulled his badge. "Alex Sight and Megan Detalio from the FBI. We have to talk to Dr. Joulie. It's urgent."

The receptionist's head tilted back, her voice firm. "He's with a patient and he's seeing patients all day. You'll need to make an appointment."

"We only need five minutes," Megan said politely.

The woman's expression didn't waver. "He's booked solid."

"Or we could start questioning patients about the good doctor," said Alex.

The receptionist gave them a stiff look but picked up the phone.

Alex turned his back on the woman, his attention wandering. The cancer division was subdued. Staff and patients walked quietly back and forth in adjacent hallways. Several dozen patients sat in a waiting room capable of seating fifty. A number of patients were in their early twenties. While they waited, nurses came to collect people.

A tall, silver-haired man entered the waiting room from a door near the receptionist. He wore a suit and had piercing gray eyes. The doctor matched the photo on Megan's laptop.

Alex walked over. "Dr. Joulie, I'm Alex Sight and this is Megan Detalio. We're with the FBI."

"We were wondering if we can ask you a few questions, doctor," said Megan.

"I'm busy with patients all day." Joulie ignored Alex's badge. "You'll have to come back."

"Or we could wait right here." Alex smiled.

"It will be a long wait," Joulie said curtly.

Leaning closer to the doctor, Alex whispered, "To amuse ourselves we'll mention to your patients that we're here to question you about murder, terrorism, and a few other nasty things, all of which you refuse to talk about." He cocked his head. "You have a lawyer, don't you? In case we want to invite you to the local police station for a chat?" Megan glanced at him, but Alex kept his focus on Joulie.

Dr. Joulie's face hardened, but he said to his receptionist, "Tell my next patient I'll be a few minutes late, Carol." He turned back to them. "A few minutes, no more." He led them through the door he had exited, past a nurse station, and down another hallway to a room that he motioned them into.

They entered a large office with a desk, chairs, air filter, and computer. Numerous plaques on the wall displayed Joulie's degrees and accomplishments. Joulie strode to the chair behind the desk, and Alex and Megan sat in the chairs in front of it.

The doctor tented his hands, his elbows on his desk. "Senator Dillon talked to me late last night." He frowned. "You accused him of complicity with Threshold. Are you going to accuse me too?"

Alex raised an eyebrow. "Should we?"

Joulie calmly sat back. "You're bumbling around, looking for suspects. I also don't believe you have proof of Dr. Crary's involvement."

"Did Senator Dillon tell you Dr. Crary's house had been ransacked?" asked Megan.

"It might have been misguided teenagers," scoffed Joulie. "There are a number of possibilities."

"What do you think of Threshold?" Megan leaned forward.

Joulie grimaced. "Atrocious. Of course, I could show you my cancer patients who have contracted terminal diseases because of the current environmental degradation. Men, especially politicians, like to say they love women, mothers, and children. But more and more women are getting cancer, and at younger ages due to policies mostly set by greedy old men. It's simple. Women have more body fat and store more toxic chemicals the liver can't process."

"You support the terrorists?" asked Alex.

Joulie lifted his hand a few inches off his chair. "Not their methods, but their goals, most certainly. Seventy-five to ninety percent of all cancer is linked to pollution. The Mayo Clinic campuses treat one-hundred-twenty-thousand cancer patients each year. And the number is growing."

"Your success is impressive," said Megan.

"Success?" Joulie gave a grim smile. "The Mayo Clinic has several billion in endowments, but that does little for prevention." His eyes glinted. "We're failing because we haven't invested in health at the industrial and corporate level. The medical community has ignored this, telling patients to exercise and eat healthy, while the air, water, and food people take in is toxic. Industry has bribed their way to requiring perfect proof that a chemical causes cancer in order to stop its production, instead of prudently deciding to err on the side of safety and discontinue its use."

Alex gestured. "You must have talked to a lot of angry physicians and patients over the years who share your views. You've probably met at least one who's capable of supporting Threshold, at least philosophically."

Joulie locked eyes with him. "I don't think any of my colleagues would be so crude. I'm sure you talk to many more people capable of such things in your line of work than I do in mine."

"Look, the real reason we're here is we've learned what Threshold is after." Alex slid to the edge of his chair.

"Really?" Joulie's brows arched.

Alex nodded. "There's a Senate hearing coming up for bill S.229, which your friend, Senator Dillon, has introduced. Do you still plan on speaking for the bill?"

The doctor smiled. "You already know that."

Megan nodded. "We think Threshold wants to draw public attention to this bill."

Joulie's voice turned cold. "Are you accusing me of conspiracy?"

"No, of course not." Waving a hand to the side, Alex added, "But you should be aware that Threshold probably regards you, Senator Dillon, and any other supporters of the bill as allies. In their own twisted way of course."

"Half the country is also in support of the bill." Joulie smirked. "Are you also accusing them of complicity with Threshold?"

"What do you plan to say at the hearing?" asked Megan.

"Everything I've just told you, along with evidence of our government agencies ignoring the medical implications of our toxic industries. Do you have any other questions?" he asked sharply.

Alex said, "Please inform us if Dr. Crary calls you again."

"If we have any more questions, we'll be in touch," said Megan.

Joulie rose. "You can see yourselves out."

Joulie's receptionist stopped them at the front desk and briskly handed over a folded piece of paper. "Emergency message for you."

Alex unfolded the paper, anger and frustration hitting him equally hard. He showed it to Megan and her face darkened, her lips mouthing the four words.

Alex looked at the receptionist, who was already on another call. "Who gave this to you?"

The receptionist said quickly, "It was called in."

They took the elevator down in silence. Outside, hot air from the sidewalk blasted them.

As they walked back to the car, Alex noted Leon keeping up with them across the street.

Megan scanned the sidewalk. "Joulie is cold as ice."

"I wouldn't care if he was Godzilla if he could cure me of cancer. And the man has a point. We poison our own children for the sake of profit, while we talk about love and family values. Hypocrites." When Megan stared at him, he added, "Hey, I'm not stupid. I just can't get worked up over a sick system we all participate in, which for the most part the majority of us are too passive to want to change."

Megan glanced behind them. "I'm glad you want to change it."

"Yeah. Back at you." He eyed the cross street ahead of them.

Leon had worked his way a half-block in front of them, still on the other side of the street. When they returned to the Porsche, Peter gave them a small nod.

Alex clenched his jaw over needing to worry about his car every time he left it.

They drove around until they spotted a small Mexican takeout. Alex parked and went in to get food, while Megan remained in the car to do a search on Joulie.

Two people were in line ahead of Alex; an elderly woman and a middle-aged man.

Leon came in after him, standing in line, not giving any recognition. Alex looked out the side windows. No one in the takeout seemed to notice them, so he handed the note from the killer to Leon.

Leon glanced at it but didn't react. After they ordered, they both stood a short distance from the counter, close enough to talk quietly without being overheard.

Alex faced the windows. "Where are you from, Leon?"

Leon spoke softly. "Chicago. Family is there. Four brothers, two sisters, and my parents. Too many cousins to stay in touch with them all."

"Wife or kids?" He was being intrusive, but he wanted to know who the man was.

"A girlfriend I want to marry. We live together. No kids. Rotten world to bring one up in."

"I can't argue with that. Where is she?" Leon had more of a life than he did.

Leon glanced at him. "D.C. She's an elementary teacher. Mobile if I relocate elsewhere. Some people dream of traveling or having things like a big house. I just dream about her."

"Sounds like a love you don't want to lose." He felt a pang over having lost his already.

Leon smiled. "I won't. I like to keep life simple. Family, friends, job. Stay in shape. Eat healthy."

"I heard you order, Leon. Five burritos."

"Two are for Peter." Leon grinned. "You do what you can on the job."

Their orders were called and they picked them up. Leon cut in front of him on the way out.

After giving Leon enough time to scan the immediate area, Alex left the restaurant, studying every car driving by, every pedestrian, and every building. He chewed his lip as he walked to his car. Getting in, he handed Megan a vegetarian burrito.

"Dr. Joulie made calls to Senator Dillon and Dr. Crary." Megan unwrapped her food. "But no one else stands out. He talks to a lot of doctors and scientists around the country. There's no patterns worth pursuing."

The heat had drained their fluids and both of them took long gulps of water, and then ate their burritos. Megan finished first.

"You want to drive?" Alex asked hopefully.

Her eyebrows lifted. "Still tired?"

Grunting, he got out and quickly changed seats with her.

She started the car. "I checked the other freeways. Still hour-long delays."

The delays were eating at him. "Then go back along the river. It's going to be faster and the water helps me think."

Shifting the seat forward, she put the car into gear and accelerated onto the road. "Something's been bothering me. Why use veterinary anesthetics at the Wheeler estate when Dr. Joulie could supply drugs?"

"Joulie wouldn't want anything tying him to Threshold. Not if he's their trump card." After chewing his way through enough food, he sat back and relaxed. "I think there's a pattern to the killings."

"I don't see one in geography," said Megan. "The murders have been in California, Texas, Louisiana, and Tennessee. Even if they're headed to D.C., they might go anywhere next."

"You're right. Not geography. They kill Wheeler as their first symbol, a GMO pesticide manufacturer and exporter. They stay on the move and hit Palmer in Texas, another manufacturer of toxic chemicals. Then they broaden their message to include politicians and lawmakers so it's clear no one's above their own prescribed law."

Megan turned on the AC and powered the windows up. "So they kill Louisiana State Senator Buford over his voting record for fossil fuels, big agriculture, and biotech."

He nodded. "They broaden their message further and kill U.S. Representative Cameron, who supported the fossil fuel industry and attacked alternative energy. They want to be certain everyone understands that anyone in the House who votes the wrong way under lobbying influences or due to incentives will be a target." He looked at her. "If they want to widen their message further, who would be their last victim?"

"Someone who's against Senate Bill S.229. Probably a U.S. senator. Two-thirds of the Senate is in opposition to the bill." She sipped some water.

"We can restrict the list to the most verbal and outspoken opponents." He got out his phone. "I'll see what Gallagher can come up with."

They had a half-day to beat Threshold to their next intended victims and his plan gave him a jolt of energy. He left a message with an assistant who said she would notify Gallagher of their request.

"You think we can find them today?" Megan glanced at him.

"Funny the people you want to meet sometimes." He studied her hair, wondering what it would be like to run his hands through it. "It'll be a mess if a U.S. senator is murdered. So many people will be involved we won't have room to breathe."

In a half-hour they were cruising along the river again, inland bluffs of brown and green grass marking the west side of the road. The right shoulder dropped off some dozen yards to the tree line below.

Megan powered her window down, allowing scents of greenery and dryness to waft in. Lake Pepin meandered to the right of them. A flock of starlings flew over the road.

Turning off the AC, Alex powered his window down too.

After another short stretch they were stopped by a line of cars slowed by the pothole work that had delayed them on the way to Rochester. Several construction workers with STOP and SLOW signs stood in the center of the road, a quarter-mile apart.

Megan slowed to five miles an hour, the sun bright through the windshield. On low volume she played Rihanna singing *Stay*.

"We don't have time for this." Alex flicked a hand in disgust.

Megan looked east at the river. "I was thinking I'd like to go for a swim."

"Glad one of us can stay calm." He regarded her. "The water's still cold this time of year. You wouldn't last more than a few minutes."

She smiled at him. "Sounds even better."

"You don't have a bathing suit."

"Hmm. Skinny-dipping."

CHAPTER 26

MAX FIGURED THEY HAD a five-minute lead on the black Porsche. They had followed Alex Sight and Megan Detalio in Rochester, and then passed them when they had taken the highway again. "Take the next left, Billy. The dirt road. I believe it's called Ski Road. And step on it."

"Right." Billy sounded bored.

Max sighed. Billy had no sense of humor. The traffic was crawling and they with it.

But Billy accelerated at the turnoff. The dirt road led directly west five hundred feet to a T-intersection.

"Right!" barked Max. "Fast now, Billy, as if your life depended on it."

Billy floored the van right, fishtailing the rear end and paralleling the highway, following the road as it veered northwest, soon curving due west with thick woods on either side. They quickly reached the bottom of the bluff on the south side.

"Stop," said Max.

Billy braked hard.

The road continued west, but a narrow dirt path zigzagged up the bluff to the right. Max directed Billy to back up to the beginning of the path and stop.

Max climbed in back. With Billy's help they muscled the two-hundred-fifty-pound Suzuki to the ground. Both of them were dripping sweat from the effort. Max slung the Carl Gustaf rifle over a shoulder, along with a pouch holding the two antitank rounds.

Billy closed the van doors and returned to the driver's seat.

Max walked around to the driver's window. "You know what to do?"

Billy nodded. "Wait here."

"Wrong, Billy." Max smiled, pulled a silenced gun from behind his back, and put bullets into Billy's chest and head.

Billy slumped to the side.

Max reached in, turned the ignition key, and dropped the shift into D. The van rolled across the road and down the sharp incline into the woods, bouncing along the uneven ground and finally hitting a tree, coming to rest mostly hidden by vegetation.

"Good boy, Billy." Max started the Suzuki and fishtailed it along the trail that wound up the bluff. It wasn't a strain for the 400cc engine and he enjoyed the ride. He was cutting things close and loving every moment of it. Dust flew, sweat ran, and the engine whined.

He parked the bike on an overlook that allowed him a view south along the highway.

Kneeling, he loaded a round into the Carl Gustaf, braced it on his shoulder, and peered through the telescopic sight. It was a pigeon shoot. His exhilaration climbed. The Porsche was stopped, trapped by cars in front and back. He sighted on the center of the car, his finger tightening on the trigger.

CHAPTER 27

ALEX GAZED IMPATIENTLY ALONG the road. The sooner Gallagher called him, the sooner they would have a plan to intercept Threshold.

As Megan eased the car to a crawl, he looked ahead. A bulldozer pushed a mound of dirt on the shoulder, then backed into the road, forcing traffic to wait. He stared at it, something gnawing at him—the premonition on the way down...*bulldozer...a bright burst of fire...*

Leaning over, he wrenched the steering wheel to the right and jammed his foot against the gas pedal. The Porsche clipped the rear bumper of the car in front of them and careened over the embankment in a nosedive.

Megan shouted.

An explosion rocked the road above them. The Porsche struck a tree hard at the bottom of the trench and slid sideways, jerking to a stop.

"Run!" yelled Alex. Megan leapt out, and he opened his door and scrambled out, immediately sprinting.

The overwhelming *whomp!* of an explosion, followed by a hot blast of air, turned his world topsy-turvy. It was as if his feet sprouted wings, sending him in a wild somersault that tumbled him along the trench. His arms got mixed up with his legs, dirt and grass covered his mouth and skin, and then everything went silent.

He came to a stop, his mind still spinning, his body numb. It felt as if he was still twirling, while the clouds above drifted in bizarre patterns.

Panic struck him. His fingers came alive and he scraped dirt, bringing partial relief to his swirling thoughts. His toes passed the next test when he wiggled them.

Leon's face hovered over him.

Alex contracted the muscles in his legs and arms for sensation.

"God almighty," the big man said, shaking his head.

Alex panicked, imagining a gaping hole in his chest or the top half of his skull blown away with only a small part of his brain able to function. "How bad is it?"

Leon lifted his chin. "You look all right."

He extended a hand. "Help me up."

Grabbing his shoulders from behind, Leon carefully helped him sit up. There were no jolts of pain, just dull aches all over his body. The Porsche's twisted frame was shattered, pieces spread along the gully. Black smoke trailed up and the odor of gas filled the air. People stood along the shoulder of the road, shouting and gawking at the sight.

Anxious, Alex looked along the ditch. Peter was walking beside Megan, her hair disheveled and her suit full of dirt and in disarray. But she seemed unharmed. Seeing her made him sag. "What the hell?"

"Yeah," said Leon. "What the hell."

CHAPTER 28

ALEX GLANCED ACROSS THE plane aisle at Gallagher, who seemed enthralled by *People* magazine. He wondered if the man even cared that he and Megan had almost died.

It had been determined that someone had used a Carl Gustaf recoilless rifle to fire two antitank rounds at his Porsche. The killer had abandoned a van, leaving a dead driver and an origami white crane inside, and escaped the bluff on a dirt bike. Other than that, they had no clue as to the identity of the killer who stalked them, and no reason to believe it was over.

Gallagher had discovered that Senator Trenton was the leader of the opposition to bill S.229. Six members of the United States Capitol Police had secretly escorted the senator with his wife and three children from his Santa Fe home to an unnamed hotel in Albuquerque. All of Threshold's suspected targets, the top senators opposing S.229, had been told to change their routines for the evening and had also been given protection.

Gallagher had decided to fly into Albuquerque because the FBI office there could supply gear, cars, and two agents he trusted that he wanted to have join them. But neither of the agents had been informed about what was involved or that they would be heading to Santa Fe.

Alex found it ironic that with hundreds of FBI agents in the field tracking information on Threshold, they were limited to using only a few out of fear of a security breach.

Deputy Director Foley had been notified, but because of previous commitments he had decided to fly into Albuquerque later in the night and meet them in the morning. They were to call him if anything developed.

Alex's thoughts flashed back to the Palmer massacre. He couldn't help but worry. Anyone who was following Gallagher, Megan, or him might deduce their final destination. A traitor in the Bureau might also put things together. Thus even if Threshold had planned on going after Senator Trenton, they might change their plans and go after someone else. The local police had also been kept on a need to know basis. If the FBI wasn't secure, there was no guarantee any police department was either.

Unable to think of any further precautions to take, Alex studied the photo of Jerry Peiser on Megan's laptop, trying to see the man behind the picture. Peiser had a straight forehead, a blunt nose, and a wide chin with a cleft. In the photo the man had brown eyes and hair. Peiser's family hadn't granted a request to exhume their son's body and it gnawed at him.

Megan sat next to him, her shoes off, fingering the silver dolphin on her neck.

Watching her, tension rose in his throat. He closed the laptop and handed it to her. "Who gave you the necklace?"

"My brother. He sent it to me from Afghanistan." Blinking, she lifted the dolphin up in front of her, studying it absently. "My father was a career officer in the army, but my brother wasn't sure he wanted to enlist. I used to listen to my father argue with him about loyalty to your country and democracy. I was a teenager and gave my brother some of my dad's rhetoric. Love it or leave it crap. Then he died over there." Her face hardened as if it had happened yesterday.

He could empathize. He always wondered if he could have done more for his brother. "Do you blame yourself?"

Her voice softened. "I was young and naïve, but my father never forgave himself. He's not as happy as he used to be."

He heard the pain beneath her words and saw it in her eyes. "That's rough."

She leaned back and her fingers on the armrest brushed over his, seeming to pause for a moment. When he glanced at her, she had her eyes closed and her hands clasped in her lap.

They arrived at Albuquerque International Airport at nine p.m. The burning sun had already set, yet it was still ninety degrees. Except for Wheeler, the terrorists had killed all their victims late at night so Alex believed they had time.

Sweat coated his skin as soon as he stepped outside. He had little luggage, though Megan had checked an oblong hard gun case, which she slung over her shoulder on a carry strap. She must have kept it in one of her suitcases, because he hadn't seen it before.

Two cars waited for them at the airport terminal. Gallagher directed Leon and Peter to the second car to ride with the other two FBI men. He conferred with them briefly, then returned.

"I'll sit in back," he said gruffly. "One of you can drive."

Alex looked at Megan. "Do you mind?"

Her lips showed a hint of a smile. "Not complaining." She took off her jacket, tossed it in back, and climbed behind the wheel, setting her gun case in the passenger foot area.

Alex noticed a duffel bag and three Kevlar vests on the back seat beside Gallagher.

Gallagher sat behind Megan and directed them. They led the other car west onto the interstate, racing northeast toward Santa Fe.

They were soon out of Albuquerque city limits, but it wasn't until a half-hour later that the desert on either side of the freeway was free of lights from the spreading suburbs and developments. Darkness claimed as much as it could, hiding the Nacimiento Mountains to the north and the Sangre De Cristo range to the northeast of Santa Fe. The air was dry and Alex found himself repeatedly licking his lips and swallowing on a papery mouth.

Gallagher put on his vest, and handed a vest to Alex. From the duffel bag on the back seat he dug out a two-way radio that he clipped to his collar. Next came a Heckler and Koch MP5A3 submachine gun with a red dot sight. From the same box he retrieved a magazine and loaded the gun. "My men have extra firepower too. We've got two more for you."

"I brought my own." Megan gazed into the mirror at Gallagher. "But I'll take a vest."

Alex slipped on the Kevlar vest.

Sweat coated Alex's palms as Gallagher handed the gun to him. He cradled it on his lap.

The southeastern corner of Santa Fe's suburbs greeted them with lights dotting the countryside on both sides of the road. They swung off the freeway and passed a golf course on the right.

Several blocks later they entered a development where darkened houses were an acre apart. Among the landscaping of desert grasses, stone, and crushed gravel were scattered desert willow and pinyon trees—black specters that gave the houses privacy from each other and the street. Alex studied the houses, hoping they were right.

Megan drove to the next side street.

"This is it," said Gallagher. "Take a right here, pull past the first drive on the right, and back in."

Megan complied and backed the car into the driveway, which angled across the street corner so the owners of the house could exit their property onto the street in front or the street to the side of their lot. Their car faced the front street. Megan turned off the engine.

Using the radio, Gallagher gave directions to the sedan following them. The other agents drove to the far end of the block and backed into the second driveway from the corner on the opposite side of the street. Trees on either side of the car kept it hidden. Alex thought it was a good set up.

Gallagher handed Megan a vest and she put it on. Next he retrieved a single lens night vision scope, and then shoved the duffel bag above the back seat beneath the rear window.

Six darkened houses spread along the opposite side of the road, squat one-and two-story homes. Four houses sat on their side of the block, three completely dark. The next one in from their corner was a large, two-story house. A hundred feet away, the house had several lights on, barely visible through the scattered trees. Its empty crushed-stone driveway ran fifty yards in from the street and looped in a wide circle up to the house and back out again. In the middle of the driveway loop was a rock garden.

Alex nodded to the large house. "Senator Trenton's place?"

Gallagher rolled down his window, letting in hot air. "We evacuated Trenton's family and everyone on both sides of the street. We had to sequester everyone to make sure no one made a call."

"Under what pretense?" asked Alex.

"Possible terrorist activity and national security. The last thing we need is to have someone taking an evening stroll. We have a helicopter standing close by." Gallagher met Alex's eyes. "We might need backup."

Alex nodded. "Smart."

Gallagher slumped into his seat. "Relax. Now we wait."

Alex looked at his watch. Ten-fifteen p.m. The moon appeared, previously blocked by cloud cover, dimly illuminating the surrounding landscape. Stretching his legs as far as possible, Alex powered his window down and settled into the seat. Tension rolled in waves along his back.

Megan opened the case she had brought and withdrew an MP7A1 Heckler and Koch submachine gun, equipped with a laser sight, extendable stock, and a shoulder sling. An armor-piercing upgrade from the MP5. She passed the case back to Gallagher.

"Are you a gun collector?" asked Alex. Besides the SIG and Glock, this made three weapons she owned.

"I like to be prepared," she said matter-of-factly. "This should stand up to anything they bring."

Gallagher grunted from the back seat. "Is that weapon registered?"

Ignoring him, she loaded a forty-round magazine, then set it on her lap.

Alex exchanged glances with her as she licked her lips. Sweat beaded his brow. The minutes seemed to tick off in slow procession.

Several times Gallagher moved from one side of the car to the other, the shift of his weight bouncing the vehicle like a waterbed. He stared into the night with one eye stuck to the night scope.

Appearing just as restless, Megan constantly changed her position as she kept vigil out her open side window and the windshield.

Rhythmically, Alex scanned the road and the Trenton estate. None of them spoke. Later Gallagher dug into the duffel bag and silently passed up water bottles and food. Alex was grateful for the water and chewed a granola bar. Megan had a sandwich.

Close to midnight, Megan hit Alex on the shoulder. His hands tensed on his thighs.

Gallagher leaned forward.

A jacked-up pickup truck swung around the distant corner. It crawled along the block, past the driveway with the other parked FBI car. The black truck had tinted windows, an extended cab, and a bed covered with a high red shell. Its headlights illuminated the street like search beacons.

Alex slid lower in the car, gripping his gun. Megan and Gallagher did the same.

Continuing at a slow crawl, the truck moved halfway down the block, then swept into the entrance of the Trenton drive. It sped up toward the house, stopping with a jolt parallel to the front door, its engine running.

Immediately touching his radio, Gallagher said quietly, "Move in." Simultaneously he hit Megan's shoulder and said, "Go!"

She started the car and shot down the driveway, the sedan's roaring engine breaking the quiet. As they raced into the street, the other FBI sedan sped out of the driveway at the opposite end of the road.

Clutching the automatic, Alex readied himself as Gallagher moved to the right side with his MP5 clutched to his chest. Their car was the first to reach the driveway. Megan jerked the wheel sharply, forcing Alex to hang onto the door.

The truck's doors remained closed and Alex couldn't see into the cab. As they pulled up the driveway, the pickup's tires spit gravel in a burst of power as it spurted around the circular loop.

Gallagher cursed loudly and moved to the other side of the back seat.

His eyes on the truck, Alex lifted the MP5 to his shoulder, aiming the muzzle out the side window.

Megan turned left at the entrance to the circular portion of the drive, aiming directly at the oncoming truck. The following FBI sedan shot up the right side of the circular drive to come in behind the truck.

The truck's lights flicked to high beams and blinded them. Cursing, Alex jerked his arms up. To avoid a head-on collision, Megan veered left. Their car jerked sideways as the truck clipped their rear passenger fender.

Megan slammed on the brakes.

Inertia threw Alex into the dash.

Gallagher swore as he banged into the back of the front seat.

The truck roared for the street, while the other FBI sedan backed down the driveway in pursuit.

"Move it!" yelled Gallagher.

Jamming the car into reverse, Megan slammed the accelerator. Keeping her gaze fixed on the rearview mirror, she swerved onto the straight section of the driveway and quickly backed onto the street. There she spun the wheel and gunned the car forward.

Farther up the street the truck roared ahead of the other FBI car. At the end of the block the fleeing vehicle took a sharp left, its frame tilting.

Already past the last driveway, Megan wrenched the steering wheel sharply left, across the left corner of the lot. A shortcut through grass and trees.

Alex bounced upward twice in quick succession as first the front wheels, and then the back, struck rocks with jarring thumps. Gallagher swore from the back seat.

Megan floored the accelerator. Putting down the MP5, Alex grabbed Megan's MP7. The fleeing truck raced along the street, visible to the right through a thin line of pinyon. Alex stuck his head and the gun out his window. The hairs on the back of his neck rose as he looked ahead. Two trees blocked their way like ominous sentries. Shouting, he ducked back inside.

Pine tree branches whipped across both sides of the car, the stiff limbs shrieking harshly against metal. As their vehicle barreled through the trees, pine needles and branches poked into the windows. For a few moments darkness gloved them.

Alex crouched to the side of the steering wheel, his line of sight just above the dash. Gallagher cursed from the back seat.

Abruptly they drove through, the scent of pine filling the car.

Alex lifted his head.

In the street, fifty feet in front of them, the truck shot across the path of their headlights.

Sticking the gun out the window again, Alex braced himself with his legs. He sighted the red dot of the laser on the truck's rear tire. Squeezing the trigger, staccato explosions cut through the sounds of the roaring engines.

The truck's tire blew and its rear end wiggled back and forth. In moments the vehicle screeched to a stop in the middle of the street.

Megan braked hard.

Alex braced himself against the window frame. Gallagher cursed again as his weight smashed into the back of the front seat once more. They stopped a dozen yards from the truck.

The other sedan braked with squealing tires in the street. Headlights from both cars spotlighted the truck.

Shoving his door open, Gallagher jumped out. Alex handed Megan's gun to her and retrieved his from the floor.

Running to the left a half-dozen yards, Gallagher stopped behind a tree, his gun aimed at the pickup. Megan stood behind her car door, the MP7A1 resting atop it at eye level, aimed at the truck.

Opening his door, Alex stepped out and positioned his gun on it. Shoulders hunched, he glanced at Megan. Wind blew her long hair. She looked utterly wild with the machine gun cradled in her arms. He glanced at the FBI car. Peter and Leon stood by the sedan with the other two agents. They all had MP5s and were using the car doors as shields.

"This is the FBI," yelled Gallagher. "Come out of the truck with your hands up!"

The truck doors cracked a few inches open.

Sweat ran over Alex's face.

"Throw out your weapons!" shouted Gallagher.

Silence continued and no one moved.

The truck doors flew open.

Alex curled his finger tight around the trigger.

A coarse young voice yelled, "Please, don't shoot! We're unarmed!"

Two male teens exited the truck, both with clean-cut hair, dressed in jeans and T-shirts. The one closest to them knelt in the road beside the truck, hands in the air, bathed in light from the FBI cars.

His voice trembling, the teen said, "Don't shoot! We just went to see if Amy Trenton was home."

"Idiots," murmured Alex.

His automatic held waist-high, Gallagher strode toward the teenagers. The four men in the road cautiously approached the teens too.

Gallagher's loud, angry voice carried to them. Alex couldn't distinguish the words. With jittery arms he lowered his gun. Megan's shoulders slumped as she returned his gaze.

"I'm sure glad you knew there weren't any trees on the other side of those pines," he said.

She said with confidence, "While we were watching the house, I noted the layout."

He rolled his eyes and leaned against the car.

In minutes Gallagher stomped back across the grass, his gun pointed down. Wiping sweat off his face, he looked at them. "Stupid kids were drunk. Thought we were Threshold after Trenton. They might have blown everything."

Alex shook his head. "They're lucky they're still alive."

Megan unslung her gun and got back into the car. Alex did the same, frowning and as upset as Gallagher.

CHAPTER 29

IN ANOTHER HALF-HOUR THE truck had been searched, its tire changed, and cell phones confiscated. The two teenagers were escorted to a local police station to be charged with a DWI and underage drinking. Alex was impatient during all of it. The terrorists could have been watching and left.

The two FBI cars took up their former positions.

Gallagher called the Santa Fe Police Department, which was fielding panicked inquiries from nearby neighborhoods about the shots fired. When he put his cell phone away, he said, "They received calls from dozens of citizens. I'd be surprised if half the damn country doesn't know about it at this point."

"Threshold still might show," said Megan.

"They have to." Alex looked out his window, wondering what to do if they didn't. Trying to relax his cramped legs, he stretched them to the end of the floorboard. The hot air made him drowsy. After a while the silence felt uncomfortable, and he glanced back at Gallagher.

Gallagher snorted. "You don't like me, do you, Sight?"

He was tired of Gallagher. "I probably wouldn't ask you to prom."

Gallagher smirked. "Don't worry, the feeling's mutual. You two have been nothing but a pain in the butt. If we're lucky, maybe after tonight we can say goodbye to each other. All you two have to do is make sure you don't screw things up."

Megan stared into the mirror and said coldly, "Could you please keep your opinions to yourself, sir?"

Gallagher scowled but didn't reply.

Not interested in trading insults, Alex looked away, shaking his head.

Megan looked at him. "Did you go to prom?"

He smiled. "Ashley Ruard. First date and kiss. You?"

She rolled her eyes. "No one asked. I was devastated."

"Their loss. First kiss?" He enjoyed the banter.

"College. Larry Basque. One date and we were through. Smoker. Like kissing an ashtray."

"That's rough." He wondered how many relationships she had been in.

"Are we done with the high school reunion crap?" asked Gallagher.

As they waited, Alex's thoughts turned to Megan. Her empathy tugged at him, along with her kindness, intelligence, and humor. Maybe his nagging doubt was his own reluctance. But he had to wonder if he would have been drawn to her under different circumstances. Still, the case, working together, and the danger had brought his emotions out again, forcing him to recognize his needs and fears.

Quietly drumming his fingers on the armrest, he stared at the adjacent lot. The next time he pulled his watch up to his bleary eyes its luminous dial read two a.m. He hadn't had a decent night's sleep since the case started. Tonight wasn't going to break the pattern.

When he glanced back, Gallagher was motionless, hidden in shadows. Megan looked half-asleep. He flicked her shoulder lightly. When she turned to him, he pointed to his watch. Anxiety filled him that Threshold might be elsewhere, killing their last victims, and then vanish for good. Watching Trenton's house had been a long shot, but he knew deep down he had hoped it was the right choice.

"How much longer are we going to wait?" Megan's gaze shifted to the mirror.

"Until I say so," murmured Gallagher.

There was a muffled explosion.

Alex jerked upright, his MP5 instantly in hand.

Flames lit the night beyond a clump of pinyon at the far corner of the street, beyond the other hidden FBI car. Fingers of fire licked the air above the greenery.

"No one move," Gallagher called into his radio. "Can you see what it is?"

"No, sir. Maybe a car."

"One of you find out what's going on." Gallagher looked through the night scope.

Megan straightened stiffly, then rapidly bent over toward Alex. "Get down!" she yelled.

He looked out her window. In a flash he saw a dark van alongside them, facing the same direction as their car. Quiet. Had to be electric or a hybrid. A driver in the front seat. In the open side door two figures knelt, both holding machine guns. The moonlight revealed all three figures wearing black Lycra suits and hoods.

Alex threw himself over Megan as the first bullets tore into their sedan. Dull pops of punctured metal surrounded them. Loud overlapping staccato filled Alex's ears as the bullets tore through the car ceiling in violent spurts. His free hand gripped the edge of the seat until his knuckles hurt, while bits of metal and glass pattered against his back and head like raindrops. Megan was below him, their bodies pressed tight. Gallagher yelled something into his radio.

The firing into the car stopped, but one MP5 continued firing short bursts, but in a different direction. Grabbing the door handle to get out, Alex felt a heavy prod on his right shoulder. He slowly sat up, facing the barrel of a gun held by a massive figure. Menelaus. Turning, Alex saw a slender man in the driveway facing Megan. Achilles or Odysseus.

"Drop your guns," hissed the man near Megan. "Knives on the floor."

The MP5 slid from Alex's fingers and Megan released her weapon. Alex drew his OTF knife and dropped it near his feet. Megan pulled a knife from a lower leg sheath too.

Alex glanced at the back seat. Slouched over sideways, Gallagher looked unconscious. His shirt showed a dark stain on one shoulder.

The car door swung open and Menelaus gestured Alex out. "Turn around, shut the door, lean through the window, hands behind your back."

Alex followed the directions. He was handcuffed and his 9mm and phone taken and tossed onto the ground. Megan suffered the same ritual on the other side of the car.

The van driver stood behind the van's driver door, still firing bursts down the street. There was no return fire. Helicopter blades whirred not far away, but the terrorists didn't seem panicked. They moved quickly and efficiently. Alex wondered how long it would take the local police to get calls and send units to the scene.

With his gun trained on Megan, the slender man shoved her through the side door of the van. With an MP5 shoved into his ribs, Alex was shoved around the sedan's trunk.

The van driver rounded the front of the van, leaned into the FBI sedan, and popped the trunk release. Next he retrieved Gallagher's cell phone and radio from the backseat. Speaking into Gallagher's radio, he said, "If you shoot at us, all of your friends are dead."

Alex stared at the man. The authority of the speaker fit Odysseus—thus the other man had to be Achilles. There was no reply on the radio as Alex was shoved into the van. The inside of the vehicle was a bare metal shell. He instinctively turned to avoid ramming the opposite van wall, and sat with his back against it, his feet flat on the floor, knees up.

Megan sat stiffly beside him.

While Achilles aimed his gun at them, Menelaus climbed into the van, moving to the front where he knelt on one knee near Alex, his gun shoved into Alex's ribs.

Achilles jumped into the van, tossing in Megan's laptop—retrieved from the FBI sedan's trunk. He moved to the rear and knelt out of sight of the open side door, his MP5 pointed at Megan. He slowly reached out and flicked a finger against her forehead.

Megan arched her neck but said nothing.

Alex wanted to hit him.

Odysseus quickly returned to the driver's seat. The van sped forward with a roar as it switched to an internal combustion engine.

Alex felt Megan's body pressed against his. He readied himself for any opportunity to act.

Careening out of the driveway, the van stopped abruptly, broadside in the street, its lights off.

Achilles shone a flashlight on Alex and Megan, while Odysseus spoke into Gallagher's radio; "These two agents are alive, as is the third one in the sedan. We'll release all three, if you give us a chance to escape. If you shoot or refuse to bargain, we'll kill all of them."

Alex stared down the block. Along with the moonlight, the fire at the far corner provided an eerie backdrop to the FBI sedan parked broadside in the road fifty yards distant. The four FBI agents stood behind the car, aiming their guns at them.

None of it made sense to Alex. Odysseus and Achilles seemed too calm. Then he realized the fourth terrorist was unaccounted for. Patroclus. "It's a trap!" he yelled.

Achilles shut off his flashlight, and Menelaus shoved his gun barrel into Alex's cheek.

"One more word and I'll put a bullet into your mouth," whispered Menelaus.

Alex knew the FBI agents wouldn't bargain, but they also didn't have clear shots at the terrorists. They would be wondering if there was some way to save him, Megan, and Gallagher.

The chop of the helicopter was louder now. Its lights shone from the west, closing in on the street.

Odysseus exited the driver's door and stood protected behind the front of the van.

Achilles exited the van's rear door, leaving his MP5 hang from his shoulder on its carry strap. The terrorist reached into the van and pulled out a tube.

Alex recognized the RPG launcher. Achilles wasn't the one that tried to kill him and Megan in Billings, and thus possibly Minnesota too—that man had a different build than the three terrorists.

Odysseus spoke into Gallagher's radio; "Tell your helicopter to leave or your agents are dead."

Achilles remained out of sight behind the van's rear door, but hoisted the RPG to his shoulder. The helicopter began to turn away.

In a moment the flare of an RPG rocket lit the night and moments later a loud explosion ended the chop of the helicopter blades. The burning chopper fell from the sky near the far end of the street, hitting the ground with a jarring crash fifty yards behind the FBI sedan.

Alex's heart pounded in his ears. He doubted the terrorists ever intended to bargain for anything. Menelaus pressed the gun barrel harder into his face.

Machine gun fire erupted to the west of the FBI car. Odysseus and Achilles immediately opened fire. Their MP5s tore holes in the FBI car in dull pops. The car shook, the tires were punctured and sank, and the windows shattered. Two of Gallagher's agents crumpled to the ground. A third ducked and ran down the street toward the far corner. Gunfire clipped the fleeing agent, sending him crumpling into a heap on the street.

The fourth FBI agent had run onto the Trenton estate, dodging and keeping low. Alex didn't want to watch but couldn't turn away. The size of the fleeing figure fit Leon's build. Alex's throat thickened as Leon raced for a small stand of trees on the Trenton estate. Machine gun fire erupted near the FBI sedan, but Leon kept running. Odysseus and Achilles quickly brought out fresh magazines from their waist belts as they moved into the street in front of the van door.

"Come on, man," whispered Alex.

Menelaus used his gun barrel to push Alex's head sideways. Alex grunted, but watched Leon run a zigzag pattern across the grass, partially illuminated in the FBI car's headlights.

Not caring what Menelaus did, Alex said, "Achilles, Odysseus, we have a perimeter waiting for radio check-ins. They'll be coming for you."

Both of the terrorists turned to look at him, but neither responded. Alex figured his lie had given Leon another second or two to flee. Facing forward, Achilles and Odysseus took a few quick steps, and then sprayed bursts from their MP5s at Leon.

Leon shouted, stumbled to the ground in the trees, and was immediately lost in the night's shadows.

Odysseus and Achilles quit firing and turned to the van, aiming their guns at Alex and Megan. Menelaus got out and stood, his weapon trained on them too.

Alex stiffened, thinking they were dead, but Odysseus and Achilles turned and ran toward the FBI car while Menelaus kept his gun on them.

Alex watched with Megan as Odysseus and Achilles bent over to check the bodies—he guessed they were retrieving cell phones and radios. A third figure joined them—Patroclus. Odysseus and Achilles hustled in the direction of the trees, but stopped when a burst of automatic fire rang out. Alex felt a surge of hope in his chest for Leon.

Crouching, Odysseus and Achilles returned short staccato gunfire, but then ran back to the van with Patroclus.

Alex estimated the whole event had taken minutes.

The four terrorists jumped into the van, and Odysseus gunned the vehicle, turning around in the street until he faced the driveway they had exited. He drove in and braked to a sudden stop.

Alex guessed they were going to finish Gallagher. When Odysseus pointed his MP5 out his window, Alex said, "Don't do it, Jerry."

"Shut up," snapped Menelaus, shoving his gun into Alex's cheek again.

Odysseus hesitated, and Achilles glanced back at Alex.

A burst of automatic gunfire spit bullets into the ceiling of the van's front cab. It had to be Gallagher.

Odysseus ducked sideways and gunned the van along the driveway.

Wondering about Gallagher's fate, a gnawing sense of guilt filled Alex. He had brought everyone to the Trenton estate and they might all die because of it. Glancing at Megan, he found her gazing at him. He couldn't help but think of Jenny's words then; *But what if you didn't see the whole picture?* He wondered if Leon was still alive.

CHAPTER 30

LEON SAT WITH HIS back against a pinyon tree. It felt like the right side of his head had been blown off. The one thing competing with that fear was the certainty that his left foot had also been shot.

Afraid to find out what was there, he gingerly touched his face. Using his fingers, he followed the blood running along the side of his cheek up to a deep gash in his ear lobe. At least it wasn't his head. He forced himself to feel along his left leg to his foot, along the inside of his shoe. With his finger he lightly probed a hole in the leather. He assumed the tip of his big toe had been shot. It burned like it had been dipped in an acid bath.

Gripping the machine gun, he glanced around the tree trunk. He wanted to sit and wait for help, to avoid increasing the pain searing his skull and foot. His hand went to his jacket pocket. His cell phone was missing. Rolling to his knees with a groan, he wiped his hands over the grass. No luck. He didn't have time to waste on it.

The terrorist van roared out of the driveway. He saw their headlights through the trees and noted their next turn. He had to find out if anyone else was alive.

Gasping, his foot on fire, he pushed himself upright and leaned against the tree. Taking a deep breath, he stumbled over the dry ground, across Trenton's front yard. His stomach tumbled over what had happened. He glanced at the shot-up FBI sedan and helicopter wreckage in the street. Three dark shapes lay in the road. Had to all be dead.

He jogged toward Gallagher's car. Every time his weight pressed down on his injured foot he wanted to scream. He modified his gait so he didn't run on the front of his foot. Sweat ran over his chest and the left side of his face felt numb.

When he reached the sedan, he noted the shot-out windows and bullet-sprayed panels. At least the tires were intact. The rear passenger door was partly open. Gallagher lay half-in, half-out of the back seat of the car, the MP5 clenched in his hands. Moaning, his eyes closed, he didn't seem aware of Leon's approach.

What gave Leon hope was that Alex and Megan might still be alive. Sirens blared in the distance. That prompted him to move fast. He couldn't afford to be delayed by questioning. More importantly, he didn't know who he could trust.

Mercilessly he grabbed Gallagher's good arm to pull him from the car. The big man was heavy and difficult to move, and Leon's foot screamed with the effort, making him gasp. Gallagher's lower body dropped unceremoniously from the car seat to the ground. Leon pulled him a few feet farther.

Wavering in pain, he looked at all the blood on Gallagher's vest and shirt. The man's eyes blinked open, appearing glassy. The Kevlar vest Gallagher wore made Leon thankful for his own vest. He probed one of Gallagher's upper pockets and found the man's cell phone. It had taken a bullet and was cracked—dead when he turned it on.

"Get them," whispered Gallagher, releasing his gun.

Leon leaned over, seized the MP5, and hurriedly looked in the car. Spotting the night scope on the back seat, he tossed it up front and shut the door. Stumbling around the trunk, he closed it, and continued to the driver's door, every step burning. He climbed in behind the wheel. Relief washed over him that the keys were in the ignition.

Megan's and Alex's guns lay on the passenger floor. His brows arched at discovering the MP7. Between it and the two MP5s he would have a heavy punch. The other thing visible was a gun case and duffel bag in the back.

He started the car but kept the lights off. Quickly he backed the sedan out of the drive to the street, where he swung the wheel, still in reverse. Facing the direction the terrorists had fled, he put it in drive and gunned it.

Images of what had happened made him grip the wheel with bunched fists. Accelerating the car, he took the first right the van had taken. He tromped on the gas and at the next T-intersection he took a left.

Accelerating to fifty, he continued straight to the next intersection, braked hard, and looked left. The road ended in a housing development. Punching the engine, he turned right, the moonlight marginal for driving. At the next intersection he took another left, soon another right. Once more he followed this progression, guessing the terrorists were headed to the freeway for their escape. The streets were level and empty, giving him a long view.

If he lost them, Alex and Megan had no chance—if they weren't already dead. His spine stiffened.

A half-mile later he spotted a vehicle making a left. He accelerated to the corner and made the same turn, spotting the van taking a right a few blocks ahead.

"Yeah!" he shouted. Gripping the wheel, he raced to the corner, cautiously making the right turn. The van was two hundred yards away. Wanting to remain undetected, he slowed just enough so he wouldn't risk losing them.

Suddenly he felt dizzy. The hot air, pain, and adrenaline made his limbs wilt.

There wasn't anything else he could do except follow. His isolation hit him. There was no way to call anyone and he was one against four. But his car had a GPS unit. The FBI could track him.

His gaze settled on the gas gauge. The needle was steadily moving to E. A bullet must have punched the gas tank. He was losing fuel fast.

CHAPTER 31

TWO GUNS POINTED AT Alex and Megan. No one spoke. Alex watched their captors, waiting for any kind of opportunity. Megan eyed the terrorists, but she kept her shoulder pressed against his.

In five minutes the van stopped. With guns pushed into their backs, they were motioned out of the van into a small garage, and then quickly led out through a side door. Alex walked in front of Megan under the moonlight. They were herded across the backyard toward a semitrailer parked on a paved parking space on the opposite side of a small house.

Odysseus trotted past them, carrying Megan's laptop, and climbed into the back of the open trailer. Patroclus ran to the cab of the truck. Reappearing with an aluminum folding step ladder, Odysseus slid it to the ground and leaned it against the trailer bed.

The semi's diesel engine rumbled to life.

Achilles and Menelaus motioned Alex and Megan up. Unable to use his hands, Alex climbed up first, needing to lean forward to keep his balance. Achilles and Menelaus kept their guns trained on them.

At the top of the ladder, Odysseus pointed a gun at Alex's head, grabbed his arm, and pulled him into the truck cab. Pushing Alex to the side, he helped Megan up in the same way. He motioned them to the side of the interior, while Menelaus and Achilles climbed up. Odysseus then hurried into the truck.

Achilles kept his gun on Alex and Megan as Menelaus pulled up the ladder and pulled down the overhead door.

Lifting his chin, Achilles motioned them forward with his gun.

Walking into the trailer, Alex looked ahead. A one-foot-diameter fluorescent spotlight lit up the trailer's interior. Standing ahead of them in the truck, Odysseus had his gun aimed at them. He motioned them forward, while speaking into a handheld radio.

The truck started moving.

Working to keep his balance, Alex walked forward. The stale air in the trailer felt oppressive. It was an oven inside. Carpet covered the floor, ceiling, and walls. Soundproofing. To the right, a swivel armchair rested in front of the floor lamp near a small desk.

A mini Bobcat was parked next to the left wall. Stacked beside the bobcat were two six-foot-long narrow plywood boxes.

The images and sensations Alex had experienced on the drive to interview Dr. Joulie swam back into his mind—*feeling compressed, dirt covering him, wrapped like a mummy...* Swallowing, he pushed the memories aside.

Two-thirds of the way into the trailer a wall blocked passage. A large black-tinted window was centered in the wall, a door visible to the far right. Odysseus backed up to the door.

The semi turned and jerked, changing gears. Alex braced himself, his gaze finding Megan's. She showed more resolve than fear.

Odysseus raised a hand to stop them. He pointed his MP5 at Alex, and then to the chair in front of the floor lamp. "Sit."

Alex stepped forward and sat in the chair, while Megan was ushered through the forward doorway. Odysseus followed her out, closing the door behind him. His stomach wrenching, Alex couldn't take his eyes off the door.

Achilles shoved the barrel of a MP5 into his upper back, while Menelaus went to the desk and opened a drawer.

Slipping his left leg off the side of the chair, Alex simultaneously twisted and rose, using his upper left arm to push the barrel of the MP5 to the side. He kicked out as Achilles turned to him, hitting the terrorist between the legs. Achilles groaned and bent over, and Alex kneed him in the jaw.

Footsteps.

Alex whirled. A gunstock swung at his head. He ducked it and charged into Menelaus. It was like ramming a tree. A fist ploughed into his ribs. He doubled over. A knee connected with his chin, followed by a heavy blow to his back, sending him to the floor.

CHAPTER 32

LEON PANICKED.

His car ran out of fuel near the end of a block. The van had just turned right and was halfway down the next street.

He jumped out, two machine guns slung over his shoulders while he carried the third. Running and hopping across the short lawn of the house on the corner, he fell to one knee, the MP7 up as he aimed at the van's rear tire. The brake lights came on so he kept his finger stiff on the trigger.

The vehicle pulled into the driveway of a small house near the end of the street, disappearing into the unattached garage.

His foot on fire, Leon hurried across the lawns in the shadows, quickly slowing to a painful limp while he considered his options.

He could rush the terrorists. One against four. Doubtful he would survive or save Megan and Alex. Moving closer, he hugged the front walls of houses, wary of being seen. He decided to go into a house and find a phone to call for help. One lot away from the small house, he stopped.

A diesel engine started. Peering between the garage and house, he spotted part of a semitrailer on the far side of the house the van had pulled into. He wavered, waiting to see what would happen next.

In a minute the semitruck edged out from behind the far side of the house, nosing into the street. Leon hobbled closer, wondering if the terrorists had transferred to the semi, taking

Megan and Alex with them. As the truck pulled away, he put the night scope up to his eye. Stenciled on the trailer's rear gate were the letters AVI. Meaningless as far as he knew, the acronym would at least allow him to track the truck.

The semi surprised him. But he had to be certain. He made a hobbled run across the last lawn to the small house. Cradling the MP7, he limped up to the side door of the garage. With the automatic in front of him, his finger tense on the trigger, he put a cautious hand on the door and tested it. Locked.

The semi engine was fading in the distance. Slamming the gun butt through the door window, Leon moved to the side and listened as glass tinkled on the cement floor inside. Quiet. Sticking an arm through, he released the lock.

Opening the door, he rushed inside, the automatic leveled at his waist. He found the light switch and stared at the empty van. The keys were in the ignition. He ran to the house and kicked in the door with his good foot, needing to be sure. After a quick search he knew they had all gone with the semi.

Limping quickly out through the front door of the house, he looked down the street. The semi had disappeared. Carefully he listened to the quiet night. In the distance he barely detected the rumbling of the semi. Again he debated if he should find a phone. But if the terrorists did another vehicle switch, he could lose them. Also Alex had confided in him that there was a mole in the FBI. Their stakeout tonight had most likely been betrayed. If he made a call it could tip off his only advantage.

His foot screamed as he hobbled back to the garage and hit the garage door opener. Once inside the van he made the engine and wheels whine. After reversing into the street, he floored the vehicle, checking cross streets as he raced through them.

After five blocks he coasted the van with the window down. Listening. Thinking he heard a semi engine's coarse growl, he made a left and accelerated.

After another three blocks, far down a cross street to the right he glimpsed a trailer turning. He made a sharp turn. The van careened around the corner. Driving another half-mile, he coasted across an intersection, scanning the cross streets. A few blocks away to the left, the back end of a semi-trailer disappeared around a turn.

Braking hard, he came to a stop, reversed, and then wheeled into the cross street. When he made his next turn, the semi was a half-mile in front of him. Accelerating along the street, he chewed his lips. When he felt he was close enough, he lifted the night scope to his eyes. The letters AVI marked the back of the truck. With a trembling hand he wiped perspiration from his brow.

Lightheaded, he allowed the semi to build a small lead as it rolled south. He put on his low beams. Worried about what was happening to Alex and Megan, he wondered why the terrorists hadn't killed them at the stakeout, and why had they switched to a semitruck?

The second answer came to him first. The police and FBI would be looking for a van, not a semi. Still it felt like overkill. Why not a box truck or something easier to maneuver? Not coming up with a satisfactory answer, he let it go. But the answer to why Alex and Megan were still alive became crystal clear; Threshold wanted to find out what they knew before they killed them. The more he thought about it, the more that rang true.

He imagined different rescue scenarios, like pulling his van in front of the semi or shooting at the driver. But in each of these scenarios he predicted two things he didn't like; his death, and the certain death of Alex and Megan. The terrorists were facing multiple murder counts—they wouldn't hesitate to kill hostages now. Worst case scenario, the semi would smash his van and escape, leaving him injured or dead, and without any means to follow them.

He thought about trying to attract attention, but a police car would immediately tip off the terrorists, again ending up in the deaths of Alex and Megan. In any case, no patrol cars appeared along the way so it wasn't an option. And he didn't have GPS anymore. No one would be tracking him.

In minutes he ended up following the truck without interruption to Turquoise Trail—Highway 14—which led south into the desert. The air felt warmer. He had to hope the terrorists were taking Alex and Megan somewhere where he would have a chance to get them both out alive. It was the best scenario for Alex and Megan, and also might allow him to surprise the terrorists and kill all of them.

He checked the gas tank. It was one-quarter full. He hoped the semi wasn't going far. If gas became an issue, he wouldn't have a choice. He would have to try stopping the truck.

CHAPTER 33

Alex blinked twice. Blinding light forced him to close his eyes to slits. His stomach ached from where he had been hit. They had tied his torso and legs to the chair this time. And he was still handcuffed. He couldn't move.

One of the terrorists appeared and stood in front of him, a silhouette in front of the light.

A blow snapped his head to the side. He tasted blood in his mouth. Before he could recover, he was backhanded in the other direction, just as skillfully and hard. Swearing, he looked up. The only response was a fist to his ribs.

After a few more body punches he allowed his head to hang—hoping to end the beating. Mercifully, it did. The semi hummed steadily. He wondered how long they had been moving. Bright edges from the lamp lit the floor and he was glad the light wasn't in his face anymore.

A pair of feet appeared in his field of vision, quickly joined by another pair. He lifted his head a few inches.

There was a sick, harsh laugh. Alex swallowed. Achilles. Something bright and silvery was thrust into his field of vision.

***

Megan Detalio sat in a metal chair in front of the small desk that faced the one-way window, staring directly at her partner.

Odysseus sat on a stool six feet to the side of her at the back of the small room—far enough away to discourage an attack. Yet close enough so he could see Alex Sight through the window. A small ceiling bulb provided ample light.

Odysseus said casually, "Push your chair back, spread your legs, and lean over so your head is beneath the desk." When she complied, he said, "Edge your feet closer to the desk, so your back is beneath it."

Detalio followed directions, and he stepped closer. "Lift your hands. If you move any other part of your body, I'll shoot you."

Slowly she raised her hands off her lower back, and he unlocked the handcuffs. Removing the one from her right wrist, he fastened it to the side rung of the chair, so her left arm was attached to it.

Satisfied, he stepped back. "Sit up and open the drawer."

Detalio pushed back in the chair, sat up, and opened the center drawer with her free right hand. A legal-sized pad of paper, three ballpoint pens, and her laptop were inside. She slowly turned to him, her gaze questioning, but hard.

Odysseus kept his voice level. "Log-in to your laptop. I want access to your files. Then write down everything you've learned about this case that isn't on the computer. Every single detail. Print clearly."

The furrows on her forehead deepened. "Why?"

"We know your capabilities, and Alex Sight's abilities." He motioned to the window in front of her. "Your partner gets tortured until we have something useful that you know about us and our operations." He forced a smile. "We have all night."

Sight yelled, the sound muffled as it came through the wall.

Odysseus didn't like torture, but they had no choice. The deaths of these two would give their pursuers something more to fear and satisfy the loss of being denied Trenton.

He stared with satisfaction at Detalio. She had pulled out the laptop and paper and was logging onto the computer. Once she had logged on, she glanced at him and pushed the laptop to the side of the table.

He had her push back and put her head beneath the desk again before he approached the table and took the laptop. Then he gave her permission to sit up, and she started to write. Sweat beaded her brow. Every time her partner yelled, she glanced through the window. Odysseus buried any sympathy that tried to surface.

Detalio wrote fast. Odysseus doubted any information she provided would change their plans, or that she would give them anything useful. But it was obvious she cared about her partner so she might give something voluntarily or slip up. Their handler had suggested it.

It bothered Odysseus that Alex Sight had used his name in the van. His cover was blown. It made him a liability to the whole operation. But maybe Sight had been guessing and the FBI weren't sure. He had heard of Sight's clairvoyant ability. That was a wild card he wanted removed.

He looked at the files on the laptop. Seeing his photo added to his concerns. They also knew about his sister Kristen and bill S.229. He couldn't see how they had come up with his name and his sister's. Alex Sight. Another reason to kill the man. Dr. Frank Crary, Dr. Seth Joulie, and U.S. Senator Brett Dillon were listed. He hadn't heard of Dr. Crary before, but he knew Dr. Joulie was testifying for S.229 and Senator Dillon backed the bill. He wasn't sure if they were part of Threshold, and it seemed as if the FBI didn't know either.

Some of the files were too large and he didn't bother looking at them. When he was satisfied, he set the laptop on the floor.

In a few minutes he had Detalio repeat the procedure of lowering her head beneath the desk. Then he walked up and looked at what she had written. She had repeated the main points he had read on the laptop, with the addition that they had contacted his family to ask to exhume his body—and had not received permission.

Not giving any reaction, he stepped back and ordered her to sit up and continue writing. A shout came from the other room.

A thin line of blood marked a cut on Sight's forearm. Achilles poured salt on it and Sight writhed in the chair. Achilles laughed.

Achilles was taking things too far, enjoying it. Suddenly Odysseus didn't want to be associated with this man anymore. Then and there he decided to kill him as soon as they reached their destination.

CHAPTER 34

Deputy Director Foley paced the corridor of Saint Vincent Region Medical Center in Santa Fe. His gaze often returned to the patient door. His lips pursed as he waited for the nurse to give him permission to see Gallagher. A police officer stood guard beside the door, but otherwise the hallway was empty.

Agents had briefed him about the attack after he landed in Santa Fe at midnight, and he had driven directly to the hospital. Six men were dead—two in the street and four in the helicopter crash. Peter had been treated for a concussion and a flesh wound in his side—his Kevlar vest had saved him—and the whereabouts of Leon Mason, Alex Sight, and Megan Detalio were unknown.

Prior to going into surgery, Gallagher had managed to give a useless description of a dark van. The FBI sedan had surfaced on a neighborhood street, but provided no leads. Foley found it frustrating, given the size of Santa Fe and the hundreds of police officers and FBI agents looking for Leon, Alex, and Megan.

The female nurse finally appeared in front of him. "You can see him now."

Foley nodded and walked in. The room was dimly lit. Gallagher lay on his back, his upper left arm and shoulder bandaged. As Foley walked up to the bed, Gallagher eyed him, appearing sleepy but lifting his head slightly.

"Any news?" Gallagher's voice was hoarse and weak.

Foley shook his head. "We've started a city-wide hunt."

"No word of Leon?" Gallagher dropped his head into the pillow.

"No. We found the sedan near an associated house, but that's it. The house was leased by a person who doesn't exist. We haven't traced it to anyone." He really didn't want to be grilled by Gallagher now.

Gallagher grunted. "I'll be out of here by morning. I lost some blood and just need a good night's rest."

Foley doubted that. "I'll be able to handle anything in the field tonight."

"Yeah, great." Gallagher stared at him.

Foley shifted his gaze away. If Gallagher's animosity was any more obvious it would be lethal. Did the idiot blame him? "I'm glad you're all right, Bill."

"Marvelous, isn't it?" From the table at the side of the bed Gallagher grabbed a pack of gum with his right hand. Using his teeth, he pulled out a piece and slowly unwrapped it with one hand.

Foley didn't offer to help.

"Anything else?" Gallagher shoved the gum into his mouth.

"Senator Dillon called me again." Foley didn't want to talk to Gallagher any longer.

"Well?"

Foley hesitated. "Same as the first meeting. The senator expressed concerns over the safety of congressional members. He also wanted to know why we bothered Dr. Crary and Dr. Joulie."

Gallagher balled the gum wrapper up in his fingers. "What did you tell him?"

Foley frowned. "The obvious. We're doing everything in our power to protect members of Congress."

"And?" Gallagher stared at him.

Foley tried to think of a way to end the conversation. "I told him we have nothing on Dr. Joulie or Dr. Crary."

Gallagher smirked. "I bet that's not all the senator wanted."

Foley exhaled. "He wondered if we're going to release any information to the press. He again stated his wishes that we keep his name and Joulie's out of our investigation. He didn't want any bad publicity or image problems."

"Always worried about their damned reputations." Gallagher tossed the gum wrapper at Foley's feet.

Forcing down angry words that leapt to his lips, Foley dug his index fingernail hard into his thumb pad. "His credibility is a legitimate concern, especially since he's backing S.229. We have to act properly on this."

Gallagher smirked. "I suppose it wouldn't look good if people thought he might be connected to Threshold, would it?"

Foley decided he had to leave. Now. He had enough of Gallagher's sarcasm and he had better things to do. "I'll check with you in the morning, Bill. Sleep well."

Gallagher ignored him.

Foley turned and left, wishing he hadn't come.

CHAPTER 35

Alex Sight's yells were weaker. Odysseus didn't think he would be conscious much longer. Just as well. He wanted to get out of the stifling air of the trailer.

Megan Detalio twisted in her chair. "Tell them to stop or I won't write a single word more."

Not moving from where he sat, Odysseus said calmly, "It can be much worse, I assure you."

Detalio didn't move. "You're planning to kill us anyway."

He stiffened. Raising the MP5 an inch off his thigh, he curled his finger around the trigger. "Keep writing."

"I'm not afraid to die," she said quietly. "I'm not a psychotic who murders to satisfy his frustrations with the world."

Odysseus' jaw tensed.

"You must be very sick inside, Odysseus. Or should I call you Jerry Peiser? Does this help you feel better about Kristen? It's too bad, because you're giving environmentalists a bad image. Now everyone will think we're all crazy, like you."

"Who's Jerry Peiser?" He stood up, glad his hood hid the anger on his face. When she didn't answer, he said, "You believe environmentalists have accomplished anything? We've brought more attention and righted more wrongs in a single week than Greens ever have. Some of America's most prestigious environmental groups have worked for many decades on environmental issues and the environment is worse off than ever. That's progress? They've sold out." He couldn't keep the fury out of his voice.

Her voice held contempt. "You're no different than any other crazy person with a gun. You're too scared to show your face to the public, to me."

Realizing she was baiting him, he calmed himself before he replied. "There are bigger things at stake than you or me. The future is on the line."

"You're a coward, killing unarmed people that can't fight back."

"The cowards are the corporations and politicians who are slowly killing our planet and everyone on it for their selfish pursuit of money and power." Holding the MP5 at his waist, he slowly approached her, his anger rising again. When she continued to glare at him, he stepped behind her and jammed the gun into the back of her neck. "Keep writing or die."

Slowly Detalio turned in her seat to the desk.

Jerking her neck violently to the left, she caused the gun barrel to slide off. Odysseus was astonished at how fast she moved. Detalio twisted in the chair, simultaneously jamming her right palm up into his chin.

The blow wasn't enough to move him but jarred his teeth. Enraged, he swung the gun barrel back toward her, but she stopped the gun with her right hand, crossing it over in front of her body. In the same instant she stood, shoved the chair toward the desk with her left hand, and brought her left knee up into his crotch.

Gasping, fire between his legs, he fell to the floor. He dropped the gun and doubled up in agony on his side. White-hot pain shot through him. She was crouching, reaching for his weapon, and he kicked her thigh with his left leg, crying out in pain from the effort.

Detalio fell to the floor on her back, the chair falling partially atop her, her chest near his feet. He tried to kick her head, but she pulled it back and he missed. She partially sat up, using her right arm to push her feet closer to his head. He kicked out again, hitting her shoulder. This time he connected and she gasped and flopped down onto her side.

Grabbing the gun, he slid the barrel across the floor to aim it at her.

She pushed closer, avoiding another of his kicks, and kicked his forearms hard, jarring the gun out of his hands. Then she kicked his ribs. Sledgehammer blows. A flash of fire ran up his side.

Groaning, again astonished by her strength and speed, he reached once more for the gun, but her foot slammed into his forehead, snapping his neck back. Rolling to his back, his skull and torso felt like spikes had been driven into his flesh. He wanted to shout, warn the others, but he had no control over his lips.

Then she was hunched over him, a blurred image before his teary eyes. But he still cringed over what he saw in her twisted lips and set jaw. Revenge. Hatred. The desire to rip and tear and kill. He gasped for air as another spike of pain hit his sternum. His nose was banged. Numb. Then something hard as steel rammed the front of his neck.

***

Alex was conscious but gave his tormentors the appearance of fading. It wasn't much of a stretch. He had a high pain tolerance, but the cuts on his arms burned. It was also hard to breath, the air thick with heat. Like a man using one finger to hang from a high wire, he just wanted to let go. But if he did, he might never wake up, so he grasped at staying alert. If he remained conscious, he had a chance to stay alive. Though he didn't expect any opportunities to come his way.

The inner wall door opened quietly, but no light shone through from the forward compartment. Still, the floor lamp near him sent enough light to outline a figure he recognized. It stunned him. He refrained from saying anything. When Megan stepped through the door, he tried to focus his gaze. She held a gun and started firing.

With surprising speed, the two men ducked low. Menelaus shattered the floor lamp bulb with his fist. Pitch black. Megan's MP5 spit bullets across the trailer.

Worried he could be hit, Alex ducked, his ears ringing. Some of the bullets struck the bulldozer, ricocheting off its metal frame in angry whines.

A yell broke through the MP5's staccato burst and there was a dull thud.

Megan stopped firing.

A knife pressed against the front of Alex's neck, cutting into his skin. Another hand pulled his forehead back.

"I'll slit the throat of your friend unless you drop the gun," snarled Achilles.

Megan's voice was calm. "Do it and you'll never get out of here alive. Alex, talk to me, tell me you're okay. If he kills you, I'll spray the whole room. If I don't hear you, I'll assume you're dead."

Alex kept mute, wanting her to fire. He sensed from her voice that she had moved to the other side of the trailer. The knife cut deeper and blood seeped over his neck. He gasped.

"Talk," hissed Achilles.

"Kill him," Alex said weakly.

"He's still alive," said Achilles. "But if you move any closer, he's dead."

The truck was slowing, which meant the driver would soon join them.

Alex's head was released and the knife was removed from his throat. He heard movement behind him. "Watch out!" he gasped.

He heard a groan, something small falling to the floor, quick footsteps. Blows. A struggle. Quiet.

"Megan?" he asked softly.

"She'll be joining you soon."

CHAPTER 36

ODYSSEUS COULDN'T BELIEVE THE pain sweeping his body. Like he'd been run over. At least one rib was injured and he had a broken nose. Achilles had taped both. His neck ached.

Megan Detalio had almost managed to escape and Menelaus was dead because of a mistake he made. It was inexcusable. His anger at Detalio was tempered by a grim determination to stay on task. They had to finish what they had planned, nothing more, and then get out of New Mexico. Revenge had to be put aside.

"Are you all right, Odysseus?" Achilles played with a knife in his hand.

Odysseus swiveled in the chair, knowing Achilles was smirking behind his face mask. He wished it had been Achilles, not Menelaus, who had been killed. But he couldn't kill Achilles now, not with only three of them left. And he grudgingly had to admit that if Achilles hadn't managed to throw his knife into Detalio, and pummel her, they would all be dead or going to jail now.

Turning, he looked at Sight and Detalio. Both were lying on the floor, facing each other, their ankles zip-tied, wrists cuffed behind their backs, gagged, conscious, and still bleeding.

They had traveled south, then east across the desert to the next highway, then south again. In another hour Patroclus drove them off the pavement onto a dirt road. It soon faded to a faint path in the headlights as it ran west into the desert. Patroclus slowed the truck over the rougher terrain. Thirty minutes later he steered the vehicle counterclockwise around an open pit in the center of a cleared circle of land until they faced east—out the way they had come in.

Achilles opened the overhead door of the trailer and Patroclus joined them and pulled out the ramp.

Painfully leaning against the inside of the truck, Odysseus watched. The repaired spotlight from the trailer bed lit the nearby area.

Ten yards from the truck, a large mound of excavated sand and dirt rested near a five-foot-by-eight, four-foot-deep rectangular pit. Others had dug the pit for them some time ago.

That others were helping with logistics of vehicles and other necessities made Odysseus feel supported. They weren't alone. Carefully scanning the desert, he took a ragged, shallow breath. Even with careful planning everything had gone wrong. His fist curled.

The Bobcat broke the quiet as Patroclus started it and drove it down the ramp. Burned fuel made the air noxious. Achilles dragged the empty wooden boxes down the ramp to the pit, undoing the half-dozen draw-pull latches bolted around the edges.

Odysseus hobbled down the ramp to the edge of the pit, MP5 in hand.

***

When Leon saw the truck turn around ahead of him and aim toward him, he panicked. His lights had been off for some time, but he couldn't risk being seen and ruin any chance of surprise.

Slamming on the brakes, he reversed the van on the road until the semi's headlights were just small points of light.

Chewing his lip, he decided this was as good an opportunity as he was going to get.

He backed the van off the road, fifty feet south of it, bouncing over rocks and small scrub. If the semi drove out on the road when he was on foot, they wouldn't see the vehicle. Grabbing the guns, he limped as fast as he could toward the truck.

The terrorists had turned off the semi headlights, but there was a small light coming from the back of it. He wondered if they planned on remaining here overnight. That made no sense. The other idea was more chilling. This was where they planned to kill Alex and Megan. The sound of a small diesel engine made him hurry faster. What were they doing?

Keeping to the side of the road, he ignored the searing pain in his foot and forced himself to jog. Both machine guns were slung over his shoulder and he gripped the MP7A1 with both hands. He kept scanning the area ahead of him, especially near the truck— he didn't want to be surprised by a terrorist on guard duty.

Clouds blocked the moon so the landscape was hard to see. Wanting to limit the amount of pressure on his injured toe, and to keep his footsteps quiet, he skimmed the ground with his feet. Rocks and brush were just darker clumps on the uneven terrain that he strained to see and avoid.

His foot hurt even worse than before, his gait more awkward, but he still pushed himself. The idea of Megan and Alex dying in the next minutes made him run faster. If he was lucky, the terrorists would be completely unaware of him. He hoped to take out two or three of them before they even knew he was here.

One moment he was hurrying along, the next he was tumbling down hard, unable to break his fall with his arms because he was still gripping the gun. He hit something hard with his head and his mind went as dark as the night.

***

After parking the Bobcat near the mound of dirt alongside the pit, Patroclus helped Achilles carry the two captives out of the truck. They dumped Sight and Detalio into the boxes on their backs and quickly closed and latched the lids.

Achilles pushed one coffin halfway over the pit. Patroclus climbed down into the hole to drag the box into it. The other box was hastily lowered next to the first. Menelaus was carried out of the truck last and thrown into the pit on top of the two boxes.

Patroclus hopped back onto the Bobcat, started it up, and pushed the mound of dirt and sand into the pit. Dust swirled up and hung in the air. Odysseus backed away. After smoothing the grave over, Patroclus drove the Bobcat back into the truck.

Odysseus stared at the leveled dirt with satisfaction. Turning, he shuffled to the truck's cab and painfully climbed into the passenger seat. Patroclus started the engine, while Achilles closed the trailer door.

"Your cover's blown," said Patroclus.

Odysseus hesitated. They had all heard Alex Sight call him Jerry in the van, and they had also seen Detalio's notes and the files on her laptop. "Yes."

"Achilles talked to me about killing you." Patroclus glanced at him.

Odysseus froze.

Patroclus said quietly, "Don't worry. I said no. We need everyone. But we're going to have to get rid of him at some point. He's out of control."

"I agree." He relaxed. His watch read three-thirty a.m. They were late. Leaning his head back, he closed his eyes as they drove out of the desert. The grave had originally been dug for Trenton and his politically active wife. Odysseus was dismayed that the Trentons weren't in it. Trenton had opposed all clean air legislation for years; the oxygen-deprived tomb would have been a fitting punishment for him.

It bothered him even more that they had lost one of their members. They were lucky they had received the tip about the FBI trap. In the routine morning check-in call he had been told to call again in late evening. He had, and the voice on the other end of the phone had given him the warning.

Given the option of going after a different political target or the two FBI agents, Odysseus had chosen the latter. Sight and Detalio were supposed to have been taken care of in Billings, but whoever had been hired had failed. Even with the loss of Menelaus, Odysseus was satisfied with his choice. They had killed their worst hounds, but he knew others would quickly replace them.

When he considered how his name might help the authorities, he couldn't see that it gave them much to work with. The risks were a little higher, but if they were careful, and made no more mistakes, everything was manageable. Nonetheless, a sense of impending doom invaded his thoughts.

CHAPTER 37

ALEX KEPT HIS EYES open in the darkness. His arms were on fire and his body ached. Groggy, he tried to shift his weight to relieve his cuffed arms, which were numb beneath his body. The hot air, thick with dust, choked his lungs and he coughed. The gag made it harder to breathe.

Fragments of the last hours, mixed with memories of Megan's failed rescue, trickled through his thoughts. He felt helpless.

Muffled thuds came from the left. Moving his ear closer, craning his neck, he heard soft beats. When they stopped, he turned slightly on his side and used his heels to pound the wood three times in succession. Three beats came back to him. Megan. He didn't repeat the effort. The air would last longer if he remained inactive. Megan didn't repeat it either.

His throat convulsed. He wondered what else she had suffered. Had she been tortured like him? Raped?

His mind played with ridiculous scenarios, but he knew any rescue attempt would arrive far too late. They might never be found. Gloom swept his thoughts. The salt in his wounds seared his skin and the pain it gave him begged for relief. Failing the case and failing Megan brought dullness to his eyes. The image of Jenny came to him and he tried to push it away.

It became harder to breathe, and at one point he fell asleep. Dull thuds to the left pulled him back to foggy consciousness. He didn't have the energy to respond. Images swirled in his mind.

Twice he actually believed he lay above ground, beside the box. He was hallucinating and didn't care. It was better than reality.

Louder bangs. Maybe his heart beating out its last efforts. His lungs labored, the heat in the box suffocating. Trying to inhale the dead air, his breaths shortened to gasps. His eyelids fluttered. Flashes of Megan and Jenny floated through him. He groaned. Too late again...failure...he couldn't form an idea anymore and his awareness drifted.

There was a tremendous explosion of splintered wood and something poured in on his legs. Fingers groped along his knees and a deep voice called his name.

"Alex! Alex!"

Air filled his nostrils and his lungs heaved in reflexive convulsions to suck it in. He coughed harshly on inhaled dust. The top of the box was broken in two with a tremendous crash, the pieces banging against his chest, and then lifted up. A dark shadow hovered above him, outlined by light.

The shadow bent over close enough for him to recognize. Leon. Holding a rock.

"What are you doing here?" Alex mumbled into his gag.

The big man quietly watched him for a few moments; Alex assumed Leon was making sure he was all right.

"Be right back. Going to free Megan." Leon disappeared.

Alex could hear him in the box next to his. He didn't try to sit up, preferring to just lay there and breathe. Leon soon returned and climbed down into his box. Relief hit Alex over seeing Megan standing in the light at the foot of the pit. She was cradling her left arm, but watching him.

Leon used a car key to cut the bindings on Alex's ankles, then Alex rolled onto his side so Leon could use his handcuff key on the cuffs. Lastly Leon removed his gag.

Leon helped Alex stand in the box, and Megan offered her right hand. Alex took it, grimacing as Leon partially lifted him up and pushed him out onto his knees. When Alex finally stood up, he saw relief and empathy in Megan's expression. He also noted the body of the terrorist to the side of the pit. Menelaus.

Alex offered a hand to Leon to help him out of the pit. They both groaned over that exertion.

They all stumbled to the van and sagged against the hood, not talking.

Leaning against the vehicle, hunched over, Alex didn't want to budge. Every exertion brought more pain to his arms. He held them lightly crossed in front of his middle. His ribs hurt whenever he twisted the slightest bit. Leon was covered in dirt and looked exhausted. The side of his face was covered with dried blood. Megan had a bruise on the left side of her face and held her left arm across her waist.

"How did you dig us out?" Alex looked at Leon.

"Car jack plate." Leon smiled wearily. "Hardest thing I've ever done in my life, given my pain."

"You're my hero." Megan touched the big man's arm gently.

"Superhero." Alex coughed but managed to wink at him.

Leon chuckled and nodded. "You know what's funny? I thought the coffins were nailed, but after I broke the second one, I saw they were just latched shut."

Alex shook his head, still unable to smile. "I'll laugh at that later." After a short rest, he said, "Let's check the windshield washer fluid."

Megan shuffled to the side with him, while Leon opened the hood and the washer fluid reservoir. After tasting a drop of the liquid, the big man said, "It's water."

Alex watched Leon wrestle with the reservoir, knowing he had to be hurting the way he stood mostly balanced on one foot. He had also seen Leon limping. Waiting, hunched against the side of the van, he coughed intermittently as his lungs cleared out the rest of the dust he had inhaled.

Leon removed the plastic container and crimped the hose at its bottom. Alex and Megan moved in front of the headlights.

Alex felt some relief as Leon carefully poured water onto the cuts on his arms.

Megan gingerly washed the salt from his wounds. Several times she asked him if he was all right, but stopped when he looked at her and said, "I am now."

After finishing with him, Leon tore off Megan's bloodied shirt sleeve. Alex was relieved to see her injury wasn't severe. A slice across the triceps. It needed stitches. Two wounds on the same arm.

Leon rinsed off Megan's arm wound, and then handed the container to Alex while he tore his shirt apart for a makeshift bandage to wrap around her arm.

Alex helped Leon take off his shoe and sock, and Megan used the rest of the water to wash off Leon's ear and his toe—which had the tip shot off. Megan tore the lower part of her blouse apart, wrapping one strip around Leon's head and ear, the other around his foot.

When they were finished, Leon fell into the driver seat of the van. Megan slumped into the passenger side, holding her injured arm.

Alex sat behind them against the van wall, resting quietly as pain and fatigue had its way with him.

Leon spoke softly. "I followed them into the desert. When they stopped, I parked and was coming in on foot." He shook his head. "I fell and hit my head. I didn't come to until the semi pulled past me on the road. Then I drove down here. I saw the freshly leveled area and began to dig. I expected to find you two dead." He sighed. "We're all lucky."

"Some of us weren't." Alex wondered how many agents had died. After a few moments he broke the silence with soft words. "Leon, I'm going to recommend you for a medal, but right now I've had enough of the desert."

"Let's see what we can do." Leon slowly straightened in his seat.

"What's wrong?" murmured Megan.

Leon sounded apologetic. "We're out of gas. Maybe we can go a few miles."

"Exactly what I wanted to hear," said Alex.

Leon started the van and turned on the lights, illuminating the pit and the body of the dead terrorist. After driving around the grave, he drove east on the dirt road, gently increasing the speed.

Megan leaned over, eyeing the dash. "How long has it been on E?"

Leon hunched over the wheel. "Most of the way in. Truth is, I wasn't sure I'd be able to get this far."

Alex snorted. "You mean we've been shot at, kidnapped, tortured, buried alive, and rescued, and now we're in the middle of the desert and out of gas? Let's call roadside service."

"I should have thought of that right away," said Leon.

Alex gave a weary smile. "I want to thank you for saving us, Leon. Next time, top up the tank first." A soft chuckle escaped his lips.

Megan laid back against the headrest. "You saved our lives, Leon."

Leon sighed. "This makes up for the mess in Billings."

"That wasn't your mess," said Alex.

"It was Threshold's," said Megan.

Alex stared at the ceiling. "Maybe this thing can drive on vapors."

Minutes later the engine sputtered and died. The van rolled a little farther and stopped. The three of them were silent.

Megan glanced at Leon. "One of us will have to go for help."

"I need a rest," said Leon. "I'm spent. We could fire the guns."

"I'm going." Megan sounded certain. "I'm the least injured."

Alex adjusted his position. "Leon, how far are we from the main road?"

"A few miles maybe." Leon cleared his throat. "I could do it."

"No way." Megan patted his shoulder. "But thanks."

"I agree with Megan. Shot toe and possible concussion. Not a good idea." Alex ran through options. "Even if any of us reached the road, we might be standing out there a long time." He paused. "The sun's not up and I'm already warm. Isn't the desert supposed to be cool at night? Damn climate change." To the east the horizon was a dark line. When no one spoke, he said, "Check the glove compartment."

A quick search by Megan turned up a screwdriver, the vehicle manual, a cigarette lighter, and some tissue. "Not much here," she said.

Leon twisted to him. "Looking for anything in particular?"

"Let's burn the van." Slowly, painfully, Alex opened the side door. "Someone will see the smoke and investigate."

"Good idea," said Leon.

Megan leaned back. "We have to wait for more light."

"Damn." Alex stared east.

In two hours the sun peeped over the horizon, illuminating yucca plants and cacti, tufts of desert grass and scattered stones, along with craggy buttes and mountain ranges in all directions. Hues of red and yellow splashed across the landscape.

Alex slowly climbed out of the van. He walked a short distance from it with Megan. His left knee ached fiercely and movement tortured his arms. They sat on a two-foot-high flat rock, huddled together.

A horned toad lizard beneath a nearby bush cocked its head at Alex.

Using the screwdriver, Leon tore the seats apart. With tissue, paper, and bits of cloth he started a fire in the front seat. The doors were left open, and wisps of gray smoke lifted skyward.

Leon limped over to them and sat down on the rock. The three of them watched the van burn.

Megan leaned her head against Alex's shoulder. "Tired," she murmured.

"Thirsty," said Alex.

"Hungry," added Leon.

In minutes the van was sending dark smoke belching into the air.

Another hour went by before a thin trail of dust in the distance announced the approach of a car on the dirt road. In minutes they could see it was a police car.

"Leon," said Alex. "For the rest of my life, every time I see a casket I'm going to be thanking you."

CHAPTER 38

Alex winced at the sharp, biting sensations his body gave him whenever he moved. Pain pills helped. His ribs still hurt. His arms were bandaged. Swinging around to appraise the others, he sensed what was going to happen. He already knew what his response would be.

They were in the study of a ranch-style safe house in a suburb of Albuquerque. The interior was cool.

Deputy Director Foley had called the early morning meeting. He sat in a chair with a cup of cold coffee in his hands. His eyes had dark circles, but his suit was fresh.

Gallagher sat across the room, frowning, his left arm in a sling.

Megan looked as worn out as Alex felt. The police car had taken them to the Santa Fe hospital, where they both had received medical attention, before moving to the Albuquerque safe house for some much-needed rest over the last two days.

Fatigue still underlined Megan's eyes and she moved carefully to keep her left arm stable. Stitches were hidden beneath her white blouse. Apparently she hadn't needed anything more serious. She still had a bruise on her cheek where Achilles had hit her. Alex's face showed bruises too.

"We lost six agents." Foley stirred. "Leon is on sick leave. Peter's vest saved him, but he's also on leave. A formal congratulation is in order, Alex. Your idea to move the Trenton family saved their lives. For their safety we've kept Trenton's current location out of the press."

"It's nice to know they can hide somewhere." Alex couldn't deny the satisfaction that Threshold had been thwarted at least once. The trouble was he didn't believe it was over.

Foley regarded him. "Threshold's latest list of criminals is anyone who opposes Senate Bill S.229. There's panic among Congress. Legislators are pushing for a postponement of the bill's hearing until the terrorists are apprehended. There's a large public outcry for the hearing to go ahead on schedule. The government position of not giving in to terrorists also supports that. The terrorists achieved what they wanted. Public awareness and pressure."

"Four days." Megan glanced at Alex.

Foley added, "We've identified the dead terrorist known as Menelaus. Michael Beator. A computer technician by trade, he was a past activist, originally from Boston."

"Why wasn't he on your lists of extremists?" asked Megan.

"He was supposed to have died over a year ago." Foley glanced at Gallagher. "We identified him from his dental records. The I.D. and passport found on him were forged. Which means this wasn't a suicide mission. They planned to survive and escape, and maybe Trenton was their last target."

Alex gave Gallagher a sharp look.

"You were right." Gallagher shrugged. "Jerry Peiser's body will be exhumed immediately. We're also doing a search for any other extremists who supposedly died around the same time Peiser and Beator faked their deaths. It won't take more than a day to get some results."

"There's an APB for Peiser," said Foley. "Since there haven't been any more murders, they might have left the country."

"No," Alex said softly.

"Why not?" asked Foley.

Alex shrugged. "Just a hunch."

Foley frowned. "Alex, Threshold sent emails to news agencies across the country this morning and posted the same message on a bogus Twitter account that went viral before it was shut down. They guarantee a million dollars deposited in an offshore account for anyone who kills you in the next three days. Supposedly the money's already been secured with an unidentified bank. Every thug in the country will be after you."

"Maybe I should offer a bounty for Threshold," said Alex. "Make it two million."

"If you don't know when to back off, go ahead and put your life on the line," scoffed Gallagher.

Ignoring him, Alex looked at Foley. "Your offices are clean?"

"As far as we can tell." Foley's jaw tightened. "Obviously there's a leak somewhere if Threshold knows you're alive. We'll conduct a full investigation. That's all I can promise. I'm advising both of you to remain here under protection, at least until the hearing for Senate Bill S.229 is over."

Alex traded glances with Megan.

"The papers have plastered your photograph everywhere," said Foley. "Threshold considers you a threat to their goals, Alex."

He shook his head in disgust. "Sure, and I don't want to crowd them."

Foley leaned forward. "I can't protect you if you leave the safe house. You've done what you could. If you develop any more potential leads you can send them to us." He turned to Gallagher. "Bill, I have to talk to them privately. I'll meet you outside."

Grunting, Gallagher rose and left, closing the door.

Foley tapped his pencil's eraser on his thigh as his voice steeled. "If you leave, I've instructed the two men here not to follow you, but you're to inform me of your whereabouts and activities. If you don't, I'll have you arrested for obstruction on this case. Understood?"

Feeling his face flush, Alex swallowed his rising anger.

From a pocket, Foley pulled out a set of car keys and a credit card, handing both over to him with a softened expression. "The keys are for the safe house car, which had its GPS tracker removed. Only people with high-level clearance can trace the credit card. ID won't be necessary. It will be good wherever you use it. You won't leave a paper trail for anyone to follow. There's a laptop on the living room table that's clean, has Internet access, and can't be tracked if you're careful. Your weapons are there too. We recovered them from the stakeout site."

Caught off-guard, Alex raised his eyebrows. "Thanks."

Foley stood. "I can't promise your safety even with these precautions."

Alex lifted his chin. "Nothing new."

"It's your neck." Foley hesitated at the door. "Good luck."

Shoulders hunched, Alex got up and closed the door, studying Megan.

"I'm in," she said.

"They're after me." Her dark, knowing eyes held his and he was unable to say anything else.

Her voice was soft. "I won't let you do this alone."

"No complaints from me." He wanted her with him anyway.

Grabbing their weapons, they loaded the gun cases into the Corolla and left the safe house. Megan didn't want the computer in case it could be tracked. As they drove away, Alex spotted one of the agents in the driveway talking into his cell phone—probably to inform Foley.

Megan glanced at him. "Who can we trust?"

He shook his head once. "No one."

They stopped at a small strip mall and bought two smart phones with prepaid plans. The sun was already hot, baking the pavement of the parking lot as they walked across it back to the car.

They checked the undercarriage, engine compartment, and inside of the car for trackers or bugs. Nothing. Satisfied, they sat in the car in the lot.

With his phone, Alex used the Bureau card to make reservations on three separate airlines for evening flights to Los Angeles, Seattle, and New Orleans. Megan used the credit card for reservations for them on two bus lines for Tucson and Chicago.

Alex scanned the parking lot. "We can't use the Bureau credit card again."

Megan nodded. "I agree. Anyone with a password and a phone or a computer terminal could track us."

Alex guided the Toyota out of the lot and into traffic. He cruised a short while to be sure they weren't followed, and then stopped at a bank. Megan waited in the car, while he went in and withdrew ten grand in cash from one of his accounts.

When he returned, Megan kicked off a shoe, putting her foot on the dash. "Where are we going?"

Alex wheeled out of the lot. "Minnesota. Macalester College." Her brows arched and he added, "The report Gallagher gave us said Joulie, Dillon, and Crary were all in the same graduating class."

Megan scanned the street. "You want to see who else might have been with them."

"Yes."

They drove east on the interstate.

Alex's thoughts circled around Jenny and Megan. The same worry ran repeatedly through his mind. Glancing at Megan, he wondered if he should have left her behind. But when she slid her hand into his, he didn't want to let go.

CHAPTER 39

ALEX AND MEGAN TOOK turns driving, heading for Des Moines, Iowa, only needing to make two quick stops along the way. At the first stop they bought fast food and juice at a taco shop. Next they stopped at an outlet mall near Kansas City, purchasing aspirin, along with jeans and tops, hats, sunglasses, and tennis shoes. They got ice cream at a small shop—Megan insisted they needed something to give them a lift.

In later afternoon, under her impatient and incredulous gaze, Alex made a quick call to Harry and kept it on speaker. Blue Shoe had lost, which put him down a hundred and ten thousand. Slumping in the car seat, the loss mirrored everything else that had occurred. He picked Crazy Dancer to win for one-hundred-twenty-thousand at seven to one.

"You already lost a hundred thousand." Megan pierced him with a steely gaze as she drove. "I can't believe you're still gambling."

He avoided her eyes. "If things go bad it's good to keep some consistency in your life."

She shook her head. "You're addicted."

He considered that, but said, "Who doesn't like money?"

She pursed her lips. "We can do this, Alex."

"We will."

They reached Des Moines at midnight and drove around until they found a cheap motel. While Megan waited in the car, Alex went in to sign for the room.

The night clerk looked tired and barely noticed him. Alex wore a baseball cap and kept his head lowered. He paid cash and used the names, Mr. and Mrs. Martin.

"ID," said the clerk.

Alex slid five hundred dollars across the counter and mumbled, "I'm with a married woman and can't give that. Take it or leave it."

The man took it.

Spartan, the room had two single beds and a small table with a TV. The AC maintained the room just below eighty degrees. Locking the door, Alex propped the one chair under the knob.

They were both exhausted. He cleaned up first, but didn't shower. His arms felt better and he didn't want to get the wounds wet. When he came out, Megan walked past him, avoiding his eyes.

"I need a long bath," she said.

He stared at the room in surprise, because with as few things as she had brought, the space was already a mess. Clothing was scattered, with some of her purchases strewn across the floor, on one of the twin beds, and on the TV stand.

Lying on the other single, he slipped beneath the sheet, not wanting to think about anything. But his mind immediately swirled with ideas regarding the events of the last twenty-four hours. He couldn't slow those thoughts down. Threshold's goals. Megan. The terrorists on the loose. All three topics continued to steamroll through him repetitively. Sleep seemed impossible. That was the last thought he was aware of before he drifted off.

Running up the stairs, already knowing he was too late, he reached the top, ran down the hallway, and swung open a door. His stride slowed as he entered the room. Jenny sat in a chair, and she turned to him, but it was Megan's face...

He woke up in a sweat. Megan sat on the edge of his bed. A thin spatter of light from the outside parking lot lamps framed the drawn curtains, giving her outline a soft shadow. She had a bath towel wrapped around her torso and wet hair hung over her shoulders. Her dark eyes were fixed on his.

"Do you want to tell me about Jenny?" she asked quietly. "Was she the woman you wanted to marry?" He tensed, and she added, "You whispered her name."

His first reaction was to say no, to tell her it was none of her business and keep it to himself as he had for three years. Instead he didn't say a thing as words choked his throat.

Gently she placed a palm on his chest. "Maybe it will help."

He said quietly, "She was my partner and we were in love. We were on a stakeout for a serial killer. I was arrogant and overconfident. A vision showed me the house across the street and we were waiting for the killer to come back. Jenny asked me, *But what if you didn't see the whole picture?*" The words seemed strangely foreign as he repeated them. "I left to get food. By the time I returned I found her tied to a chair, dead, the killer waiting. I took two bullets before I killed him."

It was the first time he could remember that the pain didn't strike quite so deeply, nor as harshly. The guilt was still there, along with Jenny's words—he didn't think he would ever be able to erase that sentence from his conscience.

He looked away from Megan, unable to hold her steady, saddened gaze. Her eyes showed empathy he didn't feel he deserved.

She held his hand. "It wasn't your fault and you need to forgive yourself."

Her words didn't help. "She trusted me. I should have been there."

"That's why you feel so responsible." She slid her hand to his shoulder, her husky voice soft. "You can't see everything. No one can."

No words came to him.

She lowered toward him until her full lips brushed his, her hand soft against his face.

Her olive skin felt smooth as he stroked her arm. His eyes wandered over her neck and shoulders which were shadowed by the faint window light. He wanted her to clear away his pain, to help him move past the memories of Jenny. He gave a gentle tug on her arm and she lowered her lips to his.

CHAPTER 40

A FTER AN EARLY MORNING start, and nearly four hours on the road, they arrived at Macalester College in St. Paul by ten a.m. The heat hadn't let up and the sun burned brightly.

The large brick-and-stone DeWitt Wallace Library looked partly out of the Middle Ages in design, with modern external additions. A flow of young people entered and exited the main doors. Wearing hats and sunglasses, Alex and Megan joined the pedestrians.

At the information desk Alex immediately requested Dillon's nineteen-eighty graduating class yearbook from the middle-aged librarian sitting there. She pointed them in the right direction, informing them that they had stopped printing yearbooks in the nineteen-eighties due to cost and lack of student interest.

While they searched the shelves, Alex exchanged another of the small smiles with Megan that they had shared all morning. She was dressed simply, wearing jeans with a new blue cotton blouse. From under her floppy hat her wild, dark curly hair fell loose to her shoulders.

Alex had felt lighter and more rested in the morning with her in his arms than he had in a long while. And for once his sleep had been free of nightmares. His arms and ribs felt better, and his heart beat hard every time he saw her eyes, her face, and her full lips—which he knew with certainty waited eagerly for him. He sensed he had a chance to be happy again.

The yearbooks they wanted were missing so they walked back to the librarian. She checked her computer.

"I'm sorry," she said. "I'm afraid I can't help you."

Alex tried to glimpse her computer screen. "Why not?"

The librarian punched keys, and in a minute looked up. "All copies of that yearbook have been taken by the FBI for an investigation."

"What about the preceding three years?" asked Megan.

"When I searched for your request, I noticed the previous years had been taken as well. There's no return date listed. The head librarian left a note saying they had been checked out. I assume we'll get them back eventually." The librarian moved off to help someone else.

Neither of them said anything as they left the library. Alex couldn't come up with anything to do, short of finding someone who had graduated in the same year and asking to see their yearbook, if they had one. Otherwise it was a dead end.

He had to hope Gallagher had already gone through the yearbooks in depth and found nothing. He tried to think of any other angles they had missed.

"The hearing on Monday will receive national televised news coverage, thanks to Threshold." He scanned the campus as they strolled across it. "News stations, reporters, the whole country will watch it. They'll all want to see if the terrorists strike again. Everyone will watch this play out until the vote on the bill is over."

She looked at him quizzically. "You have an idea?"

"I keep thinking how well-organized Threshold is. They've had everything planned down to the last detail. I wonder if a vote on S.229 is all they're after."

"It's a big step for environmentalists." She glanced around the campus.

He thought about it. "I'm not convinced so many people would put so much on the line for one bill which might not pass."

She put on her sunglasses. "You believe they're after national attention for Dr. Joulie?"

"And he'll be saying more than what's expected." He wasn't sure what the doctor had that was so important.

"There's only one person who can tell us that."

He nodded. "Joulie."

She looped her arm around his and held his hand. "What makes you think he'll talk to us?"

He grimaced. "Maybe we can do a trade, sign up for surgery or something."

"How will this help us find Threshold?"

He scanned students and pedestrians on the campus. "It might trigger something with me. Or maybe he'll let something slip or we'll find something wherever we find him. Or seeing him will pressure someone else to act. It's worth a shot."

"Sounds good, Alex."

As they walked to the car, Jenny's words were again in his head. He hunched his shoulders and didn't relax even though Megan kept his hand in hers.

CHAPTER 41

GALLAGHER STOOD NEXT TO Juanita, holding a fax. The body in Jerry Peiser's grave had been exhumed. Dental records revealed it wasn't Peiser. He grudgingly had to admit that Sight had some kind of ability that he couldn't explain with logic.

While Juanita punched numbers into her computer, he said, "Run computer variations of disguises Peiser might use and have them sent immediately to all our offices and the police. Has the information on Michael Beator come in yet?"

From a pile on her desk she picked up a few papers and handed them to him. "The rest should be here today or tomorrow."

Gallagher scanned the information. They had Beator's circle of friends, his personal data, and his arrest record for a few protests which had turned violent. One of his friends, James Watson, had been arrested with him once. Watson's whereabouts hadn't been verified, though as far as they knew he wasn't dead. Even though Gallagher believed all of Threshold's members probably had faked their deaths, he couldn't assume anything. "What's new on James Watson?"

Juanita's voice was a whisper. "Nothing."

He grimaced as he sat on a stool. Another fax came in and the machine spit out paper.

Acid burned his throat when he thought of the Trenton stakeout. They had been betrayed. But as he and Foley had discussed, nearly anyone with a small talent for deduction could have alerted Threshold.

Gallagher wanted Threshold with a vengeance. They had killed his men and abducted Sight and Detalio in the middle of his operation. What little regard he had for those two didn't diminish the embarrassment. He had seen the torture Sight had gone through and wasn't sure how he would have handled that kind of pain. His own shoulder ached. A reminder of how close he had come to death.

What scared him now was that Threshold might go into hiding. Maybe they had accomplished what they set out to do and would go underground or leave the country. Even with a massive manhunt for Peiser, he doubted they would find him. Threshold hadn't made careless mistakes, except for burying Michael Beator with Sight and Detalio.

"Look at Peiser's and Beator's past phone records and see if there's any connection to Joulie, Dillon, or Crary."

As usual Juanita didn't acknowledge his request, which irritated him. But he knew his impatience was with the case, not her. He left for his office.

Dr. Crary was another loose end annoying him. The veterinarian had yet to respond to the Coast Guard emergency broadcasts. Gallagher assumed either he wouldn't, or he had been considered a liability and was dead. The latter might at least give some credibility to the idea that Senator Dillon and Dr. Joulie were connected to Threshold. Right now they had no hard evidence against anyone else who might be involved with the terrorists.

But another thing bothered him even more.

When Alex Sight had asked Foley in Albuquerque if his offices were clean, Gallagher had kept silent. Sight had asked the question as if he assumed Foley had already done an inspection. However Gallagher hadn't been informed of any sweep for electronic bugs or that Sight had suggested one be done. It was another example of the poor communication between himself and Foley.

After returning to D.C. he had made inquiries and learned Foley had indeed requested a sweep in the last week. Gallagher had made plans do his own check tonight, after Foley left the building.

Foley understood nothing about high tech bugs, or whether the people he used were secure or not. Gallagher, on the other hand, had a few agents he trusted and he had experience with the technology involved. It wouldn't take long and then he could be certain. Foley would look like a fool if he found something.

Back in his office he slumped into his chair. If someone in the Bureau had planted a bug, they would pay for it with life in prison. And if he was the person making the arrest, he wouldn't hesitate to put a bullet into the traitor.

CHAPTER 42

BEFORE ALEX AND MEGAN left Minneapolis, they called Dr. Joulie's office and his cell. No answer. They left messages both times. Megan had obtained another address for the doctor long ago in San Diego, discovering he had a cabin in northern Minnesota.

After some quick checks on her phone, she also learned that Joulie had flown his Cessna amphibious plane out of Rochester International Airport a few days ago. It seemed certain he had gone to his cabin on Island Lake Reservoir for the weekend.

Megan did research on her phone, while Alex drove. His phone played the *Call to the Post* bugle riff and he put it on speaker. It was Joulie.

"You wish to speak to me?" The doctor's voice was emotionless.

Alex was surprised. "We have a few questions."

"Come to my cabin." Joulie hung up.

He glanced at Megan. "I don't like it. He knew we were coming."

"Maybe he guessed that would be our next stop." Megan studied him.

Alex felt uneasy. "All of a sudden he wants to cooperate."

Megan leaned back. "Maybe he's in trouble and looking for a way out."

"Or it's a trap and he's making sure we don't miss it."

In two and a half hours they reached Duluth. They continued north to Rice Lake Road. Megan studied her phone while playing Dido's *White Flag*.

He glanced at her. "It's a popular lake. There should be boats we can rent to take us to his island."

Megan looked up. "I already found a boat rental place on the southeast side of the lake, not far from Joulie's place. Island Lake Rentals." She paused. "I beat the psychic."

"I didn't have my crystal ball." He gave her a brief smile. "Island Lake Rentals it is." He hoped they were open.

Houses and businesses were spaced farther and farther apart as thick northern woods crowded out humanity for a change, instead of the other way around. Small and large lakes broke up the landscape. Once they spied three deer on the side of the road. Traffic was light, the sky blue, and the humidity intense.

Alex cleared his throat. "After this is over, I need a rest."

She leaned across and kissed his cheek. "Buy the boat."

That brought a smile to his lips. He didn't want to, but he asked, "What about your doctor boyfriend?"

"I called him four days ago and told him I wanted a break." She briefly rested a hand on his arm. "I had to decide if I was going to Europe with him, and it didn't feel right."

He regarded her in surprise. "You were that sure of us already?"

"No. I just wasn't sure of him anymore. That's been building for a few months." She paused. "When we first met, something struck me about you. Intuition. Even though I found you annoying."

"I felt the same thing." He smiled.

She rolled her eyes. "That's romantic."

In a half-hour they neared the east side of Island Lake Reservoir. Traffic increased. Cabins appeared, and the two-hun-dred-thirty-acre reservoir came into view, stretching southwest to northeast. Remaining on the east side of the lake, Alex took the south lakeshore drive which paralleled the shoreline.

Thick forest ran to the left, and to the right trees surrounded spaced cabins. The lake glistened thirty yards past the buildings. A strong wind pushed whitecaps over the surface, which was shaded by scattered clouds. Small fishing boats dotted the water, along with some large speedboats, and a few small sailboats skipped across the waves. Inlets and bays created a convoluted shoreline. The lake stretched a mile wide in some places.

In a few minutes Alex saw a tiny cabin tucked into trees with a sign stuck in the dirt reading; *Island Lake Rentals*. A logo of two crossed canoe paddles was carved beneath the words.

Alex pulled into the dirt drive and parked. They walked inside wearing hats and sunglasses again. It was good to get out of the hot blowing wind, which parched Alex's throat.

A large-framed woman stood behind the counter, stuffed into tight jeans and wearing a loose blue flannel shirt. Chewing gum, she had a no-nonsense demeanor. Brown hair curled around her cherub face and her sharp brown eyes studied them.

"We want to rent a speedboat," said Alex.

"Don't have any." The woman spoke matter-of-factly, smacking gum between her lips. "All rented."

"Fishing boats?" he asked.

"Nope."

"Motors on rowboats?" he persisted.

"Nope."

"Kayaks or canoes?"

"Nope."

"Rowboats without motors?"

"Nope."

"Sailboats?"

The woman stopped chewing. "It's too windy today and you need experience. Besides it's mine and I don't rent it."

"I can sail anything under fifty feet," said Alex.

Staring at him, the woman shook her head. "I have an old Hobie 16, but they're easy to tip in strong winds. And the water's cold this time of year."

Alex held up a hand. "I own a Hobie 18. And I'll give you a large damage deposit."

The woman considered him again. "All right."

He turned to Megan and smiled. "We don't have to swim after all."

"Seventy dollars an hour," said the woman. "And the damage deposit." She looked at him. "Do I know you from somewhere?"

"I doubt it." He peeled off two thousand dollars, knowing it was likely more than the boat was worth. "Enough deposit?"

"Plenty." She scooped up the money and led them to the boat. It took Alex some scrambling to get the beat-up Hobie 16 rigged. The woman helped him. Finished, he held Megan's hand as she sat on the dock, and then stepped onto the Hobie.

The owner threw them two life preservers. "Might be building to a blow. Come in before you tear my sails to pieces."

"I will." Alex glanced at the sails. They were already worn at the edges.

After they put on the lifejackets, the woman let go of the painter.

Alex pulled in the mainsail and tugged the tiller slightly to windward. His bruised ribs and arms stung a little from his efforts, but the pain was manageable. "Grab that line and haul." He gestured to the jib sheet lying limp on the canvas.

Megan did the best she could with her right hand and they were off. The wind blew twenty knots from the south, catching the sails and snapping them full, shooting them off like a plug out of a champagne bottle. They sailed out of the bay on a reach. Joulie's island lay a third of a mile to the west. Shaped like a pig's head, it was two-thirds of a mile long and a third of a mile wide.

Megan sat on the same side as Alex to balance the wind gusting at them. She winced while she clutched the jib sheet, making Alex wonder if this was such a good idea.

The windward pontoon lifted free of the water once; Megan glanced at him, her brow furrowed.

He grimaced. "It's all right. We'll probably only flip once or twice."

Rolling her eyes, she looked ahead.

The wind made the humidity bearable, the cool water acting like an air conditioner. Alex found it difficult to take any enjoyment from the way the boat sliced through the water, or from the rhythmic slap of the waves against the hull. There was too much tension in his chest.

In minutes they skimmed offshore of the island, flying fast.

Megan pointed. "His cabin's around the point in a bay."

It added another short leg to their sail. They rounded the southern peninsula into a large bay. A long beach appeared curving northwest, its sand looking inviting. West of the beach, an airplane bobbed in the water at the end of a long dock. Two small fishing boats were also tied up at the pier. Alex steered for the plane.

The water shot by, an occasional wave slapping at the canvas and pontoons. Spray regularly spattered their backs. Between looking for gusts threatening a knockdown, Alex scanned the shoreline. Joulie's cabin wasn't visible from the water, but it had to be close to shore and shouldn't be hard to find.

With the plane's presence the dock space was marginal, so Alex chose a spot on the shoreline near the end of the beach. Pointing the cat up in a tight tack, he steered for land. He let go of the mainsail when they were almost beached, and the pontoons slid up to the shore.

Megan kicked off her tennis shoes and scrambled over the side, stepping into two inches of water while holding the cat's painter.

Alex pulled up the rudder, took off his socks and shoes, and climbed off. The water was cold. He dragged the boat into the shoreline, tying the painter to a nearby tree with a bowline knot. His arms and side burned with the effort.

They sat on the hull to clean off their feet and put on their shoes. Quickly they walked the shoreline to the dock. The two fishing boats had outboard motors. One had *Island Lake Rentals* painted on its side. The Cessna rocked gently in the water at the end of the pier. Toward the far end of the island a man was fishing from a twenty-five-foot speedboat.

Megan stared at the boats. "Dr. Joulie has visitors."

Alex didn't like any of it. "Let's hope they're friendly."

A gravel path led up a slight incline from the dock into the trees. They cautiously followed it. Alex drew his M&P, Megan her SIG Sauer. From the top of the hill they could see the cabin, set back fifty feet amidst trees. It was an old rambler with a small wooden deck in front. The simple cabin surprised Alex. Given the doctor's income, he had expected a large house—which many Minnesotans still called a *cabin*.

They walked quietly up to the open front door and peered through the screen door.

Like many older Minnesota cabins, it had one main room—a living room with an adjacent open kitchen—and two doors that most likely led into bedrooms on opposite ends. The difference with this cabin was that its insides were shredded. The kitchen was in shambles, with pots, pans, utensils, and food items strewn over the floor. The living room furniture was ripped, lamps broken, and a bookcase taken apart.

It reminded Alex of his own abused house. His fingers tightened on his gun.

Slowly pushing the screen door open, he cautiously walked in, gun up. They each walked into a bedroom first, to make sure no one else was there. The bedroom Alex searched was simple—a bed, small nightstand, and a dresser—and just as mangled as the living room. A shortwave radio atop the dresser had been smashed and rendered unusable.

Returning to the living room, he found Megan standing behind a sofa. A large rug had been thrown back, revealing a safe embedded in the cabin's wood floor. The safe was open and empty.

"Someone found what they were looking for." Megan eyed him.

"Maybe. But then why are they still here?" Alex wondered if Joulie was still alive.

Megan walked over to the kitchen counter. Picking up a cup filled with coffee, she held her hand over the front burner of the small stove. Turning, she said, "Both are still warm, Alex."

"They must be on the island." Alex caught her eyes, but her expression remained steady.

They quietly went outside to the dirt path that forked from the front deck.

"There's a good chance the path loops." Megan motioned. "We should each take a direction."

"Whoever is here might have seen us coming. Or this is a trap." He frowned. "Let's stay together. The path might stop halfway around the island."

"If we follow the same path, they might come back on the other and leave without us seeing them." Her voice was certain.

"We could wait here." He didn't want to split up.

"And maybe whoever is here kills Joulie while we're on a coffee break." She regarded him calmly. "I can take care of myself."

Her voice was decisive and he saw it was useless to argue. His throat became dry. He tried to ignore it. Everything she said made sense and this wasn't three years ago.

"We check back here in twenty minutes," she said. "Ten out, ten back. Agreed?"

"Alright. But stick to the plan." Unable to move away, he looked at her uncertainly.

"Fine." She checked her phone and strode along the north trail quietly, the SIG Sauer ready.

Alex turned and walked down the path to the right.

The woods were quiet as he stepped into them. The scent of pine laced a warm, light breeze—all that was left of the strong lake wind once it was blocked by the trees. Humidity bathed his face as he moved into the shade of the towering evergreen and birch.

The ground was hard and gave him sure footing, but he remained tense as he walked. His gaze followed the path as it disappeared around the next curve. He tried to see ahead through the brush and trees hiding the trail, but it was too thick.

Even though it jogged left and right, the path slowly made a big arc. Megan was right. The path probably did curl around the island.

A snap made him jerk to a stop and stand still. He studied the woods until a squirrel raced over the ground, then up a tree.

As he continued along the path, he thought about Joulie's cabin. If the doctor was connected to Threshold, it didn't make sense they would harm him. But perhaps he had betrayed them somehow. He couldn't think of anyone else that might be interested in the man.

He listened for sounds from his surroundings. Nothing. He kept walking.

Staccato gun shots stopped him cold. A machine gun. It was followed by scattered pistol shots and more automatic rifle fire. The shots all came from his left, north, muffled by thick forest.

He whirled to face the woods, unsure if the quickest route was back or continuing along the path. The shots seemed farther ahead than behind, so he ran down the trail in the same direction, the 9mm clenched, his finger locked in a tight curve over the trigger. He cursed that he had let Megan talk him into splitting up. All kinds of images leapt into his mind. He had to fight to keep from yelling her name.

His side ached fiercely with every step he took and the cuts on his limbs tore at him in little bursts of sharp pain. His worst nightmare presented itself when the trail curved right, heading toward the east side of the island and the lake. It wasn't going to join Megan's trail.

He plunged into the woods to his left. To avoid the lower growth, he pumped his knees high, frantically picking the best way through the trees, finding the thinnest sections to tackle. Tree branches and low brush scraped against his arms and sweat covered his body.

Minutes after the first shots he heard Megan's SIG Sauer fire twice in succession. Two different pistol shots followed, sounding as if they had moved farther away.

Aiming himself ten degrees west, Alex ran with wild strides. A million images struck him as his legs churned; Megan hurt or dead on the ground, blood on her blouse and face. He fought panic as he peered ahead through the woods, listening for anything to tell him where she was. Oblivious to the thorns biting his limbs and the branches whipping his skin, he crashed through the undergrowth, drowning out any subtle sounds that he might hear.

A flash of empty space appeared as he stumbled out of the trees into a small grass clearing. The change of footing sent him off balance. Not fighting it, yielding to his momentum, he flung himself to the ground on his belly, clutching the M&P in both hands in front of him. His chest and stomach struck the ground hard and he bounced and slid a few inches.

A line of trees surrounded a thirty-foot-wide meadow. A wood chair sat in the middle, short pieces of rope lying on the ground next to it. Not far from the chair a man was lying on his back, eyes open in death, a gunshot wound in his chest.

An airplane engine started in the distance. Joulie's Cessna. Heaving himself up, he ran to the back of the grassy area, finding the trail Megan had followed. The deeper growl of a high-powered boat blended with the whine of the plane.

"Megan!" he yelled harshly, unable to contain himself any longer.

There was no reply. In his mind he envisioned the worst. Expected it. He knew his memory of Jenny was driving the panic, but he couldn't help it. With no hesitation he saw retribution. Joulie dead. Tracked down no matter how long it took, a gun shoved up the doctor's mouth and emptied into his brain.

The trail zigzagged. He scrambled over corners, through bushes, and under limbs of trees. Pounding up the last yards of the path to the cabin, he gulped air, hoarse from yelling. There was no sign of Megan so he ran toward the water.

Halfway to the shore another man lay still, curled up on his side, his midriff covered with blood. Alex ran onto the dock, his gaze flying south to the Cessna which was already a spot of white in the sky. Nearly as far away on the waterline he spotted the speedboat they had seen earlier racing across the lake, a number of figures onboard.

"Megan!" he shouted.

But it was pointless. She was gone.

***

An hour later the Duluth police finished taking his statement. They were unable to identify the two dead men—they had no ID on their person. He also learned the FBI car he and Megan had driven to the boat rental had been broken into and Megan's gun cases taken. Odd they had left his. He wondered what else the thieves had been looking for. He figured the gun cases were taken to make it look like a routine robbery.

He sat like stone, his left knee aching, while the police talked with Deputy Director Foley. Limping to a water fountain, he swallowed two aspirin.

The detective came out of the office, nodding to him. Walking into the office with wooden legs, Alex closed the door and lifted the phone.

"I'll do everything I can to find her." said Foley. "The trouble is, unless we're contacted we're out of leads. We tried tracking the Cessna and found nothing. It could have landed anywhere. The country up there has thousands of lakes to hide in."

Alex stared woodenly at a point on the office wall. "Alright. I want to hear as soon as you learn anything."

"Of course." Foley hung up.

Alex took out his phone and dialed Megan's cell number for the third time. Thus far no one had answered.

This time it was answered immediately in silence.

"I'm here," said Alex.

"Someone wants to talk to you. Immediately. Alone."

Alex's fist bunched against his thigh. He didn't recognize the voice. It didn't matter. "What do you want?" he asked quietly.

"If you call in any reinforcements, we'll know it, understand? Then she's history. You're being watched. A ticket will be waiting for you at the airport. When you arrive at your destination, we'll have a car waiting for you. You have an hour to catch your flight."

"If she's hurt—" he began hoarsely.

The line went dead.

CHAPTER 43

AFTER HE DROVE OUT of New Mexico, Odysseus entered Texas, driving around Dallas and continuing through Arkansas, Tennessee, and North Carolina to Virginia. The heat wave seemed to follow him from state to state.

He finally parked at a truck stop, sitting in a blue Ford Focus, just outside of a small town in central Virginia. Though he wasn't tired, he could feel tension building inside. Now that the end was in sight he wanted to get out of the country.

He tried a number on his cell phone and received a recorded message saying the number was no longer in service. Impatient, he punched in another number, waiting while it was scrambled. If the first number had been discarded, it might mean they were finished and could leave. His brow furrowed as the line rang several times. When it was answered his shoulders sagged.

The voice said, "You've been identified. Continue as planned until your next contact."

"What—"

The call ended. Odysseus stared at the phone. He knew the rules. No conversation. No questions. Though the message was expected, he panicked. It took several deep breaths to calm himself.

The man on the other end of the phone had coordinated information, logistics, and a hired killer. And the man was an unknown entity to him. Better for everyone that way. But he did wonder if the man was Dr. Crary, Dr. Joulie, or Senator Dillon. That sounded risky and unlikely, at least for Joulie and Dillon, given their public exposure. Supposedly Threshold had contacts in the FBI and plenty of resources. Odysseus had never questioned who it was—contact had always been indirect—but for the first time he wondered what risks the unknown man was taking when ordering them to risk their lives.

Ever since they had left Menelaus' body in the desert, he knew he had made a mistake. They should have buried the body elsewhere, where the authorities never would have found it. Of course he hadn't expected Sight and Detalio to be rescued either. After hearing about their escape the following day, he had wanted to find and kill the two investigators. Not only had they lived, but they had managed to save Senator Trenton too.

Slowly he drove back onto the highway, considering things. Even with his identity known it would be nearly impossible for the authorities to find him. He had shaved off his long hair and he wore a baseball cap. A pair of large sunglasses hid his bruised nose, while facial makeup covered the circles under his eyes. He would stick to truck stops and out-of-the-way places, as he had for several days now. In one more day it would all be over.

Hopefully Achilles and Patroclus hadn't run into any problems. They had split up with one more planned rendezvous.

As he accelerated the car, he wondered how much they had accomplished. The whole country was up in arms over the issues they had made public. Yet he had expected a stronger reaction, with more people ready to take up their cause in the streets. Most of the public was satisfied to let the same system that was destroying the environment decide on the justice for the destroyers. One step at a time, he thought. No revolution was an easy process.

His thoughts drifted to the Rockies and Yosemite, and all the beautiful places he had climbed. He wondered if he would ever see them again. That filled him with sadness. Long ago he knew he might end up a martyr to the cause, but he had never embraced that idea. He always believed he would survive.

One more check-in call. Then on to Europe.

His pursuers were closing in on him like a net around a tired fish, with only one opening to freedom. Not far to go, he consoled himself. Not far to go.

CHAPTER 44

I T WAS EARLY EVENING and already dark when Alex arrived at Billings Logan International Airport. He picked up his gun case and walked outside into the heat. One of Senator Dillon's young, wide-shouldered bodyguards waved him across the pick-up and drop-off lanes to the express parking lot.

The man walked away and Alex followed him. At the rear corner of the lot Alex finally caught up to the bodyguard. Smoking a cigarette, the man was leaning against the trunk of a large black sedan.

Wearing a suit and a cocky smile, the man didn't move. "Senator Dillon's waiting for you." He opened the trunk of the car.

Alex tossed in the gun case. "I know you're probably dying to frisk me."

The man sneered. "You probably can't wait, can you? Turn around." He frisked Alex quickly, finding his knife and cell phone and tossing both into the trunk too. Finished, he walked to the driver's side and motioned to the front passenger door. "Get in."

Alex complied, surprised to find the car empty.

Dillon's bodyguard got rid of the cigarette and sat in the driver's seat. From a pocket he retrieved a cell phone and hit a speed-dial, putting the cell on speaker. "Senator, all is fine. Party has arrived in good humor."

"Good." The senator's voice was stern. "I'll expect a check-in twenty minutes from now. The guest better still be in good humor or else the party here will start without him."

"Will do, Senator." Shoving the cell phone into his pocket, the man eyed Alex. "Comprende? You try anything, I don't make the call, your partner is dog meat. Got it?"

Alex stared silently at the man.

The man shoved his face closer. "You got it?"

Alex chopped his left hand into the front of the man's neck and drove his right fist into the man's side. The bodyguard doubled over.

Locking his hands, Alex drove them into the back of the man's neck. The man slumped motionless.

Alex took the bodyguard's M17 9mm. "Yeah, and now we both got it."

Quickly he pulled the keys from the ignition. After waiting for a pedestrian to walk by, he hurriedly dragged the limp man into the front passenger seat.

After recovering his gun case, knife, and phone from the trunk, he backed the sedan out of the parking space. He quickly drove out of the airport, then east a few miles to Highway 87 north. There he pushed the car to ninety.

After putting on the AC, his fingers clamped on the steering wheel until they hurt, but he couldn't loosen them. Thoughts of Megan consumed him.

Senator Dillon intended to kill them, of that he was certain. And he believed if he tried to bring someone else in to help, Dillon would also keep his word and Megan wouldn't come out of it alive. The senator must have considered it too risky to kill Megan on Joulie's island—or maybe she was just bait to get him. That seemed more likely. Safest to bury them both in quiet somewhere no one would suspect to search.

The road slid by like an oily snake, the fence posts blurs to the side as the headlights flashed along the blacktop. Traffic was light. The few cars he did overtake he swerved by as if they stood still. The numbers on the car clock moved too fast. Time seemed to be measured in flashes of images in his mind more than by the minutes ticking off.

Memories of the last days swept through him. The Wheelers, dead FBI agents, conversations with Megan, his house and Mooch, the bulldozer, his torture, and last night with Megan. Several emotions overtook him, but anger ruled.

Dillon's bodyguard groaned.

Alex glanced at the clock. In one minute the guard was supposed to check in with the senator. He slapped the man twice, and the bodyguard opened his eyes. Picking up the 9mm, he jammed it under the man's chin. "Make the call, and if I don't like it, you're dead." He locked eyes with the man. "I have nothing to lose."

The man's expression showed he believed him. Remaining slumped, he took out his cell phone, put it on speaker, and hit the speed-dial. It was answered immediately, and he said, "Senator, all is fine. Party is in good humor."

Senator Dillon answered. "Good. Call me when you enter the driveway."

The guard pocketed the cell phone and looked at Alex. "I don't make the call, she's dead."

"Thanks." Alex swung his gun butt into the man's head and he went limp.

He accelerated the car. It was a forty-mile drive, with twenty left to go. If he maintained high speed to the Bull Mountains, he would have a few minutes to spare before Dillon expected his driver to reach the ranch.

The road climbed the mountain, taking several gentle curves, and Alex had to decrease his speed. Darkness hid the drop-offs on either side, making it eerie. As he began driving down in elevation, he tried to remember landmarks from his first trip to Dillon's ranch. There was a large hill which led down to a level stretch a half-mile north of Ranch Big Horn. It would have to do.

The hill appeared and he flew over it, quickly at its bottom on the other side. Turning off the AC, he opened all the windows. Hot air from the pavement flitted in, sharply whipping his neck and face.

Alex took his foot off the accelerator and veered the car to the right, off the road and across the shoulder. The sedan sailed over the ditch, bouncing and skidding as the wheels struck the dry ground. Angling the car thirty degrees from the road, he didn't dim his lights. The shocks took major jolts as the car bounced side-to-side.

Dillon's bodyguard groaned, but he didn't sit up.

Scattered trees and rocks covered the dry grassland leading to Dillon's ranch. Alex swerved a number of times to avoid hitting either. His goal was to approach the ranch house garage from the south side. There was a risk that he might be seen, but he was out of time to do anything else.

The faint lights of Dillon's house glittered in the distance, less than a half-mile away.

He slowed to thirty. When he spotted Dillon's garage, he turned off the lights and allowed the car to coast the rest of the way. Stopping fifty yards from the south side of the garage, he killed the engine.

A bright spotlight shone on the driveway in front of the garage and house, but the backyard was shrouded in darkness. He quietly cracked open the door and stepped out of the car, shoving the guard's gun into his belt.

Something knocked him back against the car frame, bending his knees. He gasped as two bright eyes appeared close to his face and white daggers reached for his throat. Dillon's dog.

His reflexes saved him. He had jerked his arms up between himself and the dog's jaws. Gurgling a hoarse cry, he pushed the animal to the right and followed the body to the ground, bringing all of his weight onto the back of the animal.

There was a muted yelp from the dog as it scrambled to get free from under him. He rolled off it, and the senator's dog limped off into the darkness. Alex rose to his knees, then his feet, and leaned against the car. Pulling the gun, he looked into the darkness to make sure the dog wasn't coming back.

Satisfied, he quickly went around to the other side of the car and hauled the mumbling guard a few yards from the vehicle. He stared down at the man, and then kicked him in the head for good measure. With frenzied movements he ripped off a piece of the guard's shirt, and then searched the man's pockets until he found the lighter. Stuffing the rag into the car's gas tank, he lit it. Grabbing his gun case, he ran to the front corner of the garage where he knelt.

A quick look at the front of the house told him no one had been waiting outside with the dog. Running alongside the garage, he knelt at the back corner. He switched the M17 for his 9mm, leaving the gun case there. Rounding the corner, he ran along the back of the house in the shadows. At the back door he paused when the car exploded. He debated killing the guards, but that would warn Dillon and the senator might make good on his threat to kill Megan. However if the guards came out the back door, he wouldn't have a choice.

Voices inside the house were followed by footsteps. He stepped back, aiming at the door. Nothing. They must have exited through the front door. Gripping the doorknob, he turned it and stepped into the shadowed hallway, staying close to the wall. The air was cooler inside.

Quickly he sidled to the door of the study. Two table lamps gave the center of the room light, casting shadows at its margins.

Dillon sat in a high-backed easy chair, one of his pearl-handled Colt pistols on his lap. The other pistol was holstered in the gun belt, which lay near his black Stetson on his desk. A bottle of brandy and a shot glass were nearby. Megan's phone lay there too.

Megan sat across from Dillon in an armchair, her lip bloodied, cheek bruised, and face drawn. Seeing her alive buoyed Alex.

Striding into the room, he aimed his pistol at the senator. Dillon's expression darkened, but he didn't move. Alex barely glanced at Megan, who stood up, relief sweeping her eyes. Silently he grabbed the pistol on Dillon's lap and tossed it to the floor. Taking the senator's holstered pistol, he handed it to Megan.

Dillon stiffened. "You're dead, Sight."

Alex whipped the butt of his gun into Dillon's head. The senator slumped quietly in the chair. Going around to the back of the recliner, keeping it between himself and the door, Alex crouched. He motioned Megan behind the other chair and she quickly hid.

The front door opened and footsteps rushed along the hallway outside the room.

Dillon's bodyguards charged through the study door.

"Drop your guns," snarled Alex.

One of the men whirled to him, gun up.

Megan shot him. The explosion filled the room. The man doubled over and fell sideways to the floor.

The other guard immediately dropped his gun and raised his hands.

Alex gaped. Peter. "Traitor."

"To what?" Peter's voice shook as he looked at both of them. "Corporations and politicians who poison the planet, their own citizens, my father? He was a farmer, growing food for everyone, and died from cancer because of corporate greed."

"Shut up." Alex walked across the room, gesturing with the gun to one of the chairs. "Sit."

Peter looked cowed but didn't move. "You don't care about any of that, do you? You just want justice for the few—"

Alex backhanded Peter across the face and elbowed him. Peter slumped to the floor on his side, gasping and looking up with fear in his eyes.

Kicking Peter's Glock to Megan, Alex straightened when sirens sounded. His fingers tightened on his weapon.

"Dillon called them." Megan picked up Peter's gun and placed Dillon's on the desk. She also grabbed her phone and pocketed it. "He told them intruders were on his ranch."

Alex looked at Peter. "On your stomach, hands clasped at the back of your head." Peter obeyed, and Alex signaled to Megan. She nodded in understanding.

The sirens quieted and car doors slammed.

Alex backed up behind Dillon's chair again, and Megan remained on the other side of the room.

Peter remained lying on the floor, his face resigned.

The outside door opened. In seconds Chief Bixby and one of his men rushed into the study, Glocks drawn and raised.

Alex aimed his gun at Bixby, his arm tense. Megan aimed Peter's Glock at the other officer, who looked young.

"Arrest these two, they attacked me," murmured Senator Dillon, as he stirred in the chair.

Bixby stopped, his attention roving over the scene. "What's going on?" His gun remained aimed at Megan, while his officer aimed at Alex. It was a standoff.

"We're arresting the senator and his men for supporting terrorist activities, and for kidnapping a federal officer." Alex kept his gun pointed at Bixby. "Dillon's man picked me up at the airport. The senator threatened to kill Megan if I didn't come."

Megan said stiffly, "I was held captive by Senator Dillon and his men, and the senator told me that Alex and I were both going to die. You need to arrest him."

"That's ridiculous." Senator Dillon slowly moved to the edge of his chair. "They attacked me for no reason."

"Arrest them and call Deputy Director Foley." Alex paused. "Two federal agents are telling you to arrest these men. Do it."

The tall police chief smoothed his droopy moustache, and then nodded. "Alright." He holstered his gun, motioning his officer over to Dillon. "Cuff the senator."

The officer holstered his weapon and approached Dillon.

Bixby's brow furrowed as he looked down at Peter.

Steering wide of the police officer, Alex walked toward Bixby, his gun against his thigh. Megan lowered her gun.

"Senator!" yelled the officer.

A gunshot exploded.

Alex whirled, his gun leveled.

The police officer had his weapon aimed at the senator. Dillon was curled up on the floor, silent and not moving. One of his Colt pistols lay near his outstretched hand.

"He was going for his gun." The officer paled.

"Almighty," Bixby said softly.

The young police officer squatted beside the senator to check his pulse.

Bixby spoke into the radio on his shoulder; "We need an ambulance at Senator Dillon's house."

Alex relaxed his shoulders and lowered his gun, as did Megan.

The young officer walked over to them with his gun holstered, his expression troubled. Having a fresh, innocent face, he looked as if he had just graduated from the academy.

"Dillon's dead," the officer said shakily. He looked down at Peter. "Hands behind your back."

Peter took his hands off his head, but abruptly rolled sideways toward Megan, trying to rise off the floor. Megan kneed him in the jaw and Peter dropped to the floor again, groaning. She aimed her gun at him.

The young officer drew his weapon, but aimed it at Megan. His innocent face had gone hard. "Drop it."

Alex tried to raise his gun, but a sharp jab in his ribs dropped him to his knees and left him gasping for air. Even though he hadn't seen it, he was aware that Bixby had elbowed him. He didn't know what incapacitated him more, the blow or the surprise of another betrayal.

Bixby stuck his gun into his neck and said, "Drop the gun."

Alex did, and the chief kicked it away and stepped back.

Megan's eyes narrowed but she released the Glock, which slid from her hand to the floor.

Peter reached out and clutched it.

Bixby said, "Toss your phones on the floor."

Alex and Megan obeyed.

"Good job, boys."

Upon hearing the familiar voice, Alex turned.

Dillon was standing, putting on his Stetson. He buckled his gun belt around his waist, and then shoved both pistols into the holsters. "I guess the deputy wasn't a good shot. We didn't want a shootout inside the house." He turned to Bixby. "Let's get rid of these vermin."

Peter slowly rose, one side of his face puffy. Wiping his bloodied lip on his sleeve, his lips curled back in a snarl as he regarded Megan. Stepping forward, his Glock aimed at her, he swung his fist. She didn't try to stop it. He hit her, snapping her head sideways, but she made no sound.

Alex struggled to his feet, pain radiating from his side to his sternum. Bixby gave a curt shake of his head, his gun aimed at him. Alex didn't care.

Megan had blood on her lip and she wiped it with a hand, her eyes filled with fire.

"Enough," snapped Dillon. "Get them out of here."

Peter glanced at Dillon, then backed away, motioning with the Glock.

CHAPTER 45

THEY WERE HERDED OUT to the backyard.

Alex couldn't shake off the bitterness of betrayal. Other things became clear. There had never been any chance to catch the killer who had tried to murder them in Billings, who had killed four people already. Bixby had guaranteed that failure.

The burning car cast a glow beyond the corner of the garage. Two large floodlights flicked on at the back of the house, illuminating the area in front of them. A wooden bench, twenty feet long and four feet high, ran parallel with the house. A cell phone rested on it, along with several bottles of liquor and a few glasses.

Senator Dillon turned to Peter. "Get the truck."

Peter nodded and scurried back into the house.

Dillon threw a switch on the bench near him. Another floodlight went on farther out from them, lighting up a longer bench some thirty paces distant. A row of beer bottles lined it.

"Watch this, young man." Dillon drew his guns fast and fired at the bottles on the bench.

The pistols' explosions shattered the quiet of the night. A bottle disintegrated with every shot he fired.

When the senator finished, Alex said, "Looks easy. Want to give me a try?"

Dillon lowered the Colts, holstering one. Plucking bullets from his gun belt, he loaded the pistol in his hand. "Used to be your quick draw would save your neck in a fair gunfight, but usually fights weren't fair. You would get shot in the back while facing your adversary." He continued to load bullets. "Just like today."

"It's nice to see you've kept those principles intact." Alex scanned the visible area in the floodlights. There was nowhere to run or hide.

Megan's eyes narrowed, showing as much anger as he felt.

Dillon looked up. "I used to believe in due process and legal maneuvers. The whole system. Now I believe in results." He holstered the gun, then drew the other. After loading it methodically, he set it on the bench. Calmly he poured himself a drink and downed it in one gulp.

A pickup truck with a raised body and oversized tires whipped around the garage corner. Peter parked it twenty feet away. A large, thick-wired dog cage rested in its open bed.

Alex's mouth turned dry.

Peter stepped down from the cab and walked toward them. "The dog's hurt, senator."

Dillon's lips pursed but he said nothing.

Alex faced him. "And the innocent police officers, bystanders, whoever, should just stay out of the way, right?"

"My wife, Katie, was innocent." Dillon's voice was gruff. "Innocent when she drank the contaminated well water. Innocent when she got cancer. Innocent when she died. She drank water a company in Billings had fouled with chlorinated solvents for years, knowingly, within the guidelines of the law. Dr. Joulie's wife died of cancer ten years ago, Dr. Crary's five years ago."

Alex scoffed. "What a novel approach. Murder to drown your sorrows."

Dillon shook his head. "We don't want revenge, but we're going to demand change. We'll force it upon a government so corrupt in its laws that the only thing they care about anymore is profit, lawyers' fees, and criminals' rights. It doesn't matter that my Katie died, was murdered. It doesn't matter that people die every day due to sanctioned criminal acts by greedy corporations and bribed politicians. All that matters is the corrupt legal system." He scoffed. "It used to be if you took a man's horse you were hanged. Now you can kill someone's wife and nothing happens."

"What about you?" Alex stared at Bixby, wanting to keep them talking. He was aware of Megan inching toward the other side of Bixby. "Lose a wife too, or you just like to kill people?"

Bixby's face hardened. "My son died of cancer related to the same chemicals in the water." He nodded at his deputy. "His cousin."

Alex lifted his chin. "So your son's death justifies murder?"

"We're protecting the innocent," said Bixby. "Our government isn't."

"My congressional colleagues give speeches about family values, love, and integrity," said Dillon. "And then they sanction poisoning the air, food, and water of our children and loved ones. Moral hypocrites, no matter what church or religion they worship."

Alex couldn't find any words, especially since he agreed.

Bixby noticed Megan moving and shook his head.

Megan stopped. "What is Joulie reading at the hearing?"

"Senator." Bixby nodded to the truck.

"Patience." Dillon turned to Megan. "Joulie will expose connections of industrial pollution to cancer and death, and connections of paid officials to that same death. Proof of illegal CIA involvement in corporate gains abroad. Proof of how EPA officials have knowingly allowed toxic chemicals to be used on our food supplies. Proof the EPA, FDA, and the presidency has been owned by the GMO biotech companies for decades."

Dillon grimaced. "The list is endless and Dr. Joulie with his sterling reputation at Mayo will make national news and trigger an international public outcry for change. Some of it isn't new, but we have a better platform now. Threshold woke people up."

"Life, liberty, and justice for all," said Alex.

"Justice?" Dillon's face was taut. "We're in the new Middle Ages and the new feudal lords are the corporations. They control the politicians and the government—all of us—and everyone is expendable to their profits."

"You expect the public to respect terrorists?" asked Megan.

Dillon faced her. "The Boston Tea Party men were called terrorists. The men who began the Revolution against England started a war because common people didn't have fair representation against the king and queen. Today's royalty are the corporations and their paid-off politicians."

"You think a handful of men are going to change that?" asked Alex.

"Gandhi and Martin Luther King did. We have a sophisticated, failsafe network, supported by some of the country's most influential people. No one person can take down the network, and no one person's fall can stop what we've started. It will continue until we've succeeded." He poured himself another drink.

"Doesn't all this hard work cut into your golf time?" asked Alex.

"You're not the enemy, but you're in the way." Dillon tossed back his drink. "My spread is pretty big. If someone thought you two had met foul play here and wanted to search for bodies, it would take them years to find you." He motioned to Bixby, who nodded to his officer.

The young man took a step toward Alex and wagged his gun toward the pickup. "Let's go."

Alex glanced at Dillon, but the senator stared at the firing range and poured himself another drink. Bixby and the officer remained far enough away to avoid even a lunging rush.

"You can go dead or alive." The young officer raised the Glock.

Alex hesitated.

The officer extended his gun farther.

"Alex," whispered Megan.

Stepping to her side, they walked together to the back of the truck, where Bixby stopped them with his gun.

The young officer climbed into the truck bed and opened the cage, gesturing them in.

Alex climbed up first, so he could help Megan up. Then he crawled into the cage. Megan followed. Once inside, Alex turned around, his face near the wire mesh as it was shut.

The officer sneered at him, then left to join Peter in the truck's cab. Peter drove the vehicle west, away from the ranch, the pickup bouncing in the darkness. Illuminated by the lights, Bixby and Dillon could be seen talking to each other.

Alex immediately inspected the cage door with Megan. "Let's kick it open."

Megan sat on her butt beside him, and they kicked the cage door with both feet, trying to time their kicks with the vehicle's bounces.

They hadn't gone more than a hundred yards when a loud-speaker blared, "Senator Dillon and Chief Bixby, drop your weapons. You're surrounded."

The truck skidded to a stop. Peter and the officer craned their heads out the truck windows to look back at the ranch.

Alex peered out the back of the cage with Megan.

Dillon and Bixby drew their guns and fired at the corners of the house. Automatic weapons quickly overwhelmed their gunfire. The senator and sheriff crumpled to the ground.

Peter gunned the engine and sped off into the darkness, away from the ranch. Alex didn't know if he should feel hopeful or threatened over Dillon's death.

Clinging to the side of the cage, he and Megan continued kicking at the rear gate as hard and fast as they could. Alex didn't think Peter would stop the truck now anyway. After a few more attempts the door finally sprang free.

Two Jeeps appeared from around the side of the garage, four men in each vehicle. The Jeeps had one-foot-diameter spotting lights attached to U-bars on their frames, and the lights shone in their direction.

"Anyone shooting at Dillon has to be on our side." Megan crawled to the edge of the truck bed.

"Let's be sure." Alex sat beside her, his legs dangling. "Maybe Dillon is expendable."

Alex jumped off the bouncing pickup, landing hard and going prone. Megan ended up beside him.

His ribs and arms hurt, but Alex remained silent on the baked earth. Turning, he watched the truck as it fled west, its headlights bouncing wildly as it was driven too fast over the terrain. The Jeep engines roared in pursuit.

Alex waited until both Jeeps drove past them. Then he nudged Megan and rose with her. Crouching, they ran for the ranch.

One thought motivated Alex's legs; the gun case he had left by the garage. Bixby's and the senator's guns were a few steps closer, but they lay under the floodlights, which he wanted to avoid.

Glancing back, he saw the Jeeps had closed to within a hundred feet of the truck on both sides. Peter and the officer fired on them, their guns louder than the sounds of the revving engines. The men in the Jeeps responded with automatic gunfire.

Alex circled just wide of the firing range, remaining in the bordering darkness. Megan peeled away from him, heading for the bodies and the guns on the ground.

Shots echoed in the distance. Alex glanced back as he ran.

The Jeeps sped closer to the pickup truck. One of the men lifted a bullhorn and shouted, "Stop the truck and throw out your weapons."

Peter and Bixby's deputy responded with more gunfire. The Jeeps roared in at angles and fired automatic weapons at the cab of the truck. The glass of the cab shattered and dull pops punctured the metal like hammered spikes. The truck swerved and tipped over onto its side.

Alex reached the garage and squatted by the gun case. Flipping it open, he gripped the guard's M17 and stood up. Megan ran up beside him, Bixby's Glock in her hand.

"Drop the guns," said a voice amplified by a loudspeaker. "We have automatic weapons trained on you from two positions."

Alex froze and stared out to the sides of the smoldering car. Shadowed figures were kneeling on the ground, aiming weapons at them.

"Drop them. Last warning."

"Let's do it, Alex," Megan said softly. She tossed Bixby's Glock to the ground.

Licking his lips, Alex tossed the M17 too.

A spotlight bathed them. Alex raised his hands with Megan to shield his eyes from the light.

The man on the speaker said, "Alex Sight, you have a choice. We'll get you out of this if you come with us. We'll even give you a plane ride home. All we want is to talk with you. And we want you off this case."

Alex jerked his head back and asked coldly, "Who are you to make that kind of offer?"

"CIA."

CHAPTER 46

ALEX WONDERED ABOUT MEGAN.

She was quiet in the car ride from Dillon's ranch to the dirt airstrip, where a small plane waited for them. As they boarded and took off, she continued to remain distant. He didn't try to talk with her. During the flight they never had any privacy.

In addition to the two pilots, three men were onboard and two sat facing them. One was the bald man who had followed Megan in San Diego, his smile glued to his lips. Another of the men was six-four and had a thick chest, thick arms, and a wide face. The third man, tall and nondescript, sat near the pilots.

"I'm Lou." The bald man seemed amused. He bent his head sideways at the big man. "And this is Frederick."

"How about Laurel and Hardy?" Knowing he had been given false names, Alex ignored Lou's calm gaze. Megan took his attention.

Yet if they had been alone, he wasn't sure there would have been anything to say to her. A small fear played at the edge of his thoughts that she somehow provided some type of hidden key to the case that he had missed all along. But that idea seemed too far-fetched.

The plane ride felt endless. Nodding in and out of poor sleep, he always woke to find one of the CIA agents watching him. Curiosity and confusion made him interested in the CIA presence. And despite their rescue, the violence at Dillon's ranch disturbed him. It felt too much like a planned attack instead of an attempt to arrest and detain. The timing was also suspicious. If the CIA knew Dillon was involved, why had they waited until now to intervene?

Hours later they landed on a bumpy runway.

Alex nudged Megan awake, but she avoided his eyes. They all exited the plane, greeted by warm rain. The CIA agents surrounded them as they hurried toward a nearby building. The rain woke Alex fully. From what he could see they had landed on a small airstrip surrounded by forest. They could be anywhere.

They entered a small, rectangular building. Scraps of paper littered the floor and the air was musty. A single naked light bulb illuminated a closed door at its far end, leaving the rest of the space dark.

Lou led them to the closed door and said, "Wait here." He went in alone, but he quickly returned and motioned them in.

Megan stared at the door, but didn't move, so Alex stepped through and she followed. The door closed behind them.

Two bright floor lamps faced two chairs in front of a desk. The lights hid whoever stood behind them. Pausing with Megan beside the chairs, Alex instantly resented the bright lights. They brought back recent, brutal memories.

"Sit, please." Pleasant and calm, the male voice had an air of unquestionable authority.

Alex hesitated, but when Megan complied, he followed her lead.

"I apologize for the cloak and dagger intrigue," the man continued. "But it's better for all of us if we do it this way, even if it isn't the nicest way to get acquainted."

"It's those special touches that make the difference," said Alex. "How do we know you're CIA?"

The man added, "Megan can verify that for you. She knows Lou."

Alex saw her stiffen. She must have been CIA at one time. Maybe that's why she had kept silent about her past. When he had spotted Lou following her in San Diego, the man must have been trying to talk to her. He turned back to the speaker. "What do you want?"

"All the information you have on Threshold. Afterward we'll take you back to Minneapolis. In exchange all you have to do is stay off the case."

Alex remembered Dillon's words, about what Joulie intended to expose at the hearing. A few other things became clear to him. "We certainly want to help the CIA keep its glossy public image."

"We all have skeletons in our closets," the man said briskly.

Alex glanced at Megan. "Most of our skeletons aren't busy doing illegal things in foreign countries."

The man's voice sharpened. "If you don't cooperate, things will get very unpleasant for you."

Alex didn't care. "You mean I'll have to spend more time with you?"

"What happened at Senator Dillon's ranch can be left in your lap." The voice was steady. "It was unfortunate he forced us to kill him."

"Did he?" asked Alex.

"His aggressiveness surprised us. It was a sloppy event, but our main goal was your rescue. More unfortunate for you is that you can never prove we were there. But we can prove you were the last person to visit Dillon."

A wave of vulnerability swept through Alex and he had to work to gather himself. "You ought to study up on your blackmail manual. Usually you need some proof for a threat like that to work."

"Yes, but the police in Billings might see it otherwise. Your plane ride to Billings. Photographs mailed to the police of your arrival. Your fingerprints on Dillon's pistols and the other guard's gun—which we have." The voice remained neutral. "It might be difficult to defend yourself. After all, who would support your side of the story?"

"Megan, for one."

"But your partner's fingerprints are on Dillon's gun too, the one that was used to kill one of his guards." The man continued. "Dillon's other guard has been removed for questioning for terrorist activities so his story won't matter much."

Alex thought of Peter. "The FBI might be upset that you killed one of their agents."

"He'll never be found." The man didn't speak further.

Alex stiffened. They only had circumstantial evidence. He wasn't concerned with the threat, but he wanted to find out what this was about. "I'll do a trade," he said. "To start, I ask, you answer."

"We ask the questions," said the man.

"Then no information." Alex doubted the CIA were prepared to kill two more FBI agents.

"You're very foolish."

Alex sat back. "Look who's talking. Until I'm satisfied, no information."

After a pause, the man said, "I won't promise answers to every question."

"The two men that were killed at Joulie's cabin were CIA, weren't they?" Alex glanced at Megan, but she showed no reaction.

"They were two of our agents who feared they would face criminal charges if Joulie's report became public knowledge. They planned to steal the doctor's file and get any copies. They were killed by Dillon's men. Dr. Joulie found out our men were following him, notified Dillon, and invited you up there. He wanted to take care of all of you at the same time."

Alex wanted to put a fist into Joulie. "Why did your agents fear Joulie's report?"

"Ask your partner. She knows."

Startled, Alex looked at Megan. She blinked at the lights.

The man continued. "You remember, Detalio, a certain person you gave information to? That person gave his information to Threshold, and they gave it to Dr. Joulie."

Megan paled and slumped in her chair.

"Why did the CIA agents go after Dr. Joulie, Megan?" asked Alex.

Her lips curled down.

"Come on, Detalio," said the man. "We don't have time for melodramatics. Tell your partner why they were worried or I will."

Turning to Alex, she said quietly, "A decade ago the CIA made sure U.S. petrochemical and mining companies gained access to exploratory sites in a number of Central and South American countries by neutralizing the local environmental activist opposition. Our politicians were paying back favors to corporations that had donated to their reelection funds. They also kept under wraps what damage the oil and mining companies did to the rainforests."

Alex eyed her. "And you gave the information to someone?"

Megan talked earnestly. "I gave it to a man who I thought was a special prosecutor. I was promised immunity. I didn't know the man gave it to Threshold."

The man behind the lights interrupted. "The current administration and leadership of the CIA wouldn't support those past activities. However we can't afford such an embarrassment now. With a confession from one of our own agents everything would be investigated. And scandals create a feeding frenzy in the media and Congress. The CIA's credibility and public trust would suffer a huge loss, as well as our operations."

"Dr. Joulie wants to give you national news coverage." Alex stared at Megan, absorbing her words.

"He won't make it to the hearing," said the man. "But you're right, that's one of his intentions. The group Joulie is part of is very clever. They're one of the more insidious homeland terrorist groups this country has ever seen. Our mandate doesn't normally allow us to interfere with domestic operations, but since the information Joulie has could threaten our international operations, we're involved." He paused. "Of course none of this would have happened if Detalio hadn't betrayed her colleagues."

Something gnawed at Alex. "How did you get the information, Megan?"

She slowly turned to him. "I was part of the operation."

His eyes widened. "You helped eliminate legitimate local opposition to petrochemical and mining companies in rainforests?"

"Detalio was the chief coordinator for our Central and South American campaigns. She has a phenomenal mind. She knew all the environmental activists, who they were, where they were, what they were involved with, and how best to eliminate them as a threat. She was very creative, suggesting bribes, blackmail, and other assorted methods of persuasion."

Alex waited for Megan to speak as something else nagged at his thoughts.

Her gaze dropped to her lap, her voice a whisper. "I was angry over my brother's death in Afghanistan. I was naïve and believed that whatever was best for U.S. interests and U.S. companies justified what we did." She looked up. "When one of the environmental activists turned up dead, I finally questioned things. By then it was too late."

"She tried to erase her guilt by selling out her peers," said the man. "For a falsely promised immunity. It's no wonder our men tried to kill her."

Clarity swept Alex. "Those cops that tried to kill us after we left the Wheeler estate—you recognized the one you shot, didn't you? Were they CIA?" She remained silent, and he remembered again when Foley had introduced her at the Wheeler house. His initial sense that she represented a threat had been correct. His voice was heated. "Why didn't you tell me?"

"Prior to the attack I thought they didn't know that I had betrayed the CIA." She paused. "I couldn't tell you—"

"Choosy on when you're direct, aren't you?" he snapped.

"Trust is a fragile thing, isn't it?" said the man. "Our men began to distrust her after she left the CIA. We were never sure of Joulie's involvement with Threshold. Even now in a court of law our proof connecting him to the terrorists would be considered sketchy at best. His attempt to expose us wasn't clear until relatively recently.

"Then our agents became convinced Detalio had talked. They wanted to talk to her first, and then eliminate her. Someone tipped off our men that you two were brought in by the FBI on the Threshold case. Possibly it was a member of Threshold who contacted them. Most likely we'll never know. It would have made a nice alibi for our agents if it had worked. Your kidnapping and subsequent deaths could have been blamed on the terrorists."

"You knew about the first attack?" Alex glared into the lights.

"After it occurred, yes."

Disgust swept Alex. "Our tax money doesn't buy much service these days, does it?"

"We didn't inform you because we didn't want to sidetrack you from your investigation. And we wanted Detalio to help you. Detalio requested a meeting with us. Unfortunately you managed to spot Lou following Megan in San Diego, and in the Salt Lake City Airport. Subsequently we were more careful and denied any further requests from her."

Alex's back arched and bitter words churned through him. Megan glanced at him, but he ignored her and asked the man, "And the attack at the Billings hotel and in Minnesota?"

"Tell me about them."

"They weren't your agents?" he asked.

"After their first miserable failed attempt in Torrey Pines, we rounded those two agents up and warned the others. A few of our men didn't heed our orders. The doctor's cabin was a mess. Now he's warned and will be harder to find."

Alex remembered the mustached killer in Billings. He had to be part of Threshold, as they had thought, and still a loose end. The brightness of the lamps hurt his eyes, but he didn't care.

There was a long silence in the room. He didn't want to speak, but as the silence lengthened, he asked woodenly, "So now what?"

"It's simple. You give us the information you have and we'll go after Dr. Joulie and the rest of Threshold. You're finished with the case. This meeting will be forgotten. In fact we never met. If you should later decide to tell the FBI, the police, or anyone else, we'll deny everything. Also evidence about Dillon's murder might appear and inconvenience you."

Alex looked at Megan, who sat stiffly in her chair. Her dishonesty bit deeper into his frustration. Turning back to the light, he couldn't see a clear path through his conflicted emotions. Even stronger was the urge to get away from Megan. The reality of losing what he had with her made him swallow. For a few moments he drummed his fingers against the arm of the chair, and then he gripped it. "Where should I begin?"

"At the beginning."

CHAPTER 47

I T WAS AFTER MIDNIGHT when they walked out of the warehouse. The rain had stopped, leaving the air thick with humidity. Alex found his feet dragging as slowly as his thoughts. Every time he glanced at Megan his throat swam with words he wanted to spit at her.

It had taken hours to give the information they had. Through it all Megan had been methodical and emotionless. He wished she would have completely fallen apart or exploded in fury. Or shown anything besides the neutral face she had insulated herself with.

After telling their separate stories, Megan typed into a laptop any relevant information from the phone lists she had seen, and from other files Foley and Gallagher had given them. They had no reason to hold anything back.

They were flown to a larger airport and then loaded aboard a small jet with Lou and Frederick. On the plane ride to Minneapolis, Megan sat rigidly in her seat, not looking at him. Alex stared out the window. Besides his mixed feelings for her, he also experienced another pain running nearly as deep.

Everything seemed more corrupt to him, more twisted. Too many betrayals had occurred. And the recent information about CIA involvement increased his disgust. Dillon's death also bothered him. The man had lost a wife, then waged war against the enemy—a corrupt system powered by greedy corporations and politicians who showed neither empathy nor willingness to change. Alex wondered how he would have reacted.

He found it ironic that he now shared Megan's distrust of the CIA. Perhaps only a few in the Agency had gone bad or betrayed their responsibility. But enough had so he knew in the future he would question things and people that previously he had accepted. His world had become more tainted.

He wanted to yell at Megan, take her by the shoulders and demand why she had kept things from him. But like her, he remained quiet.

In less than two hours they landed in a steady rain at the Minneapolis airport where a sedan waited. They got into the car with Lou and Frederick. Frederick drove.

Lou asked, "Where to?"

Alex thought on it. "The Marriot by the Mall of America." His house was too obvious, and Threshold still had a bounty on his head. And he couldn't jeopardize friends with his presence in their homes.

Lou punched it into a GPS and Frederick soon pulled their car in front of the hotel.

Lou said, "We're to make sure you remain off the case. Highly recommended."

Alex said nothing.

Frederick retrieved a large suitcase from the trunk, and they all hurried out of the rain into the protection of the modern and spacious hotel lobby.

Without explanation, Frederick set the suitcase down next to Alex. Megan stood a few paces away, looking as if she'd been cast adrift. Lou registered them for two adjoining rooms.

Alex picked up the suitcase, noting it had some weight to it. They all rode the elevator up in silence. Lou handed over their phones.

They walked to their adjacent rooms and paused. Lou and Frederick leaned against the wall in the hallway close to their doors.

Megan opened her door, but then turned to him.

Alex could barely stand to glance at her, but he did manage to say stiffly, "Let's get something to eat in a few hours." He said it for Lou's benefit.

"You're not going to forgive me, are you?" Her eyes seemed vacant.

"Would you?" he snapped.

She shut the door in his face.

Shaking his head, he walked past a smiling Lou to his own room, stopping after he opened the door. "I'm not going anywhere."

Lou didn't move. "Wonderful."

Alex entered the room, shut the door, and threw the suitcase on the bed. After staring at it, he opened it. Their gun cases were inside, along with their guns and knives.

His side, arms, and knee throbbed with dull aches. He took a shower, some pain pills, and then sat on the bed.

He scanned his phone for news. Threshold hadn't attacked anyone the night before and the press hadn't received any faxes from them. The Senate committee was going to hear bill S.229 in a public session on Monday as scheduled. Dr. Joulie, unable to be contacted, would supposedly testify. There were headlines about Dillon's murder.

He turned on the TV. Senator Dillon's murder was on every channel. The police had no clues. The house had been ransacked and several paintings and other items had been stolen.

Alex clenched his teeth, forcing himself to watch. The FBI had been called in on Dillon's murder, but he doubted they would find any evidence. Peter's body wasn't mentioned in the news. He didn't want to call Deputy Director Foley or Gallagher about Peter—it would implicate he was at Senator Dillon's ranch and they might bring him in for questioning. He didn't have time for that.

The news did mention that Chief Bixby and another officer were found dead on the senator's premises. The theory was that

Bixby and his officer had gone to Dillon's ranch to answer a call for help, and then had been killed by the same people who murdered Dillon and his bodyguard. There was a search for the missing bodyguard, who was also a suspect. Threshold wasn't implicated, especially since Dillon was an ardent environmentalist.

Alex viewed it a little longer, but there wasn't anything useful. The newscaster stated Senator Dillon's demise might hurt the chance of passage for bill S.229, since Dillon was its main sponsor in the Senate.

Scowling, he turned off the TV. One thing occurred to him. CIA agents had probably ransacked Dr. Crary's and Senator Dillon's houses, and Dr. Joulie's cabin, looking for Joulie's files. He hoped the records had survived. If the CIA managed to capture Joulie, it was over. If not, he wondered how far the CIA would go to stop the doctor.

He again considered contacting Deputy Director Foley. However communication with him might not be secure and his trust of everyone had ebbed to zero. Besides, officially he was off the case. He felt boxed in. Even if Foley believed his story of what had happened at Dillon's, there was no proof, and the CIA might carry out its threat. He wasn't ready for that yet. It could get him arrested and he didn't have time to waste.

One option was to help ensure Joulie's file made it to the Senate committee. It would expose the CIA and lend credibility to his story if they decided to try to frame him for Dillon's death. On a personal level he wanted Joulie's file to go public anyway. His conclusion put him in Threshold's camp. Ironically any effort on his part to protect Joulie's file would help accomplish the terrorists' goals. It brought a bad taste to his mouth. There didn't seem to be any way he could come out of this feeling good.

He booked the next available flight to Washington D.C. at three-thirty p.m. Joulie would be in D.C. to testify, and thus the CIA would be there to try to stop him. He wasn't sure what he was going to do yet. And even though he had promised the CIA to stay away from the case, he had done it under duress. He had no problem breaking his word.

Afterward he stared at the door joining his room with Megan's. Eventually he picked up her two gun cases and knife and knocked loudly.

She answered, wearing a blue blouse, her eyes dark, shoulders lifted, and her hands shoved into her jean pockets. Wordlessly he set the gun cases and knife on her side of the door. He started to turn away but stopped.

Wavering, anger and disgust competed for control of his tongue. "Isn't love sweet?" Other words choked his throat.

"I wanted to tell you—" she began.

"It's nice to see how you put your own moral comfort ahead of any inconvenience a few bullets might have done to me." His voice had risen and he couldn't keep the fury out of it.

She bit her lip. "Immediately after the first attack one of the rogue CIA agents sent me a text. He said if I told you anything, he would kill you. The man was a sniper."

"Kind of you to protect me," he scoffed.

She stiffened. "The second call I got while shopping before Lou arrived. It was from the CIA. They warned me that if I told you anything, they would bring both of us in and make you a national security risk. They could hold you indefinitely who knows where." She paused. "At the time they wanted us to stay on the case."

"Very selfless of you." Even if true, he didn't want to listen to her anymore.

She gazed at him, her voice defiant. "I've felt enough guilt over what I did. I tried to rectify things by talking to a special prosecutor. I thought it would be in the papers, exposing everything. After I didn't hear anything, I thought the CIA had set me up. I became frightened. I had given them an oath of silence, which I broke. I didn't know that I gave the information to a Threshold conspirator. I didn't talk to anyone again and thought it would all disappear." She finished quietly with, "I'm still paying for it."

"Join the crowd." He slammed the door.

He called Harry. Crazy Dancer had lost. In little over a week he had lost two-hundred-thirty thousand. He gripped the phone, everything but horse racing on his mind as emotions swirled through him.

"What'll it be, Alex?" Harry asked gently.

"Put two-fifty on Easy Pitch to win." It gave him odds of two-to-one.

There was silence on the other end, then Harry said, "You've had a run of bad luck, no one can deny it. And you've always been on the winning side, I'll not deny that either. But are you sure you can handle another loss as big as this, lad?"

The word *loss* triggered a shudder in his shoulders, and he said woodenly, "No, Harry, I can't. But do it anyway."

There was another pause, and Harry said, "Right."

About to hang up, he asked, "Harry, do you still have the house in Maryland?"

Harry didn't hesitate. "It's there. Locked up until I return from Florida. Do you need it?"

"For the weekend."

"It's yours, lad."

"Thanks, Harry."

"Is everything all right, Alex?"

"No, but thanks for asking." He dialed the front desk and asked for a wake-up call. Then he went to bed with an empty feeling in his stomach.

He slept fitfully until his wake-up call at eleven a.m., and quietly got dressed. Carrying the suitcase, with the gun case inside it, he left his room. The hallway was empty.

Taking the elevator to the first floor, he strode into the lobby. There was one man whose face he couldn't see, sitting in a chair holding an open newspaper in front of him. He didn't look large enough to be Frederick or small enough to be Lou. Still he might be another of the Agency's men.

He went into the hotel's restaurant, seating himself. He called an Uber.

The waiter arrived and he ordered a simple lunch of a croissant sandwich and cup of tomato soup, which he finished quickly. After paying the bill he returned to the lobby. Without pausing he walked outside to the front entrance and waited for the Uber. When it arrived, he boarded it without anyone trying to stop him. As expected.

After giving the driver several directions, to see if anyone was following, he directed the man to the airport.

He checked in for the flight to D.C. There hadn't been a welcoming party at the airport and he hoped his luck would continue. After getting through security, he located a clothing store and bought a full change of clothes, including jeans and a shirt, which he put on in the restroom, stuffing his other clothing into the shopping bag.

At another shop he bought several bars of dark chocolate and some aspirin. In another fifteen minutes he sat at the boarding gate with over an hour to kill. Reflections about the last days swam through him, most of them painful. Megan's face kept appearing in his mind. He was glad when boarding began.

As he stood in line, he sensed someone approaching from the left. Three people separated him from the boarding entrance and he resolved he wouldn't be stopped now. No matter what. As the person neared, he jerked his head around and his eyes widened.

"Hi, dear." Megan wore a gray suit, her jaw set stiffly. She looked fresh, alive and beautiful, but her expression seemed lifeless. She stepped up to him with a forced smile and kissed his cheek. Smiling at the man behind them, she asked, "Do you mind if I get on with my fiancé?"

"No problem." The man smiled and gestured her into the line.

Alex stared ahead coldly as she stood beside him, looping her arm around his. After they passed through the gate, they separated and walked along the gangway together. He asked through gritted teeth, "What's the matter, did you get lonely?"

"I knew you were going to D.C.," she said just as stiffly. "I knew you wouldn't stay off the case. It didn't take long to learn which flight you were on. Don't worry, I was careful."

Words boiled in his head.

"You have a right to be angry with me, Alex, but I'm coming. Whether you like it or not, we work well together."

He fumbled for a response but was unable to argue with her.

After they seated themselves, she said, "They'll figure it out, if they haven't already. They might be waiting for us at the airport in Washington."

She was right. He didn't know what he would do if they tried to stop him. Even though he wasn't tired, he closed his eyes. It was painful to look at her, be around her. He barely managed to shove down the words he wanted to hurl at her.

Blue and white. Those colors filled his mind before he understood what was happening—*a young man holding boxes smiled at him, holding them out to him. Something twisted the young man's face into a grimace as he slid into darkness...*

Alex twitched in his seat, his hands gripping the armrests tightly. Blinking his eyes open, he noticed Megan watching him, but he turned away and closed his eyes again.

CHAPTER 48

OVER THE LAST HOUR Deputy Director Foley had repeated the same routine. Stare at his pictures. Take a sip of cold coffee. Pop mints.

His attention focused mainly on the photo of the spotted owl in the dark forest. The photo had always intrigued him because the dim light of the woods didn't quite hide the owl—which seemed as though it was tucked deep in a black box. Safely observing the world. Protected and ready to pounce on any intruders. It was a position he had always favored. To be secure and ready to target your enemies before they attacked you.

He checked his watch again, as he had every five minutes for the past hour. It was almost five. They would be here soon. Turning back to his desk, he set his coffee mug to the left. Resting his forearms on the top, he stared at his office door. His big hands were steady. He was ready.

The intercom buzzed and his office assistant announced, "Mr. Gallagher is here to see you."

"Send him in."

Gallagher opened the door and stomped in, sitting in the chair in front of the desk, popping a loud bubble with the gum stuffed in his mouth. Foley noticed his suit was wrinkled, but for once it looked clean. Probably an accident. His arm was still in a sling.

"Do I have to ask every time I come in here?" Gallagher frowned at the computer.

Foley grimaced and swiveled in his chair, turning off Garth Brooks' *Shameless*. Turning back to Gallagher, he asked, "What do you have?"

"Nothing turned up on Jerry Peiser's or Michael Beator's phone history or any other records. Beator's friend, James Watson, is a dead end. He has ironclad alibis, as do the two guys at the IMF-World Bank D.C. demonstrations."

Foley studied Gallagher. "Is security ready for the Capitol hearing?"

Gallagher straightened. "Press and other congressional staff will be allowed in first. A number of spectators will be given a pass at the door for the hearing on a first-come, first-served basis. We expect a big crowd which will be kept back at special gates and allowed in single file. Everyone permitted to enter will go through metal detectors and have to agree to be searched. Streets will be blocked off to traffic in all directions a half-mile from the Capitol."

Foley cleared his throat. "How many agents are going to be assigned?"

"One hundred. We'll also have the support of the Capitol Police for crowd control and premises security. They'll clear the building tonight and they've doubled their staff for Monday. The rest of the building will be closed off and secured." Gallagher sat back. "There will be several hundred people inside the Capitol."

Foley heard Gallagher's implied statement of risk. "We can't keep everyone out."

Gallagher gestured impatiently. "What's the sense of getting this security ready for Dr. Joulie when he hasn't even shown?"

Foley leaned back in his chair. "What about Dr. Crary?"

Gallagher unwrapped another piece of gum and shoved it past his lips. "Crary responded to the emergency Coast Guard message. Says he was fishing and he'll bring his boat back in a few days."

"After the hearing is over." Foley wanted Crary to pay if he was part of Threshold.

Gallagher nodded. "Exactly."

Foley lifted his chin. "Joulie has shown up."

Gallagher sat rock still. "Where?"

Foley leaned on his desk. "He turned himself in to our office an hour ago, asking for our protection until he testifies."

"Where is he now?" Gallagher's free hand formed a fist on his thigh.

Foley hit the switch on his intercom. "Could you please send in Dr. Joulie?"

Gallagher's eyes widened as he twisted to face the door.

Dr. Joulie walked in. The doctor wore a black suit and carried a small briefcase, appearing confident, his gaze sharp.

Foley motioned to the other chair in front of his desk.

Joulie sat, setting the briefcase on the floor beside the chair.

Foley eyed the doctor. "Dr. Joulie, this is Bill Gallagher. He heads up our counterterrorism division."

Joulie nodded at Gallagher, then regarded Foley. "Can you guarantee my safe passage into the hearing?"

Foley lifted a few fingers. "I can."

"Wait," said Gallagher. "Two CIA agents were killed on your island."

"How did you learn that?" Foley frowned.

Gallagher shrugged. "One of my contacts in the agency reached out."

"I'm innocent," said Joulie.

Gallagher frowned. "What did they want from you?"

Joulie turned to him. "They seemed to think I had some file of interest."

"About what?" Gallagher's face tightened.

"They never said." The doctor regarded Foley.

Gallagher snorted and looked at Foley. "We should contact the CIA. They'll want to talk to him."

"Dr. Joulie has committed no crime," Foley said firmly. "Unless charges are publicly brought against him, he'll remain under our protection. There is no evidence of his complicity with Threshold. This is not the Agency's business, nor is it their jurisdiction. As a citizen, Dr. Joulie has a right to our protection."

Gallagher glared at him. "He's wanted for questioning by the police over the two CIA agents killed on his island."

"I've already questioned him and I'm satisfied," said Foley. "I notified the Duluth police of the interview and they're satisfied that he's in our custody until the hearing is over."

Gallagher glared at Foley, then at Joulie. "Do you have anything to tell us that we haven't already heard?"

Joulie hesitated. "I'm tired."

Gallagher got up. "All right. See everyone Monday." He stomped out of the office and slammed the door.

Joulie brought his briefcase onto his lap. "Some of what I want to say is already in the transcripts I've handed to the Senate committee members. The rest is in here." He patted the briefcase.

Foley wondered what was in the briefcase. "Anything else I need to know?"

"Just get me to the hearing."

Foley clasped his hands. "You took quite a risk coming to us like this."

Joulie gave a thin smile. "Senator Dillon was my friend and he held you in high regard."

Foley spoke casually. "If Senator Dillon had anything to do with Threshold, now that he's dead, you have to wonder if anyone is running the terrorists anymore."

Joulie's voice softened. "There's no proof Senator Dillon was part of Threshold. But don't you think it would be a mistake to assume only one person is at a high level in their organization?"

Considering the underlying message, Foley saw Joulie in a different light.

"Some members of the CIA seem invested in preventing me from testifying," said Joulie. "Where are you going to put me tonight?"

Foley had already considered that. "FBI safe house. You'll be heavily guarded so you won't have to worry about the CIA."

"Good."

Foley added, "My men will report to me hourly. I won't take any chances."

"And you won't have any regrets."

Foley heard the implied promise of *vice president*, which Dillon had made to him not long ago in his limousine. Not wanting to be direct, he said, "Senator Dillon supported me for the deputy director position."

Joulie smiled again. "He mentioned that quite a few of his colleagues were just as impressed by you."

Foley found that only slightly reassuring. "Have the terrorists ever contacted you? Do you know where they are?"

"No." Joulie shrugged. "Probably leaving the country."

Foley didn't like it. "You think they're done?"

"If they accomplished their goals." Joulie's eyes narrowed. "If I had to guess, I would say their highest priority now would be escape."

"They killed FBI agents. It would be a good thing to bring them down." He knew Joulie understood the emphasis in his voice. This wasn't a request.

Joulie sat back, his eyes neutral like his face. "I would like to help you, but unfortunately I don't have any contact information."

"You're doing all you can, aren't you?" Foley said it with a wan smile.

***

Later, after Joulie had been escorted out and was on his way to the safe house, Foley sat in his chair listening to country music and looking at his wall photos. Joulie had told him what he wanted to hear. And he felt the risks were low, the potential gain high.

After contemplating the different elements of his plan, he considered his motivations. Protecting the environment. Justice. Power. They all rang with equality. And with power the other two components would be easier to accomplish.

He thought about all the loose ends. Considering Gallagher, the CIA, Joulie, and the terrorists, there were too many variables. And Alex Sight and Megan Detalio were wild cards. Equally troubling, since CIA agents had gone after Joulie, there was a chance they had also killed Senator Dillon. Thus the CIA, or at least some of their agents, might resort to desperate measures to stop Joulie. There were too many uncertainties. Some of them needed to be accounted for.

And Gallagher was capable of anything. The fact that Gallagher hadn't told him the two dead men on Joulie's island were CIA grated on him. Also an agent had informed him that Gallagher had found surveillance devices in their offices, yet Gallagher had said nothing. Foley wouldn't put anything past Gallagher now. He needed some insurance. With one call he could get all he needed.

After giving Joulie enough time to make a call, he left his office. Taking the elevators down to the garage, he sat in his car. The warm air made him sweat.

From the glove compartment he took a voice changer already plugged into a disposable cell phone. The voice changer could make his voice sound like a woman.

On the cell phone he punched the number Dillon had given him a few days ago. He hoped it wasn't the dead senator's phone.

The phone was answered with silence.

Foley waited a few seconds, and then said, "I'm calling about a mutual acquaintance, Senator Dillon." His heart pounded.

There was another pause, and then, "I've been expecting your call."

Foley quickly stated what he needed. Firepower to stop the CIA from taking Joulie—and the Threshold terrorists dead. He wasn't sure the man on the other end of the phone would agree. To make it easier, he gave the safe house address.

After a short pause, the listener on the other end said, "All right. Agreed." And hung up.

Foley walked back into the building, glad he would have reinforcements. Even if they were expendable.

CHAPTER 49

GALLAGHER SQUEEZED HIS WATER mug so hard his knuckles were white. It had been over an hour since he left Deputy Director Foley. Since then he had sat in his office and brooded. Foley's protectiveness of Dr. Joulie was like a barb in his throat. He wasn't sure what motivated Foley to protect the doctor, but it made him distrust the deputy director even more. Foley was playing by the rules he chose. Essentially the Bureau would protect one of Threshold's members. There was no proof of it, of course. They might never have proof of Joulie's complicity.

An hour ago he had checked in with Juanita, but nothing new had materialized. And he had also put in a call to his CIA contact. He hoped he didn't have long to wait.

Selecting a Mozart song on his MP3 player, he turned the volume low. He needed something to help soothe his anger and frustration.

The previous night's efforts sat on his desk. A half-dozen rice-grain-sized opaque disks had been found in his and Foley's offices, and in the phone of Foley's assistant. Transmitting listening devices. They had discovered the bugs manually. The electronic sweeps hadn't detected them. They were super high resolution, long distance, self-adhesive units tuned into one receiver, so no one else could listen in. Gallagher had never seen anything like it. His friends thought they were originals. Very expensive.

The surveillance had been conducted through long-range receivers which were untraceable. It meant whoever had tapped the Bureau, and it had to be one of their own agents, would probably lay low and remain untouched. Whoever it was, it would be nearly impossible to identify the person.

He kicked his trash can in frustration, sending it banging into the wall. Whoever the traitor was, the man was scum. Gallagher wondered how Threshold had turned an agent.

Since Peter had survived the Trenton stakeout without serious injury, and had been involved during much of the case, Gallagher planned to do a phone check on the man. Peter hadn't responded to calls. Maybe he was on the run. They would have to search the man's apartment as soon as possible. If Peter or someone else supported Threshold, it explained how the two dead men posing as cops at the Palmer massacre had no identity. Someone might have deleted records on databases.

Gallagher had all kinds of suspicions, but no proof of anything. Even with all the victims and murdered Bureau agents, Threshold was still at large. Suddenly he understood how someone might get so fed up with the system that he might reach a boiling point and want to blow someone away.

His cell phone rang. He answered it, recognizing the voice that greeted him. Walter Zimmerman. One of the CIA's top operations officers, and the CIA contact who had informed him that the dead men on Dr. Joulie's island were CIA.

Gallagher had worked with the Agency in the past. The Bureau and Agency had different mandates, but it was in the country's best interest for both to cooperate. And they were out of time.

"Bill." Walter always sounded relaxed, as if he had just come back from a great vacation.

Gallagher cleared his throat. "Walter."

"We've got a problem," said Walter.

"He's right here." Gallagher stiffened. "Dr. Joulie turned himself in to Deputy Director Foley." After a few seconds of silence, he continued. "Foley won't give him to you and he'll ensure Joulie arrives at the hearing. He'll be heavily guarded." He couldn't keep the acid from his voice when speaking Foley's or Joulie's name.

"Not much justice these days, is there?" asked Walter.

"It makes me want to puke." Gallagher blamed Foley for much of it.

Walter spoke slowly with emphasis. "We can't let Joulie go public with the information in his briefcase."

"What's in it?" Gallagher wondered if he should hang up. Playing outside the rules wasn't his expertise or value system.

"A few past mistakes the Agency was involved in. The problem is that Threshold will look like martyrs to a cause." Walter nonchalantly continued. "What about tonight, Bill, where will Joulie be?

Gallagher's insides screamed that he should get off the phone immediately, but he didn't. He decided to treat it as a discussion, which didn't commit him to anything. He swallowed hard. "A Bureau safe house, under heavy guard."

"You know where the safe house is, don't you?"

Gallagher hesitated. "Sure. But Foley will assign the men that guard Joulie."

Walter continued matter-of-factly, as if they were planning a fishing trip. "You could take us there tonight and tell Foley's men to go home."

Sweat covered Gallagher's upper lip. "And why would they do that? Just up and leave someone that the deputy director ordered them to guard?"

"We'll have a transfer of custody order signed by the Attorney General authorizing the CIA to take possession of Joulie." Walter made it sound like he was giving him a grocery list.

Gallagher's mind raced. "Under what pretext? Joulie isn't a prisoner."

"Terrorist ties. And with you there, Foley's men won't put up any resistance."

"Foley will fire me, Walter." There was no way he would put himself on the line like that. He imagined his career ending, with Foley smiling.

"You're interested in the deputy director position, aren't you?"

Gallagher held his breath.

"We believe we can help you, Bill. We have some people close to the president's ear who can pave the way. We need someone like you, who knows the score and has the right set of priorities. Someone who has demonstrated he can work cooperatively with the Agency."

"Is the Agency really behind this?" He needed time to think, to slow his panic. What if this was a rogue bunch of—

"The people who count are."

He got himself under control. Deep in thought, it was his turn to remain silent. He trusted Walter. And the truth of the matter was that Foley could get rid of him anytime he wanted. He would always be looking over his shoulder, worried about losing a job he had busted his butt for. Besides, there was no way he wanted to stand idly by and let Threshold win. Damn them all. Damn Foley and Joulie. They were scum.

He wiped his brow. "What happens to Joulie?"

"He'll be treated like any other terrorist. He'll be locked up in complete isolation, probably out of the country until we learn everything. He'll never be able to go public with anything."

Gallagher was glad Walter couldn't smell his sweat. Fear swept over him and he didn't care if Walter heard it now. "Why not go to Foley if you have a legal order to take custody of Joulie?"

"He won't obey it. Or at least he'll delay the handover with some technicality so Joulie can attend the hearing. Worse, he might go public with it and expose our involvement. You, on the other hand, won't have a choice. You don't have the authority to delay a handover. We'll come to you, show you the legal order, and you'll be bound to take us to Joulie. Foley can't fire you if you obey a written order of custody transfer signed by the Attorney General." Walter sighed. "Maybe he'll reprimand you. That's all."

Gallagher gripped his chair. On his desk a rose stood in a slender vase. He planned to bring it home tonight for his wife's birthday. It brought a pang to his chest. He thought of his kids and abruptly he had no more qualms. If Threshold was allowed to get away with multiple murders, backed up by traitors in the Bureau and society, the country wasn't far from anarchy. It wasn't the kind of world he wanted to leave his children.

"Did CIA agents kill Senator Dillon?" He had to ask, since CIA agents had attacked Dr. Joulie.

"There was a shootout. Self-defense. It wasn't intended." Walter's voice remained calm. "Murdering senators isn't our mandate, Bill."

The answer didn't put him at ease, but he didn't care about Dillon anyway. Taking a big breath, he felt as if he was about to dive from a hundred-foot platform into a bucket of water. But he didn't see he had any other choice. "Where do you want to meet?"

CHAPTER 50

A T SEVEN P.M. ALEX and Megan landed at Reagan National Airport and picked up their gun cases. Alex had managed to get an hour of sleep. After eating some dark chocolate, he felt recovered.

He rented an Accord. Megan remained quiet, and he found other places to look besides her eyes. The air was sultry when they left the terminal.

Wary when no one greeted them at the airport, Alex took his time driving to Harry's house. He followed the George Washington Memorial Parkway north, driving slowly, switching lanes, and sometimes speeding up to see if any cars followed. In a quarter hour he took the Interstate north, and a half hour later they reached Germantown.

He exited near the residential neighborhood of Waters Landing Drive and drove to a big two-story walkout with brick on the lower half.

It was a quiet neighborhood and he was happy to be off the busy expressways of D.C. They took their gun cases and walked up to the front door. Hanging from a hook, an overhead wind chime made of metal strips tinkled lightly in the breeze. Alex unhooked the chimes, sorting out the magnetized one with a key attached.

Megan raised her eyebrows, and he said, "Harry's an old friend with mutual trust."

"Good for you." Megan sounded weary.

Her hurt expression didn't make him feel good and he decided to end the digs at her. He unlocked and pushed the door, waiting for her to walk in first. He stepped inside after her.

Something hard pushed against his back, and he stopped.

"Don't move."

Alex recognized Lou's voice.

The hallway light came on, and Megan stopped a few steps in. Lou's partner, Frederick, appeared in front of her, a silenced SIG Sauer in his left hand.

Alex turned slightly.

Lou stood behind him, smiling. "We missed you too. We left last night for D.C., and they listened to your calls. Now set the gun cases on the floor and take a walk to the couch."

Alex set down his case, as did Megan.

Lou pushed Alex forward, and then shut and locked the door.

Frederick stepped aside as they walked through the tiled entryway into a large living room with an open ceiling. Two sofas and two easy chairs were spaced apart. A few tables held decorative clay art pieces. The warm air was stagnant.

Megan sat on one end of a large couch which partially faced the front door. Alex took the other end of it. Lou used his foot to shove the gun cases to the side of the hallway.

Frederick sat in an easy chair against a wall adjacent to the front entryway.

"Get comfortable." Lou dragged a chair from a small table to the other side of the front entryway, opposite Frederick, and sat. "Slide your knives to the far wall."

Alex and Megan followed his instructions.

"You haven't been good at all." Lou's lips formed a pout. "Very naughty in fact. Isn't that right, Frederick?"

Frederick nodded once, his face granite.

"You two make a cute couple," said Alex.

Lou smiled. "So do you two. Still fighting?"

Alex exchanged glances with Megan. "No, we made up."

Lou continued smiling. "Good, because we're going to stay here until the hearing is over. Then you're free to go."

Regarding both men with distrust, Alex couldn't help but gaze at their silenced SIG Sauers.

"These," Lou waved his gun, "are just in case you're foolish."

Alex slumped into the couch.

"We've been monitoring your conversations with Harry." Lou grinned. "That last bet you made, two-fifty. A bit hefty, wasn't it? Feeling desperate?"

Megan glanced at Alex, and then glared at Lou.

Alex tried to think of anything to give them a chance. "I'm hungry."

Lou looked at Frederick. "Want to order some dinner?"

Frederick nodded. "Sure."

Lou smiled. "We'll buy." He plucked a cell phone from his pocket. "What does everyone want on their pizza?"

Recent images swam into Alex's mind. "Green olives and onions."

"Veggies," said Megan.

"Sausage and pepperoni." Frederick lifted his right hand. "Order me a large."

Lou's smile widened. He pressed a few keys, saying, "Already found a delivery place and put it on speed-dial." He winked. "Knew you would be hungry." He was quickly talking to a clerk and placed an order for four pizzas. After listing the types, he asked, "How long will it take? All right. Thank you." He smiled again. "Half-hour."

CHAPTER 51

I T HAD BEEN DIFFICULT, but not impossible, for Max to follow Sight and Detalio from the airport. Sight had driven around, obviously looking for a tail. But Max was even better at not being detected.

From a block away he had watched them go into the house. Afterward he pulled a little closer, parked in the street, and considered things.

He was sullen over his two failures with Sight and Detalio. And upset further that his employers had fired him. But the million-dollar bounty on Sight was even better. And this was personal now. He wanted Sight and Detalio as much for his pride as for his desire for the money.

The neighborhood was quiet, mostly dark with a little light from soft lamps at the street corners. The ambiance suited Max. He wondered what everyone did in these neighborhoods, which seemed more like graveyards.

A number of options presented themselves to him as he sat in the car, some more clever than others. But in the end, he chose to be practical. He figured the back door would be best. After giving them a half-hour to settle in, he left the car, his guns under a long trench coat. The style suited him and hid the weapons nicely. It was hot and sweat ran down his back, but he didn't mind.

He walked along the street, enjoying the stroll.

A pizza delivery car turned into the driveway of the house he was approaching. The driver got out, wearing a blue and white pizza coat and a hat.

Max smiled, noting the young man was the right size. He walked up the driveway, smiling at the delivery man who pulled a warmer bag from the back seat. The scent of pizza made him hungry

"You're fast," said Max.

The man turned around, smiling. "You bet. Do you want me to carry it to the door for you?"

Max winked. "Actually I'm going to need a few other things too, if you don't mind."

CHAPTER 52

AFTER SITTING IN SILENCE, Alex said to Lou, "I have a bad feeling about the pizza delivery guy."

Lou's brows hunched. "What's that?"

"Someone's going to kill him." Alex waited for laughter.

Lou became wide-eyed. "I've heard of your abilities and I take them seriously. What do you want me to do?"

Alex lifted his chin to the front hallway. "Go to the front door and make sure he's alright when he arrives."

Lou looked at Frederick with a grim expression. "Okay, Frederick, listen up. I'll go to the front door and wait for someone to shoot the pizza guy, while Sight and Detalio try to put one over on you."

Frederick remained serious, but his lips trembled until he chuckled, finally bursting into laughter. Lou joined in for a few moments.

They both stopped abruptly, and Lou said, "Sight, you're not too bright, are you?"

Unable to come up with anything that sounded plausible, Alex said, "Can I use the bathroom?"

"Be my guest." With a smile, Lou got up and motioned left down a short adjacent hallway.

The doorbell rang.

Putting up a hand, Lou said, "You'll have to wait. It's the dead delivery guy." He waved his gun. "No tricks. Frederick's finger might slip if you do anything funny." With quick strides he walked to the front door and peered through the peephole. Frederick sat against the wall, gun in hand.

Alex gave a slight twitch of his eyes in the direction of Frederick. Megan slid her feet closer to the couch, inching out on the cushion she sat on.

Frederick's gaze shifted to Megan. He pointed his gun at her and slowly shook his head.

The doorbell rang again. Tucking his gun in his belt at his back, Lou opened the door halfway, the delivery man hidden from Alex's view.

"Evening, sir. Max here with your pizza delivery."

"Hello, Max." Lou reached into his pocket for his billfold and pulled three twenties, handing them to the delivery man, who handed Lou four pizza boxes.

Alex turned rigid when he saw the blue and white colors on the boxes.

"Keep the change." Lou started to shut the door, but the delivery man stuck a hand through, holding a note.

"The cook sent this note, sir."

Frowning, Lou took the piece of paper from the man's hand. Confusion, then tension creased Lou's face as he read it.

The door slammed into Lou's forehead, sending him flying backward into the entryway where he landed sprawled on his back. The pizza boxes slid along the tiled floor.

Frederick got up immediately and in one stride stood at the corner, peering around it.

Megan was already off the couch, rushing Frederick from the side.

Simultaneously a big-shouldered man strode in, wearing western boots, jeans, and a trench coat. He held a Mossberg Shockwave. Alex recognized the pump-action fourteen-inch barrel immediately. It held five shells and could be fired using one hand.

The man in the entryway stared at Alex and aimed the gun.

Alex's eyes widened when he recognized the man's puffy face and handlebar moustache. He rolled off the end of the couch as the shotgun *whomped!*—making a hole in the sofa where he had been sitting. Alex scrambled behind the couch, peeking above it.

Frederick absorbed several body blows from Megan's fists, and still managed to shove her to the floor where she landed on her back. He pointed his gun at her, and then peeked around the hallway corner at the killer.

Kicking the door shut, Max fired the shotgun at Frederick, who pulled back from the corner—which was left with a big gouge. Max took one step and kicked a slowly rising Lou in the neck. Lou collapsed and his head lolled to the side.

Megan scrambled across the room behind an easy chair.

Remaining silent at the corner, out of sight, Frederick kept his gun waist high.

Hurrying to the side wall opposite Frederick, Alex heard the killer's boots on the tile floor. He quietly moved the chair away from the corner, and nodded once to Frederick. The big man lifted his chin in acknowledgment.

Max's shotgun came into view first. But in his right hand he now held a Taurus 9mm that he shoved around the corner, firing blindly at Frederick.

The shot hit Frederick's left upper arm. The big man cried out, dropped his gun, and slumped against the wall.

Simultaneously Megan rose from across the room and threw one of the clay art pieces at Max. Max ducked it and fired the shotgun, which blasted a hole in the easy chair she leapt behind.

Lunging, Alex barreled into Max from the side, but it felt like running into a telephone pole. His shoulder ached on impact. He tried to push with his feet as he grappled with the man's barrel chest. The cuts on his arms burned. His ribs exploded with pain as Max drove the butt of the shotgun into him. Gasping, he fell to his knees and slumped against the wall.

Frederick slid off the wall and encircled Max's neck with his right arm. Alex lunged at Max's legs from behind, knocking the man down to his knees. Frederick twisted sideways to keep Max from targeting him with the Taurus.

Max fired the shotgun again at Megan to keep her pinned down. Alex hit the killer in the back. Growling, Max somehow managed to stand up, even under Frederick's weight. The killer quickly stepped backward, smashing Frederick into the wall.

Alex stood and hit Max from the side in the head and ribs, but the man ignored him.

Dropping his Taurus 9mm, Max elbowed Frederick twice in the head, sending the big man collapsing to the floor.

Megan was rising, and Max swung the shotgun.

Alex jumped on Max's back and gouged his eyes with his fingers.

Giving a hoarse shout, Max dropped the shotgun. Slamming Alex back into the wall, he turned and held Alex in a bear hug, lifting him off the floor. Alex chopped at Max's bull neck with both hands as Max spun them around.

Megan scrambled toward Frederick's gun.

Max saw her, swore, and kicked the Taurus 9mm, sending it skittering over the tiled hallway into the bathroom. He rolled Alex and himself along the wall until they were through the bathroom door. Alex's last glimpse of Megan was of her picking up Frederick's SIG Sauer.

Locking his feet behind Max's knees, Alex tripped him. They dropped hard onto the bathroom tile, with Max rolling atop of Alex. Glimpsing the handgun several feet away, Alex reached for it.

Max released him and punched his arm and chest. Gasping, Alex's arm and hand spasmed, knocking the gun farther across the floor.

From his knees, Max kicked the bathroom door shut, then reached up and locked it.

Alex's legs were pinned by Max's weight. Sitting up, he threw punches at the man's chin.

"Alex!" yelled Megan.

"Don't fire!" he shouted, imagining a shotgun blast through the door.

Roaring, Max butted Alex's head, knocking him down, and lunged past him for the gun.

Megan kicked the bathroom door.

Twisting, Alex grabbed one of Max's ankles and yanked it. Max swung an arm wildly for the gun, but instead swept it around the corner of the L-shaped room, past the bathtub. Alex twisted from under Max's legs and hauled himself along the killer's back, while the big man crawled on his stomach.

Megan kicked the door again.

Max jabbed an elbow, sending a stab of pain into Alex's ribs. Gasping, Alex lifted and pounded the man's head into the floor three times.

Max went limp.

With heaving breaths, Alex pulled himself past Max as the bathroom door was kicked a third time. A growl erupted behind him. Alex reached the corner, extending his arm around it to grab the gun.

Alex heard a click, twisted around, and jerked his face to the side as a switchblade flashed past, sticking into the wall next to his cheek. He was eyeball to eyeball with Max.

The door was kicked in with splintering wood. "Alex!"

Sweeping his hand, Alex grasped the handgun and shoved it into Max's chest as the knife was drawn back.

Alex fired three shots—and heard Megan firing too.

Max slumped onto him, forcing him onto his back. Gasping, Alex struggled to push the dead weight to the side.

Everything seemed to slow down.

Alex was aware of Megan kneeling beside him. She quickly left. He wasn't sure how long that interval lasted. Sometime later he blinked, and she was beside him again. His vision slowly cleared and his mind returned from the brink of blackout.

The pain had sorted itself out. It was all over his body and hammered at him with deep aches. His left cheek burned too. The killer must have sliced his skin.

Megan dabbed at the cut on his face with cotton balls. Wincing, he slowly rose, wanting to get away from the dead man. Megan helped him. Together they stumbled from the bathroom to the couch where he collapsed onto his back.

Megan swung his feet up and put a pillow beneath his head. She left, soon back with antiseptic and bandages for his face.

Finished, she knelt on the floor close to him. "Oh, Alex," she said softly.

"I hate delivery pizza," he whispered. He avoided her gaze. He didn't want to acknowledge her concern for him, but also couldn't deny the panic he had felt when the killer had shot at her. "The note," he whispered.

She looked at him in confusion, and then left his side. In seconds she returned, holding up the piece of paper Max had handed to Lou through the doorway. It read; *Road kill can't run.*

He grunted.

Tossing the slip away, she said, "We need to get you to a hospital."

"No. It's mainly the ribs. Everyone seems to go for them. Lou and Frederick?"

Megan leaned closer. "Both alive, unconscious. I bandaged Frederick's gunshot. We can't leave him here."

It came as he lay there, not vivid as it usually did, but sharper than his senses had been moments earlier. He was first aware of Megan's dark hair shining like velvet on her shoulders to the side of him. But his attention shifted to the vaulted ceiling, pulled upward to detailed patterns in the wood beams—*people ran through trees and smoke, guns fired into darkness, vague shapes, shouts, a fence...*

Not wanting to see any of it, Alex stared without blinking, the images taunting his sensibilities. There wasn't anything cohesive about it so he waited until the darkness shifted—*a tall man stood over a bloodied woman's body, pointing a gun down, leering... Alex's view slowly panned around the two figures until he stood behind the tall man, beneath a low branch on a large tree...*

The ceiling abruptly came into focus again. His body had gone completely stiff and his back was arched off the couch. Slowly he sank into the cushions and closed his eyes, his mind swirling with the images that had come to him. As he drifted off, Jenny's words haunted him once more, floating to him from the fringe of consciousness...*But what if you didn't see the whole picture?*

He blinked his eyes open with panic clawing at his throat, remembering the images, wanting to call Megan's name. Lifting his head, he saw her and fell back, gasping.

Megan stroked his forehead with a damp cloth. "It's all right," she said softly.

"How long?" he gasped.

"Ten minutes."

It felt like an hour. "Get me some chocolate. And pain pills. In the car."

Leaving his side, she returned with both.

After swallowing the pills, he took a bite of chocolate, unable to tell her what he had seen, not wanting to admit it himself.

"What is it?" she asked.

"I want to be alone. Could you go somewhere else, please?" He knew she wouldn't leave.

Looking as if he had struck her, she sat back, hurt visible in her eyes. Eyes narrowed, she leaned closer. "Was it that bad?"

"I don't want you with me."

Her voice remained steady. "Too bad. Regardless of what you think might happen, we both want the same thing."

He glanced at her. "What's that?"

"Joulie testifying, Threshold destroyed." She rested a hand on his arm. "I'm not Jenny, and this isn't three years ago."

It took a few moments for him to speak. "If we do this, you give me your word to stay by my side."

"Sure."

"Damn you." He heaved a breath. "If you were Joulie, where would you be safe from the CIA, where even they couldn't touch you?"

"He might turn himself in to the police," said Megan.

He gave a small shake of his head. That hurt his neck. "The CIA would trump their jurisdiction."

"The FBI."

He eyed her. "How much access did Foley give you to FBI databases?"

"I told him if he wanted this case closed fast, I needed full access." She studied him. "I researched safe houses in D.C. at the hotel."

He slowly sat up. "Then I assume you know the location of an FBI safe house convenient to D.C., not in the city proper, most likely gated, somewhat isolated, maybe near a forest."

"I do." She helped him to his feet.

"I need a clean shirt." He heaved a deep breath. "Then it's time to see our terrorist doctor."

CHAPTER 53

RELIEF WASHED OVER ODYSSEUS when two cars drew up close to the storage locker he was parked in front of. Their lights flashed on and off twice in the evening twilight.

Odysseus got out of his car. Elation filled him over seeing Patroclus and Achilles as they exited their cars. Like him, both wore Lycra and black hoods.

He walked up to the storage locker and punched in the security code. Quickly lifting the small garage door, he led the others in. It was stuffy inside. Achilles found the light switch and Patroclus pulled the door down.

Odysseus gave Patroclus a warm embrace. Achilles ignored them. No one said a word as they walked forward to see what waited for them.

Wooden crates were piled at the back of the locker, covered but not sealed.

Achilles threw back a lid and lifted a Remington 700 rifle with a telescopic sight and adjustable cheek piece. Silencers were in the boxes. "Beautiful."

"We should be running." Patroclus stood in the center of the locker, looking at Odysseus.

Pivoting, Achilles slowly swung the rifle toward Patroclus' chest. "You should be shot for even thinking something like that, you coward."

With the back of his hand Odysseus calmly pushed aside the barrel of Achilles' rifle, ignoring the anger evident in the man's voice. Stepping closer to Patroclus, he put a hand on his shoulder. "One last action, then we go to Europe," he said softly. "Joulie has to make it to the hearing."

Achilles snorted in derision and turned back to his box.

Patroclus was silent, then nodded and went to another of the boxes.

Odysseus couldn't tell Patroclus that he felt the same thing. That they should run. It wasn't a lack of commitment he felt, but fear. He went to a box and began to get ready.

CHAPTER 54

ALEX SAT IN THE Accord, parked near a four-way intersection, kitty-corner to the safe house Megan had directed him to. It was less than ten miles south of Harry's house, in Montgomery County, one of the most affluent in the country. But not this section of it. Most were tract homes on small lots—except for the one they were looking at.

The four-acre lot took up the whole corner, with an empty lot on the east side of the house. Its backyard ran up to a thick grove of trees, past which lay Great Seneca Highway. On the other side of the road was Seneca Creek State Park where Megan said some of the *Blair Witch Project* had been filmed amid dogwood, maple, and oak trees.

A ten-foot-tall chain link fence topped with three strands of barbed wire, all covered in vines, surrounded the lot. With the help of some well-positioned trees, the house and lot remained hidden from the two streets bordering it. The driveway opened onto Morning Light Terrace, where they waited a hundred feet away.

A full moon softly lit the area.

While they waited, Alex tried to answer questions that kept running through his mind. Questions about himself and Megan, and about his life.

The death and violence of the last days had taken a toll on him, and the last incident in Harry's house seemed to bring it all into focus. Killing Max, the prone bodies of Lou and Frederick, and the young pizza delivery man they found dead in the car outside, had all added to the conclusion that he didn't want violence, any of it, in his life anymore. He had to get out. That first day at the Wheeler's he had felt it, but now it was undeniably crucial. It was time to rescue himself.

While driving away from Harry's house, they had used Lou's cell phone to call for an ambulance for the CIA agents, and then wiped the phone and tossed it into the street. Alex decided he would come forward the next day. Minimally he owed Harry an apology and a cleaning fee for the mess they had left.

Megan had remained quiet during the ride, her expression drawn. Her long, wild curly hair framed her face. Alex thought she had never looked more beautiful or more subdued.

Chewing chocolate, he stared at the nearby estate, cocoa and aspirin giving some semblance of energy to his body.

"So you're never going to forgive me?" From behind the steering wheel Megan stared at him, her eyes showing vulnerability.

Sitting there in quiet, he swallowed on her words, trying to frame his. He heard the sadness in her voice and it bothered him, but he turned away.

Three black SUVs arrived, coming from the direction of the highway. The vehicles rounded the corner in front of them and pulled up to the front gate of the safe house.

Alex drew the M&P and Lou's SIG Sauer and set them on his lap. Megan had her SIG Sauer holstered, her Glock tucked into her slacks, and she reached back and swung the MP7A1 from the rear seat to her lap.

Across the intersection in front of them, and down one block on Morning Light Terrace, a black sedan with tinted windows slowly rolled along. It parked on the opposite side of the road, fifty yards from the front gate, facing them. The vehicle's lights went off as it came to a stop.

"Everyone's been invited," Alex said bitterly.

CHAPTER 55

AS THEIR SUV PULLED up to the gated driveway of the safe house, Gallagher's pulse raced. He looked at the transfer of custody document Walter had given him. It was official and signed by the Attorney General. That helped. But he had gone behind Deputy Director Foley's back and knew his neck was on the line. Walter would have to protect it.

He stepped out of the cool SUV and showed his badge to the FBI agent on the other side of the gate. Farther inside he saw agents armed with machine guns. The trees and hedges hid them from the streets. Gallagher was amazed at the firepower. Foley had prepared for anything. He hoped there wouldn't be any surprises.

The agent recognized Gallagher and nodded. Gallagher punched the security code into the gate box and returned to the SUV to wait with Walter. The automatic gate slid open and the three SUVs rolled through.

The driveway ran straight a hundred feet up to a wide circular turn-around, with one branch of the driveway going past the house to the back garage. A number of FBI agents stood outside on the grounds, all armed with MP5s.

Walter directed their driver to stop the SUV behind the FBI sedans parked in front of the house.

Gallagher got out, walking toward the front door.

The lead FBI agent walked out of the house onto the landing, and quickly down the half-dozen steps along the wall of the house to greet him. A big burly man with a nose that had been broken at one point, he nodded to Gallagher. "Agent Banks, sir."

"We're giving custody of Dr. Joulie over to the CIA." Gallagher said it matter-of-factly, while pulling the custody transfer order from his shirt pocket.

Banks took it, read it, and looked at Gallagher. "I'll call Deputy Director Foley and let him know."

"No," Gallagher said firmly. "You'll get your men together and leave the premises immediately. Understood?"

"No offense, sir, but Deputy Director Foley outranks you and I have to follow his orders. I'll call him."

Gallagher stepped closer. "The AG got involved because there's a leak in the FBI and the risk of a terrorist attack. That's why the CIA is taking over. You make that call and it's your responsibility if anything happens."

Banks frowned and hesitated, but then signaled his men with his hand. "Let's go."

He walked back up the steps, opened the house door, and gave the same order. Then he returned to the closest sedan and entered the back seat. A dozen FBI agents retreated from the grounds and the house, and quickly piled into the sedans.

Dr. Joulie stepped out of the front door of the house onto the landing, gaping as the FBI agents drove away.

Gallagher approached him as Walter and the other CIA agents exited the SUVs. Except for Walter, the eight agents either held Remington 870 shotguns or had FN P90 machine guns slung over their shoulders.

"What's this about?" demanded Joulie.

"Justice," said Gallagher, climbing the steps. He wanted to hit the man.

CHAPTER 56

FROM BEHIND A TREE outside the metal fence, Odysseus used the night scope to watch the SUVs arrive. He had been informed that the CIA would try to take custody from the FBI—so the SUVs had to be CIA.

The FBI agent near his section of fence was called to the sedans.

"Cameras disabled," Achilles whispered over coms.

Odysseus put the scope away and painfully climbed the fence. He used wire cutters on the barbed wire.

Once over the other side, he unslung the Remington sniper rifle, knelt, and sighted. Across the compound he spotted Achilles running to a tree. Swinging the rifle farther, he glimpsed Patroclus hiding by some hedges, closer to his own position. Both carried backpacks and multiple weapons, waiting for his signal.

***

FBI agent Banks got out his cell phone as soon as he sat in his car. His fist was tight on his thigh as his driver left the estate. He wondered what was going on. The custody transfer order was legitimate and he couldn't argue with Gallagher, who headed the counterterrorism analysis section. Still something didn't feel right and Gallagher's attitude was demeaning. Banks had Deputy Director Foley on speed-dial.

Foley answered the phone, and Banks said, "Sir, Gallagher arrived with the CIA and an order signed by the Attorney General which transfers custody of Dr. Joulie to the CIA. We complied and have left the safe house. Please advise, sir."

***

Deputy Director Foley was surprised he wasn't angry at Gallagher as he listened to Agent Banks. He had followed Gallagher when the man left the J. Edgar Hoover Building and was pleased at the accuracy of his predictions. From his sedan he had observed the three CIA SUVs arrive, and he watched now as the FBI sedans exited through the front gate. Perhaps he wasn't upset about Gallagher's betrayal, because his own betrayal ran much deeper.

He didn't listen to what Agent Banks had to say. He just waited for him to be quiet. Then he said, "I want you to drive across the intersection and park on the side of the road, Agent Banks. Wait for further instructions."

"Yes, sir."

The three FBI sedans drove across the intersection, a hundred yards down Morning Light Terrace, and pulled over.

Foley knew now what it was like to be a shark on a reef, able to move the little fish around with your size and strength. It made him feel in control of the whole reef and he liked it.

***

Alex watched the FBI sedans exit through the gate and drive past them a short distance before parking. "Damn. The CIA is taking custody of Joulie."

"How?" asked Megan.

"Gallagher must have sold out Foley. Doesn't matter how he did it. Turn off the dimmer switch."

Megan complied, and he opened his door. He paused when she said, "Alex, it's over."

He got out and leaned back in. "You think Threshold isn't going to protect Joulie, their trump card?"

"Alex—"

"Stay here. I'll find out what's going on." He shut the door, holding his guns in front of his thighs to hide them from the FBI agents in the sedans. No plan in mind. Anger and frustration guided his actions now. It wasn't a good combination, but he didn't care.

Pushing her door open, Megan stepped out too, the machine gun slung over her right shoulder, also kept hidden from the sedans on the opposite side of the street. Coming around the front of the car, she interlocked a hand around his arm to make it look like a couple out for a stroll, with five guns between them.

It took seconds to reach the corner and cross the street. Alex knew whoever sat in the darkened sedan ahead of them might see their guns. They continued until they stood across from the gate. Megan put an arm around his neck, as if they were two lovers whispering to each other. He looked past the side of her face at the front gate.

"I never would have let them hurt you," she whispered. Hesitating, her voice softened. "I care for you."

He didn't want her beside him, but she wouldn't leave. Tension wound from his stomach to his chest. Wavering and wanting to speak to her, the words still not ready, old images of Jenny swept unbidden into his head.

Swallowing hard, he glanced at the darkened sedan parked in the street, and whispered, "Foley's here."

***

Odysseus didn't move as the FBI sedans left, but he tensed when one of the CIA agents walked up the front steps toward Joulie, bringing out handcuffs. Another man was already on the landing beside Joulie, talking to him. When the CIA agent reached Joulie and turned him around to cuff him, Odysseus clenched his gun.

He took a deep breath. He needed to focus. No mistakes. No second chances tonight. He sighted on the CIA agent's back and squeezed off the first silenced shot.

***

Walter bent backwards, as if he had been punched hard in his spine, and then toppled silently to the bottom of the steps in a lifeless heap, a dark stain on the back of his shirt. Gallagher immediately pulled Joulie in front of himself for protection, pushing back his shock and fear. He shook his injured arm out of the sling and drew his Glock.

The CIA agents nearest him immediately went to their knees, guns up, while the agents on the far side of the SUVs fired into the darkness on the grounds.

Three agents by the SUVs crumpled to the ground, again accompanied by suppressed shots from the attackers. Of the remaining five agents, three were firing FN P70s staccato blasts into the yard in wild sweeps, covering all areas of visible lawn, while using the doors of the SUVs for protection. Remington shotguns exploded on both sides of the SUVs, swung in wide arcs by CIA agents hoping to hit hidden attackers.

Gallagher felt he was a witness to a small war. Swinging right, he detected a shadow by nearby bushes and fired, while keeping one arm tight around Joulie.

Two more of Walter's men fell. Gallagher realized he might die here tonight. And for what? The scum in his arms? He wanted to see his wife and kids again.

Putting his gun in a pocket, he kicked the front door open and dragged Joulie inside. Fumbling to get out his cell phone to call for help, he paused when noises came from the back of the house. He retrieved his gun instead.

CHAPTER 57

WHEN THE FIRST SOUNDS of gunfire erupted, Alex ran across the street to the left side of the gate and stopped. Megan ran to the other side, hiding by a gate post. Leery of the darkened sedan parked on the street, Alex made certain no one exited it. It was unlikely Deputy Director Foley would join a firefight.

Seventy yards farther along the driveway, Alex spotted fallen agents. Three agents stood between two of the SUVs, firing FN P90s wildly into the yard at unseen targets.

Two canisters sailed through the air from different directions, landing near the CIA agents. The canisters immediately released thick, billowing smoke. Alex's stomach tightened as he witnessed the first part of his vision.

Even from a distance he could smell the acrid tear gas as it spread into the air. He glanced across the driveway. Megan was gone. His heart pounded as he looked up the driveway, spotting her near a tree fifty yards up the lawn on the other side of the SUVs. Swallowing, he cautiously walked forward, both guns held out at chest level.

The CIA agents retreated into one of the SUVs and backed down the driveway, the engine roaring.

A man in black Lycra, wearing a gas mask, stepped from behind a tree with a machine gun and sprayed the SUV as it went by. Some of the bullets punched through the bulletproof glass.

Recognizing Patroclus' build, Alex ran at him, firing with his guns extended. Patroclus twisted around, staggering backward when he was hit. The terrorist fell but still managed to fire a burst at Alex.

Alex's left leg gave out and he tumbled to the grass. There was a crash to the right as the SUV hit something. He ignored it.

Patroclus fired wildly from where he lay on the ground.

Keeping his chin on the grass, arms extended, Alex returned fire, hitting the man in the chest. Patroclus jerked back but remained on his side. He had to be wearing a vest.

A burst of staccato broke through the shooting—Patroclus collapsed to his back spread-eagled. Megan stood across the drive, her MP7 aimed at the terrorist. She glanced at Alex, and then ran forward into the darkened yard.

Getting to his knees, Alex looked over his shoulder. The SUV had swerved off the driveway into a tree. He didn't see any movement inside the vehicle. Stumbling to his feet, his thigh burning under his weight, he holstered the M&P and felt his leg. His fingers found wet stickiness. Wiping his hand on his shirt, he pulled his gun again.

With a limping gait he ran toward the dead terrorist. Hurriedly he pulled off the man's gas mask and put it over his face. His eyes were already burning from the tear gas.

***

Agent Banks heard the gunfire and immediately barked at his car driver, "Back to the safe house!"

All three cars swerved to make one-eighties in the road.

Banks' phone rang. To his surprise it was Deputy Director Foley.

"Agent Banks, hold your position."

Banks yelled, "Stop!"

All three cars skidded to a stop in the middle of the street.

Waiting, his chest tight, Banks listened to the thumping of automatics coming from the safehouse. He had observed the two armed figures running across the street to the gate, not knowing who they were. Foley had to have seen them too. The situation was out of control and his back stiffened. "Please advise, sir."

"The site is too hot. Hold your position until I give the order, Agent Banks."

"Yes, sir." He leaned back, realizing Foley had to be in the sedan parked a hundred yards away, facing them. He didn't understand what was going on, but he made a decision and called for backup, giving their location and that they were hearing a firefight with unknown parties engaging CIA agents at the FBI safe house holding Joulie. Sirens blared in the distance. The police would be here in minutes.

It didn't make sense to him, holding back when CIA agents were engaged in a gun battle. Foley had little field experience. Banks considered the possibility of men dying in the yard, including Gallagher, while they sat and did nothing.

He made another decision and said to the driver, "Go!"

***

Gallagher had his back against a living room wall, holding Joulie in front of him. As far as he could tell that was his mistake, thinking a wall would protect him. Gunfire erupted and he found himself without any strength as he let go of Joulie. At first he didn't realize he had been shot through the wall. As he slid down, Joulie turned to watch him.

"Going to give me first aid?" mumbled Gallagher as his eyes closed.

***

Odysseus ran from the dining room to the living room, glancing from the slumped man to Dr. Joulie. "Let's go."

Gripping the doctor's arm, he ran for the back door. They had minutes at most to leave the premises or they would be trapped here with no exit strategy.

Joulie snatched a briefcase from a table they passed.

Odysseus ran through the back door with Joulie in tow. The driveway curved around the back of the house and led to a three-car garage. At the very back was the fence with forest beyond it. They ran across the crushed gravel onto the grass.

Odysseus scanned the yard. A little farther and it would all be over. They had a minivan parked close by. They needed to reach it, then drive a short distance on the highway to transfer to another vehicle. He had seen Patroclus fall, but he wasn't sure about Achilles. He might be on his own.

A figure stepped out from the shadow of a tree.

Megan Detalio.

***

Stumbling toward the house, Alex peered through the drifting smoke. A man dressed in Lycra knelt twenty yards in front of him, holding a tube on his shoulder.

Alex threw himself to the side behind a tree as the terrorist fired an RPG in his direction. The rush of the rocket filled his ears as he hit the ground. An explosion rocked the yard and the lead FBI sedan entering the gateway flipped over onto the car behind it. Alex saw agents inside the trapped car trying to get out. The wreckage effectively blocked the entrance through the front gate.

Alex rose to his knees, but remained behind the tree when bullets bit the bark near his face. In a few moments he risked a glance around the other side of the trunk.

The RPG rocket launcher was on the ground and the man holding it gone. Focused on only one thing, he got up and ran for the front door of the house. His thigh was on fire, but adrenaline kept his legs churning.

A muffled gunshot came from the backyard.

CHAPTER 58

ODYSSEUS STOPPED. EVEN IN the dark he recognized Detalio—holding a machine gun. His rifle was pointed away from her, but he gripped it tightly, aware of Joulie frozen at his side. He held his breath. Long ago he had decided he wouldn't allow himself to be captured.

"Drop it," said Detalio.

He ignored her.

"Last chance." She took another step toward him, her gun aimed at his chest.

Odysseus was suddenly ready, the fear that he had expected over the last days absent. About to swing his weapon, he hesitated when a muffled gunshot surprised him.

Detalio groaned and fell to her knees on the road, dropping her gun, her shoulder bloodied.

Odysseus jerked his head around.

Achilles ran toward them, a silenced Glock in his hand.

***

Alex ran into the house, nearly tripping over Gallagher who was slumped on the floor against the wall. He paused, seeing the red stain on the wall and unsure if the man was alive. He didn't check.

Taking off his gas mask, he ran to the back door, kicked it open, and ran through, his momentum carrying him down three steps to the crushed gravel, where he lurched to a stop.

At the back fence a dark figure turned to him. Alex threw himself onto the grass behind a tree as the muffled staccato of a machine gun filled the air. Bullets cut into the ground and bark as Alex rolled to the other side of the tree and fired three shots at the terrorist who was already disappearing in the forest.

"Megan!" he yelled. The backyard was empty.

"Alex." Her voice was faint, nearly choked off.

Stumbling to his feet, he ran from the tree to the corner of the garage, which blocked line of sight of any remaining shooters. He carefully edged out. Darkness hid everything, but he heard twigs snapping in the woods. Taking a chance, he ran toward the fence, following the sounds.

On the run he pushed against a vertical cut in the fence and slid through. He stopped a few steps into the dark grove of trees. Thick forest blocked his sight in all directions. Hearing soft footfalls, he ran left, northwest, his leg on fire and his chest heaving. Megan's cry echoed in his mind, churning his thoughts. That they hadn't killed her yet only meant they wanted her as a bargaining chip if they needed one.

Abruptly he stopped at the edge of the trees near a street. Sixty feet away a minivan was parked on the road adjacent to the curb. Odysseus was shoving Joulie into the front passenger seat, while Achilles pulled Megan's hair and pushed her into the side of the van.

Whirling, Achilles let loose a volley from his machine gun, forcing Alex to slide behind a tree. Bullets thudded into the trunk and tore at branches.

Hearing a screech of tires, Alex stepped into the open again. The van rocketed forward. Running into the street, he knelt and emptied his guns at the closest tire of the fleeing vehicle.

The rear passenger tire was punctured and the van sagged right. Speeding through the stop sign, Odysseus took a left onto the highway, across traffic. A Ford Explorer hit the van's back bumper, sending the vehicle skidding as it fishtailed. Another car veered out of the far lane to avoid the van, clipped the front fender of the Explorer, and slid across the road and up the curb, crashing into trees.

Tires squealed and several cars piled into the Explorer.

Both guns were empty, so Alex dropped the SIG. He ejected the M&P magazine, grabbed another from his pocket, and reloaded on the run. Cautiously he passed the Explorer, until he was sure traffic had stopped, and then he ran to the center grass divide in the highway.

The van was parked on the far side of the road, sixty yards down from him.

Waiting for a break in headlights, Alex ran across the highway, still forced to stop between lanes as horns sounded and cars swerved. He made it across the rest of the road, his gun held in both hands and aimed at the van until he reached it. The vehicle was empty, the passenger doors open.

He ran into a small ditch filled with high grass, then up a longer incline to level forest. Running through trees and brush, he looked west, his stomach tight over the idea that the terrorists might have already killed Megan.

In fifty yards he reached the park road. West of his position, four shadowy figures ran across it. He recognized one of them as Megan. Achilles pushed her with a gun in her back.

Leaning against a tree, Alex paused. His leg throbbed. Crouching, he ran across the street at an angle, hoping the moonlight didn't reveal him. He almost made it before Achilles whirled, the muffled staccato of machine gun fire chasing him.

Reaching a tree, Alex remained behind it, breathing hard, listening. Gasps from the west. He peered around the trunk.

A hundred feet away he spotted Achilles still pushing Megan through the forest. He would never be able to approach the terrorist without being spotted. Looking ahead of Megan, and west of her position, he saw a large tree with a low branch. Part of his vision from Harry's house. He hesitated, wary of following his premonition.

The trees were thick ahead of the terrorists too, and would provide enough cover for him if he just ran northwest. But that wouldn't put him beneath the low branch from his vision. Swallowing hard, he gave in to it. He ran due west, from tree to tree, his hands sweaty on his gun. As he advanced, the forest thickened with less space between the trees.

Achilles either heard or spotted him, and turned.

"Megan!" yelled Alex.

Megan whirled and kicked Achilles' thigh. The man stumbled forward but managed to turn, his gun on her. She raised her arms. Achilles yelled something, and Megan fell to her knees on the ground, clasping her hands behind her head.

Alex kept running west, his gun up, but trees blocked any shot he might take. Achilles fired at him, moving sideways to keep him in view. Ducking, still running west, Alex caught only glimpses of the terrorist tracking him with his gun. The thick forest protected him from the shots.

Small gaps between tree trunks gave him a fragmented view of Megan rolling sideways, rising very fast, and kicking Achilles in the ribs. The man dropped the machine gun and fell to the ground, rolling away from her. Megan reached for the automatic, but the terrorist pulled a silenced pistol from behind his back and fired.

Megan clutched her stomach and stumbled a few steps away, bent over.

"Megan!" As he ran, Alex watched her slump to her knees, and then to her back.

Trees still blocked any good shots. Panic. He veered north.

Achilles rose to his feet, picked up the machine gun again, and sprayed another burst at him.

Alex couldn't stop his flying legs. The large tree appeared in his peripheral vision. He turned east. He wasn't going to be in time. Thick bushes and a stand of trees blocked everything except for a glimpse of Megan.

Turning, Achilles strode toward her sprawled figure.

The imagery from Harry's house flashed through Alex. Wanting to scream, he ran harder. Abruptly a large space opened up in front of him. Arm outstretched, he shot repeatedly at Achilles, the noise of his own gun in his ears, uncertain if Achilles had fired into Megan's figure.

Achilles swung toward him, firing, bullets ripping in an arc toward him.

Running directly at the terrorist, Alex kept pulling the trigger on an empty chamber. He barreled into the man, knocking him into the grass, striking him with a fist and the empty gun. It took three swings before he was aware of the dark stain on the man's neck and his lifeless response.

He jerked off the man's hood. Glassy eyes stared back. He scrambled over the ground to Megan, his chest heaving. Unconscious. The moonlight showed her abdomen and shoulder darker than the rest of her clothing. Her neck gave a faint pulse.

Something made him glance up. The low branch on the large tree stretched above him.

Another shot rang out.

Hating to leave Megan, he heard sirens and picked up the machine gun. Sprinting through the trees, in seconds he saw Joulie. The doctor was pointing a gun at a fallen figure on the ground.

Joulie saw him and dropped the pistol, raising his hands high, still holding a briefcase.

Ignoring Joulie, Alex snatched Megan's SIG Sauer from the soil and limped to Odysseus, who was prone on the ground. He knelt and tore off the man's hood. Jerry Peiser.

Pain evident in his expression, Peiser looked up at him. "Not like this," he murmured.

"Why?" Alex felt no empathy, already certain of the answer.

"The victims. Kristen." Peiser closed his eyes. "Nature." His head lolled to one side.

Alex stood up and walked stiffly toward Joulie.

"I had to shoot him." Joulie was talking fast while backing up. "He was trying to kidnap me for who knows what—"

Alex swung hard on the doctor's jaw to cut off his words, sending him flying to the ground. Without waiting he ran back to Megan, who lay crumpled and still. He took out his cell and dialed 911, telling the operator an officer was down, his name, and location.

Then he knelt and gently pulled her up to him, holding her, with one hand keeping pressure on her stomach wound. Images of Jenny flashed through his mind. "I'm sorry," he murmured as he held her. "I'm sorry."

FBI agents and EMTs found him a short time later, still holding her.

CHAPTER 59

D R. CRARY TENSED IN the leather chair he sat in, but knew he had to stay calm or he would have another problem on his hands. He listened, holding the cell phone tightly.

"What do we do now?" asked the man on the other end. "Deputy Director Foley may be finished."

"Foley was never part of us." Crary paused. "Do nothing. Run. Hide. Stay put. It's up to you, but for now it's over."

"The network isn't finished. We can't just fold."

"Fold?" Crary couldn't keep the anger out of his voice. "I've lost one of my best friends and the other is in jail. What have *you* lost?"

"Sorry."

Crary heaved a breath. "We've won for now. It's enough. Let's see what develops. You have to get a grip and let the emotions go. They'll be watching everyone."

"It's not over."

Crary's voice hardened. "For now, it is over."

"Maybe for now."

Crary hung up. Sighing, he tore apart the cell phone and tossed it into the garbage. Leaving his study, he walked to the back porch where he gazed at his sister playing with her two kids on the swing set. The heat wave had finally ended, the temperatures normal.

Maybe his sister's children would have a better world and someday grow up with clean air, clean water, and clean food. And the platitudes politicians liked to utter about family values and love would be a reality and not a farce. A world free of greedy corporations and bribed politicians.

He couldn't be sure what they had accomplished. It was too early to tell. And too early to see what the established opposition of business, power, and money-controlled news media would do with it all. In a few weeks Threshold's gains would be relegated to yesterday's news, possibly rendering it meaningless and trivial.

The caller was right. It wasn't over.

After another deep exhalation he walked into the sun to be with his sister and her children.

CHAPTER 60

PIERRE NUZZLED AGAINST ALEX'S leg. Alex scratched the cat's back.

The compass bearing was southeast, the boat on autopilot. The forty-foot sloop, *Dreamer*, handled the two-foot waves as if gliding; the twelve-knot wind filled the sails without stressing them. A number of different islands among the U.S. and British Virgins lay close by to the north, and one was visible a quarter mile ahead. Alex looked up, allowing the sun to bathe his face. Somehow the heat felt tolerable on the water.

Taking a deep breath, he enjoyed the clear-headed feeling that came with it. A month of trouble-free sleep had done wonders for him. Isolating himself had also helped.

Before he had left the States, he learned Deputy Director Foley and Gallagher were on extended leave, pending an investigation. Dr. Joulie had given his testimony, producing an uproar in the country. And a version of bill S.229 had passed.

Joulie was now in jail, facing charges of conspiracy for murder and terrorism. His lawyers were confident he would be found innocent. That troubled Alex, but one way or another Threshold was finished. At least its heart was cut out.

The bounty on him had expired, and the CIA hadn't acted on its threat to frame him for Senator Dillon's murder. He figured with Joulie's testimony they had enough problems to sort out.

Whenever he thought about the case the results left him with distaste, especially the victims he hadn't saved. Their deaths, including Senator Dillon's, and even Jerry Peiser's, gnawed at him. Such a waste.

And the rotten system Threshold wanted to destroy chugged on, but maybe with a tiny bit less steam. He knew the victims of Threshold, and the truth of Threshold, had a voice in the changes which had occurred. All the deaths had some meaning, however small. He had to hope that was true.

He sighed, letting it all go. The sun, quiet, and lack of responsibility was healing him, slowly washing the stronger emotions away. For that he was grateful.

There was clatter from below in the galley and a head appeared above the steps.

"Hi." Megan's dark, curly hair framed her face, her olive skin shining in the light. A yellow sari was wrapped over her bathing suit and she still moved a little slowly from her wounds. But she was healing, as he was. She smiled.

"Hi." He couldn't remember seeing her smile as freely any time before in the last weeks.

She stepped out. "Crackers and cheese for lunch. Chocolate for dessert."

He smiled. "My kind of food."

She sat beside him in the cockpit, setting the plate on his lap. In a moment she reached a hand to Pierre and scratched his head. Pierre wasn't satisfied and climbed into her arms where she cradled him like a baby.

Looking at her, his gaze wandered to her full lips. Warmth stirred in his chest. She had been given immunity in exchange for her testimony. Prosecutors were going after the CIA's involvement in South America and at home.

More importantly he had learned he could forgive. Himself and her. He knew who she was, and who he was. It was more than enough. He felt free.

A pair of dolphins were surfing the bow wave of the boat, and they watched them for a few minutes until they left.

Alex sighed. "Another hour to Norman Island, supposedly the island described in Robert Louis Stevenson's book, *Treasure Island*."

"You're dating yourself." She flashed him another smile.

After he took it in, he looked out at the ocean where the sun danced on the water and the wind pushed the waves into small mounds. "You think we could sail to Tahiti someday?"

"Why not?"

"Maybe you'll be bored." He knew he wouldn't be.

"I'll bring a laptop and music in case I get tired of listening to you." She held his eyes, serious for a moment. "I like helping people, making things right."

"I do too."

"Maybe we can do more of that." She caught his eyes.

He thought he could do anything with her. "I love you."

"I know."

He added, "It has nothing to do with Jenny."

"I know that too, but it's nice to hear."

Sliding an arm around her, he said, "I took a break from gambling." Feeling lightheaded all of a sudden, he added, "Ever since Easy Pitch came in at a half-mill."

"It's about time." She sounded unconcerned as she stroked Pierre.

"I'm winning every moment I'm out here with you," he said softly.

"So am I." She nestled up beside him, her lips finding his for a few moments.

Jenny's words came to him again; *But what if you didn't see the whole picture?* He was finally at peace with those words, with Jenny, and with everything for the first time in many years.

The U.S. Army *Call to the Post* bugle riff sounded from the cabin below.

Megan stared at him inquiringly.

"I think that's my phone." He ran his hand through her hair.

"Amazing deduction, Mr. Psychic." She rolled her eyes. "Who would be calling you out here?"

He grinned. "It's Harry. The Belmont Stakes run tomorrow."

* * *

If you like hi-octane thrillers, try my Jack Steel series.
The Jack Steel Series is now in development
for a major motion picture.

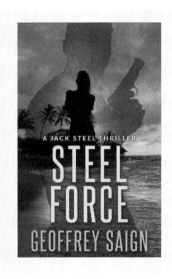

**He stood up for justice.
Now they want him
dead. Can he defeat a
conspiracy before he
becomes the next hit?**

Read the following excerpt or
buy *STEEL FORCE* on AMAZON.

* * *

AUTHOR'S NOTE

Thank you so much for reading *Kill Sight*! Environmental issues are looming, and I thought it would be interesting to have terrorists pushing for change, while hunted by a conflicted, psychic detective. I've met people with amazing abilities, similar to Alex Sight's, and that grounded my view on Alex's character.

Reviews help me keep writing, and encourage other readers to take the chance on a new author they haven't read before. So if you enjoyed the book, please leave a review. Every review—even a few words—helps!

Thank you!

~ Geoff

Excerpt from STEEL FORCE

OP: KOMODO

CHAPTER 1

Komodo: 2200 hours

MAJOR JACK STEEL'S INTUITION was screaming at him—*things don't feel right!*
Everyone at the site was to be terminated, but he hadn't signed on to murder unarmed civilians. Maybe he just needed more information. He'd be out of here in two hours. Home in twenty-four. That's all he wanted, to return to Carol.

You just have to get through two hours, he told himself.

He clenched his jaw as the plane splashed down on the quiet waters of the lake. He pulled the black Lycra hood at the back of his neck over his head so only his eyes and mouth were visible. Even though his black fatigues were vented, he still sweated profusely.

Stepping out from behind the massive kapok tree, he waited.

The twin-engine DeHavilland Twin Otter float plane was almost impossible to see except as a dark shape moving against the far tree line. Painted all black and gutted for weight so it could carry extra fuel, it also had no registration numbers on it.

The aircraft angled over to the shore, the engine noise overwhelming the rainforest sounds until it was cut. A side cargo door slid open with a rasp and a rope was tossed out.

Steel caught it and pulled the aircraft into the shore, securing the line around a tree. Picking up his silenced SIG Sauer MCX Rattler, he gripped it with both hands. The folding stock made the rifle-caliber machine gun easy to conceal and it had little recoil.

A large hooded figure jumped out of the plane into a few inches of water, also holding a Rattler. Steel recognized the height of the man. Colonel Danker.

"Good to see you, PR." Danker was using Steel's call sign for this mission, *PR*, which stood for *point & recon*. The call sign wasn't very inventive, but Danker had assigned it. Heavily muscled with a gravelly voice, at six-five Danker had three inches on Steel.

"Good to see you, BB." Steel heaved a silent breath, finally relaxing. Danker was U.S. Army and always did things *by the book*, thus his call sign of BB. Steel trusted him.

Everyone else on the Op worked for Blackhood, the private security contractor that signed their checks. But Danker would know all their profiles and made sure they had excellent skill sets for the Op.

Over a year and a half ago Steel had been asked to resign from the Army to join the secret Blackhood Ops program to target terrorists. The missions had been named Blackhood Ops to further distance the U.S. military and put the private military contractor on the hook for responsibility. Except for Danker, the U.S. government wanted no ties to these missions.

Four more hooded men exited the plane, one of them its pilot. Steel didn't know their identities, and they didn't know his—another precaution to maintain Blackhood mission secrecy.

He led them a dozen yards from the shoreline vegetation into the trees, where they squatted in a tight circle.

Each man was equipped with a Rattler, Glock 19, fixed blade knife, and a belt pouch that contained a night monocular scope, first aid, and a GPS tracking unit should things go bad. They also all had small wireless radios, earpieces, and throat microphones. The guns all had their identification numbers erased.

In addition, Steel had a Benchmade 3300BK Infidel auto OTF blade in a small, horizontal belt-sheath built into the inside back of his belt. For his fixed blade he carried a seven-inch Ka-Bar— he liked the leather handle. A small sling bag on his back held rations, a soft-sided canteen, and some first aid supplies.

He looked at Danker. "There are unarmed civilians at the building."

Danker nodded. "Brief us."

From his pouch Steel brought out a piece of white folded plastic and an iridescent red marker. He marked off the position of the site and guard positions.

Glancing around the circle, he said, "Two guards on the roof, two at each of the building's two entrances, four more in the jungle. We'll be coming in due east of the objective. The building has two main wings. Our target will be in the south wing. The target site is in a large clearing, but thick surrounding undergrowth vegetation will give us a lot of cover in our approach."

He showed them the position he would lead them to, then made quick suggestions on how to take out the guards and secure the area and building. Finding optimal strategies was one of his specialties and he didn't expect any objections.

"All civilians should be inside at this time of night." He looked up at Danker.

The colonel said softly, "No warm bodies. No one leaves the site. I'll take care of the primary target. Radio silent unless you're in trouble."

Steel's neck stiffened. He stared at Danker, but the colonel was already upright, waiting. Standing, he whispered, "There are at least four noncombatants at the site, including a Franciscan friar."

Danker spoke matter-of-factly: "Orders stand."

Glancing at the other four sets of eyes, Steel saw only acceptance. "Our drones will record it."

Danker shook his head. "No drones tonight. Take point, PR."

Fifteen years of following orders compelled Steel to nod and move past the others as he returned the plastic and marker to his pouch.

Leading them at a brisk pace through the rainforest, he walked up the gently sloped mountain. The heat produced rivulets of sweat over his torso. His thoughts were racing.

Danker had more intel than he did about the Op and the terrorist. Still, Steel had enough missions under his belt to recognize the difference between uninvolved civilians and those supporting terrorists. The female cook and maid were pushing fifty and were never armed. Like the driver and friar, they didn't act, talk, or move like terrorists in hiding worried about an attack.

He had no problem killing armed guards to get to a terrorist. But his job was to protect civilians, not actively target them. That view had inspired his entire military career. It was the cornerstone of his life.

Danker hadn't even asked how many nonmilitary personnel were on the premises. The colonel didn't care.

Steel's trust in the mission evaporated. Danker was following orders, but Steel questioned the motive of whoever gave them.

He gripped his gun. *No warm bodies.* This wasn't a planned assassination of a known terrorist. It was going to be a massacre.

How could he do anything, when he was the only one who objected?

One against five.

Hell.

CHAPTER 2

Komodo: 2230 hours

STEEL KEPT MOVING ON the narrow trail, focused on just one thing—surviving the next hour. What sent chills down his arms was that he wasn't sure how far he would—*or could*—go to stop what was coming.

The fluorescent needlepoint of his wrist compass guided him, but he didn't need it. He had traversed this same trail for two nights in a row to make sure he could do it with speed when the time came.

Now he was desperate to know where they were. Over the last three days he heard the guards speak Spanish, but he couldn't place the dialect. They could be anywhere in Central or South America. And the high canopy and the overcast sky prevented any fix on location using stars.

To protect Op secrecy, Blackhood operatives were never given mission locations or terrorist names. Even the GPS unit was rigged so it didn't show numerical coordinates, but they could track him. Real-time tracking via satellites wasn't used on Blackhood Ops to avoid any record and to minimize the number of personnel aware of the Ops.

Except for seeing a photograph of the primary target, Steel knew next to nothing about Komodo Op, other than Blackhood intel indicated the terrorist would be at the termination site for five days.

When he considered the current conflicts and problems, and everyone in power in Central and South America, he concluded they might be in Venezuela. Nicolas Maduro supported Hezbollah and Al Qaeda. Venezuela's embassy had even sold passports to operatives of ISIS.

Maybe Blackhood Ops had decided to take out someone in Venezuela's armed forces that interfaced with terrorists.

That might explain Danker's orders of *no warm bodies.* Even though ISIS had been routed from Iraq, they still had a web presence and there were splinter groups. This might be a preemptive strike to give anyone in the Venezuelan government with terrorist connections a warning: *We can hit you anywhere we want, even in your own country.*

It was the presence of the Franciscan friar that had first triggered Steel's concerns. The diminutive man wore short hair and a brown ankle-length habit with a hood. An image out of the Middle Ages.

Every evening the friar had taken a walk in the forest. Birds flocked into trees near the man. Steel had even witnessed a songbird landing on the friar's shoulder. Amazing. And there was something familiar about the man that Steel couldn't quite grasp.

Once the friar had taken a stroll with the primary terrorist target, who dressed in civilian clothing. Neither were armed. The guards had remained in their positions, seemingly unconcerned about the target's increased vulnerability. That also didn't fit a terrorist camp under heightened security.

In twenty minutes Steel summited the low mountain, and in another ten minutes he led the others down the other side to a large plateau. The building wasn't far ahead. Steel stopped behind a hollow strangler fig tree and held up a hand as he scanned the terrain. He had to estimate where the guards would be, given the lack of light and waist-high undergrowth that filled in between the trees. The others watched and waited.

A laughing falcon gave its intense *ha-ha-ha-guaco* call in the distance. From much closer came the low-pitched guttural rumbling of a gray-bellied night monkey. Insects buzzed and hummed everywhere. Normally Steel would drink in the teeming life that enveloped his senses. He had a deep abiding love of nature.

But right now he felt trapped.

Shoving panic aside, he focused on his own motto for when a plan blew up: *Stay calm, assess options, look for a solution.* He didn't believe in the Kobayashi Maru principle. He trained in his virtual reality simulations under the belief that there was always a way out of even seemingly impossible situations.

He signaled left and right. The men spread out, Danker to his right. Steel would take the middle, while the others would circle around to the back and sides of the building.

Using the carry strap, he positioned the Rattler against his back and lowered himself to his knees, and then his belly. Motionless, he looked ahead for any signs of movement. Crawling around the buttresses, snakelike, he pressed his hands and arms into the thick detritus. A rich brew of earth filled his nostrils.

He had practiced this part of his plan each day he was here, visualizing the enemy in a position similar to what the guard held now. This was also a maneuver he had repeated a hundred times in his VR sims. Using one foot and arm at a time, he quietly pushed and pulled himself forward. In minutes he spotted the faint outline of the guard sitting on one of the waist-high tree buttresses of a hundred-foot fig tree.

Moving at an angle, he kept crawling until the tree hid him from view.

All the guards wore nondescript tan uniforms and they never changed their nightly positions. Their lack of caution felt amateurish, supporting his doubts about the mission.

He paused at the back of the gnarled tree. No sounds. Methodically he drew himself to his knees, then his feet. Moisture and sweat beaded his face and hands, and the light rainfall patter disguised the quiet whispers of his movements.

Drawing his fixed blade knife, he gripped the handle and slipped over each buttress in turn until only one separated him from the guard. He checked his watch: twenty-three-hundred.

Taking a deep, silent breath, he fluidly slid one leg at a time over the last buttress, allowing his boots to make a slight rustle.

The guard whirled around, wide-eyed.

Steel swung the butt of his knife into the man's temple. The soldier slumped to the ground. Clenching his knife, Steel stared at the limp body. The guard looked young, maybe eighteen. A novice. Not an experienced soldier guarding a terrorist camp.

It cemented his distrust in the mission. Maybe the mission had nothing to do with terrorists. He swallowed. They would be out of here before the guard came to. The risk was that one of Danker's team would discover the man alive.

He picked up the guard's assault rifle, ran forward, and flung it away. Racing through the darkened forest, he slowed when the ranch-style stone building appeared, a lighter shape against the dark forest. Stopping behind a tree, he paused when he heard footsteps.

The friar broke from the surrounding trees in a run, his ankle-length habit flying out behind him as he yelled, "Intrusos! Intrusos!" The small man darted past the startled guards and into the building.

Steel was glad the friar had made it out of the forest without getting shot. He remained behind the tree—he was Danker's backup.

Machine gun fire erupted from several different locations.

Colonel Danker sprinted up beside a nearby tree. He dropped to one knee and sprayed a short burst at the two guards crouched in front of the building. Both men fell to the ground and Danker charged across the open clearing. A guard on the roof leaned over. Danker dove to the ground, rolling toward the building.

Steel stepped out from behind the tree and fired a spray of bullets to cover Danker, his shots much quieter than the staccato bursts coming from the guards around the compound.

The guard of the roof reeled backward.

Rising to his knees, Danker paused only a moment before he rose and ran through the door.

Steel followed at a dead run, adrenaline pumping his legs. More gunfire erupted in the forest. The other guards were fighting back, but he doubted it would help them. The radio silence from the Blackhood team confirmed it.

He rushed through the main entryway, past a large living room to the right. No civilians or soldiers. And none of the other Blackhood operatives were inside yet. A short hallway ran left. At the end of it stood Danker, facing a closed door. Steel kept his feet quiet on the stone floor as he ran forward, hoping the colonel didn't look back.

Danker kicked in the door and stepped into the room.

Steel ran harder, his hands like stone on his gun. He heard Danker's gun fire.

He stopped in the doorway just as the colonel swung his machine gun from one corner of the small darkened room toward the other. He glimpsed a desk and chair to the left. An interrupted line of bullet holes streaked across the wall behind the desk—it probably hid a corpse—most likely the target.

To the right, over the colonel's shoulder, he saw the friar—his small hands empty, his face hidden in the shadows. Steel snapped a kick into the side of Danker's left knee.

Danker grunted as his knee bent and his back twisted, but he remained upright. He tried to twist around, swinging his gun.

Steel jarred a knife hand into the side of Danker's neck and the colonel collapsed. Adrenaline flooded his limbs and his ears roared as he stared at Danker's crumpled body on the floor. Glancing at the gaping friar, he motioned his gun to the waist-high open window.

The friar's eyes widened, but he ran to it and climbed through.

Steel crossed the room, keeping to the side of the window. He watched the friar disappear in the forest. Shots were fired almost immediately in the direction of the friar's flight. He grimaced. All of it for nothing. And there was nothing he could do for the other civilians. Now he had to worry about his own survival.

***

To continue reading buy STEEL FORCE on Amazon!

Read all the Jack Steel and Alex Sight Thrillers.

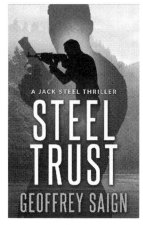
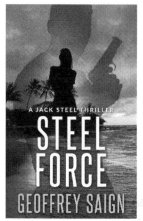
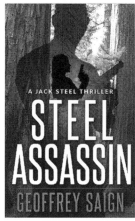
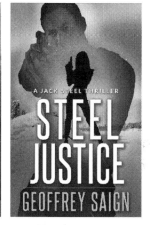
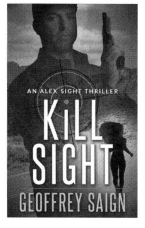

ACKNOWLEDGMENTS

I WANT TO THANK Stanley Blanchard who used his extensive military background to strengthen the character of Alex Sight and give him the nuances he needed to play the part. Any mistakes or omissions in anything procedural is my fault alone. I wish to thank Steve McEllistrem who gave the book a read for grammar, and my parents who have always had a sharp sense of what makes a great action thriller.

The looming man-made environmental disasters are heating up politics and communities worldwide, and I hope saner minds will find a way to peacefully end the current course of technology on our planet.

Alex Sight is a character who is challenged to decide what is the right course of action. He cares about his values above all else. As a child, doing the right thing is something you learn from the adults around you. My parents did a great job of teaching that to me.

Lastly I wish to thank all the men and women who act heroically every day to ensure our safety. We owe you our thanks, gratitude, and support.

Award-winning author Geoffrey Saign has spent many years studying kung fu and sailed all over the South Pacific and Caribbean. He uses that experience and sense of adventure to write the Jack Steel and Alex Sight mystery thriller action series. Geoff loves to sail big boats, hike, and cook—and he infuses all of his writing with his passion for nature. As a swimmer, he considers himself fortunate to live in the Land of 10,000 Lakes, Minnesota.

For email updates from Geoffrey Saign and
your FREE copy of the novella STEEL TRUST go to
http://www.geoffreysaign.net

See how the Jack Steel series began!

Made in the USA
Monee, IL
17 June 2021